MISTER TEACHER

Another riotous year in the life of Ragley-on-the-Forest village school.

It's 1978, and as Jack Sheffield begins his second year as headmaster of a small Yorkshire primary school there is a letter on his desk from nine-year-old Sebastian, suffering from leukaemia in the local hospital, who writes a heartbreaking letter to 'Mister Teacher'. So begins another year in the life of the school and community, in which Jack is accompanied by many colourful characters, including Vera, the school secretary whose greatest ambition is to be President of the Women's Institute, and of course, Beth Henderson, a teacher from a nearby school who with her sister Laura presents Jack with an unexpected dilemma.

MISTER TEACHER

MISTER TEACHER

by

Jack Sheffield

Magna Large Print Books
Long Preston, North Yorkshire,
BD23 4ND, England.

British Library Cataloguing in Publication Data.

Sheffield, Jack
    Mister teacher.

    A catalogue record of this book is
    available from the British Library

    ISBN   978-0-7505-2959-4

First published in Great Britain in 2008 by Bantam Press
an imprint of Transworld Publishers

Copyright © Jack Sheffield 2008

Cover illustration © Paul Hess by arrangement with Arena

Jack Sheffield has asserted his right under the Copyright, Designs and
Patents Act, 1988 to be identified as the author of this work

Published in Large Print 2009 by arrangement with
Transworld Publishers

Magna Large Print is an imprint of Library Magna Books Ltd.

Printed and bound in Great Britain by
T.J. (International) Ltd., Cornwall, PL28 8RW

For Jenifer, Sarah, Aimee, Emily and Lucy

Contents

Acknowledgements

I am deeply indebted to my editor, Linda Evans, and all at Transworld for their support, especially Stina Smemo, Katie Espiner and Sophie Holmes. Also, thanks go to my agent, the indefatigable Philip Patterson of Marjacq Scripts, for his hard work, good humour and deep appreciation of Yorkshire cricket.

I am grateful to everyone who assisted in the research for this novel – in particular: Alan Beddows, paediatric nurse, Roald Dahl Haematology Centre, Sheffield; Anne Butler, ex-President of the Women's Institute, Sutton-on-the-Forest, York; Janina Bywater, nurse and lecturer in psychology; Steve Bywater, headteacher, Cornwall; Tony Cleaver, international flower arranger; Maria Demkowicz, and all the 'Literary Girls' of Sutton-on-the-Forest, York; John Everton, ex-Sheffield steelworker; John Kirby, ex-policeman and Sunderland supporter; Eileen Lavender, amateur dramatic producer and ex-dancer, York; Roy Linley, Solutions Architect, Unilever Europe IT; Sue Matthews, primary school teacher, York; Don Pears, musical director and Newcastle supporter; Canon Bob Rogers, York; Mike Smith, gentleman's clothing expert, Clarkson's, The Shirt Shop, York; Caroline Stockdale, librarian, York Central Library; Gwen Vardigans, African aid worker and friend of teddy bears.

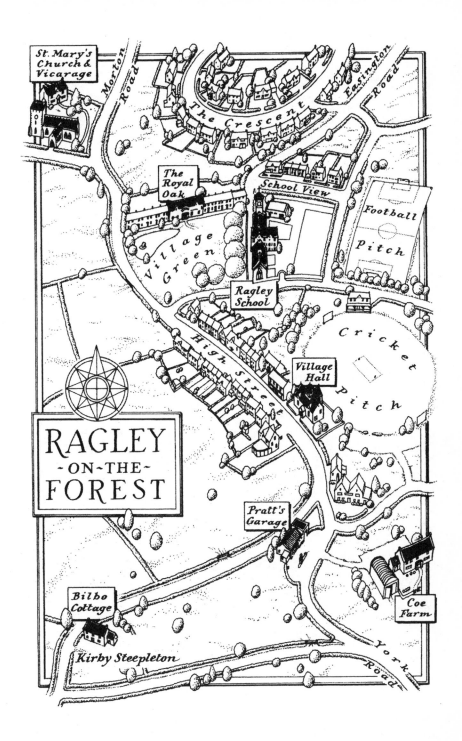

St. Mary's Church & Vicarage

Morton Road

The Crescent

Easington Road

The Royal Oak

School View

Football Pitch

Village Green

Ragley School

Cricket Pitch

High Street

Village Hall

RAGLEY
-ON-THE-
FOREST

Pratt's Garage

Coe Farm

Bilbo Cottage

Kirby Steepleton

York Road

Prologue

There were three letters on my desk: one made me smile, another made me sad and the third was destined to change my life.

It was Friday, 1 September 1978, and I was alone in the school office. My second year as headmaster of Ragley-on-the-Forest Church of England Primary School in North Yorkshire was about to begin.

I picked up a brass letter-opener and looked at the first envelope. The flowing, expansive hand-writing was distinctive and the Northallerton postmark confirmed it could only be from the formidable Chair of the Education Committee, Miss Barrington-Huntley. I unfolded the thick cream writing paper and underneath the impressive coat of arms her busy script raced powerfully across the page.

County Hall, Northallerton, 28 August 1978

Dear Jack,
I do hope you have had a restful summer break. Congratulations on your successful first year in headship.
I shall be visiting your school to make an assessment of your premises on Monday, 9 October at 9.00 a.m.
Yours sincerely,
Fiona Barrington-Huntley

17

(Chair of the Education Committee)

PS On this occasion I shall not be wearing a hat!

I smiled. Following Miss Barrington-Huntley's last annual inspection her expensive peacock-feathered hat had met an unexpected end.

On that occasion, she had been accompanied by Beth Henderson, a local deputy headmistress who had been seconded for one year to support English and Physical Education in primary schools. After a whirlwind romance at the end of the summer term, Beth and I had driven off into the sunset in my Morris Minor Traveller for a holiday in France. Two carefree weeks later, I had left her at her parents' house in Hampshire, where Beth had decided to spend the end of the school holiday, and I had returned to Yorkshire.

To my surprise the second letter was from her. It was written on floral-patterned, lilac-coloured paper.

Austen Cottage, Little Chawton, Hampshire, 27 August 1978

My dear Jack,

I'm sorry to be writing instead of phoning, but I wanted you to have time to think this through before I return to Yorkshire.

As you know, my next career move is to look out for headships of small village schools. There's a lovely school down here in Hampshire in need of a headteacher and I've decided to apply!

Looking forward to telling you all about it!

See you soon,
Love,
Beth

With a tinge of sadness in my heart I sighed and stared at the address. Hampshire seemed such a long way off. I suddenly realized that Beth had become an important part of my life. She was different from any other woman I had known: dynamic and exciting. With my mind elsewhere, I picked up the third envelope.

It had a York postmark and felt bulky. Inside was a handwritten letter on crisp white hospital letterhead. It read:

York Hospital, 28 August 1978

Dear Jack,
Following the success of last year's pen-friend project with the local special school, I wondered if we could arrange something similar with the Children's Ward in York Hospital. We have a small number of children with very serious illnesses who would benefit from contact with children of their own age. If you can help, please let me know and I'll call into school to arrange the details.
I also enclose a letter from a wonderfully creative little boy called Sebastian, age 9, who has leukaemia.
With best wishes for the new school year,
Sue Phillips (Staff Nurse)

Sue Phillips was a very active member of our Parent Teacher Association and, in between shifts at the hospital, she was also our school nurse.

19

I looked inside the package and took out a small bright-yellow envelope on which the words 'MISTER TEACHER' were scrawled in thick pencil.

It was a letter I would keep throughout my career. It read:

Dear Mister Teacher,
My name is Seb. I am nine years old. I am in hospital. There is something wrong with my blood. I have no hair and I feel poorly.
I have three wishes. The first is to be an artist. The second is to make a snowman. The third is to go on a magical journey with a special friend.
Mrs Phillips says I should write to you.
Love from
Seb

I stared at the letter for a long time, folded it carefully and replaced it in the envelope. Then I unlocked the bottom drawer of my desk, put the envelope there for safekeeping, and took out the large, leather-bound school logbook. I opened it to the next clean page, filled my fountain pen with black Quink ink, wrote the date, and stared at the empty page. The record of another school year was about to begin.

A year ago, the retiring headmaster, John Pruett, had told me how to fill in the official school logbook. 'Just keep it simple,' he said. 'Whatever you do, don't say what really happens, because no one will believe you!'

So the real stories were written in my 'Alternative School Logbook'. And this is it!

Chapter One

Nits and the New Starters

86 children were registered on roll on the first day of the school year. The school nurse completed a head-lice inspection. Skateboards were banned following a directive from County Hall.
Extract from the Ragley School Logbook:
Tuesday, 5 September 1978

'Ah don't want this school giving my Damian no nits, Mr Sheffield!'

Mrs Brown was our least favourite parent and had the build and manner of a raging buffalo. It didn't seem to be the right moment to correct her use of a double negative.

'What seems to be the problem, Mrs Brown?' I removed my Buddy Holly spectacles and polished the lenses in an attempt to look composed.

'Ah'll tell y'what t'problem is,' she shouted. 'It's nits!'

She advanced through the office doorway, dragging four-year-old Damian with her. Clutching a Curlywurly bar, he was cheerfully oblivious of the chocolate and sticky toffee smeared across his face.

'Them little buggers are everywhere. My Eddie says a midget bit 'im last night in t'back seat of 'is car. So ah want summat done!'

I took a deep breath and tried to remain calm. 'We've heard about the outbreak of head lice in the village, Mrs Brown, and the school nurse will be in this afternoon to do a check on all the children.'

'Well, she better do it reight!' yelled Mrs Brown. She yanked little Damian's arm, causing his Curlywurly bar to leave a chocolate skid mark on my office wall, and rumbled out into the entrance hall. As I closed the door I heard her final tirade: 'We never 'ad no nits when Mr Pruett was 'eadmaster.'

I glanced up at the clock on the office wall. It was exactly 8.45 a.m. on Tuesday, 5 September 1978, and my second year as headmaster of Ragley Church of England Primary School in North Yorkshire had begun.

Back in the sanctuary of the staff-room, Ragley's other three teachers were collecting their new class registers from Vera, the secretary.

'Were those Mrs Brown's dulcet tones, Jack?' asked Anne Grainger.

Anne, a slim, attractive brunette in her mid-forties, was a superb deputy headmistress. She taught the youngest children in school in Class 1 and Damian Brown was one of six four-year-olds about to start full-time education in her class.

'Yes, and she's just about blamed me for the arrival of head lice in the village.' I picked up my old herringbone sports jacket from the back of a chair, frowned at the worn state of the leather patches on the sleeves, and straightened my brand-new tie.

Sally Pringle passed me a mug of coffee. 'Nice tie, Jack,' she said, nodding towards my fashionable flower-power tie sporting a bright pattern of yellow daisies.

Sally, the lower junior class teacher, was a tall, curly-haired thirty-something who clung to the last vestiges of her rebellious hippie days. She took her hands out of the pockets of her purple tie-dyed apron, which clashed violently with her frilly lime-green blouse and buttercup-yellow waistcoat, and grinned at Vera.

'What do you think, Vera?' asked Sally.

Vera Evans, a spinster in her mid-fifties, had been the school secretary for over twenty years and her opinion was always important.

'I'm sure the children will think it's cheerful, Mr Sheffield,' said Vera tactfully.

Vera pressed the creases from the skirt of her immaculate Marks & Spencer's two-piece navy suit, and distributed the new registers.

'Thanks, Vera,' said Jo Maddison, staring a little nervously at her smart new register. 'I promise there will be no mistakes this year.'

Jo, a diminutive twenty-three-year-old, was about to begin her second year as teacher of the top infant class. She flicked her long black hair from her eyes and scrutinized my new fashion statement.

'I think it's an excellent choice, Jack,' said Jo, with an encouraging smile. 'Where did you get it?'

'Beth bought it for me,' I said.

You could have heard a pin drop.

'And how are things with you and Beth?' asked Sally.

23

Anne and Vera gave Sally a startled look, while Jo immediately found the small print on the front cover of her new register particularly interesting.

'Not sure, but thanks for asking,' I replied cautiously.

They all nodded in unison, in the way women nod when they know more than they say they do.

Beth Henderson had visited Ragley School almost a year ago. She was the deputy head-mistress of Thirkby Junior School and had been assisting Miss Barrington-Huntley, Chair of the Education Committee, on her first inspection of the school. Beth and I were both single and in our early thirties. For me, it had been an eventful meeting, not least because it felt like love at first sight. A few weeks ago, in the school summer holidays, Beth and I had enjoyed a carefree holiday together but now she was applying for headships in Hampshire, so I guessed the feelings I had were not reciprocated. With a sigh, I put on my jacket, drank the coffee, picked up my new register, and headed for the door.

'I'll leave you ladies to it,' I said. 'I'll check on the children in the yard and then I'll ring the bell.'

The front door of the school creaked on its Victorian hinges as I walked under the archway of Yorkshire stone. Above my head, the date 1878 was carved into the rugged lintel and the grey slate roof reflected the bright September sunshine. My flared polyester trousers flapped in the breeze as I walked across the small playground that was alive with skipping feet and the shouts of over eighty red-faced four- to eleven-year-olds.

24

The mothers of the new starters were gathering in a corner of the playground. Betty Buttle, a local farmer's wife, hung on to her sturdy, rosy-cheeked twin daughters, Rowena and Katrina, and absent-mindedly picked straw out of their hair. Ominously, both girls were scratching their heads. Sue Phillips, our local nurse, looked relaxed as she watched her four-year-old Dawn wander off to chat with her friends. Sue's elder daughter, Claire, had been in my class last year and she had seen all this before. Alongside her, Margery Ackroyd, the local gossip, shouted to her son, Tony, to look after his little sisters, Charlotte and Theresa, and then proceeded to tell Sue Phillips about a certain local plumber who had offered to do more than lag her cold-water pipes.

Meanwhile, Mrs Dudley-Palmer, by far the richest woman in the village, slammed the door of her Oxford Blue 1975 Rolls-Royce Silver Shadow and hurried up the drive with six-year-old Elisabeth Amelia and four-year-old Victoria Alice. When she reached the playground, she dabbed her eyes with a lace handkerchief and clutched Victoria Alice, as if she was about to lose her for ever. Such sentiment was lost on Mrs Brown, who pointed little Damian towards the school entrance, gave him a push, and then turned on her heel and waddled towards the school gate. She gave me one final withering look before lighting up a cigarette and heading for the bus stop.

I walked under the magnificent avenue of horse chestnut trees that bordered the front of the

25

schoolyard and looked around me. Instantly, I remembered why I loved working in this beautiful part of the north of England. Ragley was a pretty picture-postcard Yorkshire village. On the far side of the village green, a group of farmers sat on the benches outside the white-fronted public house, The Royal Oak. The High Street was flanked by wide grass verges and terraced cottages with reddish-brown pantile roofs. Villagers were going about their daily lives, shopping, chatting, cleaning windows and watering hanging baskets.

It was an age of innocence. There was no National Curriculum, computers in schools were a far-off dream, and a teacher's salary was £400 a month. For this was the autumn of 1978. Average house prices had shot up to £17,000, one-third of the population of York, some 30,000 people, had paid to see *Star Wars* and *Close Encounters of the Third Kind,* and John Travolta and Olivia Newton-John were riding high in the charts with 'You're The One That I Want'. Suits had wide lapels, trousers were flared, and men often had longer hair than women. Also, the skateboard had arrived.

In fact, it was about to make its first appearance at Ragley School. Dominic Brown, elder brother of Damian, was racing towards school on a skateboard at that very moment.

'Gerrin t'school, Dominic,' screamed Mrs Brown. 'Y'neither use nor ornament!'

He ducked as his mother tried to clip him round the ear and promptly fell off. With his skateboard tucked under his arm, he ran through the gate and into the safety of the playground.

I glanced at my watch. It was almost nine o'clock. Down the High Street, the owners of the Post Office, Diane's Hair Salon, Nora's Coffee Shop, Pratt's Hardware Emporium, the Village Pharmacy and Piercy's Butcher's Shop were also beginning to look at their watches and unlock their doors. Prudence Golightly's General Stores had been open for over an hour and she had just switched on her Bush radio in time for the pips preceding the nine o'clock news. I walked across to the school belltower, grabbed the thick, ancient rope, and rang the school bell that had summoned children to their lessons for the last one hundred years.

Back in my classroom, twenty-four ten- and eleven-year-olds sat down in their seats, and looked excitedly at their brand-new exercise books and tins of Lakeland coloured pencils. Their cheerful faces reminded me why teaching was the best job in the world. I took the top off my pen, opened my class register, and began to fill the small rectangular boxes next to each child's name with black diagonal lines.

'Tony Ackroyd.'

'Yes, Mr Sheffield.'

'Dominic Brown.'

'Yes, Mr Sheffield, an' me 'ead's itching!'

'Jodie Cuthbertson.'

'Yes, Mr Sheffield, an' so's mine!'

I gave in to the inevitable, scratched my unruly, dark-brown hair and carried on with the register.

Outside the classroom window, a few mothers

were waving goodbye to their loved ones, while Mrs Dudley-Palmer wept uncontrollably into her handkerchief. Sue Phillips seemed to take charge. She put her arm around Mrs Dudley-Palmer's shoulders and guided her out of the school gate, pausing only to pick up a Curlywurly wrapper and put it in the bin.

Soon the children were writing in their English books about their recent summer holiday. Jodie Cuthbertson had just written, 'On holiday my gran kept getting up in the nite. My mam says she is intercontinental.' I recalled with a certain irony that, a few minutes earlier, Jodie had approached me with her dictionary and asked how to spell 'intercontinental' and I had been impressed.

It was a few minutes before lunchtime when ten-year-old Jodie made her first announcement of the year. Her older sister, Anita, had left last summer and she had clearly inherited her skills for never missing anything that went on outside the classroom window.

'Fella with a big case coming up t'drive, Mr Sheffield,' said Jodie, in the style of a British Rail announcer.

A small man with a flat cap and a huge black case was staggering towards the front door. At twelve o'clock, I walked into the school office and noticed that Vera looked harassed. She was counting dinner money.

'I can't get used to these new smaller pound notes, Mr Sheffield; they're like Monopoly money,' said Vera. 'The way things are going, they'll have pound coins next.' She chuckled to herself at the absurdity of the idea. 'Oh, and there's a circular from County Hall, Mr Sheffield.' She waved a sheet of official-looking notepaper. 'It says that, following a spate of accidents, skateboards have been banned. So I'll prepare a note for parents, shall I?'

'Thanks, Vera,' I said. With a class to teach, as well as being a headmaster, I appreciated that a secretary like Vera was worth her weight in gold.

'Also,' she continued, 'there's a book salesman waiting for you in the staff-room.'

'Oh dear,' I said. 'I'd better see him now.'

Vera beckoned me over to her desk and whispered, 'It's Ernest Crapper from Morton village, Mr Sheffield, and his wife's our pianist at the Women's Institute. She's on tablets for her nerves, poor thing.'

When I walked into the staff-room, I began to understand why.

Mr Crapper had opened the lid of his black case, on which his initials were stamped in gold-blocked letters. He looked like a magician about to begin a performance but, instead of white rabbits, he began to produce a collection of very large books. I felt like applauding.

'You look like an intelligent man to me, Mr Sheffield,' said Ernest Crapper, Morton village's finest encyclopaedia salesman.

A year ago, I would have been flattered by this astute observation but now, as a headmaster in my second year, I knew this was delivered with the sincerity of a beauty queen who promised to end poverty and deliver world peace if she won the Miss World Beauty Competition.

'This is your lucky day,' gushed the effusive Mr Crapper.

I had heard this line before. At the start of a new school year, the book salesmen of North Yorkshire gathered like vultures. Our precious school capitation was safely in the bank but this little bald-headed man in the dark pinstriped suit was determined to take a large slice of it. He was now in full flow.

'There's a free set of Ladybird Books with every gold-blocked, hand-stitched, top-of-the-range, superior volume,' said Mr Crapper. His large black leather suitcase, like *Doctor Who*'s Tardis, clearly defied all spatial logic as yet another huge encyclopaedia emerged and was added to the teetering pile on the staff-room coffee-table.

'Perhaps you would like to display your books on the big table in the entrance hall. The rest of the staff can look at them later this afternoon,' I suggested. 'Then you can come back at the end of school.'

'Certainly, Mr Sheffield,' said the enthusiastic Mr Crapper, as he repacked the sum total of human knowledge into his case.

Back in the school hall, our first school dinner of the year had already begun. Shirley Mapplebeck, the school cook, looked anxious. It was the launch of the cafeteria system and the children were lining up with their new plastic trays that had separate partitions for the main course, sweet course and a beaker of water. Because of this new arrangement, Mrs Critchley, our dinner lady, had become Shirley's assistant. She was serving a rectangle of steak-and-kidney pie, a portion of mashed potato, a spoonful of cabbage, followed by a splash of gravy and, in the hollow alongside, a helping of rice pudding.

I picked up a tray and joined the queue. Mrs Critchley was clearly not a woman you would want to meet in a dark alley. It was rumoured in the Ragley Sports and Social Club that she could crush a snooker ball in her right hand. As if to prove the point, with effortless ease she squeezed the strong spring on the handle of a large aluminium ice-cream scoop to release a hemispherical dollop of mashed potato on to Heathcliffe Earnshaw's tray.

Heathcliffe was queuing up with his little five-year-old brother, Terry.

'Ah don't like greens,' said Heathcliffe, looking dubiously at the cabbage.

'There's children starvin' in Africa,' growled Mrs Critchley.

'They can 'ave my cabbage, Miss,' said Heathcliffe cheerfully.

Mrs Critchley defiantly slapped a large portion of cabbage on his tray.

'Gerrit eaten,' she said.

Mrs Critchley did not take prisoners, as Mr Critchley would no doubt confirm on the very rare occasions she allowed him to visit The Royal Oak. With a flick of her other wrist, a slice of meat pie landed on little Terry's tray.

Terry looked closely at the pie, wiped the snot from his nose on the back of his sleeve and looked up at his big brother for support.

''E won't be able t'chew that, Miss,' said Heathcliffe, ever protective of his little brother.

31

'Why not?' snapped Mrs Critchley.

''E's no teeth, Miss,' explained Heathcliffe. 'Show 'er, Terry.'

Little Terry smiled shyly at the fierce dinner lady. All his front teeth were missing.

'Well, 'e can suck it, then,' retorted Mrs Critchley.

It occurred to me that a future in the diplomatic corps for Mrs Critchley was unlikely. Meanwhile, her magnificent biceps rippled once again, as she gave the rice pudding a quick stir.

Anne was sitting with the six new starters, so I lowered myself onto a tiny plastic chair and placed my tray of rapidly cooling food on the octagonal Formica-topped table. Next to me, Damian Brown was putting spoonfuls of gravy onto his rice pudding and stirring it to make a muddy brown paste.

'Don't do that, please, Damian,' said Anne Grainger.

Anne was showing her usual patience, as all the children seemed to be speaking at once.

'Please may I have a napkin?' asked Victoria Alice Dudley-Palmer.

'We don't use napkins, dear,' said Anne.

'My cat was sick this morning, Mrs Grainger,' said Charlotte Ackroyd.

'I'm sorry to hear that, Charlotte.'

Damian looked up from his rice-gravy compote. 'That's nowt: our cat bit 'ead off a mouse las' night, Missus,' said Damian, not to be outdone.

The appeal of the steak-and-kidney pie was fast fading.

'Eat your dinner, please, Damian,' said Anne.

32

'My mummy's coming to look at our nits,' said Dawn Phillips cheerfully. 'She says they come from little white grubs.'

My rice pudding had also lost its appeal.

Opposite me, the Buttle twins were sharing their dinner, while scratching each other's hair. They were the youngest members of a local farming family and they obviously enjoyed their food. Rowena was eating Katrina's cabbage and Katrina was eating Rowena's rice pudding. In seconds both trays were spotless.

'Please can we have...?' said Rowena.

'...Some more?' said Katrina.

Victoria Alice was still waiting to begin. 'Mummy says I must never eat without a napkin.'

I looked across at Anne Grainger and thought to myself that infant teachers were definitely a breed apart.

In the office, Vera was typing a letter on her huge old-fashioned Royal typewriter. She swept the chromium arm of the carriage return for the final line of a note to parents entitled 'Skateboards Banned in School'. Then she wound out the Gestetner master sheet from the typewriter, smoothed it carefully onto the inky drum of the duplicating machine, peeled off the backing sheet, and began the laborious process of winding the handle to produce the copies of her letter.

'Pity we haven't got one of those fancy photocopying machines, like they have in my husband's office,' said Sally, as she scanned the first, slightly smudged copy of the letter.

'Twenty-seven ... twenty-eight ... twenty-nine...

33

Schools will never afford them until Mrs Thatcher takes charge... Thirty ... thirty-one,' said Vera, as she steadily wound the handle. Vera firmly believed the world would be a better place with Margaret in charge of the nation's handbag.

During the afternoon, Sue Phillips got to work with her special metal comb and identified the children who had nits. She made a list and gave Anne three dozen bottles of strong-smelling shampoo. At a quarter past three, the parents of the new starters came into Anne's classroom to collect their children. Mrs Buttle and Mrs Ackroyd picked up their letters about skateboarding and were delighted to receive the free shampoo.

Mrs Winifred Brown was less pleased when she received her bottle. She barged into the school office, where Vera was tidying the contents of the metal filing cabinet. 'It's a disgrace,' she shouted, holding up the bottle in one hand and the skateboard notice in the other. 'My Damian 'asn't got no nits an' my Dominic doesn't do no 'arm on 'is skateboard.'

Vera stood up with a fierce gleam in her eyes. The school office was her empire. Mrs Brown, momentarily unnerved, took a step backwards. She quickly worked out she had underestimated this apparently mild-mannered sister of the local vicar and retreated through the doorway.

'Good afternoon, Mrs Brown,' said Vera firmly. She closed the door and returned to her filing, a smile flickering on her lips.

Meanwhile, Mrs Dudley-Palmer was more interested in the collection of encyclopaedias in the entrance hall.

Mr Crapper, who had noticed his potential customer's Rolls-Royce at the school gate, was not
Morton village's finest, and only, encyclopaedia
salesman for nothing. 'These encyclopaedias will
guarantee your children'll get to Hoxford an'
Cambridge,' he said, caressing Volume XVI.

'My husband was thinking about buying one of
those new computers from America,' said Mrs
Dudley-Palmer.

'Compooters, compooters!' cried the astonished Mr Crapper. 'Them'll never catch on. If
you 'ave an electric cut you've 'ad it. But y'can
still read y'encyclopaedias.'

'Except if it's dark,' added Mrs Dudley-Palmer
somewhat dubiously.

'Tell y'what,' said Mr Crapper, producing his
final ace. 'Ah'll chuck in a free torch. Y'can't say
fairer than that.'

Minutes later an Oxford Blue Rolls-Royce,
with the latest in luxury – namely, adjustable
headrests – reversed smoothly up the drive,
pulled up at the side entrance of the school, and
Mr Crapper began to load the encyclopaedias
into the boot.

At a quarter to four, the junior children filed
out of school and the staff gathered in the staff-
room. We all looked out of the window as the
children wandered across the playground. Our
first day was over.

'There goes a satisfied customer,' said Anne, as
Mrs Dudley-Palmer eased her Rolls-Royce out of
the car park.

'And there's another,' said Jo, as Mr Crapper,

35

cheque safely in his pocket, looked back at the school and doffed his flat cap.

'Not sure about that one, though,' said Sally, pointing towards Mrs Brown, who was hurrying down the drive, oblivious of the stately car silently creeping up behind her.

Meanwhile Dominic, pleased to be out of school, jumped on his skateboard, pushed off, gathered speed and hurtled towards the school gates. Winifred Brown, clutching Vera's 'Skateboard' letter in her plump fist, and cursing at the top of her voice, suddenly became aware of the car and jumped back onto the path. At the moment Dominic pitched into her, Mrs Brown looked momentarily as if she was auditioning for the cancan, as she pirouetted on one leg and fell forwards into the prickly hedge. The skateboard crashed against one of the stone pillars, and the front wheels fell off, while Dominic had the good fortune of a soft landing on his mother's backside.

'An' that bloody skateboard's goin' in t'bin!' screamed Mrs Brown at the retreating figure of Dominic. She walked off, rubbing her ample backside.

'Looks like she's got a bee in her bonnet!' said Anne.

'Or ants in her pants,' said Sally.

'More like nits in her knickers,' said Vera, buttoning up her coat in a very determined way.

'Oh, Vera!' everyone chorused.

Occasionally, I reflected, even a vicar's sister has her moments.

Chapter Two

The Sound of Ruby

County Hall requested a copy of our most recent school curriculum document. Miss Evans informed the School Maintenance Officer that we wish to proceed with the painting of the staff toilets.
Extract from the Ragley School Logbook:
Wednesday, 20 September 1978

Ruby, the caretaker, was singing 'Edelweiss' as she mopped the ladies' toilet floor. It was the end of the school day and Ruby was in good voice.

I found myself humming along with her as I marked Tony Ackroyd's English book. Tony had written 'Christopher Columbus circumcised the globe' and I put a tiny red question mark in the margin.

Ruby Smith was forty-five years old and had a heart of gold. At twenty stone, Ruby was a large lady but she skipped around the school like a dancer with her mop and galvanized bucket. On this sunlit September afternoon, she seemed to be working even harder than usual.

'Ah'm trying t'finish a bit smartish if that's all right, Mr Sheffield,' said Ruby, her rosy cheeks glowing bright red.

'That's fine, Ruby,' I replied. 'Is it something special?'

'Big night t'night in t'village 'all,' shouted Ruby, as she moved out into the entrance hall and began to mop the wood-block floor with even greater effort.

Curious, I stood up and leaned round the staff-room door. 'What's happening tonight, Ruby?' I asked.

'It's Talent Contest night, Mr Sheffield, an' me an' Ronnie are tekkin' t'kids,' explained Ruby.

With six children, life was always a struggle for Ruby, but somehow each day she managed to put food on the table for her family. Her eldest son, Andy, a strapping twenty-seven-year-old, was in the army, serving in Ireland, and her eldest daughter, Racquel, a twenty-five-year-old choco-late-sorter at the Joseph Rowntree factory, lived with her new husband in York. Her other four children, Duggie, Sharon, Natasha and Hazel, lived in their council house at number 7, School View. The youngest, Hazel, a cheerful, pink-cheeked five-year-old, attended Ragley School, while Sharon and Natasha were teenagers with a keen interest in local teenage boys. Duggie, a twenty-three-year-old undertaker's assistant, was known by the affectionate nickname 'Deadly' Duggie. Ruby's husband, Ronnie, was an un-employed pigeon-racer with a liking for football, the betting shop and Tetley's bitter. Even so, Ruby loved them all. She asked for little, received less and gave a lot.

'Sounds interesting, Ruby,' I said. 'I might even go myself.'

'Y'could tek your young lady,' added Ruby, with a cheerful chuckle.

I pretended to give her a stern look but privately admitted it was a good idea. Acting on impulse, I walked through to my office and picked up the telephone.

The headmistress at Thirkby Junior School had become accustomed to my calls. 'I'll get Miss Henderson to call you in about half an hour, after her netball practice, Mr Sheffield,' she said.

The familiar butterflies in the pit of my stomach were there again when Beth finally called and I explained about the Talent Contest. There had been no contact for the past week but, surprisingly, she seemed relaxed.

'I'd love to come, Jack,' said Beth. 'I'll see you outside the village hall about twenty past seven.'

Once again, Beth filled my thoughts as I drove home to Kirkby Steepleton to wash and change.

On Ragley High Street, the end of another busy day was near at hand in Diane's Hair Salon. This was a popular meeting place for all the women of Ragley village, and for a small number of adventurous young men with Kevin Keegan bubble-perms.

Diane Wigglesworth, a cheerful and friendly woman in her mid-forties, had left school with no qualifications, except for a natural ability to cut hair like a professional. But if degrees had been awarded for hairdressing psychology, Diane would have graduated with honours. She was particularly skilful at handling Nora Pratt, her next-door neighbour and owner of Nora's Coffee Shop.

Diane glanced up at the clock above the

canisters of hairspray and the poster of Bo Derek. As usual, Nora was late for her appointment.

The bell above the door jingled madly.

'Sowwy, Diane,' gasped Nora. 'Me an' Dowothy 'ave been weally busy. We've 'ad a wush on.'

Nora had difficulty pronouncing the letter 'r'. In spite of this, as President of the Ragley Amateur Dramatic Society, she always landed the star part in the annual village pantomime. This year she was due to be the princess in *Aladdin* and rehearsals had just begun.

'Don't worry, Nora,' said Diane. 'Come and sit down.'

Nora was clutching a copy of the *Daily Mirror* and pointing to a full-page picture of Charlie's Angels. 'It's the Wagley Talent Contest tonight an' ah'll pwobably win it,' she said breathlessly. 'So ah weally want t'look like 'er.'

'Which one?' asked Diane, with suitable restraint.

'Fawwer Fawcett,' said Nora eagerly.

Diane looked down at the photograph of the nubile, slim and athletic movie star with the perfectly coiffured, artfully fly-away, highlighted hair. Then she stared thoughtfully into the large mirror at the reflection of plump, forty-one-year-old Nora with her limp brown hair that at present resembled rats' tails.

Thirty years of hairdressing had prepared Diane for this moment. 'No problem, Nora,' said Diane, with glassy-eyed sincerity and a Mother Teresa smile. 'Let's gerrit shampooed and set.'

Nora breathed a sigh of relief.

'So what y'singing tonight, Nora?' asked Diane,

40

putting a warm towel round Nora's shoulders.

'A song fwom *The Sound of Music*,' replied Nora.

'Which one?' asked Diane, amid a lather of shampoo suds.

'"Favouwite Things",' mumbled Nora, from under the towel. 'An' they've got that weally handsome entertainer from Easington, Twoy Phoenix, to pwesent it.'

As Diane plugged in the hairdryer and collected the tray of plastic rollers and a big hairnet, she glanced at the clock. There was now no doubt in her mind where she would be at half past seven.

Three miles away, in Trevor the Barber's Shop in Easington, Shane Ramsbottom picked up a *Playboy* magazine, rested his size-eleven Doc Marten boots on one of the battered wooden stools, and lit up a Piccadilly King-Size Filter cigarette.

Trevor Brearley, affectionately known as Chainsaw Trev, had learned his trade as a boy apprentice to his uncle, Tomahawk Tommy, whose speciality, after giving one of his trademark severe short back and sides, was to singe hair with a lighted taper to prevent the customer from getting a cold!

This was definitely an old-fashioned, no-frills barber's shop where, according to Trevor, men were men and women knew their place.

'Usual, Shane?' asked Trevor curtly. Chainsaw Trev never wasted words.

'Usual, Trev,' replied Shane gruffly.

'Owt 'appenin'?' asked Trevor, making an

attempt at conversation.

'Nowt much,' answered Shane.

As Trevor shaved Shane's skull with the finesse of an Australian sheep shearer, Shane had an afterthought. ''Cept f'Little Malcolm,' said Shane. ''E's playing 'is 'armonica in t'village 'all t'night.'

''Ow come?' asked Trevor.

'It's Talent Night,' explained Shane. 'Me an' t'lads are off t'watch 'im.'

Trevor grunted in a non-committal way. This was his usual way of ending a conversation. Also, while he had no time for theatrical show-offs, he was reluctant to mention this deep-seated prejudice to Shane in case he took offence. Trevor was aware that the members of the Ragley football team were a band of brothers, and an insult to one was taken as an insult to the whole team. Also, Shane had the letters H-A-R-D tattooed on the knuckles of his right hand and this tended to command respect. As Trevor reduced Shane's scalp to the appearance of a plucked chicken, he reflected that, if you valued your kneecaps, it was wise always to agree with Shane.

At twenty past seven, Beth's pale-blue Volkswagen Beetle pulled into the High Street. She climbed out, locked her car, caught sight of me outside the village hall and waved. As she walked towards me, a light breeze tugged at her pale-cream summer dress and outlined her slim, athletic figure. A wisp of honey-blonde hair trailed across her cheek and accentuated her perfect English beauty. She looked simply wonderful. A cool silk scarf that exactly matched the colour of her green eyes was thrown casually across her tanned shoulders and her smile, as usual, made me feel weak at the knees.

'Hello, Jack.' She reached up to peck me on the cheek and the scent of Rive Gauche perfume lingered.

'You look lovely,' I said. 'Then again, you always do.'

She smiled and we walked in to find a seat.

By half past seven, Ragley village hall was packed and latecomers were each given a folding picnic chair and told to fill up the aisles. As usual, Ruby and Ronnie Smith and their family were on the front row. Beth and I found two spare seats on the third row behind Vera Evans and her brother, the Revd Joseph Evans. As the lights went down, Beth slipped her hand into mine and, once again, contentment filled my heart.

The curtains opened and Troy Phoenix, the local entertainer from Easington, strutted out onto the stage like a turkey cock into an avian harem. Troy, whose real name was Norman Barraclough, was on good form. Deep down in his heart he knew he was destined to star at the London Palladium, and that these village audiences worshipped the ground he walked on. As he strode to the middle of the stage, microphone in hand, he knew he looked a million dollars in his imitation gold lamé suit. However, as Troy's day job was delivering fresh fish in his little white van, sadly his suit smelled strongly of Whitby haddock.

'Ah can smell fish,' said Ronnie Smith, on the

front row.

'Shurrup an' be'ave y'self!' whispered Ruby, who could also smell fish, but didn't want to cause a scene. Next to her, Natasha and Sharon stared in admiration at Troy's Boomtown Rats hairstyle, John Travolta shirt and four-inch, Cuban-heeled, white boots. The Christmas tinsel Troy's grandmother had sewn around the turn-ups of his thirty-two-inch flares sparkled in the single spotlight, fixed to the roof beam by Timothy Pratt.

That afternoon Timothy, or Tidy Tim as he was known in the village, had been busy in the back room of Pratt's Hardware Emporium, and he was intensely proud of his plywood 'clapometer'. It was mounted on a table at the back of the stage, flanked by two primitive microphones. A maze of wires wound their way to a flickering metal dial, fixed to a semicircle of timber painted bright red and graduated around its circumference. A small ripple of applause caused the small arrow to move to number 1 on the scale. A few extra cheers moved the arrow further to number 2. Timothy Pratt guessed that nothing short of a Russian atomic bomb would persuade the arrow to reach number 100 at the top of the scale.

Troy stood, feet astride, and shook his shoulder-length hair.

Sharon almost swooned.

'Good evenin', pop fans, an' welcome t'Talent Night. Ah'm 'ere in person t'entertain you, the one an' only, sex-on-legs, Troy Phoenix!'

A small smattering of applause, led by Ruby's daughters, rippled round the hall.

Troy swelled out his puny chest and felt proud that his Cuban heels enhanced his height to five feet six inches. Then he gyrated his pelvis. This was clearly his Elvis impersonation but, sadly, he looked more like a vertically challenged fishmonger with haemorrhoids.

Sharon, Ruby and Ronnie all went red in the face with passion, embarrassment and hilarity respectively.

'Ah can still smell fish,' said Ronnie.

'Shurrup, Dad,' chorused Sharon and Natasha in unison.

Troy was now in full flow. 'We're gonna see some crème de la crème of t'local talent tonight, an' then y'can clap 'em an' see who wins on this 'ere clapometer.' He stroked the softwood frame of the clapometer suggestively and flashed a leering smile at Sharon Smith in the front row.

'First act t'night, guys 'n' gals, is Malcolm Robinson, Ragley's very own bin man. 'E's gonna play "Mull of Kintyre" on 'is 'armonica. So let's 'ear it f'Little Malcolm!'

Malcolm scowled at Troy as he walked onto the stage and polished his Dad's harmonica on the back pocket of his cleanest pair of jeans. At five feet four inches tall, he didn't mind his cousin and fellow refuse collector, Big Dave, calling him Little Malcolm, but he did object to being called 'little' by a fishmonger who, without his Cuban heels, was two inches shorter than he was.

Malcolm's hidden talent on the harmonica had been a surprise to the rest of the Ragley Rovers Football Club, who were seated in the back row. Soon they were in full voice.

'Give it some welly, Malcolm,' shouted Shane Ramsbottom.

'Y'easy best so far,' yelled Stevie 'Supersub' Coleclough.

''E's a proper little Larry Adler is our Malcolm,' said Big Dave proudly. Big Dave and Little Malcolm shared a council house in Ragley and, during the past week, Dave had grown used to his little cousin practising each morning in the toilet.

At the end of his performance, and to thunderous applause from the back row, Little Malcolm, looking very relieved, bowed and shook the spit from his harmonica in the direction of Troy as he walked off.

Troy pointed dramatically at the clapometer. 'Little Malcolm scores a thirty-three,' yelled Troy triumphantly. 'That'll tek some beating, folks.' He consulted a list that he pulled from a pocket in his skin-tight hipster trousers. 'Next one up is t'bird man of Alka Seltzer,' he then shouted, laughing at his own joke. Sadly, no one else did. 'So let's 'ear it for t'one and only Ernie Crapper from Morton, who will whistle some bird songs of Yorkshire.'

Ernie Crapper walked on purposefully, reversed his flat cap so that the neb did not get in the way of his flying fingers, and launched into a dawn chorus of strange whistles. The sympathetic applause he received was probably down to the fact that he had forgotten to remove his cycle clips, there being little of artistic merit in his performance. His wife, Elsie, hiding behind the piano at the back of the hall owing to her nervous

46

disposition, was glad she had taken her Valium.

The clapometer barely flickered.

After that, the range of talent was thin on the ground.

Elvis lookalike Lionel Higgingbottom, the Prudential insurance man, was suffering from a sore throat and a bad back during his rendition of 'Jailhouse Rock'. At the end, only his deaf mother clapped and Troy added insult to injury by flicking the dial on the clapometer to see if it had stuck on nought.

Would-be ventriloquist Gary Greaves, clearly in pain, with his teeth apparently super-glued together, could say his own name perfectly well, but struggled to introduce his dummy, Bobby Button.

Sixty-six-year-old Tommy Piercy, an excellent piano player, misguidedly chose to play the Warsaw Concerto on a pair of spoons. A sympathy vote put him briefly into second place, only to be immediately surpassed by Rocky the Talking Dog. Rocky had remained stubbornly silent but, after urinating on the back table leg of the clapometer, he received the second-best cheer of the night.

Deke Ramsbottom, seated near the back of the hall, turned up the sleeves of his John Wayne cowboy shirt, leaned over to his sons, Wayne, Shane and Clint, and mumbled, 'Bloody amateurs!'

Deke, the local cowboy singer and occasional snowplough driver, had won this competition so often in the past he had now retired. His rendition of 'Rawhide', complete with cracking whip and jingling spurs, had yet to be surpassed.

Troy eventually swaggered on to introduce the final act.

'Ah can still smell fish,' said Ronnie, blowing his nose very loudly.

'Ronnie, f'last time, shurrup,' whispered Ruby.

Troy frowned at Ronnie and then, undeterred, read the notes supplied to him by Nora Pratt. 'An' now, last but not least, we 'ave Ragley's very own star of stage and screen.' Troy paused for effect and those in the audience with long memories could vaguely recall the day Nora played a non-speaking extra in *Crossroads*. 'So, let's 'ear it for the Julie Andrews of Ragley, the beautiful Nora Pratt, singing a song from *The Sound of Music*.'

Nora walked on as if she was top of the bill. Once again, she was clad in the alpine leather corset she had worn for the last Ragley pantomime, when she was Snow White. It was laced up so tight she could barely breathe. But, with her Farrah Fawcett hairdo, Nora oozed confidence. As the introductory bars played on her ghetto blaster at the side of the stage, she invited the audience to join in.

Ruby was delighted and right on cue began to sing in a perfectly pitched voice. 'Raindrops on roses...'

'Waindwops on woses,' sang Nora.

Laughter began in the back row and gradually spread throughout the audience. Diane Wigglesworth quietly smiled to herself. Beth looked at me with wide eyes. Vera turned round and frowned at the footballers but it was too late.

Troy tried the gallant approach of a true Yorkshireman. He rushed on, leaned over to Nora's microphone and yelled, 'C'mon, lads, give t'poor cow a chance!'

Nora looked at him in horror, stopped singing and rushed off in tears.

Meanwhile, Ruby, eyes closed in contentment, continued to sing one of her favourite songs, completely oblivious of the uproar.

Soon the laughter died down, the backing music continued to blare out and Ruby, in a world of her own, carried on singing. As she sang the last few bars, spontaneous applause broke out and grew into a tumultuous roar. Everyone loved this cheerful village girl whose moment of recognition had unexpectedly arrived. Ruby's daughters and Duggie stood up and clapped. Ronnie leaned over and gave her a big kiss. Vera and her brother Joseph shouted, 'Bravo!' Everyone rose from their seats and joined in. The football team in the back row, led by Big Dave and Little Malcolm, stood on their chairs and began chanting, 'Ruby for England!'

Troy took one look at the clapometer, declared Ruby the winner and stepped down from the stage to give her a small shield engraved with the words 'Ragley Talent Show – WINNER'. Ruby having given him a hug that nearly broke his ribs, Troy was relieved when Natasha and Sharon took the opportunity to hug him a little more gently.

'C'mon, our lass,' shouted Ronnie, above the cheering, 'let's go t'pub t'celebrate.'

The tap room of The Royal Oak heaved. Big Dave ushered Ronnie and Ruby into the bench seat near the dartboard and Don, the barman, pulled pints as if there was no tomorrow. His wife, the buxom Sheila, put a double gin and tonic in front of Ruby and Little Malcolm staggered under the weight of a tray full of frothing pints of Tetley's bitter. Beth and I were crushed together near the bar and I wasn't complaining.

'I'm so pleased for Ruby,' said Beth, pushing a few strands of hair from her face. 'She deserves a night like this.'

'So do we,' I said, and looked steadily into her green eyes. I put my arm around her waist and held her even closer.

She raised her glass of white wine and tapped it gently against my half pint of Chestnut mild. 'To the future,' she said softly.

'The future,' I replied, hoping her thoughts were the same as mine.

With the thumping of a pint pot on a table, Big Dave broke the spell. 'Horder, let's 'ave horder!' he shouted.

'Horder, a bit of horder,' agreed Little Malcolm.

'Our Ronnie wants to say a few words,' shouted Big Dave. 'So shurrup!'

Ronnie stood up in front of the dartboard, pushed back his Leeds United bobble hat, shook the birdseed from his handkerchief and wiped his forehead. 'Ah'd just like t'say a proper well done t'our lass f'winnin' Talent Contest,' said Ronnie. 'Ah've allus said our Ruby 'as a reight good voice an' t'night she's proved it. So let's 'ear it f'our Ruby.'

Everyone, including a few sympathetic souls in the lounge bar, clapped and cheered. Ruby wiped tears from her eyes and Sharon and Natasha kissed her on the cheek. This was Ruby's day.

Soon the crowds tumbled out of The Royal Oak and, with shouted farewells, everyone made their weary way home.

As Beth and I walked back to our cars in the High Street, I put my arm round her shoulder. 'Do you know, Beth,' I said, 'I really love this village.'

On the other side of the road Ruby's family passed by. Ruby was singing again.

'So do I,' said Beth. 'At times like this.' She looked thoughtful.

'Are you going straight home, or would you like to come back with me for a coffee?' I asked.

She was silent.

'What is it, Beth?' I asked.

She took a deep breath. 'I wanted to tell you and I've been waiting for an opportunity.'

'Tell me what?'

She appeared to search for the right words. 'Well, you know that I've started to apply for headships of small village schools...'

I nodded slowly.

'I've got an interview,' she said suddenly. 'It's next month, on the sixth of October.'

'That's great news, Beth; you would make a wonderful headteacher,' I said. 'So which one is it? Tell me about it.'

'I'm sorry, Jack,' she said, and let go of my hand.

'What do you mean?' I asked.

'It's the one down in Hampshire, near my parents' home,' Beth replied hesitantly.

The walls of my world seemed to tumble down around me.

'Oh,' I mumbled. 'Well, I wish you luck.'

'It's a great opportunity for me, Jack,' said Beth evasively.

'I know it is, Beth.'

'I'm very fond of you, Jack, but at the moment I don't want any permanent commitment.'

I didn't know how to respond.

There was silence between us.

A breeze sprang up and a flurry of fallen leaves whirled round our feet.

'I don't want to stand in your way,' I said quietly.

Beth looked up into my eyes. 'You're a lovely man, Jack, but...' She didn't finish the sentence. Instead she stood on tiptoe and kissed me softly on the cheek. 'I'll ring you soon,' she said.

Then she walked quickly away into the darkness towards her car and I stood looking after her.

'Look back, Beth. Look back,' I whispered.

But she didn't.

On the other side of the village green, Ruby, arm in arm with her daughters and flanked by Duggie and Ronnie, walked home laughing and singing. I stood there staring at the tail lights of Beth's Volkswagen Beetle as it turned onto the Morton Road.

I shivered and felt very alone.

From a distance, on a chill September wind,

came the faint sound of a female voice. 'Edelweiss,' sang Ruby, but my homeland no longer
felt blessed.

Chapter Three

A Brush with the Law

*County Hall authorized the painting of the staff
toilets. Miss Barrington-Huntley, Chair of the
Education Committee, confirmed she will be visiting
the school on Monday, 9 October to check the
premises.*

Extract from the Ragley School Logbook:
Monday, 2 October 1978

'Y'toilets need painting, Mr Sheffield,' said Cecil
Trump, the School Maintenance Officer, with a
voice of authority.

He wrote 'Ragley School – £65.00' with a
dramatic flourish on his paint-speckled clipboard,
as if he had just signed the Magna Carta.

It was lunchtime on Monday, 2 October 1978,
and Miss Barrington-Huntley, Chair of the
Education Committee for North Yorkshire, had
allocated some much needed funds to maintain
our Victorian building.

I pushed my spectacles further back onto the
bridge of my nose and studied the pink maintenance sheet.

Anne Grainger looked as if she was about to

dance with delight. 'Oh, thank you, Mr Trump,' she said. 'We've put up with that horrid dark-green colour in the ladies' toilet for years.'

'It's actually Eucalyptus Echo Green,' announced Cecil, with an affected cough, and the superior smile of a man who had just won *Mastermind* answering questions on shades and tints in the living world.

Anne raised her eyebrows and gave me a warning look, but there was no need. After one year in my post as headmaster, I had learned to be subservient when the time was right and this was clearly one of those moments. We both nodded vigorously, partly to demonstrate our appreciation of Mr Trump's superior knowledge, but mostly because we liked the idea of toilets that no longer reminded us of the Amazon jungle.

'So 'ere's y'colour chart,' he continued, taking a thick rubber band off his wad of Crown paint booklets. 'Jus' pick the code for the gents an' another for the ladies, an' then ring Patrick O'Leary in Easington on this number an' 'e should do it by the weekend.'

By the time his little white van had rattled down the cobbled school drive, Anne had spread out the colour charts on the staff-room table. 'So, what do you think, Vera?' she asked. 'We've got to choose wisely, particularly as Miss High-and-Mighty will be coming to inspect the school soon.'

'I prefer lavender,' said Vera. 'It's such a sensitive and refined colour and I'm sure Miss Barrington-Huntley will think it's a sensible choice.' She

54

stroked her greying, carefully permed hair thoughtfully and pointed a long, elegant finger at a coloured box at the top of the chart. 'I'm sure that's the colour Margaret Thatcher has in her office,' she said. 'So it should be perfect.'

Sally Pringle, the lower junior class teacher, was not convinced. Her politics and dress sense were poles apart from Vera's. 'Looks a bit boring to me,' said Sally defiantly. 'But, as long as we don't have a signed photo of Maggie Thatcher on the loo wall, I don't mind.'

'What about you, Jo?' asked Anne.

Jo Maddison looked up from her *Nuffield Book of Science Experiments*. 'I'm happy to go along with your choice,' she said tactfully. 'Anything will be better than that dismal green. But, personally, I prefer this one: "Pink Perfection".'

Everyone nodded in agreement. It looked as though Jo had picked a winner.

I glanced at the clock. 'I'll just get some fresh air before afternoon school,' I said.

The playground was full of activity. Children skipped, bounced tennis balls against the school wall, and played hopscotch in the autumn sunshine.

'Hello, Mithter Theffield,' lisped Jimmy Poole, a sturdy six-year-old with a mop of ginger curls, who had just moved up into Jo Maddison's top infant class. He was poking a stick through the iron railings fixed to the top of the low stone wall that bordered the playground.

'Hello, Jimmy,' I said. 'What are you doing?'

'Collecting conkerth,' said Jimmy. 'An' you thaid we muthent go out of thchool but I thaw

Tony Ackroyd climb over the fenth.' Jimmy never had any problems informing on his friends.

I walked round one of the huge stone pillars that guarded the school gateway and bent down under the avenue of magnificent horse chestnut trees at the front of the school. The leaves were turning brown and the fruits hung heavily like spiky green sputniks. I collected a few of the shiny brown conkers that had burst out of their shells.

'Here you are, Jimmy,' I said, as I thrust them through the railings. 'Take these.'

'Thank you, Mithter Theffield. I'll give them to Mith Maddithon for our dithplay,' said Jimmy, the informer, with a self-righteous smile.

I stood up and surveyed the village green. On the far side, near the duck pond, the toddlers in the local playgroup were being encouraged by a group of mothers to feed the ducks. Deke Ramsbottom had parked his tractor outside The Royal Oak and was chatting with a few farmers. They glanced up in surprise as a small grey police van drove past them and then pulled up near the school gates.

A huge, athletic, six-feet-four-inch policeman somehow extricated himself from the front seat. He looked smart in his navy-blue uniform with a small coat of arms on each collar. A polished whistle chain glinted on his tunic and a pair of new-looking handcuffs hung from his belt. He was in his early twenties and sported a fashionable 'Sergeant Pepper' drooping moustache.

'Is it Mr Sheffield, by any chance?' he asked, in an accent that sounded as if he hailed from the north-east of England.

At six feet one inch tall, I wasn't in the habit of looking upwards when greeting someone.

'Yes, I'm Jack Sheffield,' I said, and shook his hand. I was reassured by his big, honest, friendly face.

'I'm PC Hunter, but call me Dan,' he said with a smile. 'Pleased to meet you. I'm new here – just moved into Easington. I've come about the cycling proficiency training.'

'Oh, I see,' I said, feeling relieved. 'Thanks, Dan, we've been expecting you. Come on in and meet Jo Maddison. She's organizing it this year.'

As I followed his size thirteen, black polished boots up the driveway alongside the tarmac playground, Jimmy shouted up at the giant policeman.

'I haven't thtolen any conkerth but I know who hath,' and he pointed to Tony Ackroyd, who was trying to stuff his pile of conkers through a hole in his pocket and into the lining of his shorts.

But at that moment Dan Hunter had other things on his mind. Jo Maddison was standing on the steps, by the entrance door, wearing a tight-fitting, navy jogging suit in preparation for the girls' netball practice that afternoon. She looked slim and full of life and her jet-black hair fluttered in the breeze. At five feet three inches tall and standing on the top step, Jo Maddison found her eyes met Dan Hunter's as he stood transfixed on the bottom step. It was like a scene from *Love Story*.

I coughed politely to break the spell. After a few hesitant and mumbled introductions, they quickly forgot about me and walked off towards Jo's class-room, deep in conversation, to plan the dates for the after-school cycling proficiency training.

Back in the staff-room, the Crown Paint Selection Committee had completed their task.

'Everybody's happy, Jack,' said Anne, smiling. 'We've selected "Pink Perfection" for the ladies'.'

'It's light, delicate and ladylike,' said Vera, with a knowing look at Sally.

Sally grinned and pointed to a pale-blue box near the top of the chart. And we've picked "Air Force Blue" for your loo, Jack, but, obviously, it's up to you,' she said.

'That's fine with me,' I said.

'We've put Jo in charge,' said Anne. 'We thought it would be a good idea to give her this as her first responsibility. So she's going to ring Patrick O'Leary with the order numbers.'

'Good idea, Anne. I'll see her later. She's a bit preoccupied with PC Hunter at present.'

Sally's eyes rolled. 'Oooh, isn't he dishy. Looks just like a young John Newcombe, the tennis player.'

'Yes, they would make a good match,' said Vera knowingly.

All three of them looked at me. There was a pause.

Happily, the bell for afternoon school broke the spell and we all walked back to our classrooms.

I called into Jo's room as she was saying good-bye to Dan Hunter. He looked reluctant to leave.

'I'll pop back tonight with all the equipment and you can store it in school,' said Dan.

58

'Thanks, Dan,' said Jo cheerfully. 'I'll look forward to seeing you then.'

They shook hands hesitantly and were not distracted by the children who had rushed in eagerly for afternoon school.

First in his seat was six-year-old Heathcliffe Earnshaw, who had arrived last year from Barnsley, in South Yorkshire. Jo Maddison had told him he would be making crab-apple jam that afternoon and Heathcliffe was so excited he picked up a pencil and began to stab a crab-apple with the measured demeanour of a crazed axe-murderer.

I crouched down next to him. 'What are you doing, Heathcliffe?' I asked gently.

Heathcliffe leered up at me with manic delight. 'Ah'm killing crab-apples, Mr Sheffield,' he said confidently.

Life was uncomplicated for Heathcliffe.

Meanwhile Jo's eyes lingered on the massive frame of Dan Hunter as he left the classroom.

'Anne says you're looking after the painting order, Jo,' I said.

'Yes, Jack,' she replied dreamily. Her thoughts seemed far away.

As I walked back into my classroom, Jungle Telegraph Jodie was quick off the mark. 'Big copper goin' down t'drive, Mr Sheffield.'

'That's Police Constable Hunter, boys and girls,' I explained. 'He's helping with the cycling proficiency you'll be doing with Miss Maddison.'

Afternoon school passed slowly and at a quarter past three a large posse of parents collected their infants from Anne's and Jo's classrooms. Many of them stared in surprise at the little grey police van that crawled up the cobbled school driveway. The impressive blue light atop its roof flashed on and off, adding to the drama. The technology of the 1970s was such that this illusion was created by a small plastic cylinder, with a gap in it, revolving slowly round the fixed lamp. Unfortunately, as the car battery died, so did the lamp.

'That big copper's back,' said Jodie, looking up from her English comprehension exercise. Sadly, she was struggling again. In answer to the instruction 'Complete the sentence: The four seasons are...' Jodie had written, 'Salt, pepper, mustard and vinegar.'

At a quarter to four, we said our end-of-school prayer and soon the junior children wandered across the playground towards the school gate. Dan Hunter and Jo Maddison were unloading cardboard traffic lights, plastic traffic cones and old fire-hoses from the back of his van and their laughter filtered through the classroom windows.

From the entrance hall, the crash of a galvanized bucket announced the arrival of Ruby, the caretaker.

'Ah've just heard t'news from Miss Evans, Mr Sheffield,' she said. 'Patrick O'Leary 'as said that, seeing as it's just t'staff toilets, 'e'll do t'paintin' after 'is tea on Thursday, so I'll come back late an' lock up.'

I was impressed that Patrick was prepared to work so late and pleased that the school would be ready for Miss Barrington-Huntley's visit next Monday morning. Patrick O'Leary was the most laid-back man I had ever met; he liked his beer, but always did a good job. He had sailed from Belfast to Liverpool in the Sixties and, after moving from job to job, had finally settled in Easington and begun his own one-man painting business. His low tenders meant that he regularly secured the painting contracts for the local schools.

By Thursday evening, painting toilets was the furthest thing from my mind. I had telephoned Beth at her parents' house to wish her luck for her interview the next day. She sounded tense at the prospect. It was her first interview for a headship and she peppered me with questions. She said she was spending the night at her home in Hampshire and would ring me on Friday.

The evening news came on the television and dragged my thoughts back into the present. A Member of Parliament, called William Rodgers, was explaining why his new seat-belt bill would save lives, but all I could think of was Beth. Suddenly the telephone rang again. It was Patrick calling, but there was no hint of a problem from his cheerful message.

'Sorry t'disturb you, Mr Sheffield, but oi've finished de painting an', to be sure, it looks a lot broighter,' said Patrick.

I thanked Patrick for his speedy work and settled down to watch Anna Ford, the first female news-reader on ITV, explain how Prime Minister Jim Callaghan was going to restrict pay rises to five per cent. When she moved onto the next item, about life for Princess Margaret after her divorce, I stood up to make a coffee, happy in the knowledge that the school would look good for Miss Barrington-Huntley's visit. I should have guessed that life was not that simple.

On Friday morning I arrived at school at the same time as Anne and we walked in together. Ruby was in the entrance hall with an armful of toilet rolls.

'Still smells o' paint in there, Mr Sheffield,' said Ruby, nodding towards the gents' toilet.

I walked into the tiny room and was surprised at the midnight, dark-blue colour. It was like walking into the London Planetarium. Tactfully, I said nothing and thought privately that 'Air Force Blue' was obviously a good camouflage colour for night flying.

Then I froze as a high-pitched scream rent the air.

I ran into the staff-room, towards the door that led to the ladies' cloakroom.

Anne staggered out and slumped into a chair. 'I don't believe it!' she mumbled, as if in a daze.

'What's happened?' I asked.

'Just look in there,' said Anne, and pointed incredulously at the closed door.

I pushed open the door and looked inside. It was like walking into a vision of hell. The dark crimson walls and ceiling were matched by the equally vivid, bright-red gloss on the doors and skirting board.

I sat down, dumbstruck, as Jo and Sally arrived.

They both walked into Satan's kitchen together. Sally shouted 'Wow!' and Jo just stared in absolute horror and then ran back into the staff-room and grabbed the colour chart from the table.

'Oh no! I've used the code numbers *above* the boxes instead of *below!*' Jo groaned. 'Instead of "Pink Perfection" we've got "Geranium Fire" and instead of "Air Force Blue" we've got "Moroccan Moonlight"! I'm so sorry.' She burst into tears.

Sally and Anne quickly put their arms around her.

Ruby looked bemused. As she reloaded the toilet-roll holders, she looked around at the traffic-light-red walls and shook her curly head. Garish colours did not affect her, particularly since in 1972 Ronnie, her football-mad husband, had painted the walls of their cluttered bedroom with blue, yellow and white vertical stripes in celebration of Leeds United's FA Cup victory.

Sally tried to console Jo. 'Perhaps if we put up some posters?' she suggested.

'Or drapes?' said Anne, in desperation.

A thought struck Vera. 'What's Miss Barrington-Huntley going to say?'

A look of horror crossed everyone's face.

I decided to be noble. 'Don't worry, Jo,' I said gently. 'If necessary, I'll explain to Miss You-Know-Who that I made an innocent mistake.'

'It was my first responsibility and I've blown it,' said Jo, drying her eyes. 'It's my fault and I have to solve it.'

She walked out to her classroom followed by Anne and Sally. Vera sat at her desk, unlocked the bottom drawer and took out her late dinner-money cash box.

'Something will turn up, Mr Sheffield,' said Vera optimistically.

Friday morning dragged towards lunchtime and even the sunny Dan Hunter could not raise my spirits as he prepared the playground for the first cycling proficiency session. Jo Maddison walked out disconsolately and began to help but her body language reflected her despair and soon they were deep in conversation.

Anne joined me in the staff-room after lunch. 'Don't worry, Jack,' she said. 'Miss B-H might not go to the Ladies if she's busy in the class-rooms and she may rush off like last time.'

Vera said nothing, but I knew what she was thinking. Miss Barrington-Huntley put great store by the appearance of her schools and she would not be impressed by a room painted to resemble a Russian brothel. After school, I drove the three miles home to Bilbo Cottage and my weekend began with troubled thoughts and no telephone call from Beth.

It was Saturday morning when she eventually rang.

'Morning, Jack,' said Beth. 'Sorry I didn't ring last night.' She sounded tired. Her voice was empty and hollow. 'My parents sort of took over after the interview and we got back late from the restaurant.'

'So, how did it go?'

'I didn't get it, Jack.'

A mixture of emotions ran through me, first relief and then disappointment for Beth. 'I'm really sorry, Beth,' I said.

'The feedback was OK. I feel I did reasonably well, but there were a few questions that I struggled on.'

'There'll be other opportunities, and you'll learn from this.'

'I know, Jack,' she said with a sigh.

'If I can do anything to help, you know I'm here,' I said, trying to lift her spirits.

'Thanks. I'll ring again when I get back to Yorkshire.'

'OK, Beth, safe journey home.'

'Bye, Jack.'

I put down the phone and stared at the receiver. My emotions were mixed and I wondered what Beth would do next. On Sunday I tried to brighten up Bilbo Cottage by painting the kitchen. By the evening, I had a smart new kitchen with barley-white walls and paint-splattered spectacles but no further message from Beth.

Monday dawned. The weather looked ominous. Heavy clouds filled the grey, overcast sky and it was the day of Miss Barrington-Huntley's visit. Just for luck, I polished the shiny yellow and chrome AA badge on the front grill of my car before I drove to Ragley village.

As I turned into the cobbled school driveway, to my horror I saw that a strange car was parked in the car park. I grabbed my old leather brief-case and hurried into school. Miss Barrington-Huntley, an imposing, stylish woman in her fifties who exuded power and authority, had arrived early and was talking to Vera in the school entrance hall. Vera was immaculately dressed in her favourite charcoal pin-striped suit and a crisp white blouse. Both women looked relaxed as they chatted together.

'Good morning, Jack,' said Miss Barrington-Huntley calmly. 'I just adore the smell of new paint, don't you? Miss Evans has kindly shown me round.'

'Oh, I see,' I replied hesitantly.

At that moment Anne and Sally arrived together in the entrance hall and their eyes widened as Miss Barrington-Huntley continued in full flow.

'Good morning, ladies,' said Miss Barrington-Huntley. 'I'm pleased you have spent the maintenance money wisely. I always found that dark-green colour so depressing. Your choice for the ladies' cloakroom is a most sensitive selection. Well done!'

Anne and Sally looked astonished and I was nonplussed.

Vera gave us all a knowing look as if she was trying to convey a secret message. Then she opened the staff-room door and we all trooped in behind Miss Barrington-Huntley.

Inside, two familiar figures were deep in conversation. Dan Hunter, casually dressed in a green rugby shirt and blue jeans, was smiling at Jo Maddison.

Dan jumped up when he saw me. 'My day off, Jack,' he said. 'Just called in to fix up a date with Jo ... er, I mean for the test at the end of the cycling proficiency training. Anyway, I'll see you later.'

He leaned forward to shake hands and something caught my eye. I noticed that his hands were flecked with tiny splashes of paint and I smiled in recognition. The paint was 'Pink Perfection'.

It was then that I understood a little more about love. Love is more than never having to say you're sorry. Love is painting toilets together on a Sunday afternoon!

Chapter Four

Jam and Jerusalem

Reading tests were completed for all infant children. The Parent Teacher Association agreed Miss Evans, school secretary, could borrow their crockery on behalf of the Women's Institute.
Extract from the Ragley School Logbook:
Wednesday, 18 October 1978

The ladies of the Ragley and Morton Women's Institute were singing 'Jerusalem' with gusto – in fact, rather too much gusto. The pianist, Elsie Crapper, had clearly forgotten to take her tablets.

It was just after 7.30 p.m. on Wednesday, 18 October, and I was a few minutes late in delivering Vera's crockery. I squeezed through the back door of the village hall and put down the huge box of cups and saucers on the kitchen worktop. The louvre doors of the hatchway were slightly open and I could see rows of ladies in the main hall, and at the front, behind a large trestle table, stood Vera Evans with the rest of the committee.

Vera did not look happy. She liked decorum and Elsie's piano-playing definitely lacked it, especially when she had failed to take her Valium. With a flurry of chords that sounded like the theme tune from *The Archers*, Elsie raced to the end of 'Jerusalem', slammed down the lid of the piano and rushed into the kitchen to switch on the Baby Burco boiler for a cup of camomile tea.

Elsie was startled to see me. 'Hello, Mr Sheffield,' she said in surprise.

'Sorry to disturb you, Mrs Crapper,' I whispered. 'I'm delivering this box of crockery for my school secretary, Miss Evans.'

Elsie, after a lifetime of distrusting men, opened the cardboard lid of the box suspiciously and looked inside. 'I see,' she said thoughtfully. 'What's this?' she asked, picking up a large jar of jam from the top of the pile of crockery.

'Oh, that's Miss Evans's jam,' I explained.

Jo Maddison's class had just finished their jam-making project and Jo was keen that Vera should be the first to sample it, particularly as she had provided all the jam jars from her collection at the vicarage. When she heard that I would be seeing Vera after school, Jo had written 'Miss Evans, Crab-Apple Jam, October 1978' on the sticky-label on the front of the jar and asked me to deliver it.

'Vera will be free in about fifteen minutes,' said Elsie, rummaging furiously in her handbag for her tablets. 'So how about a cup of tea?'

I nodded, peered through the hatchway again, and turned my attention to the strange rituals

68

that were part of Women's Institute folklore history.

The President of the Ragley and Morton Women's Institute, the tall and distinguished Mrs Patterson-Smythe, rose from her seat, took a deep breath, smoothed her presidential green sash, adjusted her spectacles and read from her handwritten script.

'On behalf of the Ragley and Morton Women's Institute, it gives me great pleasure to introduce Miss Edith Fawnswater, who is our visiting speaker this evening. Miss Fawnswater has travelled all the way from Bridlington to give us a fifteen-minute talk entitled "The Sex Life of an Ant".' Mrs Patterson-Smythe looked at her wristwatch and prayed it would not last more than fifteen minutes. After all, ants were simply awful little creatures. 'So I'm confident we will find it most illuminating,' she added, with another anxious glance at her wristwatch.

There was hesitant applause and Vera frowned. She was sure ants were very interesting and industrious insects but their sex life was surely a private concern. If, one day, Vera achieved her life's ambition and became President of the Ragley and Morton Women's Institute, she was determined not to have visiting speakers who delivered talks about the sex life of any of God's creatures.

Miss Fawnswater was now in full flow. 'The young males and fertile females fly from the nest to mate, after which the males die.'

Mrs Patterson-Smythe gritted her teeth, Vera looked to the heavens and the Treasurer, Miss

Deirdre Coe, sister of Stan Coe, the notorious local pig farmer, gave an evil chuckle.

'Serves t'randy little buggers reight!' muttered Deirdre to her friends in the front row. Their sniggers were cut short by an icy stare from the President.

Thirteen tortuous minutes later, the talk finally ended and Mrs Patterson-Smythe gave a vote of thanks, while secretly vowing to visit Timothy Pratt's Hardware Emporium at the earliest opportunity in order to purchase a tin of his most potent ant poison.

'I have two more notices,' said Mrs Patterson-Smythe. 'The first, which Miss Evans, our excellent Programme Secretary, has typed up, is the programme of monthly competitions for 1979 along with the hostesses for each event. This list will be displayed on the notice board in the entrance hall.'

Vera flushed with embarrassment and smiled modestly at Mrs Patterson-Smythe.

'The second notice,' continued the sharp-eyed President, looking in my direction, 'says that we are grateful to our local headmaster, Mr Sheffield, who has kindly delivered a box of crockery from Ragley School. This crockery is on loan until we can replace our own crockery, which, I'm sure you ladies will agree, has seen better days.'

There were murmurings of approval around the hall and Vera spotted me sitting in the kitchen and mouthed a thank-you.

'And now, ladies, it's time for welcome refreshment,' said Mrs Patterson-Smythe, with an air of finality. The sudden rush of activity made it clear

70

that the main business of the evening was about to begin.

A group of ladies, known as hostesses, leapt into action with surprising vigour. A trestle table, covered in a snow-white linen tablecloth, was quickly filled with large plates and dishes from the kitchen. A succulent joint of ham, eight pounds in weight, was displayed alongside two tongues, a vast quantity of sausage rolls and a large bowl of mixed nuts. Mary Hardisty, wife of George Hardisty the local champion gardener, had brought a large bowl of bright-red tomatoes and two cucumbers from her greenhouse.

Around the edges of the table an assortment of cakes covered in glacé cherries, shredded coconut and colourful hundreds and thousands were placed on delicate doilies. Unfortunately, the aesthetic quality of this wonderful presentation was somewhat reduced when Deirdre Coe went out to her mud-splattered Land Rover and returned, carrying one and a half gallons of fresh milk in an aluminium milk-churn, which she propped on the end of the table. She rubbed the splashes of milk from her beefy forearms, picked up a sausage roll in each ample fist, and wandered off, munching happily.

Mrs Patterson-Smythe and Vera immediately made a beeline for me and two of the hostesses began to unpack the box of crockery, while Elsie Crapper enjoyed the calm that accompanied her first cup of camomile tea.

'Thank you so much, Mr Sheffield,' said Vera. 'That was good timing.' She glanced up at the elegant Mrs Patterson-Smythe. 'And may I introduce our President?'

It was like being introduced to the Queen. I felt I should be bowing.

'Mr Sheffield, I do appreciate your giving up your time to help us out like this and I insist you stay for some refreshment,' said Mrs Patterson-Smythe.

I didn't need asking twice. Minutes later I was munching ham-and-cucumber sandwiches and perusing the latest addition to the WI notice board. I smiled as I read what challenges lay in store for the ladies of Ragley and Morton in the year ahead. Vera's neatly typed notice read:

The Competitions for 1979 are as follows:

January   Prettiest Egg Cup
February A Decorated Milk Bottle
March   6 Butterfly Buns
April   Cleanest Pair of Shoes
May   Most Uses of a Lemon
June   The Longest Dandelion
July   A Posy in an Egg Cup
August   A Painted Doily
September Prettiest Tea Cosy
October   Best Hat Using a Piece of Paper and 2
*   Safety Pins*
November Most Articles on a 2-inch Safety Pin
December Most Attractive Christmas Present

Vera and Mrs Patterson-Smythe were soon alongside me.

'Our WI cups and saucers definitely look rather dated,' said Mrs Patterson-Smythe, with a sigh.

72

'It's just that crockery is so expensive these days and it's vital we choose something appropriate.'

'I agree,' said Vera. 'I shall have to keep my eyes open.'

'I hope you do, Vera: it could be a vote winner at next year's elections,' said Mrs Patterson-Smythe, with a knowing wink.

Vera looked surprised. Then the penny dropped. It was well known that Mrs Patterson-Smythe wanted Vera to succeed her as President of the Ragley and Morton Women's Institute. The member who introduced a new range of crockery would clearly be seen as someone to be reckoned with.

'And we must keep out the riffraff from our committee,' said Mrs Patterson-Smythe, with a steely glare towards Deirdre Coe, who was, as usual, expounding the virtues of her infamous brother, the local landowner and bully.

'Jus' you wait an' see, ladies, our Stanley will be a councillor one day,' announced Deirdre to a group of browbeaten hangers-on, as she devoured yet another sausage roll. Her double chin wobbled as she turned to stare in our direction with a smug grin and the innate confidence of ignorance. 'It's good 'aving powerful relations,' she added menacingly.

It was clear that Deirdre blamed me for her brother's enforced departure from the school governing body at the end of my first year at Ragley.

Mrs Patterson-Smythe shook her head. 'And we've simply got to make sure that dreadful woman doesn't become President,' she said.

'She has a lot of support,' said Vera, 'and she did win a monthly competition once, which is more than I've ever done.'

'I'm sure your turn will come one day, Vera,' said Mrs Patterson-Smythe confidently.

Sadly, Vera had never won a monthly competition in all her twenty-five years as a member of the Women's Institute. She put it down to her non-competitive instincts. Although she had received a Highly Commended for her bacon-and-egg pie in April 1957 and was runner-up in the open-sandwich competition in August 1969, a first prize had always proved elusive. Unfortunately for Vera, in every village there is always someone deeply dedicated to producing the ultimate, perfect chocolate cake.

'What did Deirdre Coe win?' I asked.

I was soon to learn that Mrs Patterson-Smythe had an astonishing encyclopaedic knowledge of Women's Institute affairs.

'She won the "Best Bowl of Bulbs" in March 1973,' she said, with a shake of her head. 'And I still swear she bought it in Thirkby market.'

The internal politics of Women's Institutes were becoming apparent to me.

'No one has given finer service to this Institute than Vera, Mr Sheffield,' said Mrs Patterson-Smythe emphatically. 'She was Cupboard Supervisor in 1958, Outings Secretary in 1962, Produce and Handicraft Secretary in 1969, Press Secretary in 1974, and she has also been in charge of "Flowers for the Sick" for the past eleven years.'

Mrs Patterson-Smythe's attention to detail continued to amaze me.

'Well, it's been a pleasure meeting you, Mr Sheffield, but, if you will excuse me, it's time for our monthly competition,' said Mrs Patterson-Smythe, with calm authority.

With that she walked briskly to the front of the hall, where a long row of jars of jam had been lined up on a trestle table. It was announced that Ragley village's outstanding cook, Mary Hardisty, was to judge the October Jam-Making Competition. Mrs Patterson-Smythe made it clear that, prior to tasting, the anonymity of each of the seventeen competitors would be ensured by wrapping a paper napkin round each jar.

The jar of crab-apple jam came to mind. 'By the way, Vera,' I said, 'Jo said thank you for all your help with the jam-making. The children were very proud of their results and she sent a jar for you. It's in the crockery box.'

'Thank you, Mr Sheffield,' said Vera enthusiastically. 'I'll sample it tonight with Joseph back at the vicarage.'

'Well, I'll go now, Vera. Thank you for the hospitality and I'll see you tomorrow afternoon.'

I walked towards the main doors and then looked back at the bustle of activity. Vera appeared animated among her friends in the Women's Institute. She was clearly well-liked and respected and I felt lucky to have her as my school secretary. Vera had proved a trusted and loyal colleague during my hectic first year as headmaster of Ragley School. One of her strange old-fashioned foibles was that she preferred me to call her by her first name, whereas she insisted on calling me Mr Sheffield. 'That's right and proper,' she had said to me on our first day together, just over a year ago.

Vera was an interesting village character. She lived with her younger brother, Joseph Evans, who was both chair of the school governing body and vicar of the parish of Ragley and Morton. They shared the spotless and beautifully furnished vicarage in the grounds of St Mary's Church along with Vera's three cats, Treacle, Jess and Maggie. Vera clearly loved all three, but undoubtedly her favourite was Maggie, a sleek black cat with white paws, named after her political heroine, Margaret Thatcher.

As I walked out of the village hall, I paused to read a notice advertising the next meeting of the Ragley and Morton Women's Institute. The ladies met on the third Wednesday of every month at half past seven. On 15 November, Lady Alexandra Denham from Harrogate was to be the special guest with a reading from her book *Vegetable Dyes Through The Ages*. This was to be followed by a demonstration on how to make a plate-drying rack by Miss Duff from the Ragley Post Office.

I climbed into my car with the feeling I had just discovered a strange lost world and lived to tell the tale.

When I walked through the front door of Bilbo Cottage there was a note on the mat. It was from Beth and had been scribbled hastily on a page torn from a spiral-bound exercise book. It read:

Jack, just called round for a chat on my way to a residential course for deputy headteachers. Nothing

76

urgent. Will catch up with you sometime.
   Beth.

The word 'sometime' clattered around in my brain. I wanted to ring Beth, but I didn't know where she was going. Cursing my bad timing, I sat at the kitchen table, stared at the note again and wondered what it was she wanted to say.

The next morning, as I drove into school, autumn leaves carpeted the narrow back road from Kirkby Steepleton to Ragley village. The hedgerows had turned to brown and the school field to burnt sienna. Midges danced under the russet canopy of the horse chestnut trees and airborne, fluffy thistle-heads lost their freedom in among the countless spiders' webs lacing the iron railings. In spite of the uncertainty surrounding Beth, I knew I had found peace in this lovely Yorkshire village and I breathed in the clean air as I walked across the playground and pushed open the giant Victorian oak door under the archway of hand-carved stone. Another school-day had begun.

As Vera worked only half-days on Tuesdays and Thursdays, it was lunchtime when she drove into the car park in her spotless Austin A40 and walked into school for her afternoon's work.

'Good afternoon, everybody,' said Vera, but without her usual cheerfulness. She made a cup of tea in the staff-room, walked through the open door to the office we shared, sat down at her desk and opened her *Daily Telegraph*. However, instead of searching out the latest article on the triumphs of Margaret Thatcher, or following the problems of US President Jimmy Carter at the Middle East summit, she sipped absent-mindedly at her tea and stared vacantly at a photograph of Muhammad Ali, who had won the World Heavyweight Boxing Championship for a third time.

This went unnoticed among the other ladies in the staff-room as Sally Pringle was showing seven-year-old Theresa Ackroyd's topic folder to Anne and Jo. Theresa had written, 'Louis Pasteur discovered a cure for Rabbis.'

Curious to understand why Vera looked a little tense, I walked casually into the office and sat down on the other side of her desk. 'Hello, Vera,' I said. 'How are you?'

Vera looked thoughtful and gripped her teacup very tightly. 'Fine, thank you, Mr Sheffield.'

I decided to probe further. 'Is everything all right?'

Vera took a deep breath and then exhaled slowly. 'I have a moral dilemma, Mr Sheffield.'

I pushed the door closed to shut out the conversation in the staff-room. 'Can I help, Vera?'

She looked straight into my eyes. 'I've always been an honest person, Mr Sheffield.'

I didn't know what to say.

'It's just that I feel as though I've transgressed.'

'What do you mean, Vera?' I asked. 'What's happened?'

'I've always wanted to win a competition at the Women's Institute and, at long last, last night I finally won one.'

'But that's marvellous news,' I said enthusiastically. 'So did you win the jam-making?'

'Yes,' replied Vera. 'I entered my usual raspberry-and-strawberry preserve that I make every year.'

'But you've waited twenty-five years for this, so why are you looking so glum?'

'It came second, Mr Sheffield. My raspberry-and-strawberry preserve was the best I've ever made and it was the runner-up.'

I was confused. 'So how did you win, Vera?'

'It was that silly woman, Mrs Crapper,' said Vera. 'When she hasn't taken her tablets she gets confused.'

'I don't understand,' I said, shaking my head.

'You brought a jar of jam up to the village hall last night, Mr Sheffield.'

'That's right: it was in the box of crockery.'

'Well, Mrs Crapper put it with all the other jars in the competition.'

'Oh, I see.'

'So I have a favour to ask,' said Vera.

'Anything, Vera – just name it.'

'Perhaps it would be wise not to mention this to anyone.'

'Of course,' I said, in the whisper of a fellow conspirator. 'But don't you see, Vera, you were still the winner. Of all the ladies who made jam in the Women's Institute, yours was the best. So, morally, you've nothing to worry about.'

She appeared to weigh this carefully in her mind. 'I believe you're right, Mr Sheffield. It's just that I've waited so long for this moment and it hasn't quite worked out as I thought it would.'

'But the outcome is you were the winner,' I said.

Vera sat back in her chair, visibly relaxed and began to chuckle. 'You should have seen Deirdre Coe's face,' she said. 'It looked a picture!'

It was good to see Vera looking happy again.

'There's just one thing, Mr Sheffield. I know the crab-apple jam came from Miss Maddison's class but exactly which child was it that made this particular jar?'

I looked through the office window. Heathcliffe wasn't hard to find. He was one of our noisiest children. 'It was Heathcliffe, Vera. Look, he's over there by the far wall.'

Out on the playground Heathcliffe Earnshaw was playing conkers. The shattered remains of his opponent's horse chestnut lay at his feet, largely because Heathcliffe's father, an ex-conker champion himself, had hardened Heathcliffe's conker in the oven. With the tribal yells of the victor, he punched the air and then leaned back against the school wall in order to resort to his favourite activity. With the expertise born of a lifetime of practice, Heathcliffe stuck a filthy index finger up his equally filthy right nostril. After some serious excavation he took his finger out and stared at it thoughtfully. Then with assured deliberation he put the sticky finger in his mouth and sucked it clean.

Vera visibly winced in horror. 'Oh dear, so is that the little boy who made the jam?' she asked incredulously.

'Yes, Vera,' I replied.

Vera considered this for a moment. To my complete surprise, she appeared to see the funny side of it all and began to laugh. She laughed so hard she had to dab her eyes with her lace-edged handkerchief. 'I was just thinking of the certificate that was presented to me last night,' she spluttered.

'Why is that, Vera?'

'Well, after the judging had finished, Mrs Patterson-Smythe stood up and praised my jam in a most particular way.'

I was puzzled. 'And what exactly did she say?' I asked.

Vera opened her Marks & Spencer's blue leather handbag and took out an elegant white card, which was edged with a green border and inscribed FIRST PRIZE: JAM-MAKING: OCTOBER 1978. She passed it over to me and I read it carefully.

Underneath the inscription, Mrs Patterson-Smythe had written in neat, cursive script, *Congratulations! The small chewy particles in this excellent jam added greatly to the flavour and gave it a unique consistency!*

We both laughed.

Then Vera put a sheet of carbon paper between two sheets of typing paper, fed them into her typewriter and began to hammer the keys for her first letter of the afternoon.

Meanwhile, Heathcliffe, at the tender age of six and completely oblivious of his talent as a supreme jam-maker, contentedly picked his nose in the October sunshine!

Chapter Five

Whistling John and the Dawn Chorus

87 children on roll. Police Constable Hunter visited school today in response to a complaint made by Mr Stanley Coe. The situation was resolved.

Extract from the Ragley School Logbook:
Friday, 3 November 1978

It was the turning of the season and the first frosts had arrived. Dense November fogs had descended upon the Vale of York, shortening the days and chilling our bones. Along with the dawn chorus of the birds, someone was whistling Johnny Tillotson's 'Poetry in Motion' outside my lounge window.

It was Friday, 3 November, the day I met John Paxton, the village odd-job man.

I put down my cereal bowl, walked into the hallway, opened the front door and peered out into the gloom. The whistling stopped.

''Ow do, Mr Sheffield,' came a loud voice. 'An' a champion morning it is an' all.'

Out of the mist, a giant walked towards me.

'It's John, isn't it?' I asked. 'Vera Evans asked you to come about the broken gate.'

'Aye, that's reight,' said John. 'Ah'm diggin' 'oles now, then ah've a job in Ragley t'price up. Ah'll be back t'concrete y'posts when t'frost 'as gone. Then ah'll fix y'gate tomorrow.'

'Thanks, John,' I replied. 'That sounds fine.'

I glanced down at my watch. It was just after half past seven and the frosty path sparkled as the first rays of sunlight began to emerge.

''Ope y'don't mind me startin' early, Mr Sheffield. Old 'abits die 'ard.'

'You sound cheerful,' I said, shivering in my shirtsleeves.

'I allus whistle when ah'm content, Mr Sheffield.'

Vera had told me John's nickname in the village was Whistling John, so I guessed he was content most of the time. It was also obvious that Whistling John did not appear to feel the cold.

'Would you like a mug of tea?' I asked.

'That's reight kind, Mr Sheffield. Two sugars, if y'please, an' thanks for all y'doin' for my little Molly. She's lovin' it in Mrs Grainger's class.'

Molly Paxton was five years old and a popular newcomer to Ragley School.

I filled the kettle and looked out at Whistling John, who was digging furiously at the frozen earth. At six feet three inches tall and in his early thirties, John Paxton was built like a Viking warrior. A mane of long, wavy blond hair hung down on his huge shoulders and his bright-blue eyes twinkled with the deep satisfaction of manual labour. He had the strength of a Russian weight-lifter and, while he worked, he whistled his considerable repertoire of his favourite songs of the Sixties.

As the kettle boiled, he had reached the Beach Boys' 'Sloop John B', and the rhythm of his

83

digging exactly matched the rhythm of the song.

Vera had told me that she knew an excellent gardener and general labourer who had recently arrived from Sheffield. 'He's as honest as the day is long,' she said.

John's lungs had been badly damaged by inhaling manganese dust while working as a grinder in the 1960s in one of South Yorkshire's giant steelworks. Although he was proud that he could grind twenty-four-foot lengths of railway lines to an accurate profile of one-thousandth of an inch, he was nevertheless relieved when the giant klaxon horn shattered the dusty air on his very last day. No longer would the flying red-hot sparks burn his arms and scorch his overalls.

Following his redundancy, he had gradually recovered his health and made a new start in life. He had moved into a small cottage on the Morton Road with his wife and daughter, and Vera had said you could always tell his mood by the songs he whistled.

John thanked me for the tea and, as I left for school, he said he would call back for his money when the job was finished.

I thought no more about him as I drove carefully to school. Little did I know it but this gentle giant was about to have his peaceful life unsettled by a formidable enemy, one who had caused me many problems in my first year as headmaster of Ragley School.

Stan Coe was one of the wealthiest men in the area and owner of much of the land that surrounded Ragley School. His pig farm provided him with a steady income, but it was well known that it was his other deals that made him rich. He wore his ignorance like a badge of honour and had been a bully all his life. At the end of my first year as headmaster, Stan had been forced to resign as a school governor. However, he was now trying to gain support to become a local councillor and was determined that no one would stand in his way; but that was furthest from my mind when I arrived in the school car park.

Anne's husband, John Grainger, a tall, bearded man in a thick Arran sweater, was untying sections of a large wooden construction from the roof-rack of his battered Cortina Estate. It looked as though he was unloading a mini garden shed.

'Morning, John,' I said. 'Can I give you a hand?'

'Thanks, Jack – it is a bit awkward,' said John, as the wind lifted the first piece of framework like a plywood kite.

'What is it, John?' I asked. 'This isn't quite your style.'

John was a well-known craftsman and wood-carver who turned trees from the local forests at the foot of the Hambleton Hills into hand-carved, solid oak and pine furniture. Such was the quality of his work, he had a waiting list of over eighteen months.

'Knocked it together last night, Jack, from a bit of spare softwood and a few sheets of ply,' he said, lifting another huge wooden section with his large woodcarver's hands. 'Anne needed a shop in the corner of her classroom so that the children could practise buying and selling. It could probably do with a lick of paint to brighten it up.'

Once in the classroom, John screwed on the hinges so that the four sides could stand safely and unsupported. One side included a small doorway and the opposite side held a counter.

Anne was delighted. 'This is perfect, John. Thank you so much,' she said, quickly filling the shop with empty cardboard packets of cereal, assorted tins, a large price list and a metal money box full of plastic coins and Monopoly bank-notes.

Once again, I marvelled at how Anne brought life and excitement into her teaching and I knew I was seeing an infant teacher who made learning fun for her children. The reception children loved coming to school and it was easy to understand why they found Anne's classroom a journey of discovery. However, marking Class 4's English comprehension books was, occasionally, a slightly different journey. The first exercise book I opened that morning belonged to Tony Ackroyd. Tony had written, 'An octopus has six testicles.'

In red ink, I underlined the words 'six testicles'. A few minutes later, Tony, with a grin on his face, returned with his book.

'Sorry, Mr Sheffield,' he said, thrusting his book towards me. 'Ah know where ah went wrong.'

I looked at his book. Tony had crossed out 'six' and changed it to 'eight'.

Teaching might not be well paid, I thought, with a smile. But it has its compensations.

During morning break I joined Vera, Jo and

Sally in the staff-room. Anne was on playground duty. Vera was scanning the local newspaper and studying a large photograph of Virginia Wade, who was consoling a heartbroken Sue Barker following her crushing fifty-five-minute defeat by Chris Evert in the Wightman Cup.

'What a shame for Sue Barker,' said Vera. 'It's about time she found a nice young man.'

'That's just what I need,' retorted Sally, who frequently complained about the boring life she spent with her husband.

'What time does *Superman* start, please, Vera?' asked Jo, showing sudden interest in the newspaper. 'I'm going tonight with Dan.'

'Oh to be Lois Lane, just for this weekend,' said Sally. She gave a sigh. 'Christopher Reeve is gorgeous.'

'I've got my own "Man of Steel",' said Jo, with a grin.

'Lucky you,' said Sally. 'Meanwhile, I'm stuck at home with boring Clark Kent.'

'Oh no,' said Vera. 'Look who's coming up the drive.'

'It's Ragley's Lex Luther,' said Sally, hastily finishing her coffee. 'Good luck, Jack.'

I looked out of the staff-room window. A mud-splattered Land Rover I recognized was bouncing up the drive.

Stan Coe never wasted words. He stood in the car park, a thick polo-neck jumper stretched over his huge belly, his wellington boots coated in mud and manure.

'Ah'll keep this short,' he said, his yellow and brown teeth almost grinding in anger. 'Some money's gone missin' from our 'ouse. It were a ten-poun' note on m'table jus' inside t'front door an' it's been tekken.'

'Why are you telling me, Mr Coe?' I asked.

''Cause it's one o' your kids 'as tekken it!' he shouted. 'Name o' Paxton.'

'Surely not, Mr Coe,' I said. 'I can't imagine little Molly Paxton taking money. How did she get in your house?'

'She came in wi' that great useless lump of a father this morning. 'E came t'price up a job f'me. Told 'im it were daylight robbery and t'sling 'is 'ook. Little girl were just inside t'door. She must 'ave tekken it then.'

I realized that, although his allegation sounded unlikely, I would have to investigate. 'You had better come into school, Mr Coe,' I said. 'And please take your boots off first.'

'Let's get on wi' it, then,' said Stan, angrily kicking off his wellingtons. 'Ah've already telephoned 'er mother an' told 'er ah want me money back an' she says she's comin' 'ere. An' ah've called t'police an' they're sending someone round.'

Suddenly, this was becoming serious.

'You should have come to me first, Mr Coe,' I said.

'Nay, ah want 'em punished. It's thievin' is this. An' m'next call will be t'newspaper.'

The thought of a case like this in the local *Easington Herald & Pioneer* didn't bear thinking about.

I left Stan Coe in the entrance hall while I went into the staff-room. Anne and Vera looked up anxiously. Anne, in her usual unflustered style, immediately grasped the situation.

'Vera, please will you go to the school gate and wait for Mrs Paxton?' said Anne. 'When she arrives, bring her in the side entrance to my classroom. I'll go and find Molly. We need her mother present when we talk to her. I'm sure there's a simple explanation.'

This seemed to make sense.

'I'll take Stan Coe into the office and wait for the police,' I said.

Minutes later, much to my relief, it was PC Dan Hunter who walked in. I noted his new professional demeanour: he was on duty and it showed.

He took a black ball-point and new-looking notebook from his breast pocket. 'Now, Mr Coe,' said Dan, 'what seems to be the trouble?'

Stan Coe radiated malevolence. 'Ah want t'report a burglary,' he said. 'It's a den o' thieves is this school.'

Dan's expression never flickered. He put down his pen. 'Perhaps you should be cautious what you're saying, Mr Coe,' said Dan politely. 'Start from the beginning with the facts, please.'

Suitably reprimanded, Stan Coe launched into a graphic account of the events of the morning.

Meanwhile, outside Anne's classroom, a distressed Mrs Pauline Paxton – who had run all the way from the Morton Road – was being calmed down by Vera and Anne. Sally and Jo were hovering, anxious to help.

'Ah knew ah should've brought 'er t'school m'self, but my John said 'e was comin' into t'village so it was no trouble,' said Mrs Paxton. 'If ah get me 'ands on that Stanley Coe, ah'll murder 'im.'

As Mrs Paxton was six feet tall and an ex-South Yorkshire schools discus champion, this threat sounded entirely plausible. It occurred to me that here was a woman who could just possibly beat our own Mrs Critchley in an arm-wrestling contest.

Anne sent Jo out into the playground to find Molly Paxton, while Sally trotted off to the staffroom to make a cup of tea. Anne and Vera took Mrs Paxton to sit down behind Anne's desk.

In the cold months, the youngest children were allowed to play in Anne's classroom during the lunch break, so a few were building sand castles in the brightly coloured plastic sand tray. Victoria Alice Dudley-Palmer and Charlotte Ackroyd were playing in the new shop and Dawn Phillips was teaching Terry Earnshaw how to iron a beanbag in the home corner.

Molly, red-faced on such a cold day, rushed in excitedly, blonde curls flying, to see her mother and gave her a big hug.

'Hello, my little poppet,' said Mrs Paxton. The anger immediately left her and she looked almost tearful.

'We've gorra new shop,' said Molly, pointing towards John Grainger's plywood construction. Victoria Alice Dudley-Palmer was rearranging the empty biscuit tins, boxes of jelly cubes and a collection of red and yellow beanbags from the PE store.

'It's lovely, dear,' said Mrs Paxton, absent-mindedly untangling Molly's hair. Then she looked enquiringly at Anne Grainger, who took the lead.

'Molly,' said Anne softly, 'do you remember coming to school with your daddy this morning?'

'Yes, Mrs Grainger,' said the bright-eyed Molly.

'And do you remember stopping at Mr Coe's farmhouse?'

'Yes, Mrs Grainger. Ah saw some pigs,' answered Molly cheerfully.

'And do you remember seeing any money like this?' Anne pulled a ten-pound note out of her purse and held it up.

Molly screwed up her little face, thinking hard. 'Yes, Mrs Grainger,' said Molly.

Mrs Paxton's closed her eyes in disbelief.

'Can you tell me about it?' asked Anne very gently.

Molly took a big breath. 'Yes, Mrs Grainger.'

Everyone held their breath.

'Go on, Molly,' said Anne. 'Tell us what you remember.'

'When Daddy was talking to the shouting man, it blowed away,' said Molly.

'What blew away, Molly?' asked Anne.

'The money-note,' she replied, pointing to the ten-pound note.

'And what happened then?' Anne asked.

'I told Daddy,' said Molly.

'And what did Daddy say?' asked Anne.

Molly looked at her mother with wide eyes. 'He didn't 'ear 'cause the 'orrible man was shouting at Daddy and Daddy was upset,' said Molly.

'So what happened to this money-note, Molly?'

'It blowed all the way down the path.'

'And where did it go then?' prompted Anne.

'Ah don't know, Mrs Grainger. But Terry was walkin' past with 'is brother.'

Anne called across the classroom to Terry. 'Terry,' she said, waving the ten-pound note, 'did you find a money-note like this on your way to school?'

Terry looked up from behind the tiny ironing board and nodded.

'And what did you do with it?' asked Anne.

'Ah spent it, Mrs Grainger.'

Anne sighed. The problem was not going away. 'And what did you buy with it, Terry?' she asked.

'Bee-bag, Mrs Grainger,' said Terry, pointing to the bean bag on the ironing board.

'And who sold it to you, Terry?' asked Anne.

'Vicky,' said Terry, and he returned to his ironing, lips pursed in concentration.

Anne looked across the classroom to the shop, where Victoria Alice Dudley-Palmer appeared very much at home playing the part of a shop-keeper. 'Excuse me, Victoria Alice,' said Anne politely. 'Did you sell a bean bag to Terry?'

Victoria Alice had just completed the sale of an empty tube of Smarties to Charlotte Ackroyd for a one-hundred-pound Monopoly banknote. Charlotte was insisting she received some change.

'Yes, Mrs Grainger,' said Victoria Alice, rummaging in the money box. 'And he gave me this.' Smiling, she held up the ten-pound note.

Mrs Paxton looked at Anne with relief written all over her face. 'Thank you so much, Mrs Grainger,' she said, and gave Molly a big hug.

Anne picked up the ten-pound note and walked towards the school office, followed by Vera and Mrs Paxton, who was still clutching little Molly.

As Anne opened the door to the office, Stan Coe caught sight of Molly. 'That's t'little thief!' he shouted.

Dan Hunter leapt towards the doorway to block the charge of Mrs Paxton, pulled the door shut behind him, and held the handle firmly in his giant fist.

Minutes later, Anne had told PC Hunter the whole story and, slowly, a grin spread over his face. He took the ten-pound note, told Mrs Paxton not to worry any more, and asked Vera if she would drive Mrs Paxton home again. Then he walked back into the office with a very determined look on his face.

Although Stan Coe was pleased to retrieve his missing money, he was ashen-faced when Dan had finished with him and was told in no uncertain terms that he should apologize to Mrs Paxton. Stan merely glowered and left as quickly as he had arrived.

Dan relaxed when Stan Coe had gone and arranged a time to pick up Jo for their date at the Odeon Cinema with a certain superhero who wore scarlet underwear. Unexpectedly, Beth telephoned to ask if I wanted to meet her in The Royal Oak later that evening for a drink. Vera was quick to notice how eagerly I said 'Yes'.

Back in Bilbo Cottage, I ate a hastily prepared meal of fish fingers and chips while watching the latest episode of *Star Trek*. Captain Kirk and Mr

Spock proceeded to defeat yet another strange alien life-form within the allotted fifty minutes, against a familiar backdrop of papier-mâché boulders that had clearly been recycled from the previous week's episode. When the news came on that 57,000 Ford car workers had gone on strike at the Dagenham factory in protest at Prime Minister Callaghan's refusal to budge on his five per cent pay limit, I switched off and drove towards Ragley.

Beth arrived a few minutes after me. She looked casual and confident in her tight blue jeans, cheesecloth blouse and an open-weave, knitted cardigan. Her relaxed smile put me at ease after a hectic day.

The Royal Oak was packed with its usual Friday night crowd. Ronnie and Ruby Smith were sitting with Big Dave and Little Malcolm on the bench seat under the dartboard. Old Tommy Piercy was tinkling the old piano in the corner while Deke Ramsbottom, resplendent in his John Wayne hat, waistcoat with shiny sheriff's badge, and jingling spurs on his brown leather cowboy boots, was giving his rendition of 'Home on the Range'. Stan Coe, in the far corner, was berating a group of farmers about high taxes, while Shane Ramsbottom was asking his brother Clint why he had started to wear a Bjorn Borg headband over his Kevin Keegan perm.

Sheila, the barmaid, was keeping up a good old northern tradition by serving mince-and-onion pies with a large helping of vivid green mushy peas. It was a feast on a freezing cold Yorkshire night.

When Beth and I walked through to the lounge bar, we spotted Jo Maddison and Dan Hunter, apparently deep in conversation about the possible chemical formula of Kryptonite. We pulled up two stools to join them and Dan and I walked to the bar and ordered drinks from Don, the barman.

At that moment, John and Pauline Paxton walked in. Pauline waved a greeting and set off for the taproom, while John joined us at the bar.

'Evening, Mr Sheffield,' said Whistling John. 'We managed t'get a baby-sitter.'

'Would you and Mrs Paxton like a drink, John?' I asked.

'Nay, Mr Sheffield, we're not stopping. We're goin' down t'Bluebell. We only called in 'cause my Pauline saw Stan Coe's Land Rover an' she wants a word wi' 'im.'

'Oh, I see,' I said, and glanced at Dan.

John looked at Dan Hunter square in the eyes. 'Ah see y'not in y'uniform, Constable,' he said.

Dan appeared to guess what was going on. 'I'm not on duty, if that's what you mean.'

'In that case, ah'll apologize in advance for my Pauline. She's a bit vexed. In fact, she's spittin' feathers,' said John.

Dan and I looked across the lounge bar into the taproom, where Pauline Paxton was making her way towards Stan Coe like a nightclub bouncer. She towered over him and tapped him on the shoulder.

'Mr Coe,' she said, 'ah want an apology. Y'called my little Molly a thief today.'

'That's reight. There's nowt t'say she's not,' said

Stan ungraciously.

'Ah'm askin' politely, Mr Coe,' said Mrs Paxton.

The taproom went quiet. Stan Coe was not well liked, although few would have confronted him in this way.

'Get back 'ome, woman, t'that dimwit of an 'usband,' growled Stan.

Whistling John suddenly stiffened and Dan Hunter put his hand on his arm.

'No trouble, please, John,' said Dan.

Surprisingly, John simply smiled and replied, 'Don't worry, Constable. My Pauline'll 'andle it.'

Pauline Paxton moved slowly and methodically. With immense strength, she grabbed Stan Coe by the collar of his faded shooting jacket and lifted him up, so that his feet dangled in the air. Stan Coe was paralysed with fear. Never had he met such a woman as this.

Mrs Paxton stared into Stan Coe's frightened eyes. 'Ah'm waitin' for an apology, Mr Coe.'

A group of well-lubricated farmers began to cheer. 'Watch out, Stanley,' shouted one of them. 'She used t'castrate pigs!'

'An' ah were good at it an' all,' said Mrs Paxton, not relaxing her grip or showing any sign of strain in lifting sixteen stones.

'Ah'm s-sorry,' stuttered Stan.

'Insult my family again an' ah'll show you just 'ow good,' she said, replacing him in his seat.

With that, she walked back towards the exit and beckoned Whistling John to follow. Applause and laughter broke out in equal measure, while Stan Coe looked as if he had just gone three rounds with *The Bionic Woman*.

'Ah'll be round t'morrow t'finish that gate, Mr Sheffield,' John said with a grin.

'Are you sure you don't want a drink?' said Dan, looking both relieved and amused.

John looked at his watch. 'No, thanks, Constable. We'll 'ave a swift one at t'Bluebell and then ah'm off 'ome t'watch *Match o' the Day*.'

I smiled and shook his hand. 'Will you be watching it with Mrs Paxton, John?' I said.

'Ah don't think so, Mr Sheffield. She knaws nowt abart football,' said Whistling John. 'In fact, she still thinks Sheffield Wednesday's a public 'oliday.'

And with a great roar of laughter he was gone.

It was a good night, although Beth and I stayed later than we should. When we kissed goodnight and drove off in opposite directions, we were both very tired after such a busy week.

The next morning my brain was slow to function. Dawn was breaking but, thankfully, it was Saturday and I was looking forward to a lazy start to the day. I lifted the bedcovers a little, rolled my head off the pillow and groaned as a thousand hammers beat a sickening rhythm on the inside of my skull. Outside my window, birds were twittering and, as if that wasn't bad enough, there was another piercing, ear-shattering sound that at first I couldn't place.

Gradually, I realized what it was that had woken me. It was someone who was definitely cheerful. In fact, it was someone who was clearly *very* content.

97

Out-whistling the dawn chorus was John Paxton with his jubilant rendition of 'Glad All Over' by the Searchers.

Chapter Six

Wonder Woman's Boots

The Annual Parent Teacher Association Jumble Sale was a success and raised £172.57 for school funds.
Extract from the Ragley School Logbook:
Monday, 27 November 1978

It was a bitterly cold late November evening and, on Ragley High Street, the acrid smell of wood smoke hung heavily in the air. I pulled up the hood of my duffel coat and crossed the road by the village green. The profusion of scarlet holly berries, though brightening the gloom, were also a warning of the harsh winter to come. Ahead of me, the lights of Nora's Coffee Shop blazed out brightly and, as I opened the door, Bob Geldof and the Boomtown Rats were belting out their new number one, 'Rat Trap', on the bright-red and chrome jukebox.

Nora Pratt was expecting me. 'Ah've put all the dwessing-up clothes in the twunk, Mr Sheffield,' she said. 'What Mrs Gwainger doesn't want can go in t'Jumble Sale.'

'Thank you, Nora,' I said. 'I've got my car just outside.'

It was Friday, after school, the evening before the Annual Parent Teacher Association Jumble Sale. Nora Pratt had telephoned Vera to say she had cleared out the Amateur Dramatic Society's costume store and would we like the cast-offs. Two months had gone by since Nora's débâcle at the Talent Contest, but she seemed to have recovered and emerged unscathed.

'Dowothy,' shouted Nora to her assistant, 'Mr Sheffield might like a fwothy coffee.' Nora never missed the chance of business.

'You've gorra a big chest there, Nora,' said her assistant, Dorothy Humpleby.

Nora's eyes narrowed. What went on in Dorothy's mind was still a mystery to her. 'It were Aladdin's tweasure chest,' she said curtly, and walked off into the back room.

'So what d'you fancy, Mr Sheffield?' asked Dorothy, putting down her magazine. She had just spent 25 pence on a copy of the new magazine *Smash Hits Monthly*, mainly because Blondie was on the front covet

'What do you recommend, Dorothy?' I asked.

'Doughnuts,' she replied without hesitation.

I nodded and smiled tentatively.

Dorothy served me with a two-day-old jam doughnut and a frothy coffee, but her mind was obviously elsewhere.

'How are you, Dorothy?' I asked politely, and put a fifty-pence piece on the grubby counter.

'Fair t'middling, Mr Sheffield,' said Dorothy, fingering her huge, plastic earrings in an absent-minded way

Dorothy was a twenty-two-year-old, mini-

99

skirted, peroxide blonde with ambitions to be a model. She was also five feet eleven inches tall with four-inch white stilettos, so a conversation with her was demanding on the neck muscles. Among the villagers, Dorothy was not regarded as the sharpest knife in the drawer so our conversations were usually brief.

'Ah were jus' thinking about Lynda Carter,' said Dorothy. 'She's got everything, she 'as.'

'Lynda Carter?'

Dorothy looked at me in amazement from beneath her false eyelashes. 'Y'know, Mr Sheffield: Lynda Carter. She were that beauty queen in America and, when she spins round reight fast, she turns into Wonder Woman wi' 'ot pants and red boots to die for. Ah'd love a pair o' them boots.'

In front of me in the queue, Big Dave and Little Malcolm, after locking up their council dustbin wagon, had called in for a pork pie and a mug of tea before going home to wash. They were listening in to the conversation.

'She's on telly every week, Mr Sheffield,' said Big Dave helpfully, as he transferred three heaped spoonfuls of sugar with a white plastic spoon into the chipped mug of tea.

'Y'reight there, Dave,' agreed Little Malcolm. 'An' she wears bullet-proof bracelets an' 'as a gold lasso.'

Dorothy looked down in admiration at Little Malcolm. 'Ah didn't know you were a fan, Malcolm,' she said.

'Ah think she's fantastic,' said Little Malcolm, his ears going bright pink.

100

Big Dave gave Little Malcolm his 'big girl's blouse' look, while Dorothy fingered the chunky signs of the zodiac on her charm bracelet and gazed at Malcolm with new appreciation.

Unusually for Little Malcolm, he launched into a conversation of his own, instead of merely waiting for Big Dave to speak and then automatically agreeing with him. 'Y'reight about 'er boots, Dorothy,' he said enthusiastically. 'They're jus' like Starsky 'n'Utch's car: red wi' a white stripe.'

'Yer spot-on there, Malcolm, an' it's same shade o' bright red,' said Dorothy. She gave him one of her very best toothy smiles and he went almost as red as Wonder Woman's boots.

'C'mon, Romeo,' shouted Big Dave, and cuffed his little cousin round the ear. Malcolm promptly dropped his pie in his tea. As the pastry had the consistency of cast-iron, the crockery was a slight favourite to shatter first.

'See y'tomorrow morning at t'Jumble Sale, Mr Sheffield,' said Big Dave, as he lumbered over to a nearby table. Little Malcolm followed on behind, casting wistful glances at Dorothy while drying his pie on his council donkey jacket.

I found the only spare seat, opposite Timothy Pratt, who had just locked up his Hardware Emporium for the night. As usual, Tidy Tim had left everything in a state of immaculate order.

'Hello, Mr Sheffield,' said Tidy Tim, in his monotone voice.

'Hello, Timothy,' I said, taking a sip of my lukewarm frothy coffee.

Tidy Tim picked up his mug of hot chocolate

and put the square coaster two inches from the edge of the table. After closing one eye, he made a minute adjustment. The coaster was now parallel to the edge of the table. Exactly parallel. It was only then he visibly relaxed. Tidy Tim liked parallel lines.

After losing the battle with the doughnut, I got up to leave.

''Ope t'Jumble Sale goes well, Mr Sheffield,' said Dorothy, as she pressed C7 on the jukebox, turned up the Commodores singing 'Three Times a Lady' and sat down on a high stool. She carefully readjusted the seams on her black fish-net stockings, crossed her legs, picked up her nail file and looked thoughtfully at Little Malcolm.

Next day, I was up early. Late autumn had brought with it a jewel of a morning to Bilbo Cottage. As I stood in my dressing gown and filled the kettle, I looked through the leaded panes of my kitchen window onto the back garden.

Nature had truly blessed this beautiful part of Yorkshire. Soft sunlight dappled the holly berries, and the spiky heads of russet dahlias, their sharp edges tinged in white hoar frost, stirred in the gentle breeze. At the end of the garden, a blackbird poked its yellow beak through the ochre leaves of bracken and the calling of the rooks echoed in the vast powder-blue sky. Once again, I silently thanked Vera for introducing me to this lovely little cottage on the edge of the pretty village of Kirkby Steepleton.

The PTA Jumble Sale was due to begin at eleven o'clock. This meant I had to do my morning shopping a little quicker than usual. Only pausing to put on my old duffel coat and college scarf, I hurried out to my pride and joy. There on the driveway stood my emerald-green Morris Minor Traveller with its ash-wood frame and brightly polished chromium grill, gleaming in the sunlight.

I needed petrol, so I called into Victor Pratt's garage at the end of the High Street. Victor was Timothy and Nora's elder brother. Unlike Timothy, he was very untidy and always covered in grease and oil. Also, no one could ever recall seeing Victor smile and, as usual, he was in a bad mood.

'Ah've gorra bad chest, sinus trouble, stress, an' ah'm allergic t'summat,' said Victor.

'Sorry to hear that, Victor,' I said.

'An' ah've got earache, toothache, backache an' bellyache. You name it, ah've gorrit.'

'Sounds like hypochondria, Victor,' I muttered.

'That's t'only disease I 'aven't got,' shouted Victor as I drove away.

Minutes later I drove past the huge red-brick Joseph Rowntree chocolate factory and, in front of me, came into view the magnificent West Towers of York Minster, the largest medieval building in England. I felt privileged to have this wonderful city on my doorstep and I promised myself that the next time I visited York it would be with Beth Henderson.

I wondered what she might be doing, as I parked my car on Lord Mayor's Walk alongside the ancient city walls and walked through Monk Bar, the city's tallest gateway. A little further along, the Shambles, the old and incredibly narrow cobbled snickelway that had once been a street of butchers' shops, was teeming with tourists so I cut through into the open-air market.

As always, the stallholders were on fine form and the lively banter among them was soon in evidence. They had obviously all recently seen Kirk Douglas in the gladiator epic *Spartacus*.

'I'm Spartacus!' shouted the fishmonger at the top of his voice, waving his straw hat in the air.

All the shoppers stopped momentarily in surprise.

'No, I'm Spartacus!' answered the greengrocer, from the far side of the market, brandishing a cucumber in a menacing fashion.

Laughter spread like a wave among the stallholders.

'No, I'm Spartacus!' yelled the cheerful lady in the fingerless gloves who sold Pretty Polly nonstop comfort tights at seventy-five pence a pair.

'No, I'm Spartacus!' replied a Barry Manilow lookalike peddling Barbie and Ken dolls.

'No, I'm bleedin' Spartacus!' screamed a skinhead behind a bank of posters of Showaddywaddy, Gary Glitter and the Sex Pistols.

'Watch yer language!' shouted the elderly lady in a headscarf on the opposite stall heaped with brocade cushion covers at a pound each.

And so it went on.

Half an hour later, and weighed down with two heavy bags, I stopped next to a large crowd of shoppers, when a familiar voice shouted my name.

'Hello, Jack, over here!'

It was Staff Nurse Sue Phillips with a navy-blue

gabardine raincoat loosely buttoned over her freshly starched uniform. I squeezed through the crowd to stand next to her.

'I'm going to buy one of those,' said Sue, pointing to a pile of shiny cardboard boxes on a handcart at the front of the crowd.

I put down my shopping and listened to the street trader. He was standing on an orange box and holding an item I didn't recognize. It looked as if it had once belonged to one of *Doctor Who*'s Daleks.

'Y'can trust me, ladies. Ah'm not 'ere-t'day-gone-t'morrow,' shouted the swarthy trader, his jet-black pony-tail swinging with every turn of his head. 'This 'ere is a genuine, top-of-the-range Carmen Compact Curler, straight from one o' them posh shops in Hoxford Street in London.'

I still didn't know what he was talking about. What I did know was that I was the only man in the crowd.

'So what am I askin' for this telescopic, steam stylin' wand?'

I was still no wiser.

'It folds to 'alf its size, ladies, an' it curls, it waves an' it smoothes in seconds.'

Sue leaned over and whispered in my ear, 'That's what every woman wants, Jack, and they're £9.95 in Boots.'

'Ah'm not askin' a tenner, ah'm not askin' a fiver. Who'll give me two poun' fifty?' yelled Pony-Tail.

'I'll have one!' shouted Sue.

A sudden impulse took over. 'So will I,' I echoed.

105

'Thank you to the sexy nurse an' Buddy 'olly.'

The crowd laughed and Sue blew the trader a kiss.

Self-consciously, I pushed my large, black-framed spectacles further back onto the bridge of my nose, while a scrawny young girl in hot pants and thigh-high boots snatched our money and gave us each a box in a carrier bag.

'What have I bought, Sue?' I asked.

'A present for a lady,' said Sue, with that familiar mischievous grin. 'Anyway, I must rush, Jack. I need to collect the girls from their riding lesson, get changed and go to the Jumble Sale. See you later.'

Sue lived her life at breakneck speed and with a wave she was gone. I glanced at my watch. It was ten-fifteen and the Jumble Sale started at eleven o'clock, so I drove straight back to Ragley.

When I walked into school, Anne, Sally and Jo were already classifying the mountain of jumble and Shirley, the cook, was serving hot drinks from her giant cast-iron teapot. Soon the tables were piled high with the cast-offs of the wardrobes, toy cupboards and garages of Ragley village. Some of the jumble looked vaguely familiar and Anne told me it wouldn't be the first time that children bought toys they had once owned but had discarded a year ago.

Soon it felt as though the whole village had descended on our school hall, with everyone looking for a bargain.

Five-year-old Terry Earnshaw, Heathcliffe's little brother, was concerned about his purchase. He had bought a plastic model of an extremely

106

muscular Action Man for ten pence. "E's bin in t'box too long, missus,' he shouted, in a foghorn voice that was beginning to resemble his elder brother's.

'Why's that, then?' asked Mrs Critchley, from behind the second-hand-toy stall.

"E's gorra beard,' yelled Terry, pointing to the brown plastic designer stubble on the doll's chin.

As Mrs Critchley's bedtime reading was *Confessions of a Window Cleaner* and not *Stages of Children's Psychological Development* by the Swiss psychologist Jean Piaget, she took the easy option and gave Terry his money back.

Ruby Smith loved the Annual PTA Jumble Sale. It was a high point in her life and an opportunity to clothe her large family for the price of a few coppers. She would scavenge the choice jumpers, skirts, boiler suits and footwear, and then pile them into black bags to be carried home by her daughters. Vera was determined to do her best for Ruby, for whom she had great affection. She was in charge of the footwear and handbag stall and, while many of the thigh-high leather boots, pink stilettos, Doc Marten boots and plastic Barbie doll make-up bags were beyond her comprehension, she tried hard to reserve a suitable selection for the diverse needs of Ruby's family.

Big Dave and Little Malcolm were staring at the boots on Vera's stall. 'Excuse me, Miss Evans. We're looking for a pair o' wellies,' said Big Dave.

'Yes, wellies, Miss Evans,' echoed Little Malcolm.

Vera, in her immaculate cream blouse and bottle-green Marks & Spencer's cardigan, looked slightly incongruous standing behind the huge mountain of wellington boots. She pointed a beautifully manicured finger at a particularly large pair and then a slightly smaller pair.

'Please help yourselves, gentlemen, and put whatever you think they're worth in the jar,' said Vera. Secretly, she thought that they may be bin men but at least they were bin men with manners.

As headmaster, I had been appointed to look after each stall at intervals, to give the parent or teacher a tea break. Shortly after I had taken over from Vera, Little Malcolm reappeared, looking extremely furtive. He pointed to a pair of knee-high ladies' boots in bright red for two pounds fifty pence.

'Can y'stick 'em in a black bag for me, please, Mr Sheffield?' said Little Malcolm, looking over his shoulder towards Big Dave. Fortunately his giant cousin had just found a copy of the 1978 *Roy of the Rovers Annual* on the second-hand bookstall. Big Dave was not an avid reader, but soon he was chuckling at the first comic-strip story, in which Roy Race, player-manager of Melchester Rovers, had just discovered that the Australian football team they were about to play were, in fact, a team of female footballers.

Little Malcolm quickly paid his two pounds fifty pence and looked so serious I refrained from making a joke. Seconds later, I saw him disappearing down the school drive, his parcel tucked under his arm.

Raised voices suddenly caught my attention. Sue Phillips was doing battle with Deirdre Coe.

'Twenty pence is a fair price for a hand-made apron, Deirdre,' said Sue defiantly.

'Bare-faced robbery, that's what it is,' said Deirdre, reluctantly handing over her twenty pence, before snatching the apron and barging her way to the front of another queue.

'Hello, Sue,' I said. 'Everything all right?'

'She infuriates me,' said Sue. 'Just look at her, mutton dressed as lamb!'

'Shall I get you a cup of tea?' I asked, trying to calm things down.

'Sorry, I'm forgetting myself,' she said, and took a deep breath. 'By the way, Jack, that lovely little boy, Sebastian, in the Children's Ward, was asking after you this morning. He's hoping you might find time to visit him before Christmas.'

I remembered the 'Mister Teacher' letter.

'Sorry, Sue,' I said. 'Life's been busy.'

Sue just nodded, but her silence spoke volumes.

'I'll do my best,' I said.

'I know you will,' she said. 'And, by the way, I've just spotted the person who might appreciate that gift you bought this morning.'

Beth Henderson had just walked into the hall and was talking to Vera, who, as usual, was trying to encourage her to join the church choir.

Vera ushered her towards me. 'But you've got a wonderful voice, dear, and we need a good soprano,' said Vera, persuasively.

'I'll think about it, Vera,' said Beth, but she looked distracted.

'I'll take over now, Mr Sheffield,' said Vera, with a look that brooked no argument.

Beth and I wandered through the crowded school hall and out into the car park. There was a moment when she appeared to be trying to find the right words. I gave her time.

A thought crossed my mind. 'Come on, I've got something to show you.'

I unlocked the rear doors of my car and took a carrier bag from behind the spare can of petrol. 'For you,' I said.

'Oh, thank you,' said Beth, in surprise, and looked in the bag. She read the label on the box.

'Just what I wanted, Jack. Thank you so much.' The shutters over her eyes had lifted. 'These really are the in-thing. How on earth did you know I wanted one of these?'

Sometimes it's easier to say nothing.

Back in the staff-room, Vera and Anne were counting up the money. 'Over one hundred and fifty pounds and still counting, Mr Sheffield,' said Vera. 'I'll get Mrs Phillips to verify the amount, lock it in the vicarage safe overnight and bank it on Monday.'

Sally and Jo walked into the staff-room. 'We're parked in the High Street,' announced Sally. 'So how about calling in at the Coffee Shop before we go home?'

Vera was reluctant but Beth and I joined them and we walked down the High Street together. Her summer tan had faded now but she still looked stunning in a white polo-neck jumper, blue hipster denims, white trainers and a navy-blue tracksuit top.

The doorbell jingled as we walked into the Coffee Shop but there was no sign of Dorothy.

110

Instead, Nora was talking to Little Malcolm, who was sitting on a high stool next to the counter. Gladys Knight and the Pips were singing their latest hit, 'Come Back and Finish What You Started', on the jukebox as we took our seats.

I ordered four frothy coffees and four Kit-Kats.

Suddenly, from the back room, Dorothy appeared, wearing a Lycra figure-hugging top, skin-tight hot pants and a pair of long, bright-red, patent-leather boots. The finishing touch was the vertical stripe of white insulation tape on each boot.

Everyone in the Coffee Shop turned to look at Ragley's version of Wonder Woman.

Nora stared at the red boots. 'Hey, Dowothy, they look jus' like the wed boots I wore in *Cindewella;* 'cept for them white stwipes down the fwont,' she added.

'Malcolm bought 'em for me,' said Dorothy excitedly.

Little Malcolm beamed from ear to ear. He was five feet four inches tall, but at this moment he felt like a giant.

I returned to the table with the coffees and chocolate bars.

'Why is Dorothy spinning round and round?' asked Beth.

'That's what Wonder Woman does,' I said. 'She spins round in her red boots and turns into a superhero.'

This item of knowledge clearly surprised the three women sitting round the table.

'Impressive,' said Sally, after an astonished pause.

'What's in the bag, Beth?' asked Jo.

'It's a gift from Jack,' said Beth, smiling and unpacking her Carmen Compact Curler.

'You certainly know the way to a woman's heart, Jack,' said Sally.

Beth's soft green eyes looked relaxed as the three women began an animated conversation about the benefits of high-quality curling tongs.

I sat back in my chair. Life was good again. Little Malcolm caught my eye and gave me a thumbs-up. I guessed we were both thinking the same thing.

It was two pounds fifty well spent.

Chapter Seven

A Gift for Jeremy

Mrs Pringle invited parents into school to support Class 3's topic work. Miss Golightly from the General Stores provided an exhibition of photographs.
Extract from the Ragley School Logbook:
Wednesday, 6 December 1978

Tidy Tim was polishing his apostrophe.

It was half past eight on the morning of Wednesday, 6 December, and Timothy Pratt was up a ladder cleaning his grammatically correct shop sign.

'Be careful, Timothy,' I shouted, as I stepped gingerly on the frost-covered pavement of Ragley

High Street.

'Don't worry, Mr Sheffield,' said Timothy, as he moved on to the letter 's'. 'Ladder's got non-slip rubber grips.'

Tidy Tim was cleaning his shop sign prior to decorating it with spray-on snow and a strand of Christmas lights. Next door to Pratt's Hardware Emporium, outside Piercy's Butcher's Shop, a boldly written sign read 'ORDER XMAS TURKEY'S NOW!' and on the door of the General Stores & Newsagent was the notice 'BAKERS STRIKE - NO LOAVE'S TODAY!'

I shook my head in dismay and vowed I must do another lesson with my class on the use of the apostrophe, so that the next generation of shopkeepers could write correct notices.

Each morning on my way to school I parked my car by the parade of shops on Ragley High Street to buy my morning paper. The General Stores and Newsagent was the first shop in the terraced row, and this morning it looked cheerful with a long strand of red and green light bulbs attached to the metal frame of the canvas canopy over the front window. On display were the usual large glass jars of liquorice allsorts, bull's eyes, sherbet dips, penny lollies, giant humbugs, dolly mixtures, aniseed balls, chocolate butter dainties, jelly babies, extra-strong mints and liquorice torpedoes to tempt the passing trade of children on their way to school.

I followed Heathcliffe Earnshaw and his little brother Terry into the shop. The shop-owner, Miss Prudence Golightly, peered over her pince-nez spectacles and observed with a gimlet eye the two little boys. The General Stores was always a hive of activity each morning and the villagers, who called in for their newspapers and cigarettes, were all aware that the tiny, four-foot-eleven-inches-tall Miss Golightly had a number of idiosyncrasies, as the Earnshaw brothers were about to discover.

Heathcliffe clutched his five-pence piece firmly in his grubby right hand and stared at the vast array of chocolate bars next to the counter.

'What d'you wan', Terry?' demanded Heathcliffe.

'Ah wanna currywurry,' mumbled five-year-old Terry.

Heathcliffe, clearly destined to be an expert in ancient Japanese dialects, immediately understood his little brother's request. A Curlywurly cost three pence, which left two pence for him to buy his favourite treat – namely, a Milky Way. It seemed to make sense.

'A Curlywurly an' a Milky Way,' said Heathcliffe, slamming his five pence on the counter.

Miss Golightly looked down from her elevated position on the wooden steps behind the counter at the determined face of the ex-Barnsley boy and fiddled with her hearing aid. 'Stop mumbling and speak up!' she shouted.

'AH WANNA CURLYWURLY AN' A MILKY WAY,' yelled Heathcliffe.

The stack of Cherry Blossom shoe-polish tins on the nearby shelf rattled with the force.

Miss Golightly frowned. She adjusted the mother-of-pearl comb that held in place her tightly wound bun of grey hair. 'There's no need to shout!' she said.

Heathcliffe kept a finger pressed on top of his five pence and attempted a smile. In the past he had practised his glassy-eyed smile on elderly aunts and uncles with mixed results. A few uncles had given him ten pence to get rid of him; most of his aunts thought he was in pain, and his Aunt Mavis from Doncaster said if he kept doing it his face would stay like that.

Fortunately, after a lifetime of serving generations of schoolchildren, Miss Golightly was made of stronger stuff. 'And what's the magic word?' she asked, as she folded her arms in a determined manner across her starched white shopkeeper's overall.

Heathcliffe relaxed his manic stare, unclenched his teeth and pondered the question for a moment.

The answer came to him in a flash. 'ABRA-CADABRA!' he shouted triumphantly, at the top of his voice.

Miss Golightly, for all her stern appearance, did have a sense of humour. Shaking her head in mock despair, she smiled and passed over the two chocolate bars. 'In future, boys, do remember that *please* will do very nicely.'

Heathcliffe, confused but happy to see the chocolate bars, attempted yet another variation of his smile and released the pressure on his five-pence piece.

Remarkably, Little Terry's face was already smeared with chocolate by the time he walked out of the shop and the bell on the door jingled madly.

I was next in the queue with exactly fifteen pence at the ready for my copy of *The Times*. Miss Golightly knew her customers well and was already folding my newspaper.

'Good morning, Miss Golightly,' I said. 'And how are you?'

Miss Golightly stepped onto the next wooden step so that she was on a level with me. 'Very well, thank you, Mr Sheffield,' she said.

'And how's Jeremy today?' I asked.

'A little tired after his stocktaking last night,' she answered, with an admiring glance towards Jeremy.

On the shelf behind her, sitting proudly beside a tin of loose-leaf Lyon's Tea and beneath two ancient and peeling advertisements for Hudson's Soap and Carter's Little Liver Pills, was a much loved teddy bear immaculately dressed in a white shirt, a small black bow-tie, black trousers and a white shopkeeper's apron. The name Jeremy was neatly stitched in royal-blue cotton on the apron across his chest. Rumour in the village had it that Jeremy was once the love of her life but, as a young fighter pilot, he had been killed in the Battle of Britain in 1940. Miss Golightly had never told the full story and now, as a sixty-one-year-old spinster, it was presumed she never would.

However, Jeremy lived on in the incongruous guise of Miss Golightly's favourite teddy bear. On a large notice board behind the counter, a collection of photographs depicted Jeremy on his grand world tour. With the Eiffel Tower in the background, Jeremy could be seen wearing a

116

striped onion-seller's jersey and a blue beret. On a boat in Auckland harbour, he sported an All Blacks' rugby jersey and, in the Swiss Alps, he looked the part in his green anorak, thick woollen socks and tiny hiking boots. Miss Golightly spent countless hours creating appropriate costumes for Jeremy Bear and these were packed carefully in an ancient picnic basket under the counter.

I said goodbye to Miss Golightly, put the newspaper in my duffel-coat pocket, wrapped my old college scarf a little tighter round my neck and walked out to my car. At the top of the High Street, the coloured lights on the giant Christmas tree in the centre of the village green shone brightly through the gloom. As I drove through the school gates, Ruby was shaking a carton of salt over the frozen steps in front of the main entrance.

'Good mornin', Mr Sheffield,' shouted Ruby. 'Watch y'step: it's jus' like glass.'

The warmth of the office was welcoming as I hung up my duffel coat and scarf. Strangely, Vera was not at her desk, so I walked through to the staff-room.

Jo Maddison was showing Anne her new lipstick. 'Ninety-nine pence in Miss Selfridge,' she said. 'Dan says he likes this colour.'

I had never considered the six-feet-four-inch Sunderland-born policeman to be an expert in the subtleties of lipstick shades, but I guessed that his relationship with Jo had reached another level, whereas mine with Beth was moving at a slower pace.

'Good morning, Jack,' said Anne cheerfully. 'If

you're looking for Vera, she's in the hall, helping Sally prepare for her meeting.'

I remembered that Sally had arranged a meeting with parents after morning assembly at nine-thirty. Class 3 had begun their 'Christmas Around the World' topic and Sally had invited any parents who could help with books, photographs, artwork and general advice to call in.

In the hall, Sally and Vera were sorting through a collection of Vera's postcards of European capitals. I recalled the photographs of Jeremy Bear.

'Miss Golightly in the General Stores has lots of photographs of her trips round the world,' I said.

Vera suddenly looked very interested. 'You're right, Mr Sheffield,' she said. 'The children would love to hear about her travels with Jeremy.'

'Jeremy?' said Sally.

'That's her teddy bear,' explained Vera, in a very matter-of-fact way. 'And it would do her good to get out of that shop once in a while.'

'Fine,' said Sally. Having in her youth wandered round the muddy fields of the Glastonbury Festival wearing nothing but strategically placed flowers and skimpy hot pants, she was not taken aback by the thought of someone going on holiday with a teddy bear. 'Shall I go round and ask her?'

Vera thought for a moment. 'No, it's better if I go, but we shall need Ruby to look after the shop for her. She trusts Ruby,' said Vera. 'Don't worry, Sally, I know what to do.'

Vera was deep in thought as she walked back

118

with me to the school office. I noticed that she looked particularly smart this morning in a brand-new dark pin-striped suit and she had obviously been to Diane's Hair Salon for a stylish perm. She looked very businesslike as she settled behind her desk.

'And don't forget, Mr Sheffield,' she said, checking the school diary, 'that the Major is calling in to see you at ten-thirty.'

I could have sworn that Vera's cheeks flushed for a moment, but once she had inserted a sheet of paper into her typewriter she looked her usual self.

I had met Major Rupert Forbes-Kitchener briefly on various committees but I had never spent time with him. He was a popular local character and a welcome replacement for Stan Coe as a member of the school governors. It had proved a long, drawn-out process to remove the infamous Mr Coe, but, happily, the Major had been officially proposed and seconded and was now installed on the governing body. Since his wife died ten years ago, he had immersed himself in local charity work and had dabbled in politics. After his appointment, he had telephoned Vera and asked if he might have a tour of the school and meet the staff and children.

By half past nine, a group of around twenty parents and grandparents were sitting in the hall, chattering happily, while Shirley served hot mince pies, and cups of tea from her Baby Burco boiler.

Sally Pringle had prepared a speech to launch

the project and had gone to particular lengths to dress for the occasion. She was wearing her newest outfit. Her three-tiered, gypsy-style skirt in flaming orange and yellow competed for attention with her sleeveless, quilted waistcoat, which was buttoned neatly over her favourite salmon-pink, Miss Selfridge crêpe-de-Chine blouse. Although this had added the final sartorial touch, it clashed horribly with her freckles and ginger hair.

Sally was about to begin, when Miss Golightly arrived with Vera, who was carrying the notice board of photographs from the General Stores. Ruby had taken over as temporary assistant and was, at that moment, agreeing with her first customer that the price of a loaf of bread was far too dear at twenty-eight pence and the bakers' strike would make it worse.

Miss Golightly had been thrilled to help the children in school and had quickly dressed Jeremy in a white shirt, a bright-red tie, grey trousers, a black academic gown and a mortar board with a little tassel hanging down over his black-framed spectacles. It was mildly disconcerting to note that Jeremy's spectacles were very similar to mine.

With a communal 'Aaarrhh', the sort of sound reserved for greeting new-born babies, the parents welcomed Jeremy as he was placed on a seat on the front row.

The meeting went well and soon the children in Sally's class were sitting round tables, looking at Mrs Dudley-Palmer's collection of German Christmas-tree decorations and a *Ladybird Book of Christmas Customs* belonging to Sue Phillips.

Back in my classroom and just before the bell went for morning break, Jodie Cuthbertson was quick off the mark. 'Big posh car comin', Mr Sheffield,' she announced.

A large black twenty-year-old classic Bentley was purring up the drive.

As I walked through the school hall, the youngest children in Anne Grainger's class had wandered in to meet Jeremy and Miss Golightly.

The Major had arrived in style and parked in the car park. A chauffeur in a smart grey uniform and a peaked cap got out and opened the rear door. It struck me that a red carpet would not have been out of place as Vera and I walked out to meet him.

'Good morning, Major,' said Vera. 'May I introduce our headmaster, Mr Sheffield?'

'How do you do, sir,' said the Major, standing to attention and shaking me warmly by the hand. He was a tall, athletic, sixty-year-old man with a ruddy complexion and a vigorous handshake. 'Let me assure you, I shall do my duty as a school governor to the best of my ability. And I'm delighted to see you again, Miss Evans,' he said, bowing low. 'Tomkins, the flowers, if you please.'

His chauffeur hurried to the well of the passenger seat and lifted out a plant pot in which a beautiful scarlet poinsettia defied the dark days of winter.

'For you, dear lady,' said the Major, with a gesture to his chauffeur, who carried the plant with great ceremony into the entrance hall and put it safely on the large pine table.

121

For a moment Vera's cheeks were almost the same colour as the bright-red leaves of the poinsettia. 'Thank you, Major – you really shouldn't have,' said Vera.

We all walked into the office and the Major removed his Sherlock Holmes hat and revealed a head of close-cropped, steel-grey hair. He took a neatly ironed large white handkerchief from the pocket of his cavalry-twill trousers and mopped his forehead. 'Not used to this central heating, old boy,' he said.

'Would you like a cup of tea, Major?' asked Vera, picking up the deer-stalker hat and his brass-headed walking cane and putting them on the wide Victorian window ledge.

'Spiffing idea, Miss Evans,' he said, as he stroked his military moustache. 'Quench the old fires, what?'

The Major undid the button of his Lovat Green jacket and checked the immaculate knot in his East Yorkshire Regimental tie, resplendent with its vivid white, gold, black and maroon stripes. His highly polished brogue shoes sparkled.

Vera went into the staff-room to collect our best crockery.

'Damn fine lady, what?' said the Major appreciatively.

I noticed his interesting habit of turning a statement into a question by finishing a sentence with the word 'what'.

'Vera is a wonderful secretary, Major,' I replied. 'I'm a lucky man.'

'You certainly are, my boy,' he said, casting a further approving glance at Vera's slim figure.

As the Major was old enough to be my father, I guessed he was entitled to refer to me as 'boy'. He certainly had an eye for Vera and I wondered how she would respond.

During the coffee break, the Major met Anne and Jo and then we walked into the hall to meet Sally and her class. He seemed very much at home with the small children around him and sat at a table with Miss Golightly, Vera and the new starters.

Very gently, with a finger and thumb, the Major shook Jeremy's paw. 'Good morning to you, sir,' he said.

'Jeremy says it's always a pleasure to meet the Major,' said Miss Golightly, with a gentle smile.

'The honour is all mine, dear lady, to meet such a brave pilot,' said the Major softly, so that only Miss Golightly and Vera heard. Miss Golightly had a far-away look in her eyes, but the spell was suddenly broken when all of Anne's new starters began to speak at once.

Anne had brought them into the hall to meet Jeremy and speak to the Major.

'Are you Father Christmas?' asked Charlotte Ackroyd.

'No, but I'm a friend of his,' said the Major.

'I'd like a Barbie doll, please,' said Charlotte.

'Ah wanna *Star Wars* light sabre,' said Damian Brown.

'I'd very much like a pony, please. My sister got one last year,' said Victoria Alice Dudley-Palmer.

'I'd like a nurse's outfit, please,' said Dawn Phillips.

'We'd like...' said Rowena Buttle.

'...A kitten,' said Katrina Buttle.

'Please,' said Rowena and Katrina, in unison.

The Major bent down on one knee and looked at the excited group of children. 'I know how to tell Father Christmas,' said the Major.

Remarkably, all the children stopped talking at the same time.

Anne looked on in wonderment and Vera smiled.

Unaware that he had just qualified for entry in the *Guinness Book of Records* by completely silencing six four-year-olds with a single sentence, the Major calmly proceeded. 'You have to write a letter to him, show it to your mummy or daddy and then give it to Jeremy and he will give it to Father Christmas,' said the Major, in a solemn and serious voice.

The children stared at the Major in awe and wonder. Then they looked at Jeremy Bear.

'But how will Jeremy get to the North Pole?' asked Dawn Phillips. 'My mummy says it's a long way.'

'He will fly in his aeroplane,' said the Major, with absolute authority. 'Jeremy is a pilot.' He cast a glance towards Miss Golightly and smiled. 'In fact, he is a very brave pilot.'

Miss Golightly lowered her head, deep in thought. She remembered a tiny Kentish village in the war-torn summer of 1940 when, for a short time, her life was complete. After all these years, in her mind's eye she could still see a wicker basket on a picnic rug beneath an apple tree and a sea view that, like the ache in her heart, went on for ever.

Sally's excited voice woke her from her reverie.

'We're going to make a Christmas post box, aren't we, boys and girls?' said Sally. 'So we can give our letters to Jeremy after school on Friday.'

The four-year-olds obviously thought this was a wonderful idea, while the eight- and nine-year-olds in Sally's class nodded knowingly.

Vera was soon deep in conversation with Sally, who immediately collected a safety pin, a length of coloured ribbon, some cardboard and a piece of tinfoil. While Vera gave the Major a guided tour of the school, Sally helped a group of children to make a special gift for Miss Golightly. When the Major returned, Sally asked Miss Golightly to sit down with Jeremy while all of Sally's class gathered round. Anne had allowed a few of her new starters to join in and they sat cross-legged round Miss Golightly's chair and as close as possible to Jeremy.

Dawn Phillips gently tickled Jeremy's feet, waited for a reaction and then whispered in Charlotte Ackroyd's ear, 'He's not ticklish.'

Sally pulled up a chair for herself and gestured to the Major to do the same. 'Now, before Miss Golightly goes back to her shop,' she said, 'we would like to say thank you to her for bringing in her wonderful collection of photographs.'

'You can keep them for a while if you like,' said Miss Golightly.

Nine-year-old Katy Ollerenshaw put her hand up.

'Yes, Katy?' said Sally.

'Does Jeremy get travel-sick?' she asked politely.

'No, because he's used to flying his aeroplane,'

said Miss Golightly.

'What does he want for Christmas?' asked Victoria Alice Dudley-Palmer.

All eyes turned towards Jeremy.

'I think we've already got something he would really like,' said Sally.

Miss Golightly looked puzzled.

'Some boys and girls in our class have made a gift for Jeremy,' continued Sally.

Right on cue, Katy Ollerenshaw stood up and faced Miss Golightly. 'On behalf of Class 3,' she said slowly and clearly, 'I should like to present this medal to Jeremy for being such a kind and brave bear.'

She passed the medal to Miss Golightly, who looked as if she was about to burst into tears.

Everyone clapped, the Major stood up and saluted and Vera dabbed her eyes with a hand-kerchief.

'Thank you so much, children,' said Miss Golightly. 'Jeremy will treasure it for ever.'

And so it was that, on that cold December morning, the Major escorted Miss Golightly to his car and all the children in Class 3 lined the school drive and waved goodbye. When the chauffeur opened the car door outside the General Stores, Ruby was serving four slices of crumbed Yorkshire ham to Margery Ackroyd, which guaranteed that the news of Miss Golightly's eye-catching return was circulated round the village in the time it took Tidy Tim to switch on his Christmas lights.

Meanwhile, back in school, the Christmas post box filled quickly with the children's letters and

Jeremy rapidly became the most popular bear in Ragley village.

The next morning I walked into the General Stores and, once again, I was behind Heathcliffe and Terry.

'What d'you wan', Terry?' asked Heathcliffe, clutching his five-pence piece.

'Ah wanna lorry,' said Terry.

Heathcliffe, translating instantly, barely hesitated. Lollies cost one pence. He made a swift calculation and then he looked up at Miss Golightly and took a deep breath. '*Please* can ah 'ave two Milky Ways an' a penny lolly, *please?*'

'*Preeze,*' echoed little Terry, with a toothless smile that would have melted the heart of Ebenezer Scrooge.

Miss Golightly was delighted. 'Well done, boys,' she said. 'You can have a free barley sugar each for being polite.'

Heathcliffe thought Christmas had come early and collected the sweets before Miss Golightly could change her mind. As they reached the door, Heathcliffe turned round. 'Thank you,' he said.

'Fankoo,' repeated little Terry.

Heathcliffe opened the door for his brother.

Terry seemed to remember something and he looked back into the shop beyond Miss Golightly. 'Bye bye, Jemmery,' said Terry.

Heathcliffe grinned. 'Bye, Jeremy,' he said, biting the wrapper off his Milky Way.

The door jingled as they ran off down the High Street.

Through the open doorway, I saw Vera's Austin A40 parked behind my car. She walked in and smiled at her old friend.

'Good morning, Prudence,' said Vera. 'And how are you today?'

'Very well, thank you, Vera,' said Miss Golightly.

Miss Golightly smiled, stepped up one more step behind the counter and gave me my newspaper.

'And here's your *Times*, Mr Sheffield.'

'Jeremy looks smart today,' I said, looking up at the shelf behind her.

Jeremy Bear was wearing a leather jacket, flying helmet, goggles and a white silk scarf that had been pinned up in a straight line behind him as though he was flying in an open cockpit on a windy day. He looked like Biggles about to do battle with the Red Baron.

On his little leather jacket, below a brightly coloured, striped ribbon, a round silver medal sparkled in the shop lights. In the centre was inscribed in italic lettering the name *Jeremy*.

'He looks very fine with his medal!' I said.

'It was a wonderful surprise,' replied Miss Golightly.

She went very quiet and, for a brief moment, she was a young woman again, standing in a green field that shimmered with a million blood-red poppies.

Vera leaned over the counter and put her hand gently on top of Miss Golightly's hand and then looked down in astonishment. 'Prudence,' said Vera, 'you're wearing your ring!'

'Yes, Vera,' she said. 'It's my engagement ring. I

128

haven't worn it for nearly forty years but I thought I should wear it today.'

Vera nodded. She understood. 'Yesterday was a special day,' she said.

'Yes, it certainly was. I've waited a long time for this.' She carefully arranged the medal on Jeremy's jacket. 'My Jeremy is wearing his medal and it seemed right that, after all these years, I should wear my engagement ring again.'

Vera collected her *Daily Telegraph* and we walked out onto the freezing pavement.

'She seems happy,' I said.

We both stopped and looked back into the brightly lit shop.

'The last thing Jeremy said to her was that when he returned they would travel the world together,' said Vera.

We stood there for a moment, as the first few flakes of winter snow began to fall, and we watched Prudence Golightly tape a new notice on her shop door. It read 'BREAD CAKE'S ON SALE' and it occurred to me that maybe apostrophes weren't so important after all.

Chapter Eight

The Christingle Piano

School closed today for the Christmas holidays. The school choir are due to sing at the Christingle Service in St Mary's Church on 20 December.
Extract from the Ragley School Logbook:
Tuesday, 19 December 1978

'Ah'm away tay feed the wee birds wi' this desecrated coconut,' said Aunt May.

She wiped her hands on her Glasgow Rangers apron, scooped up the shredded pieces of coconut from the worktop in my kitchen, and walked out into the back garden. Not for the first time, I marvelled at my aunt's unique vocabulary.

My mother, Margaret, looked affectionately at her sister. With their curly grey hair and rosy cheeks, they looked like twins, although my mother was two years older. It was Wednesday, 20 December, the first day of the school Christmas holiday, and Margaret and May had arrived for their usual visit before venturing up to Scotland to celebrate Hogmanay with their many relatives.

'Y'dinna get no better in this kitchen, Jack,' said my mother, staring down at the jumble of pans under the sink. 'Och aye, it's still like Fred Karno's.'

'Sorry, Mother – life's been hectic,' I muttered lamely.

'Ah thought y'wee lassie might have been here t'help,' said Margaret, with a knowing look.

I turned away to fill the kettle and changed the subject. 'The vicar will be here any minute, Mother. The school choir are singing at the Christingle Service in church tonight and we need to go over the arrangements.'

Margaret's eyes widened and she immediately turned off the radio. Thankfully, Father Abraham and the Smurfs singing 'The Smurf Song' were cut off in their prime.

'Well, dinna stand there like one o'clock half struck. Where's the best crockery, Jack? He canna drink from a navvy's mug,' said Margaret, holding up my huge blue 1972 Leeds United FA Cup Winners mug. She scuttled off to my little oak-beamed lounge to search in the old Welsh dresser for some more refined cups and saucers.

The rat-a-tat of the brass knocker on my front door announced the arrival of the vicar. Revd Joseph Evans, a tall, thin figure with a sharp Roman nose that was turning blue with cold, was shivering on the doorstep.

'Come in, Joseph,' I said. 'There's a warm fire in the lounge.'

'For you, Jack,' said Joseph, as he stamped the frosty leaves from his shoes on the doormat. He held out a bottle of wine with no label. 'My tea and banana special,' he announced proudly. 'Got a kick like a mule. Shall we give it a try?'

Joseph's sister, Vera, frowned on his wine-making hobby to such an extent that he took every opportunity to sample his highly potent concoctions when he visited friends.

'Perhaps a coffee first, Joseph,' I said apologetically. 'It's a little early for me.'

Looking disappointed, he put the bottle of murky liquid on the hall table and walked into the kitchen, where my mother was pouring hot coffee into matching crockery that I had forgotten I owned.

'Good tay see ye, Vicar,' she said, handing Joseph his cup of coffee. 'It's nae warm today.'

'Very true, Mrs Sheffield, and lovely to meet you again,' said Joseph. He sipped the warm cup of coffee gratefully. 'Mmm, this is much better than Nora Pratt's, but I presume you don't know her.'

Aunt May suddenly reappeared from the garden. 'Tits like coconuts,' she announced confidently.

Joseph looked surprised. 'Well, er, I wouldn't have put it quite like that,' he stuttered.

'No, Joseph,' I intervened quickly. 'My aunt has been feeding the birds.'

'That's reet, Vicar,' said May. 'The wee creatures love tay eat this decimated coconut.'

'What wee, er, small creatures?' Joseph looked confused.

'The wee tits, Vicar. Or t'be more pacific, blue tits.'

Joseph peered out of the window. 'They look like coal tits to me,' he said.

'Nae, that's just an optical collusion, Vicar,' said May, and walked to the sink to wash her hands.

'We're nae talking aboot wee birds, May,'

132

shouted Margaret. 'We're talking aboot that Nora from the Coffee Shop.'

'Och aye, ah know that poor wee lassie,' said May, drying her hands on the towel.

I smiled as I saw the astonished look on Joseph's face. Aunt May had her own personal vocabulary but the words she used were always close enough to the real thing to make sense. However, the fact that she was deaf in her right ear and my mother was deaf in her left ear did not help matters.

Joseph and I walked into the lounge and settled down in front of the roaring log fire. My mother followed on behind.

'Would ye like tay have some cinnamon toast, Vicar?' asked Margaret.

'Aye, she's the queen's knees at making cinema toast,' shouted May, from the kitchen.

'No, thank you, Mrs Sheffield,' said Joseph. 'Time is precious today.'

My mother skipped back into the kitchen, wiping her hands on a Glasgow Rangers tea towel, and told May that their dubious culinary skills would not be required.

'Ah hope ye have nae been casting nasturtiums on mah cooking, Margaret!' yelled May into Margaret's good ear.

'There's nae need tay shoot,' replied Margaret, also into her sister's good ear and with equal volume.

Meanwhile, Joseph stared at the flames, his mind elsewhere.

'Now, what about the Christingle Service?' I asked.

Joseph looked relieved to change the subject. 'We have a problem, Jack. We need a piano and we need it urgently,' said Joseph hurriedly.

'Why, what's wrong with the one in church?' I asked.

'Everything,' said Joseph, in desperation. 'Barely a note works. It must be the cold and, as you know, the organ won't be repaired for another three months.'

An idea struck me. Beth had an old upright piano that had been passed on to her by an elderly aunt.

She answered the telephone almost immediately. 'You're welcome to use it, Jack,' said Beth, 'although it needs tuning.'

'Thanks, Beth,' I said. 'I'm sure it will be fine.'

'Anyway, Jack, I'm sorry but I have to rush. My parents are coming up with my sister for Christmas and I've got to go shopping. The key's under the mat if you want to collect the piano. I'll see you tonight in church. Bye.'

Joseph was relieved when I told him the news. 'I know a piano tuner who would call in and check it for us,' he said. 'But we'll need a vehicle to collect it from Morton village.'

'I know just the person,' I said, picking up the telephone again.

Deke Ramsbottom answered. 'Howdy,' he said.

'Hello, Deke. It's Jack Sheffield here. The vicar and I wondered if you could help us out. We need a piano collecting and delivering to church for the Christingle Service. It starts at seven o'clock.'

'I'll get my lads on to it reight away, Mr Sheffield. Tell t'vicar not t'worry,' said Deke. 'What's the address?'

'End of the High Street, Deke, number thirty-eight,' I said hurriedly. 'She said the key's under the mat.'

'Consider it done, Mr 'eadteacher. *Adios, amigo*,' said Deke, and rang off.

By lunchtime, the church was a hive of activity. Vera was arranging a spectacular vase of scarlet poinsettias next to the choir stalls, while a group of her friends from the Women's Institute were decorating a huge Christmas tree positioned next to the pulpit. Joseph was leaning against a shiny upright piano, listening to a distinctly self-opinionated piano tuner expound words of wisdom.

'You've got to understand the Pythagorean Comma,' he said, in a loud, warbling voice. He sounded as if he had swallowed a tuning fork. 'It's the amount by which twelve pure-fifths exceeds seven pure octaves. This means I have to tune the fifths narrow.'

Joseph stared at the ceiling, clearly seeking spiritual guidance and a cure for complete boredom. My arrival awoke him from his self-induced trance.

'Oh, Jack, good to see you,' said Joseph. 'I must thank Miss Henderson personally for the loan of this wonderful piano.'

'I'm pleased it's arrived, Joseph,' I said. 'And I must say it does look rather grand. She's had it professionally polished, by the look of it.'

'It's a top-of-the-range Steinway,' announced the voice from the bowels of the piano. 'Probably worth around £18,000.'

'Good Lord!' I exclaimed.

Joseph grinned.

'Oh, sorry, Joseph,' I said. 'It's just that Beth obviously has no idea it's worth that much.'

I spent the rest of the afternoon in the vicarage, helping a group of parents and children prepare the Christingles. They were made by inserting a candle into an orange, around which wooden cocktail sticks, decorated with Rowntree fruit pastilles, had been inserted. Vera supervised while occasionally reading the *Yorkshire Evening Press*. Margaret Thatcher was once again dominating the headlines. Her latest quote was: 'We shall not bash the unions; neither shall we bow to them.' Vera smiled and muttered something like 'The day of judgement is nigh'.

Shortly before seven o'clock, the Morton Road was full of parked cars and I pulled up outside St Mary's Church behind the Dudley-Palmers' Rolls-Royce. I shivered as I got out of my car. The evening was dark and cold and a few flakes of snow had begun to fall. Behind me, in the distance, the lights of Ragley village flickered like tiny glow-worms against a vast purple sky, cast like a mantle over the plain of York.

Geoffrey and Petula Dudley-Palmer were getting their coats and scarves from the boot of their car.

'Good evening, Mr Sheffield,' called Mrs Dudley-Palmer enthusiastically. 'Do come and look at what we've just bought.'

In the expensively carpeted car boot was a large white cardboard box and on the side was printed

'Philips 610 D Microwave Oven, £323.00'.

'It's one of those newfangled microwave ovens,' announced Mrs Dudley-Palmer. 'Top-of-the-range, of course.' She stroked the box tenderly in the same way as the female assistants on Nicholas Parsons' *Sale of the Century*.

I stared in amazement at this wonder of modern technology and wondered how it worked. However, on my salary I knew I would never find out.

Geoffrey Dudley-Palmer leaned over to me. 'Just on our way back from a day's shopping in Leeds, Mr Sheffield, and she just can't resist a bargain.'

He looked tired and I could understand why.

'We're looking forward to hearing the choir,' said Mrs Dudley-Palmer. 'My darling Elisabeth has such a beautiful voice.'

'Where are your daughters?' I asked, looking at the empty back seat.

'Oh, my sister in Morton has been looking after them today. They'll be in church now.'

'Well, I hope you enjoy your evening,' I said.

'And you must come to our house tomorrow lunchtime, Mr Sheffield. We're having a buffet lunch with mulled wine and Christmas carols round the piano. It's an open house and everyone's invited: the more the merrier. The vicar and Miss Evans said they would come along.'

'Thank you,' I said. 'That's very kind.'

After giving the microwave oven a final caress, Mrs Dudley-Palmer turned up the collar of her mink coat, grabbed her husband's arm and walked with him through the church gates, past a large poster that proclaimed, 'It is better to give than to receive.'

I followed on behind. The church bells rang as we picked our way along the pathway of frozen Yorkshire stone and the drifting snow began to curve gracefully against the grey walls. Outside the vicarage, I noticed Deke Ramsbottom's Land Rover and pig trailer parked under the elm trees and smiled. Deke was already prepared to return Beth's piano.

Next to me, on a huge wooden sign, a poster read 'Peace on Earth'.

I followed the procession under the sloping roof of the stone porch at the entrance to St Mary's Church and through the giant Norman doorway, where the Revd Joseph Evans welcomed us.

'Thanks for your help with the piano, Jack,' said Joseph as I walked in.

The church was filled with families and on the narrow wooden shelves, fitted to the back of each pew, a Christingle had been placed in front of each child.

I walked through the nave, down the central aisle towards the chancel with its beautifully carved choir stalls. Anne Grainger, looking completely relaxed as usual, was busy arranging the children in the Ragley School choir in order of height. This meant Tony Ackroyd had to stand next to a girl and his face had gone bright red.

At the front of the chancel, alongside the pulpit on the north side of the nave, stood a brass lectern decorated with a wondrous eagle, upon whose outstretched wings a giant Bible rested. I checked that the page was marked for my reading.

Meanwhile Sally Pringle was preparing to accompany the Nativity on her guitar and was arranging her music on a stand. Jo Maddison and Sue Phillips were gathering together the costumes for the Three Kings and putting them in a neat pile next to the pulpit.

Beyond the chancel, a balustrade of low rails separated it from the sanctuary of the altar, where Vera was lighting the tall candles. The flickering light illuminated the stained glass in the magnificent east window.

Meanwhile, Elsie Crapper was admiring the shiny new piano she was about to play, while secretly counting the Valium tablets in her pocket. She was wondering if she could last until Mary had given birth to baby Jesus and the congregation had launched into a rousing chorus of 'O Come All Ye Faithful' before another dose was required.

As I turned to find a seat, I caught sight of Beth sitting on one of the pews at the back of the church. She was waving and pointing to the space she had reserved for me. Walking down the aisle, I tried to look casual and nodded to the parents and children I knew. Then I squeezed in next to Beth, who immediately indicated her mother and father sitting alongside her. Her father, a tall athletic man with steel-grey hair, shook my hand and smiled warmly. I could see where Beth's firm handshake came from.

Beth's mother leaned forward and gave me an elegant wave of her leather-gloved hand. Her soft blonde hair was tied back to reveal a smooth complexion and her look was inquisitive. It was clear that Mrs Henderson had still to make her mind up about me. Next to her, to my surprise, was a younger version of Beth. I had never met Beth's sister before, but I had been told she was in her late twenties and she lived life to the full. Her appearance was breathtaking. Her hair was darker than Beth's, much longer and held back in a sleek pony-tail. She had the same high cheek-bones, clear skin and green eyes, except that hers shone with mischief as she mouthed a cheerful 'Hello'. Beth frowned at her younger sister, squeezed my hand and said, 'Good luck with your reading.'

Meanwhile the service began in dramatic fashion. Joseph Evans directed two of the church wardens to light a spill from the candles on the altar, walk down the central aisle and light the first Christingle at the end of every pew. Each family then lit the Christingle next to them, until the church was bathed in a flickering sea of candlelight.

A tapestry of shadows danced on the tall stone walls behind the shimmering light of a hundred candles. Within this ancient church on this cold winter's night, a feeling of calm, reverence and dignity, touched with the faint trace of incense, descended on the congregation. Joseph walked up into the pulpit and, in a slow clear voice, explained that the candle in the orange symbolized Jesus Christ as the light of the world.

Finally, it was my turn. I stood in front of the lectern, opened the giant Bible to the gospel of St Luke, chapter two, scanned the illuminated rows of faces and began to read. *And it came to pass in*

140

those days, that there went out a decree from Caesar Augustus, that all the world should be taxed...'

On my way back to my pew, I spotted Deke Ramsbottom sitting next to old Tommy Piercy. Deke pointed to the piano and gave me a thumbs-up. Then Elsie Crapper played the opening bars of 'O Little Town of Bethlehem' and the congregation rose to sing.

In between verses I smiled down at Beth and whispered in her ear, 'Thanks for the piano. Did you know it's worth a fortune?'

Beth looked puzzled. 'My piano is still at home, Jack,' she said. 'No one came to collect it.'

I pointed to the gleaming piano that had been pushed in through the priest's door and was standing against the south wall of the chancel. Elsie was hammering the keys as if her life depended on it. 'Are you saying that's not your piano?' I asked.

'It's not, Jack. Mine's just a poor, bog-standard, Medina Victorian upright piano. It's nothing like that one,' whispered Beth.

'Well, whose is it?' I asked.

'No idea,' said Beth. 'How did it get here?'

My mind raced. Something had clearly gone wrong.

After a rousing rendition of 'O Come All Ye Faithful', Joseph announced a short interlude while preparations were made for the children's Nativity.

I took the opportunity to walk to the back pew, where Deke Ramsbottom had his two strapping sons on one side of him and the stooping figure of Old Tommy Piercy on the other.

'Excuse me, Deke,' I said. 'Beth Henderson has just told me that you didn't collect her piano.'

Deke gave me a big grin. 'Don't know nothin' about Miss 'enderson, Mr Sheffield. Ah jus' went t'number thirty-eight like y'said. 'Ouse was all dark but t'key was under t'mat, so my lads carried it out.'

'Number thirty-eight?' I asked.

'That's reight, Mr Sheffield. Number thirty-eight, the 'igh Street, like you said.'

'I meant the High Street in Morton, Deke.'

'Don't recall nowt abart Morton, Mr Sheffield. Ah jus' went t'number thirty-eight in Ragley.'

Understanding hit me with the clang of a hangman's trapdoor.

'Well, who lives there?' I asked frantically.

'Mr an' Mrs Dudley-Palmer,' said Deke. 'An' they've got a lovely 'ouse.'

At the front of the church, Mrs Dudley-Palmer was putting the finishing touches to the coat-hanger haloes balanced precariously above her daughters' angelic faces, while Mr Dudley-Palmer, yawning frequently, was sitting a mere ten feet from his own piano.

'Deke, I need you and your lads to help me right away,' I said, and I ushered them out through the main entrance, along the snow-covered path at the side of the church and back towards the priest's door. I explained along the way that it was important the piano was returned to the exact same spot in the Dudley-Palmers' house.

The distraction of children moving into their places and the entertainment of seeing anxious mothers rearrange a Co-op tea towel and an elastic snake belt to create a perfect shepherd's headdress was sufficient for Clint and Shane quickly to remove the piano.

Moments later, it was being loaded into the pig trailer. I explained to a confused Joseph what was happening and he was beginning to realize the extent of the problem. 'I feel as though I've just committed a robbery!' he said.

'Don't worry, Joseph,' I said unconvincingly. 'Everything will be fine when Deke returns it.'

Joseph took another startled look at Mr Dudley-Palmer, who caught his eye and waved. 'Oh dear,' said Joseph. 'I've just told them that Vera and I are looking forward to their house party tomorrow.'

With a dramatic flourish, Sally began to play the chords of 'Away in a Manger' on her guitar and we crept back to our places.

Later, as the snow began to fall more heavily, Mr and Mrs Dudley-Palmer called out a cheerful goodbye with a reminder to attend their Christmas gathering the following day.

On Thursday, 21 December, the day of the winter solstice, I prayed that the shortest day of the year would not turn out to be the most embarrassing.

The whole village seemed to be crammed into the Dudley-Palmers' spacious mansion at the end of Ragley High Street. Vera and Beth, blissfully unaware of the recent theft of the piano they were actually standing alongside, drank their hot mulled wine contentedly and admired the state-of-the-art heated hostess trolley, from which deep-filled mince pies, powdered with icing sugar, were being served.

Mr Dudley-Palmer, sporting a bright-red tie decorated with Christmas trees, wandered over to join us. 'Welcome to our little get-together, gentlemen,' he said. 'Aren't we lucky living in such a wonderful village?'

Joseph and I nodded and sipped our wine a little nervously.

In the distance, Mrs Dudley-Palmer was filling a second bowl of fragrant pot-pourri and complaining bitterly to Vera about the strange smell that had recently appeared in the vicinity of her piano.

Mr Dudley-Palmer surveyed the scene of Christmas joy and happiness and sighed with pleasure. 'Do you know, Vicar,' he said, 'it really is wonderful to live in a village where you can trust your neighbours.'

'I agree,' I said hesitantly.

'I couldn't agree more,' said Joseph, nervously fingering his clerical collar.

Mrs Dudley-Palmer approached us with a dish of perfectly formed triangular turkey-and-cranberry sandwiches.

'And another thing, Vicar,' continued Mr Dudley-Palmer, now in full flow: 'in spite of all our valuables, in what other village in the whole of merry England could you still leave a key under the mat?'

'I agree,' I said, adopting my most humble expression.

Joseph looked to the heavens and muttered something under his breath.

'We're fortunate to have such trusted friends,' said Mr Dudley-Palmer.

'Especially our excellent headmaster and our wonderful vicar,' gushed Mrs Dudley-Palmer, who had suddenly appeared at her husband's side.

'Of all the villages we could have settled in, we certainly made the right choice moving to Ragley,' said Mr Dudley-Palmer, patting Joseph on his shoulder.

As they moved on to chat with another group, Mrs Dudley-Palmer called over her shoulder, 'God moves in mysterious ways.'

'He certainly does,' replied Joseph.

Then he drained his glass, leaned over to me and whispered in my ear, 'And so do bloody pianos!'

It was the only time in my life I ever heard a vicar swear.

Chapter Nine

Sebastian's Snowman

During the Christmas holiday, on 30 December, the Children's Ward at York Hospital thanked the school for their contribution towards the joint pen-friend project.

Extract from the Ragley School Logbook:
Saturday, 5 January 1979

His eyes were cornflower blue.

I shall always remember the striking gaze. It was a look of honesty, of knowledge beyond his years, but most of all it was a peaceful acceptance of a life that was his and his alone. Sebastian was nine years old and the effects of leukaemia had ravaged his tiny frame.

Christmas had come and gone and my mother and Aunt May had moved on to Scotland to celebrate Hogmanay. It was Saturday, 30 December, and I had arranged to meet our school nurse, Sue Phillips, in the reception area of York Hospital. Our pen-friend project, involving the children in my class and those with long-term illnesses in the Children's Ward, had gone well. Sue had telephoned to ask if I would call in during her afternoon shift at the hospital. She had again mentioned the little boy called Sebastian who had written to 'Mister Teacher' many months ago. I had replied to him, and arranged for ten-year-old Tony Ackroyd to be his pen-friend, but there had been no communication since then and I was curious to meet him for the first time.

As I walked under the harsh glare of fluorescent lights into the sanitized Children's Ward of York Hospital, I felt as though I had entered an alien world. The noise and colour of Ragley School were far removed from the silence and starched white sheets that surrounded me now.

Staff Nurse Sue Phillips directed me into the General Acute Medical Ward and held up two medical masks. 'We have to wear these, Jack,' she said. 'It's the usual precaution against infection.'

As I donned my mask, Sue looked pensive and

146

fingered her silver General Nursing Council badge as we caught sight of the small boy sitting in his bed.

'That's Sebastian,' said Sue quietly. 'I'm so pleased you've come to meet him. He's a lovely boy: bright and cheerful, in spite of his dreadful illness.'

I nodded and smiled behind my mask. Words seemed unnecessary.

Sue and I walked to sit by his bedside. Sebastian was dressed in striped pyjamas that seemed too big for him. His face was deathly pale and he had lost all his hair. There were painful sores round his mouth. I would have guessed he was about seven years old, but I knew he was nine.

Sebastian was crouched over a drawing board that was resting on his knees. The skin on his left hand looked translucent as he gripped the wax crayon tightly.

'Hello, Sebastian,' said Sue, grinning. 'This is the teacher from Ragley School you wrote your letter to.'

Sebastian stopped drawing and looked at me carefully. His blue eyes gradually creased into a smile and he held out his skinny right hand. It was bandaged and connected to a drip on a metal stand alongside his bed.

'Hello, Mister Teacher,' he said, and I held his tiny hand gently and shook it slowly and carefully. 'Do you like my drawing?' he asked politely.

He turned his drawing board to face me. It was a remarkable piece of work. A fairytale castle with pointed spires pierced a grey sky, heavy with snow clouds. In the foreground, a forest of giant

147

fir trees guarded its walls and, at the foot of the picture, a solitary figure was making a snowman.

'It's fantastic,' I said, in admiration. 'You're a wonderful artist.'

'It's the land of Narnia. You know, from the story by C.S. Lewis,' he explained. 'Well, actually, it's my Narnia and that's me making a snowman.'

My heart ached for this little boy who was so proud of his artwork.

'I read *The Lion, the Witch and the Wardrobe* to my class last term,' I said, 'and they loved it.'

'I've read all the Narnia books,' said Sebastian. 'And I think that, one day, I'll find a magic world too, and I'll explore it with a new friend.'

I really wanted to believe him. 'What's it like, Sebastian?' I asked. 'What's in your magic world?'

He gave me that look again as if deciding whether to reveal an innermost secret. 'In my Narnia, I'm a famous artist and I can make a snowman and I'm not poorly any more.' There was a pause as he let this sink in. 'But, just for now,' he said, 'this is the only snowman I've got.'

He pointed to a hemisphere of clear plastic about the size of half a cricket ball on the bedside unit. It was a snowdome, filled with clear liquid, and he picked it up and shook it. Inside this little world, minute flakes of plastic snow whirled round in a snowstorm and then sank gently onto a tiny snowman's head and gathered at his feet in a smooth mound.

I looked closely at the snowman. He had small buttons for eyes, a plastic carrot for a nose and a straight black line for a mouth, so it was difficult to tell whether the snowman was happy or sad.

'I bet your snowman likes the swirling snow,' said Sue, as Sebastian placed it back on the bedside unit.

'He does,' said Sebastian, 'because he gets lonely in there sometimes.'

Sue glanced up at me and we both knew what the other was thinking.

'It might snow tonight,' said Sebastian hopefully.

Next to his bed was a large window that looked out onto a bare wasteland of brown earth that had been prepared for future building. We stared up into the darkening sky full of swirling blue-grey clouds.

A doctor appeared and Sue tugged at my sleeve. Another blood transfusion was imminent and it was time to go.

'I'll come back to see you as soon as I can, Sebastian,' I said.

'I'll have finished my drawing by then,' he said, nodding.

Sue leaned forward and gently stroked his cheek; then we walked quietly out of the ward.

Sue looked distressed when she removed her mask. 'I know I'm a nurse,' she said, 'but there's something really special about that little boy. He's been in there for almost a year now and it's such a lonely existence for him.'

I hardly dared to ask the next question. 'What are his chances, Sue?'

She turned to look back through the window and slowly shook her head. 'There's a limited survival rate, Jack, but we're learning all the time about leukaemia.'

She had slipped smoothly into professional mode and we both knew why. I handed my mask to her and looked back through the window at Sebastian. He was engrossed in his drawing again.

'He looks so frail.'

'That's to be expected,' said Sue. 'Nutrition is a problem and his sore mouth makes eating difficult. Also, the blood transfusions are painful for him because every blood test involves a needle in the vein.'

We walked slowly down the long tiled corridor.

'He's a talented boy, Sue,' I said. 'His artwork is exceptional. What educational provision exists for him?'

'It's a bit haphazard. There's no regular formal schoolwork and anything that is done is by the bedside. The strong analgesics make him sleepy sometimes, so you have to pick your moment.'

We reached the doors to the entrance hall.

'Thanks, Sue,' I said. 'I'm glad I came and I pray his dreams come true.'

'They will, Jack. You've got to believe it. I wouldn't be in this job if I didn't.'

Back in the brightly carpeted entrance hall, noise and reality washed over us again.

'I'm on duty in five minutes, Jack, so I guess I'll see you tomorrow night in the village hall.'

I had forgotten about the New Year's Eve Dance. Beth and I had arranged to meet for lunch the next day in The Royal Oak and then she was going into York to buy a dress for the dance.

Excited as I was about Beth being my dance

partner, the journey home to Kirkby Steepleton was filled with thoughts of Sebastian.

New Year's Eve dawned clear and cold and I pulled back my bedroom curtains and looked out. A white rime of powdered frost framed the frozen window panes of Bilbo Cottage and the silent earth slept under two inches of fresh snow. On this harsh winter morning the distant woodland was silent.

After a breakfast of hot porridge, I decided to keep my promise to Anne Grainger and put up some shelves in her classroom before meeting Beth. I expected the three-mile journey to be hazardous but, thankfully, Deke Ramsbottom had been out early and cleared the back road to Ragley village with his council snowplough.

I pulled up outside Pratt's Hardware Emporium in the High Street. Tidy Tim was standing behind the counter and had just removed the lid of his John Bull printing set.

'Good morning, Timothy,' I said. 'I need some two-inch screws, some rawlplugs and some shelf brackets, please.'

'Second shelf, above the mouse traps, Mr Sheffield,' droned Timothy.

As I searched for steel brackets, Tidy Tim inserted some tiny rubber letters into the groove in the wooden printing block, working from right to left. His brow furrowed with the intensity of dedication and, a few minutes later, he pressed the block onto the inky pad and printed the words TAP WASHERS on a small sticky label. Rumour had it that his mother had given him this very printing set when he was a boy and the first label he ever made was PRATTS HARDWARE EMPORIUM. Sadly, he had not been able to find an apostrophe in among the tiny rubber letters. However, his pride was not diminished. Tidy Tim knew that one day he would own an empire of brass hinges, steel chains and ornate gate latches.

As I approached the counter, Tidy Tim arranged a collection of tap washers in size order at the bottom of a small square cardboard box. He stuck the label on the side and inserted the box on the shelf between TAP HANDLES and TAPE MEASURES. Tidy Tim liked alphabetical order.

Two hours later the shelves were up and I tied my college scarf round my neck and fastened the wooden toggles on my duffel coat. The school seemed a cold and desolate place without the sounds of children and the giant oak door echoed as I banged it shut and turned the key stiffly in the lock. My thoughts kept returning to Sebastian as I retraced my footprints in the snow on the school drive.

At the school gate, I paused and my breath steamed in the cold air. Around me, winter had spread its bitter cloak over Ragley village. The cold wind had stripped bare the branches of the weeping willow on the village green and lichens and mosses had crept over the gnarled roots. I hunched my shoulders and set off towards The Royal Oak. Alongside the frozen pond, the paving stones were covered in dank green moss and a squirrel had cracked open hazelnut shells and left them scattered like countryside confetti under the old holly trees.

Ahead of me, Beth's snow-covered Volkswagen Beetle pulled up on the far side of the village green. She climbed out with a cheery wave and trudged through the snow towards me. I stopped to enjoy the view. She wore a waist-length quilted ski jacket, a bright-pink bobble hat and scarf, and her denim jeans were tucked into a pair of furry boots. She looked sensational. As we walked into the lounge bar, the heat of the roaring log fire enveloped us like a warm cloak. My spectacles immediately steamed up and, while I cleaned them, Beth found a table. We selected potato-and-leek soup, followed by chicken in a basket, from the menu on the chalkboard and I walked over to the bar to order.

The barmaid, Sheila Bradshaw, dressed in her usual low-cut blouse, fluttered her eyelashes and leaned over the bar, notepad in hand. I averted my eyes from her astonishing cleavage and attempted instead to show interest in the sparkling Christmas baubles hanging from her ears.

'Hello, Mr Sheffield. Nice t'see yer. Y'll be pleased t'know our Claire's doin' real well up at t'big school.'

I had taught Sheila's daughter last year prior to her moving on to Easington Comprehensive School.

'That's good to hear, Sheila.'

'Ah see y'with Miss 'enderson again,' whispered Sheila, pressing her prodigious bosom even further over the bar.

'Er, yes, Sheila. So, please could I have the soup of the day and chicken in a basket for two?'

153

Sheila scribbled on her pad. 'An 'ow d'yer like yer breasts, Mr Sheffield?'

'Pardon!'

'Big uns or little uns?'

I was beginning to sweat. 'I don't quite follow...' I mumbled.

'Well, big uns f'you an' little uns f'Miss 'enderson, ah suppose,' said Sheila, checking her notepad.

'Er, oh, I see. Medium is fine, thank you, Sheila,' I said, trying desperately not to look down.

'Y'surprise me, Mr Sheffield. Big man like you should 'ave a 'ealthy appetite.'

'And a half of Chestnut mild and a glass of dry white wine, please,' I said, changing the subject.

'I'll bring 'em over, Mr Sheffield.'

'Thank you, Sheila,' I said, relieved that Don, her husband and an ex-wrestler, was pulling pints at the other end of the bat

'Anythin' f'you, Mr Sheffield,' she replied, adjusting one of her straining bra straps and flashing me another smile.

I was pleased to get back to the table.

In a haze of cheap scent, Sheila served the drinks followed by the piping-hot soup. We broke open the crusty rolls and tucked in. The sounds of children playing on the village green outside drifted in and I looked out of the window. Most of them were in my class and they were throwing snowballs, dragging sledges and rolling a giant snowball.

I put down my spoon. 'Beth, this might seem a strange question, but...'

She looked up in surprise as I paused mid-sentence. 'But what, Jack?' she asked.

'It's just that I've had an idea.'

Beth sipped her glass of wine and leaned back in her chair. 'Well, don't keep me in suspense.'

'It might mean postponing your shopping trip,' I said apologetically.

'Nothing could be that important,' she said playfully.

I looked out of the window again. 'Beth.'

'Yes?'

'How would you like to make a snowman?'

The bright lights of the hospital pierced the darkness and streamed through the windows of the Children's Ward onto the patch of frozen snow immediately outside Sebastian's window. Night had fallen quickly and more snow was forecast. Panting with exertion, Beth and I put the finishing touches to our giant snowman. It had taken an hour of hard work, during which time more and more faces had appeared at the windows; patients, nurses, doctors and curious visitors all gazed down on us. Staff Nurse Sue Phillips, at the end of her shift, had instructed one of her trainee nurses to find a large hat and a scarf from the children's dressing-up box and a carrot for a nose, while Beth had picked some black stones from a pile of builder's rubble to use for eyes and a mouth.

Sebastian's parents had arrived to see in the New Year with their brave little son and they sat on either side of him as the snowman took shape. When we had finished we looked up at the window and Sebastian waved. The look on his face made it all worthwhile.

At the other windows alongside, people were clapping and Beth and I waved in acknowledgement. It was a good feeling, one I shall never forget. Beth looked up at me, her cheeks bright and tears of cold streaming down her face. I wiped them away with the edge of my scarf.

'Thanks, Beth,' I said. 'A job well done.'

'Beats shopping,' panted Beth.

So it was that, just before midnight on the last evening of 1978, Beth and I found ourselves in among hundreds of late-night revellers in Duncombe Place outside York Minster. The New Year's Eve Dance in Ragley village hall was forgotten as we left the hospital and had a meal in the Royal Station Hotel. We didn't feel like dancing.

It was a strange meal with many silences, as we reflected on the experiences of the past few hours. When we did talk, it was about Sebastian and what might happen to him. We both prayed he would be well again one day. Then, in silence, we walked towards Stonegate hand in hand, attracted by the bright lights and the decorated shops, and into Parliament Street, where we sat on a bench and Beth rested her head on my shoulder.

'Makes you appreciate what we've got, Jack,' said Beth quietly.

I nodded and wondered if there was more to what she meant. 'He loved the snowman,' I said.

'It made today really special,' said Beth, as she

snuggled closer.

Eventually, we walked slowly up Petergate, crossed the road by the Minster and continued in front of the black-and-white frontage of St William's College. Soon we were in the Minster Gardens with its giant trees frozen and still, when, above our heads, the bells of the Minster rang out and announced the New Year.

A year ago Beth had gone to the New Year's Eve Dance in Ragley village hall with another man but at the end of the evening we had shared the last dance. Tonight she had been my partner for the whole evening and I was blissfully happy. As the bells rang out and the crowds in front of the west doors of York Minster sang 'Auld Lang Syne', Beth stretched up and kissed me tenderly on the lips. We hugged each other for a long time.

'You're a good man, Jack Sheffield,' she said.

'Happy 1979, Beth,' I whispered in her ear. 'May your dreams come true.' I held her closer, not wanting to let her go.

'Happy 1979, Jack,' said Beth.

She was smiling as, hand in hand, we walked through the crowds and I wondered what the new year would bring.

Chapter Ten

The Plumbers of Penzance

The school was closed for the morning session only, owing to the toilets freezing because of the severe weather. The temperature today was minus sixteen degrees centigrade.

Extract from the Ragley School Logbook:
Thursday, 11 January 1979

The headline of the front page of the *Sun* screamed, 'CRISIS? WHAT CRISIS? – Rail, lorry, jobs chaos – Jim blames Press'.

Prime Minister Jim Callaghan was having a hard time. However, Scott Walmsley was more interested in the photograph of the scantily clad young woman on page three as I approached his little white van.

It was Thursday, 11 January, and we had been back at school for a week. Every day was colder than the one before. The crates of milk in the school entrance had frozen and forced the silver-foil tops off the top of the bottles. This morning the temperature had fallen to minus sixteen degrees centigrade and the school toilets had frozen.

Ruby, dressed like an Eskimo, had met me in the entrance hall with the news that, even with the school boiler going flat out, the pipes in the children's toilets were still blocked with ice. She had telephoned the Walmsley Brothers, Ragley's finest, and only, plumbers.

Scott wound down the window as he saw me doing an impression of Bambi on ice across the school car park. Grinning, he pointed at the picture of the well-endowed page-three girl. 'She could defrost my pipes any day, Mr Sheffield.'

I guessed this was good weather for plumbers.

'Our Luke's checkin' out t'damage,' said Scott, nodding towards the school boiler-house door, which was ajar, from where the clanging of metal could be heard. ''E'll fix it.'

'How long will it take?' I asked anxiously.

In the time-honoured manner of all plumbers, Scott shook his head sadly, sucked air through his teeth and uttered the immortal line, ''Ard t'say.'

He wound the window back up, propped his newspaper on the steering wheel and began to unscrew the top of his flask. It was good to know he had such confidence in his brother.

I thought I might get more sense out of Luke, who, I was told, was the brains of the outfit. When I walked into the boiler house, Luke was tapping some of our Victorian pipework with a giant spanner. He looked a pale shadow of his swarthy brother in his hand-knitted, khaki balaclava and matching fingerless gloves.

'Good mornin', Mr Sheffield,' said Luke politely. 'You've 'ad some good work done on this old beauty.' He tapped the cast-iron door of the giant boiler appreciatively and I recalled Jim, the boiler man, from Harrogate who had repaired it

159

during our last emergency, just over a year ago.

'Good morning, Luke,' I said. 'Thanks for coming out in such atrocious weather.'

'Glad to 'elp, Mr Sheffield. Ah were a pupil 'ere, y'know. If y'can't 'elp your old school, it's a poor do.'

The longer I worked in Ragley, the more I realized the importance of the village school to the community.

'I can't open school until the toilets are working, Luke. So when do you think you can fix it?' I asked, stamping my frozen feet in the coke dust on the concrete floor.

'Ah should have y'up 'n' runnin' by this afternoon, Mr Sheffield. But, y'll 'ave to close f'this mornin', ah'm afraid,' he said, checking one of the pressure gauges.

I sighed. I had never had to close the doors of our school before. Little did I know that, on this arctic morning, fifty other headteachers in North Yorkshire were about to make the same decision.

With chattering teeth, I walked back into the school entrance hall.

'They're a reight pair, them two,' said Ruby, shaking her head.

'Why is that, Ruby?' I asked.

'Let's jus' say Ruth Walmsley were unlucky in love,' explained Ruby. 'Ah went t'school wi' Ruth. She were a couple o' years older than me an' she were a lovely lass. Well, she were till she met that Frenchman.'

'What was the problem?' I asked.

'What it allus is, Mr Sheffield, an' no offence intended,' she said forcefully.

'What's that?' I asked, still none the wiser.

'Men!' grumbled Ruby, and walked off, shaking her head in annoyance.

Anne popped her head round the office doot

'Shall I start ringing parents, Jack, to tell them we're closed this morning?' she said, clutching her 'Telephone Numbers in Emergency' book.

'Yes, please, Anne,' I said, 'and I'll put a large notice at the school gate.'

Suddenly, there was the sound of a loud wolf whistle from the car park. Sally and Jo were walking up the drive.

'This should be interesting,' said Anne, looking out of the office window. 'Sally doesn't take prisoners.'

Sally walked over to the white van and hammered on the driver's window. Whatever she said appeared to have effect and Scott's ardour rapidly changed from hot to tepid.

'Flaming cheek!' said Sally, as she stomped into the office. 'Talk about fancying yourself!'

'What did he say?' asked Jo, pulling off her bobble hat and gloves.

'He said it was you he was whistling at and not me.'

'So what did you say?' asked Jo.

'I told him your boyfriend was a six-foot-four-inch policeman.'

'Bet that shut him up,' said Jo, reaching for the kettle.

'Yes, it did, but I'm still a bit fed up,' said Sally.

She took off her sheepskin coat, flung it over a chair and began to warm herself in front of the gas fire. 'I've definitely got to start slimming,' she grumbled, patting her thighs disconsolately.

'I don't understand why you're fed up,' I said.

Sally gave me a despairing look, Vera and Anne grinned like Cheshire cats and Jo paused, mid-twist, in removing the lid of the coffee jar.

'Because he didn't whistle at me, Jack!' said Sally, in disgust. 'I still have my pride, you know.'

This seemed a good moment to disappear and write the notice for the school gate. It was becoming clear to me that the older I got, the less I understood about women.

It was Vera who finally told me the story.

When Ruth Walmsley, at the tender age of twenty-one, read in her weekend paper, *Reveille*, about cheap holidays in Cornwall, she immediately told her sister, Eileen. So, at the end of May 1953, the two sisters left Ragley village for a holiday in Penzance, unaware of how it would change their lives.

They both watched the Coronation of the Queen on a small black-and-white television set and then went to their room to get ready to go out. After sharing their Morphy-Richards electric hair-dryer and unpacking their treasured, ultra-sheer, nylon stockings, they sat together at the tiny dressing table and studied their reflections in the mirror. Eileen opened up their Max Factor Colour Harmony Make-Up set. Eileen went for her favourite Elizabeth Taylor look, while Ruth's home-perm confirmed a similarity with Ava Gardner. Feeling like Hollywood stars, they went out to enjoy the street party.

Sipping a glass of red wine under the brightly

coloured bunting was the most handsome man Ruth had ever seen. His bootlace tie matched his velvet jacket, and his drainpipe trousers and crepe-soled 'brothel-creeper' shoes were the height of fashion. When he winked at the two sisters they giggled, and when he bowed and introduced himself as Pierre they both fell immediately in love with this tall Frenchman with the jet-black, Brylcreemed hair. Ruth and Eileen drank more wine than they should have and, when Pierre raised his final glass with the words 'To ze Queen', they thought they were in heaven.

But it was Ruth he chose, much to her sister's chagrin. When Pierre and Ruth walked together that evening on a lonely stretch of beach towards St Michael's Mount, he held her hand and asked her in broken English if she believed in love at first sight. At that moment, Ruth would have believed anything that Pierre told her, and when he stroked her cheek and ran his fingers through her wavy brown hair she leaned back against the prow of an old rowing boat and closed her eyes. In years to come Ruth vaguely remembered Pierre lifting her gently into the rowing boat and what happened next literally remained with her for the rest of her life. After a few minutes of passion and the rhythmic creaking of the planks at the bottom of the rowing boat, Ruth fell into a deep, blissful sleep. When she awoke, she had only the night sky and lapping waves for company. Pierre had gone and Ruth never saw him again.

The reception from her sister was so frosty,

Ruth curtailed her holiday and boarded the next train home, carrying with her a small brown leather suitcase, a photograph of the queen, a Coronation mug, a pasty for her lunch and a secret that came to fruition almost nine months later.

At 4.00 p.m. on 16 February 1954, Ruth was in hospital with a group of pregnant mothers crowding round a tiny television set. She had just watched a programme for women entitled *Leisure and Pleasure* and, with snow piled high outside and a blizzard battering the windows, had learned how to make a Mexican-style summer skirt when the *Watch with Mother* programme began. The string puppet Andy Pandy, in his vertically striped playsuit, began to dance with a slightly belligerent Teddy Bear and a definitely subservient Looby Lou.

'You c'see t'strings,' remarked Ruth, as her contractions suddenly started again. Before Maria Bird had finished reading the script and begun to sing 'Andy is waving goodbye', Ruth was on her way to giving birth to twins. Her babies came into the world while she was screaming, 'All Frenchmen are bastards!' much to the delight of the midwife, Madame Yvette Dupont, whose husband had recently run off with the au pair.

One of the twin boys was christened Luke, as Ruth had taken up Bible studies after her unhappy experience; and the other, Scott, after her father's favourite Polar explorer. Although the boys grew up to be completely different in both looks and character, they made a good business partnership and, after leaving Easington School, they both served their apprenticeships and became plumbers. Ruth always secretly assumed this affinity with water was clearly connected to their being conceived in a rowing boat.

Luke Walmsley, who had mousy-brown thinning hair, was a quiet introvert, but his business acumen was outstanding. It was inevitable that, having chosen to be a plumber, his friends gave him the nickname 'Lukewarm'. Scott Walmsley had shoulder-length, jet-black hair, an extrovert personality and a different girlfriend every week. His nickname of 'Red Hot' among the local female population had nothing to do with plumbing. The nickname was loved by Scott, frowned upon by Luke and hated by his mother.

'That's quite a story, Vera,' I said. 'Did Ruth Walmsley ever go back to Penzance?'

'She's never even been back to the seaside,' said Vera.

'Why ever not?' I asked.

'She says you can't trust sailors,' said Vera, with a shake of her head.

By nine o'clock, to announce our closure Anne had contacted County Hall and a sufficient number of parents to ensure the village grapevine had gone into action. For the first time since I arrived in Ragley, the school bell remained silent at the start of a school day, which caused Prudence Golightly in the General Stores to check that her hearing aid was working.

Soon Nora's Coffee Shop was filled to over-flowing with parents who had to look after their children and couldn't get to work. Only two children had arrived at school without parents and they were busy in the playground. Jodie Cuthbertson had made a slide on the hard-packed ice and she was challenging six-year-old Joey Wilkinson to slide further than she had.

The soles of Joey's shoes were so thin that there was virtually no resistance and he soared across the playground like an Olympic skater.

'Huh, boys are 'opeless!' Jodie shouted rather ungraciously.

'An' girls are smelly!' retorted the red-faced Joey, before landing on his backside in a flurry of frozen snow.

Anne opened the office window. 'Joey, Jodie, come here, please,' she shouted.

Thinking they were in trouble, they both walked slowly towards the window.

Anne turned back to me. 'Jodie's and Joey's parents aren't on the telephone, so we'll have to walk them home.'

She leaned out of the window. 'Is there anyone at home to look after you?'

'Yes, Mrs Grainger,' said Jodie, quickly assessing the situation. While Jodie couldn't spell 'opportunity', she certainly recognized one.

'Well, wait there and Miss Maddison will walk back with you. School's closed this morning,' said Anne.

'Is anyone in at your house, Joey?' she asked.

'Dunno,' said Joey, beginning to shiver in his thin grey jersey and his threadbare shorts.

'Just wait there, Joey,' said Anne.

She scribbled an address on her spiral-bound note pad and handed it to Sally.

'I'll take him if you like,' I said, and took the sheet of paper.

When I arrived in the playground, Joey was blowing on his bare hands. He had an open freckled face, unkempt blond hair that stuck up like a startled hedgehog and the look of a child who needs a good hot meal. His home was on the other side of the council estate at the end of a terrace of Victorian cottages.

I gave Joey my college scarf and wound it round his head and shoulders and this cheered him up.

'Thank you, Mr Sheffield,' said Joey, in a muffled voice.

At the school gate we turned right and walked past the village green and then turned right again into School View.

Deke Ramsbottom passed by on his snow-plough, followed by the council grit wagon. He yelled 'Hi-Yo Silver!' in the manner of the Lone Ranger and drove on. We both waved back as if it was the most normal thing in the world to see a snowplough driver wearing a cowboy hat and a sheriff's badge.

As we walked along the narrow streets of the council estate, a column of smoke was rising from Ruby's house. In the frozen wasteland of her front garden a small bonfire was burning merrily. Ronnie had just dropped a book into the flames and he bowed his head in sadness. He was burning his Don Revie *Book of Football Management* after the England manager's £350,000 defection to the United Arab Emirates football team.

'It's a sad day, Mr Sheffield,' said Ronnie. 'Ah've lost mi faith in 'uman nature.'

Ronnie took his football very seriously.

The further we went into the council estate, the poorer the dwellings became. Eventually, the pavement ceased and, across an unmade track of frozen mud, stood a row of six cottages, four of which were boarded up. Joey walked confidently to the last cottage. Smoke was pouring from the chimney and it gradually settled on the litter-strewn gardens as if it was too tired to blow away. On the crumbling brickwork, clinging ivy thrived in these dark days of winter and, in the overgrown field nearby, fallen branches had been stripped bare by hungry animals.

Joey opened the cracked, unpainted door and walked into the kitchen. The biting cold wind did not remove the smell of damp and decay that hung in the air.

'Joey, is that you?' came an anxious voice.

Jessie Wilkinson was twenty-four years old and a single parent. While she was an attractive young woman, hardship had begun to leave lines of worry on her forehead. She was holding a coal-scuttle in one hand and a lump of coal in the other.

'School's closed this morning, Mrs Wilkinson,' I said. 'The pipes are frozen, so I've brought Joey home again. He can come back at lunchtime.'

Jessie Wilkinson looked anxious. 'Ah see,' she said. 'An' it's Miss, by the way, not Mrs.'

'Sorry,' I said, feeling awkward.

'Not your fault, Mr Sheffield. Anyway come in – don't stand on t'step,' said Jessie. 'Ah'm just getting a fire going.'

Leading off the kitchen was a tiny bathroom

and the door was wide open. Next to a wash basin was a once-white, old enamel bath. It was filled to the brim with coal. Jessie noticed the direction of my gaze.

'Summer prices, Mr Sheffield,' explained Jessie, without a hint of embarrassment. 'Only way ah can afford t'keep warm in winter.'

'Good idea,' I said, but without conviction.

'Ah'd offer you a cup of tea, Mr Sheffield, but t'pipes 'ave all frozen an' we've no water. Ah'm trying t'fix it.'

'Is there anything I can do to help?' I said, looking around at the sparseness of the furniture.

Jessie bristled with independence. 'Ah'm all right, thank you, Mr Sheffield. Ah can look after my Joey jus' fine, so don't worry.'

I quickly sensed it was time to leave. 'I'll be off, then, Miss Wilkinson. Pleased to have met you.'

'Thanks f'bringing our Joey 'ome, Mr Sheffield. Ah do cleaning today in t'Bluebell pub, so ah'll drop 'im off at school later.'

The walk back to school was filled with thoughts of how I could help Jessie Wilkinson and I decided to contact Roy Davidson, our Education Welfare Officer, at the earliest opportunity to discuss what could be done.

By late morning, the boiler hummed back into life, hot water filled the radiators, the school warmed up and Shirley, the cook, miraculously prepared hot mince and dumplings. Parents and children drifted back into school as word spread round the village that we were open again.

I was talking to Ruby in the school entrance hall

169

when Luke and Scott came in. Luke was covered in grease and coke dust but Scott was spotless.

'Thanks for all your work, Luke,' I said. 'We all appreciate your efforts.'

'Always willin' to 'elp m'old school, Mr Sheffield,' said Luke, with a shy smile.

A thought struck me. 'You don't fancy helping a damsel in distress, do you, Luke?' I asked.

'That's more up my street,' quipped Scott, as he readjusted his head band.

'Shurrup, Scott!' said Luke.

I took the sheet of paper out of my pocket. 'It's Miss Wilkinson at this address, Luke,' I said. 'She hasn't got any water and she's got a small boy to look after.'

Luke looked at the address. 'Ah know where this is, Mr Sheffield,' said Luke. 'It's at t'far end of t'village in them derelict 'ouses but ah don't know Miss Wilkinson.'

'Ah do,' said Scott knowingly. 'She cleans at t'Bluebell an' she's fit as a butcher's dog.'

Luke looked furiously at his brother. 'Get back in t'van, Scott.'

'Don't worry, little brother,' said Scott. 'She's not my type. Too 'igh-an'-mighty is that one.'

Scott sloped off, climbed in the van and resumed his acquaintance with the page-three girl.

'Sorry 'bout m'brother, Mr Sheffield,' said Luke. 'An' don't worry, ah'll call in t'see if ah can 'elp.' He folded the address and put it in the top pocket of his boiler suit.

A thought struck me. 'Luke,' I said, 'it would help if you didn't charge her. Perhaps you could call back on me and I'll see you right for your labour and parts.'

Luke understood immediately and nodded slowly. 'Don't worry, Mr Sheffield,' said Luke. 'Ah don't imagine it'll tek long. Ah'll drop our Scott off an' ah'll see to it m'self. They'll be no charge.'

We shook hands and, as he left, Ruby reappeared.

'Nice lad, that Luke,' she said. 'Teks after 'is mother.'

'He's certainly a good plumber,' I said.

'Not like 'is brother,' said Ruby. 'All mouth an' no trousers!'

With that she picked up her box of toilet rolls and marched off.

The following morning at half past ten, I walked outside with a mug of hot milky coffee for Jo, who was on playground duty. She was in conversation with Jessie Wilkinson. The two women, who were of a similar age, but separated by circumstances, looked relaxed together.

'Ah called in t'say thank you, Mr Sheffield,' said Jessie. 'Luke Walmsley's a lovely man. 'E fixed t'plumbing in no time at all.'

Jo looked up at me and winked. 'We were just swapping notes on Luke's brother, Scott,' said Jo, with a grin.

'Aye, 'e thinks 'e's God's gift t'women,' said Jessie. 'Ah put 'im straight long ago.'

'Jessie says Luke is taking her and little Joey to see *Jack and the Beanstalk* at the Theatre Royal in York,' said Jo.

'You'll enjoy it,' I said. 'Sally Pringle says

171

Berwick Kaler is excellent as Dame Dolly and Daisy the Cow should make Joey smile.'

''E's lookin' forward to it,' said Jessie. 'In fact, so am I. It's a long time since ah've been tekken out.'

'Luke's a good man,' I said.

''E were good wi' our Joey, Mr Sheffield,' said Jessie. 'Real gentle, he was, an' 'e let 'im hold all 'is plumber's tools an' showed 'im 'ow they worked.'

'I hope you have a lovely night out,' said Jo.

'Thank you, Miss Maddison,' said Jessie. 'If Luke's owt like your policeman, ah'm sure it will be.'

With a private exchange of glances, Jo and Jessie both smiled.

'Anyway, ah'm really grateful t'you, Mr Sheffield,' said Jessie, and then she set off down the gritted cobblestones of the school drive.

At lunchtime, Luke Walmsley called in to school to deliver his plumbing bill for the work on the school boiler.

'No rush, Mr Sheffield. Pay when y'can. Ah've only charged for materials. Labour's free for m'old school,' said Luke.

'Thank you, Luke,' I said. 'And I appreciate you helping out Miss Wilkinson.'

Luke blushed slightly. 'She's a really grand lass, Mr Sheffield. Jus' 'ad it a bit tough.'

'I heard you're taking them to the pantomime,' I said.

'Aye. It seems a shame that they don't 'ave a chance t'go,' said Luke wistfully. 'Our mother used t'tek me an' Scott when we were little. Little Joey deserves 'is chance as well.'

'You're right, Luke, and I know that Jessie Wilkinson is appreciative.'

'She's a lovely person, Mr Sheffield. We got on really well.' He looked thoughtful as he walked to the door. 'Meks a change, a woman pickin' me instead o' m'brother. It's a good feeling.' He smiled, a little self-consciously, and then closed the door gently behind him.

Love blossoms in the most unlikely of places, as this modest, hard-working, quiet-spoken plumber was about to discover. Although we didn't know it then, Luke and Jessie were destined to spend the rest of their lives together and, in time, young Joey began to show a remarkable natural aptitude for the art of plumbing.

Two weeks later, Ruby and I watched Luke arrive outside school in his van. Jessie climbed into the passenger seat and Joey clambered into the back. This had become a regular occurrence.

'She's a lovely girl,' said Ruby. 'An' she deserves 'er bit of 'appiness. It'd be nice for that little lad to 'ave a proper father like Luke.'

'Who was the father, Ruby?' I asked.

'Don't know 'is name, Mr Sheffield. She met 'im on a day trip t'Skegness. 'E were a sailor from Grimsby an' she never saw 'im again.'

Ruby picked up her tub of Saxa salt to sprinkle on the stone steps. The temperature was dropping again. At the entrance doorway she paused and shouted over her shoulder. 'You know what they say, Mr Sheffield. Y'can't trust sailors!'

173

Chapter Eleven

The Winter of Discontent

A meeting of the school governors discussed the impact of the widespread strikes of public sector workers, including school maintenance, delivery of school mail and the removal of rubbish. A letter from County Hall urged all schools to try to conserve heat during this very severe winter.
Extract from the Ragley School Logbook:
Wednesday, 31 January 1979

'"Now is the winter of our discontent",' recited Vera, as she scanned the front page of the *Yorkshire Post*.

When William Shakespeare wrote the opening line of *Richard III*, he could not have imagined the turbulent state of England in the long cold winter of 1979.

It was the last day of January and, after the government had imposed a limit of five per cent on pay rises, Britain had been paralysed by the worst industrial action since the General Strike of 1926. The railways were in turmoil after a series of one-day strikes and thousands of public sector workers were marching through the streets. Hospitals turned away patients; ambulance drivers refused to answer emergency calls; and even gravediggers had downed their shovels.

174

Meanwhile, over half the nation's schools were closed owing to inadequate heating. Thanks to Luke Walmsley's plumbing repairs, we were still open, but I didn't know for how long.

As I stared out of the staff-room window at a quarter to nine, fog shrouded the school like an ethereal blanket and the droplets on the school railings were frozen pearls. Parents and children, muffled in coats and scarves, stooped like the ghosts of a Lowry painting as they crunched over the school driveway. It was minus seven degrees centigrade and the village of Ragley shivered in the grip of winter.

However, huddled next to the gas fire, Sally Pringle had other concerns. 'Well, I finally did it,' she said, fiddling furiously with the straining zip on the side of her dress.

'Did what?' asked Jo, blowing into her mittens.

'I signed up last night for the Beginners' Keep Fit evening class in Easington.'

'Well done, you,' said Anne, wiggling her frozen toes in her fur-lined boots.

'I'm not looking forward to it,' said Sally forlornly. 'I keep imagining all those slim young things in Lycra leaping around to Abba music.'

'You'll feel better for it,' said Jo encouragingly.

'Hope so,' said Sally, as she rummaged in the biscuit tin.

Vera frowned as Sally dunked a digestive biscuit in her coffee, munched it disconsolately, and then gently prodded her expanding waistline.

Sally recalled sadly that, twenty years earlier, on a summer's day in 1959, at the age of seventeen, and with a twenty-four-inch waist, she had demonstrated to her little sister how to rotate a hula-hoop around her slim hips. As she reached for a second digestive biscuit, Sally realized her gyrating days were over.

Meanwhile, a spiteful wind forced its way through every crevice of our Victorian building and the ancient casement windows shivered in protest. Anne leaned over and clicked the dial on the staff-room gas fire to maximum.

'There's a lot of rubbish next to the car park now, Jack,' said Anne. 'The bin men didn't come on Monday.'

And we've had no mail for a week,' added Vera.

'My delivery of glass prisms didn't arrive,' said Jo, who had not removed her mittens as it was her turn to pull the frozen bell rope at nine o'clock. 'Reflection and refraction will just have to wait.'

If we had needed a conversation-stopper, that was it.

Suddenly, there was a brisk knock on the staff-room door.

I opened it to be met by the sight of our most eccentric parent, holding her daughter's hand and looking anxious. I knew from past experience that conversations with her never followed a logical path.

Mrs Daphne Cathcart was a strange lady with an unusual set of teeth, bright pink hair, resembling a Sindy doll with attitude, and a distinct, heavy breathing problem that sounded like Darth Vader with sinusitis. Her uninhibited nine-year-old daughter, Cathy, gave me a smile like Stonehenge and leaned round the doorframe to wave at her teacher. Sally, self-consciously, moved smoothly out of dunking mode, brushed the biscuit crumbs from her sheepskin coat and joined me in the doorway.

'Hello, Cathy,' said Sally.

'Ah'm going to t'dentist, Mrs Pringle,' said Cathy, with enthusiasm, and dreams of yet another visit from the tooth fairy. She looked up at Sally and gave her a huge grin that resembled a lop-sided picket fence.

I looked at Mrs Cathcart, focusing as I always did on her nose to avoid staring at her hair and her teeth.

'Ah'll 'ave 'er back f'lunchtime, Mr Sheffield,' she said.

'Thank you for calling in and letting us know,' I said.

'Ah saw y'signing up las' night, Mrs Pringle,' said Mrs Cathcart, with a slightly unnerving smile.

'Oh, were you there as well?' said Sally, praying that Mrs Cathcart had not signed up for the Beginners' Keep Fit class.

'Yes, but ah'm fed up,' said Mrs Cathcart.

'Why is that?' asked Sally politely.

'I wanted to sign up for intermediate embalming,' she said.

'Embalming?' said Sally, in horror.

'Did you say embalming, Mrs Cathcart?' I asked, not quite believing my ears.

Vera, Anne and Jo stared wide-eyed at this pink-haired vision in the doorway.

Mrs Cathcart was unmoved. 'Not jus' embalming,' she said, sounding slightly affronted. 'It's intermediate embalming. Ah've already done t'beginners' course.'

'So, what happened?' asked Sally.

'Weren't you able to sign up, Mrs Cathcart?' I asked, intrigued.

'No,' she said, in disgust. 'It were full up.'

'So, what are you going to do?' asked Sally, gripped with curiosity.

We both stared at Mrs Cathcart, wondering what the possible options were if you couldn't do embalming; or, to be more precise, intermediate embalming.

'Ah've signed up f'summat else,' said Mrs Cathcart.

'Yes?' said Sally and I, in unison.

By this time Vera, Anne and Jo were crowding behind us, eager for the reply.

'Ah'm doing advanced cake decorating instead,' said Mrs Cathcart proudly.

We were speechless.

And so, with an asthmatic wheeze, a toss of her candy-floss hair and a final flash of a set of teeth that would have been a popular visitor attraction on the Giant's Causeway, Mrs Cathcart grabbed Cathy's hand and set off. 'Ah'll 'ave t'get goin',' she shouted. 'There's no buses runnin' now.'

They pushed open the entrance door and stepped precariously into the freezing cold.

'Thank God she's not doing Keep Fit!' said Sally, aghast.

'Embalming,' I mumbled.

'Intermediate embalming,' corrected Jo.

'Advanced cake decorating!' spluttered Anne.

We all stared at one another in disbelief.

'I suppose there is a strange logic in there somewhere, Mr Sheffield,' said the phlegmatic Vera.

We laughed so much, Sally was convinced she had already lost a couple of pounds by the time she replaced the lid on the biscuit tin.

Jo rushed away to ring the bell and we all set off to our classrooms. As the children tumbled happily into school, I reflected, once again, how they didn't seem to feel the cold. They all wandered in, pink-cheeked and with bare knees that were impervious to extremes of weather. As I took the register, I noticed snow had begun to fall heavily and I recalled that I had promised Ruby I would buy a snow-shifter.

During the morning, my class wrote poems about the snow; Sally's children examined hexagonal snowflake patterns; Jo helped her children to complete a weather graph and Anne's children drew snowy pictures with white chalk on black sugar paper. At the end of morning school, Anne gathered her children into the carpeted book corner and read the enchanting story 'The Elves and the Shoemaker'.

When Jo pulled the ancient rope to ring the bell in the school belltower at twelve o'clock, I pulled on my duffel coat and thick college scarf and called into Anne's class. The children had clearly loved the story and were full of questions about the magical elves who appeared mysteriously in the night to help the poor cobbler and his wife.

'Anne, I'm slipping out to buy that snow-shifter for Ruby,' I said, and set off for the parade of shops on the other side of the High Street.

179

Hunched figures, buffeted by the gusts of swirling snow, nodded in recognition as they hurried by. Everyone appeared to be unhappy, worn down by the atrocious weather and the dismal state of the country.

I trudged past the Post Office and Diane's Hair Salon and stopped outside the window of Nora's Coffee Shop. Disco culture had begun to sweep through the Western world and the Village People's anthem, 'YMCA', had just topped the charts. Behind the counter, I could see Dorothy Humpleby performing a strange aerobics routine to the music.

The jingling doorbell was the only cheerful sound in Timothy Pratt's Hardware Emporium. Big Dave and Little Malcolm were slumped over the counter, disheartened by an excess of extreme weather and a lack of work. Mrs Betty Buttle was casting a critical eye over a collection of cast-iron coal scuttles; and Albert Jenkins, loyal friend and school governor, was searching for a new brass watch chain.

Big Dave and Little Malcolm were feeling like outcasts, as their union had told them to go on strike.

'Country's goin' t'dogs,' said Big Dave, absent-mindedly rolling an Ever Ready battery along the counter to Little Malcolm.

'Y'reight there, Dave,' said Little Malcolm, rolling it back again.

Big Dave saw me step into the shop and stamp my feet on the coconut matting just inside the entrance.

'Sorry abart y'rubbish, Mr Sheffield,' shouted

Big Dave, as he rolled the battery again.

'We're on strike,' mumbled Little Malcolm, glancing up at me and missing the returning battery, so it rolled over the counter and landed at Timothy's feet.

Tidy Tim picked it up and replaced it exactly in line with the other batteries, with the label facing outwards. Then he checked its alignment and made a minute adjustment. Tidy Tim liked matching labels.

'Don't worry,' I said. 'We'll manage. These are difficult times for everybody.'

The three men nodded slowly.

'I just need a snow-shifter, please, Timothy,' I said. 'Ruby wants to clear the school steps.'

Suddenly, Betty Buttle marched up with a coal scuttle, slammed a pile of loose change on the counter and proceeded to give the two down-trodden bin men a piece of her mind. 'Ruby's mother, and all them old-age pensioners on t'council estate, 'as got rubbish piling up, an' you're twiddlin' y'thumbs! Y'ought t'be ashamed of y'selves.'

With that she stormed out of the shop.

For once Big Dave was lost for words and the two big-hearted bin men looked down at their boots.

'We'll get t'batt'ries later, Timothy,' said the crestfallen Big Dave. 'C'mon, Malcolm.' They trudged out into the snow, deep in thought.

'These are 'ard times, Mr Sheffield,' said Tidy Tim. He selected a sturdy, long-handled snow-shifter from the corner of the shop. It had a curved steel blade like the front of a snowplough.

'The world's changing, Timothy,' I said.

'An' not for the better, Mr Sheffield,' said Timothy, taking my pound note and giving me a penny change.

'One day,' he continued, 'one o' these new-fangled supermarkets will close me down, an' then where will y'get y'tap washers an' y'dome-'eaded screws?'

'You're right, Timothy,' said Albert, placing a heavy brass chain and a pound note on the counter.

'Thank you, Mr Jenkins,' said Timothy.

'We're witnessing the de-industrialization of Britain,' said Albert, who was a great tradition-alist. 'Did you know that in 1948 we made forty-eight per cent of all the boats launched in the world?'

'Old industries and old jobs have gone now,' I said.

'We've never really recovered from Ted 'eath's three-day week,' said Timothy.

'We're even importing coal!' said Albert.

'An no good'll come of these new fancy bar codes. Y'can't replace a 'uman bein',' said Timothy.

I realized I was joining the ranks of grumpy old men, so I picked up my snow-shifter and walked to the door.

Timothy had one parting shot. 'And we're getting lazy,' he shouted. 'Can you believe it? Three per cent of 'omes now 'ave a dishwasher.' Tidy Tim liked percentages.

As I walked back to school, Mrs Dudley-Palmer slid smoothly past in her heated Rolls-

Royce. It was her husband's birthday and she had been into York to buy him an Atari 2600 video game with a woodgrain console, plastic paddles and a stubby rubber joystick. Little did she know then that the games, a range including 'Tennis', 'Outlaw', 'Breakout' and 'Space War', were hugely addictive and she was about to spend the next year of her life with a man whose spare time was entirely taken up with staring at a screen full of slow-moving blocks.

However, at that moment her mind was full of the very latest in kitchen technology. That afternoon, following the purchase of her state-of-the-art microwave, she had become the proud owner of a cordless slicing knife, a fizzy-drink maker, a blender and, best of all, a Goblin Model 860 Teasmade. As she loosened her silk scarf in the tropical temperature inside her car, she reflected how thankful she was that those irritating men with their talk of pay rises did not infiltrate her strike-proof world. As she drove home, thoughts of a new, avocado bathroom suite flickered through her cluttered mind.

The afternoon passed by without incident, except for little Charlotte Ackroyd, who was celebrating her fifth birthday. One of her presents was a Play-Doh Barber's Shop and she had brought it in to show Anne Grainger and her classmates. Unfortunately, the temperature dropped so low that the Play-Doh had gone hard in the cold. Anne spent a messy afternoon playtime trying to make it pliable in front of the staff-room gas fire.

At four o'clock, everyone rushed home as darkness descended. As I walked to the car park,

I saw Ruby adding a few more bags of rubbish to the unsightly pile at the back of the school.

Driving slowly down the High Street, I recalled the frozen kitchen I had left that morning, and decided to call into Victor Pratt's garage to buy some paraffin for my spare heater at Bilbo Cottage. When I pulled onto the forecourt, there was a long queue. Victor was obviously doing good business.

'Paraffin 'eaters, Mr Sheffield. Ah love 'em,' said Victor triumphantly.

At first I thought it was a trick of the light, but then I realized it was actually happening: Victor Pratt was smiling.

'So things are looking up, are they, Victor?' I asked.

'Business is boomin',' said Victor. 'Absolutely boomin'.'

'A gallon of paraffin, please, Victor.'

'It's a pound deposit on t'cans for them that 'asn't got their own,' said Victor, in a well-rehearsed fashion.

I rummaged around in my wallet for more money.

Victor's till rang merrily once again. 'These are 'appy days, Mr Sheffield, 'appy days.'

As I drove the three tortuous miles home, I reflected that at least someone was enjoying life.

The next day, as I scraped the ice off my windscreen, the air felt even colder, although a pale sun peered out of high cirrus clouds in a slate-blue sky. I looked around me at my garden and the fields beyond. On this arctic morning, the hedgerows were frozen in time under a crisp blanket of snow. The brave white blossom of snowdrops shivered with balletic tension in the stiff gusts of piercing wind. I stared, rooted to the spot by the sheer beauty. It was a view that froze the spirit but healed the soul.

Everyone arrived at school at once. Sally had collected Vera and Jo and I followed in her tyre tracks through the smooth crust of snow on the school drive. The slim, energetic Anne had walked in from the Easington Road. Outside the school entrance, reliable Ruby was demonstrating her prowess with the new snow-shifter.

'Oh, well done, Ruby,' said Vera.

'Thanks, Ruby,' said Anne, kicking the excess snow off her boots.

'I like the snow-shifter,' said Jo.

'You're a star,' said Sally effusively.

'Thanks, Ruby,' I gasped, in the cold air. 'We're all grateful to you.'

'S'all right, Mr Sheffield,' Ruby replied, apparently unconcerned by the freezing temperature. 'There's no need t'make a song 'n' dance about it.'

Ruby, after a lifetime of dealing with lazy menfolk, considered ten minutes of shifting snow to be light relief.

We all paused at the huge oak door.

'Rubbish 'as all gone, Mr Sheffield,' announced Ruby.

'Are the bin men working again, Ruby?' asked Vera.

'Don't think so, Miss Evans,' she said, pausing to lean on her snow-shifter and tighten her headscarf. 'There's no sign of t'bin wagon.'

'Maybe they came early?' I said.

'Ah've been 'ere since seven, Mr Sheffield.'

'And there's only your tyre tracks and Sally's on the drive, Jack,' said Jo, ever the analyst.

'An' my mother said all t'rubbish 'as gone from 'er 'ouse an' all t'old folks' 'ouses,' added Ruby.

We all pondered the problem and stared at the frozen snow on the school drive.

'I had to get up during the night,' said Sally. 'It started snowing heavily at about two in the morning.'

'Maybe they came at midnight,' said Anne.

We all looked at Anne, who had a wide grin on her face.

'You know,' said Anne, 'just like the elves in "The Elves and the Shoemaker".'

'Don't know about no elves,' said Ruby, tapping the snow from her snow-shifter before walking back into school.

The others walked in, leaving me outside. I stared down the driveway as the first children and parents arrived.

Standing behind the school wall were Big Dave and Little Malcolm. Big Dave was looking over the metal railings and Little Malcolm was looking through them. Both were grinning.

'Ah see all t'rubbish 'as gone, Mr Sheffield,' shouted Big Dave.

'It's gone, all reight,' yelled Little Malcolm.

'I wonder who removed it,' I shouted back.

'Might 'ave been fairies,' yelled Big Dave, and he laughed heartily.

'Y'reight there, Dave. It'll be fairies,' shouted

Little Malcolm, and with a wave they wandered off towards Nora's Coffee Shop.

I watched them as they crunched across the snow-covered High Street: Big Dave, with his huge strides, and Little Malcolm scampering alongside, his council donkey jacket flapping in the breeze. During a time when the country was in turmoil, it was good to know there were still people prepared to do a good deed.

I supposed that elves came in all shapes and sizes. When the brothers Grimm wrote about the little sprites who helped the poor cobbler, perhaps even with their vivid imagination they would have found it difficult to imagine the elves of Ragley village, who came out at midnight to clear their neighbours' rubbish. Especially as one of them was six feet four inches tall.

Chapter Twelve

Understanding Women

The school loaned the Baby Burco boiler to the Village Hall committee for their annual Valentine Day's Dance on 14 February.
Extract from the Ragley School Logbook:
Tuesday, 13 February 1979

'Ah don't understand women,' said Big Dave, as he supped thoughtfully on his fifth pint of Tetley's bitter.

'Y'reight there, Dave,' agreed Little Malcolm, nodding vigorously and supping equally thoughtfully. It was an automatic response but Little Malcolm Robinson was beginning to wonder why, at the age of thirty-five, he always immediately agreed with his big cousin.

It was Tuesday, 13 February, and the Ragley Rovers football team had finished their training session earlier than usual. After fifteen minutes listening to their manager, Ronnie Smith, talking about tactics, they had taken one look at the frozen wasteland of the football pitch and retired quickly to the taproom of the Oak.

I was sitting in the lounge bar, waiting for Beth, who had telephoned after school, sounding quite upbeat and suggesting we meet up at seven o'clock. As I sipped distractedly on a half pint of dark mild, the raucous voices of the village football team drifted across the bar.

Chris 'Kojak' Wojciechowski's broad Yorkshire accent belied his Polish ancestry. The Bald-Headed Ball-Wizard collected another tray of frothing pint pots from Don, the barman, and launched into one of his favourite subjects.

'Ah've said it afore, an' ah'll say it again. Ah blame that 1975 sex incrimination act,' said Kojak. 'Y'know, all them women burning bras an' reckonin' they can run t'bloody country.' He scratched his shaven head in dismay and looked round at the troubled faces. 'They're even reading t'news on telly now. That Anna Ford reckons she can do it jus' same as men.'

''Ow can she read news when she knows nowt abart football?' said Norman 'Nutter' Neilson, with a hollow laugh.

'Y'spot-on there, Nutter,' said Kojak scornfully. 'Bet she dunt even know t'offside law.'

Nutter nodded in agreement, although, if truth be told, he neither knew this law nor cared. He merely head-butted opposing forwards, regardless of being in an offside position or not.

'Ah blame that Maggie Thatcher,' said Big Dave. 'She should know 'er place an' not get above 'erself.'

'She could be t'next Prime Minister,' said Stevie 'Supersub' Coleclough, the number twelve, who rarely played in any of the team's games but always turned up to carry on the oranges at half-time. Stevie was proudly wearing his latest new tank top knitted by his colour-blind Auntie Maureen from Pontefract, in West Yorkshire. Stevie liked to be noticed and the lurid purple and green horizontal stripes across his chest clashed beautifully with his ginger hair.

'Over my dead body!' said Clint Ramsbottom, peering through the ringlets of his Kevin Keegan perm. 'Y'can't 'ave a bloody woman Prime Minister. Y'll 'ave women drivin' buses next if she gets in!'

The enormity of this statement slowly sank in.

'No, they're not strong enough t'drive buses,' said Kojak.

'You haven't seen Big Brenda from Thirkby,' retorted Clint. 'Ah've seen her castrating bullocks an' changing tractor tyres. Y'wouldn't tek 'er on at mud wrestling.'

'Y'dead reight, Nancy,' said Clint's big brother, Shane, who always called him 'Nancy' since

Clint had become a regular customer at Diane's Hair Salon.

It was tough for Clint having a father who dressed up as a cowboy and who named his sons after the stars of his favourite westerns, but being called Nancy really upset him. As usual, he remained silent, largely because Shane was built like a heavyweight boxer and his muscles bulged under his Boomtown Rats T-shirt.

'Y'need t'show 'em who's boss,' boasted Shane. 'Ah jus' give 'em a bag o' crisps an' a Babycham. After that, they're jus' putty in me 'ands.'

While everyone nodded in silent agreement at this significant insight into human relationships, it was a fact that no girl had ever been out with Shane for a second night.

In the strained silence that followed, Stevie 'Supersub' Coleclough suddenly put his head in his hands and groaned.

'What's up wi' laughing boy?' asked Shane Ramsbottom, looking at Stevie.

'Ah bought a lass a bunch o' flowers once,' he confessed.

It was clearly a confession Stevie needed to get off his chest. There was a collective intake of breath. This was serious news. Everyone stared at Stevie as if he had just announced he was booked in for sex-change surgery.

Big Dave was the first to recover from this thunderbolt. 'Ow much did that set y'back?' he asked gruffly.

'Aye, 'ow much?' echoed Little Malcolm, resorting to the habit of a lifetime.

'An' did y'get y'money's worth?' added an

incredulous Shane.

'It were one pound ninety-nine,' said Stevie sadly. 'And, er, no, ah didn't get me money's worth.'

Everyone shook their heads. They were united in their disgust, although Little Malcolm did not agree with his usual enthusiasm.

'It were that skinny lass what works at t'optician's in Easington,' said Stevie forlornly.

'Y'd need y'eyes testing t'go out wi' 'er,' said Kojak, with a big grin on his stubbly face.

'Aye, that's 'ow ah met 'er,' said Stevie, missing the joke.

There was silence as this group of men, bonded by football, friendship and fantasy, supped on their pint pots.

'Ah even bought 'er a Wimpy,' added the broken-hearted Stevie.

There was another gasp of disbelief.

'Y'daft ha'porth,' said Kojak.

'Our dad says when y'go out wi' a girl, a three-penny bun costs sixpence,' said Shane, ruffling his brother's tightly permed curls. 'Reight, Nancy?'

His brother Clint grunted in agreement and carefully rearranged his ringlets, concerned that the sparkly highlights may have been disturbed.

'Y'can't trust women,' growled Big Dave.

Strangely, Little Malcolm did not immediately agree with his giant cousin, but no one noticed this gap in the conversation.

'Is anyone tekking a lass t'dance tomorrow night?' asked Norman 'Nutter' Neilson, the hard-tackling full back.

Relieved to move on to another important

subject, everyone started talking at once. It was the annual Valentine's Dance in the village hall the following night and each year the football team sat by the bar, observed the local talent, but rarely summoned up the courage to ask a girl to dance. After ten pints of Tetley's it was usual for them to start dancing with one another.

'Ah'm tekkin' her wi' t'big chest from Easington fish shop,' said Clint proudly.

'Y'mean that bow-legged lass?' asked Shane.

Clint frowned. 'Ah admit she's not what you'd call a looker,' he said.

'She wouldn't stop a pig in a passage,' said Shane, with a grin. He ruffled Clint's hair again. 'C'mon, Nancy, get some pints in.'

Clint rearranged his bubble perm and decided that the next time he visited Diane's Hair Salon he would ask for a David Bowie feather-cut.

It was at that moment Beth arrived, looking flushed. She walked into the lounge bar, sat down and sighed deeply.

'You look as though you need a drink,' I said.

'Probably more than one,' she replied. Her eyes looked tired and she wound a strand of honey-blonde hair round her fingers in a distracted way.

A few minutes later, a glass of Muscadet, with its sharp dry taste, seemed to wake her up and she sat back in her chair and closed her eyes in contentment.

'Mmmm, I needed that,' she said. 'I've come straight from a girls' netball tournament.' She stared at her glass and swirled the amber liquid round and round.

'It's good to see you, Beth,' I said, trying to

gauge her mood. As usual I was cautious, when all I really wanted to do was pick her up in my arms and whisk her off to Bilbo Cottage.

'So what's your news?' I asked. 'You sounded quite excited when you rang.'

Beth continued to stare at her glass of Muscadet. 'I'm applying for another headship, Jack,' said Beth simply.

I could barely wait to ask the next question. 'Where is it, Beth?'

She sipped her wine, set down the glass and looked me squarely in the eyes for the first time. 'It's in North Yorkshire.'

It felt like my prayers had been answered.

'In fact it's not far from where I teach now in Thirkby,' explained Beth. 'It's a tiny village school called Hartingdale Primary School.'

'That's wonderful news, Beth,' I said enthusiastically. 'If there's anything I can do, please let me know.'

'Thanks,' said Beth, relaxing visibly and settling back in her seat. 'Maybe you could check through my letter of application. It has to be at County Hall by the end of the month.'

'Of course,' I said. 'Anything to help.'

Beth smiled and I wondered if she guessed how much I wanted her to get this headship.

'I hoped you would,' said Beth, rummaging in her handbag. 'So I've brought a gift.' She pulled out a large, heavily embossed card and gave it to me. 'It's a ticket for the Valentine's Dance at the Assembly Rooms in York for tomorrow evening.'

I stared at the elegant cursive script in disbelief. 'Thanks, Beth,' I said. 'What a lovely surprise. So what time should I pick you up?'

Beth grinned and shook her head. 'No, we'll meet you there at seven-thirty,' she replied mysteriously.

'*We?*'

'It was my sister's idea, Jack. Laura is staying with me for a few days while she checks out her next job. It's a promotion for her in the fashion industry. She's being transferred next month from Regent Street in London to a management post at Liberty's in York, and she's looking for somewhere to live.'

'So who else is going?' I asked.

'That's it, Jack: just the three of us. Laura's friend can't make it, so she wondered if you would like to come. She says she doesn't want anything for the ticket.'

'Oh, er, well, thanks,' I said, a little nonplussed. 'I'd love to come.'

'It's a formal affair,' said Beth. 'You'll need a dinner jacket.'

The meal that followed was dominated by Beth's application for the local headship, but my mind kept drifting back to why I was going with two women to a Valentine's dance the following evening.

The next morning, Vera was determined to find a dinner jacket and trousers for me to wear. She was also curious to know why Beth's sister was coming as well.

'You will have to look smart for the Assembly Rooms, Mr Sheffield,' she said. 'The dances there are so elegant.'

Anne walked into the office with Sally and quickly solved the problem. 'John's got an old dinner jacket and trousers, Jack. Can't remember when he last wore it. You're about the same size, I should think.'

Vera, Anne and Sally scrutinized me from head to foot and nodded in agreement.

'I'll nip home at lunchtime and get it for you,' said Anne.

Jo Maddison popped her head round the door. 'Just heard about the dance, Jack,' she said, with a grin. 'I'm going with Dan, so we'll see you there.'

Jo sounded even more excited than usual. Dan had obviously become a big part of her life and she seemed to walk around school with a permanent smile on her face.

'Don't worry about me,' said Sally mournfully. 'Not only am I not going anywhere tonight, I didn't even get a Valentine's card. My dear hubbie said he didn't think you did things like that when you were married. That's men for you!'

'Did you send him one?' asked Jo.

'Huh, you're joking!' retorted Sally.

With that she walked back to her classroom to write the notes of 'London Bridge is Falling Down' on her chalkboard for her beginners' recorder group.

After school, I put John's rather dated dinner jacket, trousers and black bow-tie in the back of my car and drove down the High Street. As the dance ticket made no mention of dinner, I called into Nora's Coffee Shop for a mug of coffee and a jam scone. Blondie's number one hit, 'Heart of Glass', was on full volume on the jukebox as I walked in and, at the counter, Dorothy Humpleby was deep in conversation with Little Malcolm.

''Ello, Mr Sheffield,' said Dorothy, looking up. 'Ah were jus' tellin' Malcolm 'ere that ah'm an Aquarian. We're the kindest, most 'elpful and friendly people of the Zodiac.'

'That's good news, Dorothy. Please can I have a coffee and a scone?'

'It's the perfect sign to be a model,' said Dorothy, smoothing the creases in her incredibly short miniskirt.

'I'm sure that's right,' I said, looking at the state of the scones and wondering if I had made a wise choice.

'At t'moment of my birth, Mr Sheffield, the sun, moon and planets were in a special position in the sky,' said Dorothy thoughtfully.

'That's very interesting, Dorothy,' I said. 'It's just a coffee and a scone, please.'

'Aquarius is an air sign, Mr Sheffield. So ah'm likely t'get on wi' other air signs like Gemini and Libra, an' Malcolm 'ere is a Gemini.'

I looked down at Little Malcolm, who was blushing furiously and casting nervous glances in the direction of his giant cousin. Fortunately, Big Dave was deep in conversation with Old Tommy Piercy about the price of fish.

Dorothy was now in full flow. 'Not many people know that the Aquarian body area is the ankles, so dancing is important t'me,' recited Dorothy. 'An', jus' by chance, it's t'Valentine's Dance in t'village 'all tonight, Mr Sheffield.'

'Actually, I'm going to another dance in York tonight, Dorothy,' I said. 'So it's just a coffee and a scone, please.'

'What's your star sign, Mr Sheffield?'

'I'm a Leo,' I replied.

'Best girl for you, Mr Sheffield, will be a Sagittarian and t'next best sign is Aries.'

For a moment I was encouraged. Beth's star sign was Aries.

'Thanks, Dorothy. So how about the coffee and scone?'

'Do you know, Mr Sheffield,' said Dorothy, fingering her signs of the zodiac charm bracelet. 'My Aquarius sun-sign will work wi' someone wi' Leo rising because they're t'opposite sign of t'zodiac. But ah'm better off wi' a Gemini.'

I was beginning to lose the will to live.

Dorothy flickered her false eyelashes in the direction of Little Malcolm, who realized it was now or never.

'Mebbe ah could take you,' gulped Little Malcolm. His hand was shaking so much that hot tea spilled down his council donkey jacket.

'Oooh, that's a lovely s'prise, Malcolm,' gushed Dorothy.

'Ah'll call 'bout 'alf seven,' mumbled Little Malcolm, staring up at the vivacious coffee-bar attendant, who was seven inches taller than he was – and eleven inches taller in her high heels.

The queue behind me lengthened as Dorothy stared into the eyes of her perfectly matched, astrological bin man. Then she glanced back at me. 'Now, what did y'want, Mr Sheffield?' said

Dorothy. 'We've got some scones that were fresh yesterday.'

I joined Timothy Pratt at a vacant table and attempted to cut my scone in half with a plastic knife. Tidy Tim had brought one of his cricket record books with him. The sixth and final cricket Test Match between Australia and England at the Sydney Cricket Ground had just finished with another win for England. He nodded to me, sipped his hot chocolate and then began to write in his tiny, neat script that both captains, Yallop and Brearley, had each scored their one-thousandth run in Test matches.

Tidy Tim punched some numbers on his brand-new Casio calculator. I had not seen one before. 'Wonderful invention, this, Mr Sheffield,' said Timothy, staring at his new toy. 'I hardly use my slide-rule now.' Then he looked up as if he had just discovered penicillin. 'Do you know, Mr Sheffield,' said Timothy, 'Yallop's innings of one hundred and twenty-one runs represents sixty-one-point-one per cent of the Australian total and, according to my records, only four other batsmen in the history of Test cricket have scored a higher proportion.'

I bit into my scone and thought to myself that it takes all sorts to make a world.

Tidy Tim firmly believed that, outside the ordered perimeter of Pratt's Hardware Emporium, the world was in chaos and records such as these brought a semblance of order. So he added yet another neat column of statistics to his cricket almanac. Tidy Tim liked statistics.

At seven-thirty, I stood outside the Assembly Rooms in Blake Street wearing my 1950s-style dinner jacket and looking as though I was about to audition for Glenn Miller's band. The huge entrance porch around me was magnificent and I was captivated by the sheer drama of the soaring colonnade supporting the massive portico of grey stone. Vera had waxed lyrical that it was an architectural innovation of the eighteenth century and one of the earliest neoclassical buildings in Europe. I felt as if I was walking into a Roman forum.

I handed my ticket to the doorman and walked into the Great Assembly Room, where I had agreed to meet Beth and Laura. On either side of me, the tall Corinthian columns bordered a huge, polished dance floor that reflected the lights of the sparkling chandeliers. It was a majestic setting that demanded a regal partner and mine had just arrived.

I noticed that, when Beth and Laura walked in, every head turned. They both looked stunning. Beth wore a long black dress straight out of Audrey Hepburn's wardrobe in *Breakfast at Tiffany's*. I could see the smooth skin of her neck and shoulders, and her hair was tied back in a bun with stray curls framing her face. Laura wore a full-length, crimson halter-neck dress and her long hair hung loosely round her shoulders.

'You look beautiful,' I said to Beth and kissed her on the cheek. 'And so do you, Laura.'

Laura stepped closer and her green eyes looked me up and down. 'You scrub up quite well for a village school headmaster,' she joked.

I leaned over and gave her a peck on the cheek. 'Thank you for the ticket and for the invitation. I'm sorry your friend couldn't come.'

'Are you?' teased Laura.

'Let's find a table,' said Beth quickly.

Around the perimeter of the dance floor, hidden behind the columns, were a series of alternate rectangular and semicircular niches decorated with mouldings and hand-carved scallop shells. We found an alcove that was empty and sat down together round an ornate circular table. It was a grand setting with the royal arms of Queen Victoria above our heads.

Laura saw me taking in the surroundings. 'Better than the village hall, Jack?' said Laura.

'Definitely,' I said.

The cocktail of perfumes was intoxicating.

'Can I get you ladies a drink?'

'Martini and lemonade, please,' said Beth.

'Just a Britvic Orange for me, please, Jack,' said Laura.

I set off for the bar, pondering Laura's choice of drink. It wasn't what I thought a London businesswoman would drink. At the bar, a familiar figure appeared to be trying to wrench off his collar. It was Dan Hunter.

'Hello, Jack. This collar's too bloody tight,' he said. 'It was the biggest one I could borrow.'

'Hello, Dan,' I said, and shook his hand. 'What would you like to drink?'

'No, not tonight, Jack,' said Dan. 'I'm buying. Jo and I are celebrating.'

'Celebrating?'

'We got engaged this morning. I'm a lucky man.'

'This calls for champagne,' I said, pulling out my wallet. 'And I insist.'

Dan relented and, as I placed my order, we both looked across to our table, where Jo – who had joined Beth and Laura – dressed in a full-length, figure-hugging green gown, looked very different from the young schoolteacher in her familiar tracksuit.

'She looks good, doesn't she?' said Dan, proudly, as he gazed at Jo.

'She certainly does,' I replied, but my eyes were on Beth.

Jo was stretching out her left hand and Laura and Beth were examining her engagement ring.

'It's a diamond solitaire,' said Dan. 'Got it in Stonegate. Took her into the Minster gardens, got down on one knee and proposed. Felt a bit of a fool, but she said yes. She's not stopped talking since.'

As we approached the table, Jo had just finished recounting the story and all three women laughed out loud.

'What wonderful news, Jo,' I said, and I held her hand and looked at her engagement ring. 'It's beautiful and I wish you both every happiness.'

Jo was simply glowing and she reached up and gave me a big hug. 'I can't wait to tell everyone back in school,' she said. 'Vera will be so excited.'

'So when's the big day?' I asked.

Jo looked up at Dan and smiled.

'We don't want to wait long, so probably the start of the summer holidays,' said Dan, as he slipped his arm round Jo's waist and pulled her closer.

Under the lights of the ornate chandeliers we raised our champagne flutes and drank a toast.

'To the happy couple,' said Laura.

'The happy couple,' echoed Beth and I.

As we touched glasses, I looked at Beth and thought she had never looked more beautiful.

Right on cue, the band struck up a slow gentle waltz and Jo was immediately on her feet, dragging Dan onto the floor. She pressed her head contentedly into Dan's chest and, for a big man, Dan moved lightly round the floor. They looked blissfully happy.

'Young love,' said Laura, sipping her champagne.

More couples walked onto the dance floor, so I took the plunge.

'Laura, do you mind being on your own for a few minutes?' I asked.

Laura just smiled.

'Beth?' I stood up and held out my hand.

She took it and we walked onto the dance floor together. Her hair was fragrant, she was in my arms and I couldn't have been happier. I looked back at our table. Laura was sitting alone and watching us.

A few minutes later, I saw Jo and Dan return to our table. Dan asked Laura to dance and soon they were quickstepping round the floor at great speed. Laura looked full of life and Dan was panting when we all returned to our seats.

Eventually, the band took a break and a visiting disc jockey dimmed the lights and began to play Abba's 'Take a Chance on Me'. Dan took Jo's hand and they were soon dancing again.

Laura suddenly stood up and looked at her sister. 'Do you mind?' she asked.

Beth seemed to understand and smiled in acknowledgement.

Laura grabbed my hand and together we walked onto the dance floor and began to dance. Her sense of rhythm was remarkable and her lithe movement exactly matched the beat of the music.

'You're a fantastic dancer,' I said.

'You could be too if you just loosen up a bit, Jack,' she replied, and playfully pulled off my Buddy Holly spectacles. 'Do you really need these?' she teased, as the music came to an end.

When the second Abba song, 'Knowing Me, Knowing You', began, Laura moved nearer. The lights dimmed further and suddenly Laura's head was on my shoulder. For an instant she looked up at me and her green eyes looked amazing.

We danced again and I noticed Laura held me a little closer than before.

When we returned to the table, Beth looked curiously at Laura and I went to help Dan with the drinks. Standing at the bar, I looked back at them. Their heads were bowed together as they shared the secrets of sisters. I wondered what they might be.

It was a wonderful evening and I had spent it with Beth, even though she had been chaperoned by her sister. At midnight, we said goodnight to Jo and Dan, and Beth and Laura, who had come into York by taxi, climbed into my car.

As we drove through Ragley village, couples were walking home from the village hall dance.

Outside Nora's Coffee Shop, Dorothy Humpleby had her arm around Little Malcolm's shoulder and they looked blissfully happy together. According to Dorothy's reading of their star signs, it was a match made in heaven.

On impulse, I called to Laura in the back seat, 'What's your star sign, Laura?'

'Sagittarius,' said Laura. 'My birthday is the first of December. Why do you ask?'

'Just curious,' I said.

Thirty minutes later, I parked at the end of Morton High Street, outside Beth's neat little cottage. Beth set off up the path, searching in her handbag for her keys.

Laura paused. 'Thanks for coming, Jack,' she said. Then she stretched up and kissed me on the cheek and squeezed my arm just once in a parting gesture.

I followed her to the front door. Beth had opened it and switched on the hall light.

Laura lifted up the hem of her dress and stepped inside. She didn't look back. Beth took my hand and walked back down the path to the gate.

'It's been a lovely evening, Jack,' said Beth. She leaned up and kissed me softly on the lips, but with a new intensity.

I looked down at her and shook my head.

'What?' said Beth.

'I don't understand women.'

Beth smiled and walked back to her front door. 'Don't worry, Jack. You're not meant to.'

As I drove out of Morton and then down Ragley High Street, I noticed Dorothy and Little

Malcolm were still braving the cold in the entrance to Nora's Coffee Shop.

From the look of them, Aquarius and Gemini were definitely compatible star signs.

Chapter Thirteen

Mr Dibble and the Rubik Cube

Mr N. Dibble visited school today to inspect our provision for Religious Education.
Extract from the Ragley School Logbook:
Wednesday, 7 March 1979

'It's a puzzle,' said Jo Maddison.

'But did you actually see him do it?' asked Anne.

'See who do what?' asked Vera, looking up from an article on Prince Philip in her *Daily Telegraph*.

'Heathcliffe did the Rubik Cube,' said Jo.

'Oh,' said Vera and returned to the fascinating news that, after his inspection of the equestrian facilities in Moscow for the forthcoming Olympics, Prince Philip had made a recommendation for the more efficient disposal of horse dung.

It was Wednesday, 7 March, and the new month had roared in like a lion. Nature was announcing a new season and the bitter winds of a pale spring had arrived. Six-year-old Heathcliffe Earnshaw's new-found skill in solving the Rubik Cube had surprised everyone and brightened up a bleak morning.

'So what's a Rubik Cube?' asked Sally.

'It's this,' said Jo. She passed over a plastic multi-coloured cube.

Sally held it in the palm of her hand. 'So what do you do with it?' she asked.

'Well...' said Jo. 'Each side is made up of nine smaller cubes and, at the moment, each face of the large cube is the same colour.'

'Yes,' said Sally. 'I think I'm following.' She looked at the six faces. Their colours were red, orange, purple, green, yellow and white.

'Well, each section of nine connecting small cubes rotates in a different direction,' said Jo, going into her familiar science teacher mode. 'So, if I turn them to mix up the colours on each side, the problem is to get back to square one with each face made up of one single colour.'

'Is that all?' said Sally.

By the time the bell rang for the beginning of the school day, Sally was still spinning the cubes round and round, but each face was more multi-coloured than when she started. 'Oh, damn and blast!' she said, in frustration. 'You have a go, Jack.'

She tossed it over and, after studying it for a moment, I made a quick decision. 'I'll have a go later,' I said defensively.

Then I walked through to the office and left it on my desk.

After the attendance and dinner registers had been completed and returned to Vera in the school office, the children in my class picked up their chairs and we filed into the hall for morning assembly.

Anne carefully cleaned the vinyl surface of a long-playing record with her anti-static cloth and put it on the turntable of our music centre, which was, in fact, a Contiboard trolley on castors. She set the dial to 33 revolutions per minute and gradually Grieg's 'Morning', from the 'Peer Gynt Suite', drowned out the sound of the wind battering against the windows and appeared to have a calming influence on the children as they walked in.

This was one of my favourite times of the school day. It was as if we were one large family. My class sat on chairs at the back of the hall; Sally's class sat on benches in front, and then Jo's class sat cross-legged on the floor, playing with their loose teeth and rubbing sleep out of their eyes. Last of all, Anne's class trooped in and sat at the front of the hall in a neat single line. They always seemed so small and looked round to wave to their big brothers and sisters sitting behind them. The more adventurous among them would play with my shoelaces.

'Good morning, boys and girls,' I said.

'Good morning, Mr Sheffield. Good morning, everybody,' they recited in unison.

I introduced the first hymn, the children stood up and Anne sat at the piano and opened her teacher's copy of our collection of hymns entitled *Morning Has Broken*. Anne played the opening bars of hymn number 44, 'When a Knight Won His Spurs'. Sally gathered her recorder group round their music stands and, with the intensity of Last Night of the Proms, she raised her arms *à la* Sir Malcolm Sargent and conducted the opening notes. Right on cue, we all began to sing and, as we did so, Vera unexpectedly stepped quietly into the hall, followed by a small and serious-looking man carrying a black briefcase.

It was obviously another book salesman. I had begun to believe they were turned out on a conveyor belt. Vera gave me what I took to be an apologetic look. It wasn't like her to bring a visitor into assembly without an introduction.

'...and the knights are no more and the dragons are dead,' we sang with enthusiasm.

Our anti-dragon policy appeared to stir the strange visitor into action and he began to write vigorously in his black notebook. At his feet, the leather flap of his black briefcase was embossed with his initials and a gold crest that reflected the glare of the fluorescent lights.

Class 2 were the featured class this morning and Jo had hastily selected a few children to read their writing and show some of their paintings. However, since Jo's engagement to Police Constable Dan Hunter, her evenings were no longer spent correcting her children's writing books with the frequency of her pre-Dan existence. Yesterday had been such an evening.

The Revd Joseph Evans had recently visited Jo's class and told them a Bible story about Jesus raising Lazarus from the dead. Little Jimmy Poole, the ginger-haired boy with the delightful lisp, stood up, opened his uncorrected book and announced that 'Jethuth raithed Platyputh from the dead'. A few members of my class giggled, which seemed to prompt our stony-faced visitor to open his notebook once again and scribble furiously. Fortunately, seven-year-old Sarah Louise Tait, easily the best writer in Miss Maddison's class, read a wonderful description of how her daddy had made a magnificent rabbit hutch from a plan in his *Reader's Digest Do-It-Yourself Manual* and this seemed to rescue the situation.

Finally, Jo, her face slightly flushed, stood up at the end of our assembly and read the School Prayer:

Dear Lord,
This is our school, let peace dwell here,
Let the room be full of contentment, let love abide
  here–
Love of one another, love of life itself,
And love of God.
Amen.

As soon as the children began to file back to their classrooms, Vera reappeared and stood alongside our unwelcome visitor.

'Mr Sheffield,' she began.

'Good morning,' I interrupted, and stared hard at the little man with the large briefcase. 'Please don't be offended, but this isn't a good time to discuss new books and our capitation is already spoken for.'

'Yes, but Mr Sheffield–' said Vera, a little anxiously.

'That's all right, Vera,' I said abruptly. 'I'm sure this gentleman has other schools to visit.'

'Mr Sheffield–' continued Vera, in despair.

'You may not be aware,' I said, determined to drive home the point, 'but I'm a teaching head and my class is waiting for me, so, with apologies, I suggest you make an appointment next time and I'll do my best to see you then.'

The little man was looking slightly bored by now and had begun to tap the gold block letters on his briefcase. I glanced down. The letters were 'ND' underneath a crest of York Minster. I didn't know a bookseller known as 'ND'.

'ND,' I said, a little bewildered.

'That's what I was trying to say, Mr Sheffield,' persisted Vera. 'It's Mr Nicholas Dibble, from the Diocesan Board of Education.'

'The Diocesan Board of Education?' I repeated.

'Yes,' said the unflinching Mr Dibble.

'Oh!'

'Exactly, Mr Sheffield,' said Mr Dibble.

'I'm so sorry,' I spluttered. 'I had no idea, and we've been besieged with book salesmen, just like you.'

'Really, Mr Sheffield?' he said.

'Well, obviously not quite like you,' I explained. The hole I was digging was getting deeper.

'Would you like a coffee, Mr Dibble?' said Vera, with true professionalism.

'Thank you, Miss Evans, I would.'

He looked up at me with a slightly unnerving stare that I was beginning to realize was an essential part of his persona. 'I'm here until tomorrow lunchtime, Mr Sheffield,' said the unblinking Mr Dibble. 'During this time, I shall inspect the religious education taught in all four classes, talk to all your staff and make an assessment of your RE policy.'

'Of course, Mr Dibble,' I said. 'And I do apologize. I've been teaching for over ten years and I've never met a member of the Diocesan Board before.'

'Exactly, Mr Sheffield,' said Mr Dibble.

I returned to my classroom, while Vera made Mr Dibble a coffee and cleared my desk in the school office for him to use. Then she ran round all the classes to inform Anne, Jo and Sally of our surprise visitor and, finally, she relocated to the staff-room.

Mr Nicholas Dibble was alone in the school office, sitting at my desk. As the door that led from the office to the staff-room was ajar, he could be observed by the diligent and ever-faithful Vera. In front of him was the Rubik Cube.

He picked it up, weighed it in his delicate fingers and, with careful precision, rotated one of the sides. With satisfaction, he noted that he now had three orange squares in alignment. Now, if he could get the other six orange squares to appear on that face, somehow life would be more complete. Although he didn't fully understand why, he thought he would spend a few more minutes trying to achieve this.

When the bell rang for morning break and I returned to hover at the school office door, he had six orange squares on the same face but the task was becoming increasingly difficult. With great reluctance, he put the cube down and, with a sigh, turned his attention to our Religious Education policy that Vera had found for him.

Apart from brief introductions, little conversation took place between Mr Dibble and Anne, Jo and Sally, who collected their cups of coffee and left Vera to look after our guest. However, as Sally left, she called out, 'I've brought those flowers in for my class display corner, Vera, so if you get time to arrange them for me...'

'Of course, Sally,' said Vera, with a confident smile. 'I'll do them for you before I go home.'

Mr Dibble did something I hadn't seen him do before. He blinked. As I walked out, he was staring hard at Vera.

'Excuse me, Miss Evans, but did you say you were interested in flower arranging?' he asked.

'It's one of my life's passions,' said Vera. 'I do a flower arrangement for the church every week.'

Nicholas Dibble took a deep breath. 'I wonder if I might ask your advice?'

'Of course, Mr Dibble,' said Vera.

'Tomorrow evening is the Annual Spring Flower Show in my village hall in Branton,' said Mr Dibble, as he sat down opposite Vera's desk. 'I always submit a flower arrangement. Along with my Advanced Upholstery Evening Class, it's my favourite hobby.'

'I see,' said Vera.

'It's just that my arrangements don't look quite right and they usually fall over,' said Mr Dibble, with an anguished look on his face. 'I have terrible problems with my floral foam, no matter how much I soak it first.'

'I understand, Mr Dibble,' said Vera, with the quiet reassuring empathy of a caring social worker.

'I was thinking of doing something with

daffodils and maybe some crab-apple blossom,' said the earnest Mr Dibble.

Vera considered this for a moment and then began to pace the room. Mr Dibble watched her every move, waiting for the flash of inspiration.

'Mr Dibble, I have a picture in my mind's eye,' said Vera, half closing her eyes and putting a dramatic hand to her tormented brow. It was an effect she had subconsciously perfected after watching Celia Johnson in *Brief Encounter*. 'I can see five irises in a row,' she continued, staring into space.

'In a row,' repeated Mr Dibble.

'In descending order,' said Vera.

'Interesting,' murmured Mr Dibble. He was beginning to believe he was in the presence of a woman who was almost as creative as he was himself.

'Surrounded by the rounded and crinkle-edged leaves of *Bergenia crassifolia*,' said Vera, as if in a trance.

'Really?' said Mr Dibble.

'And set among fluffy-grey sentinels of pussy willow,' added Vera, with absolute authority.

Mr Dibble gasped. There was no doubt. He was now utterly convinced that he was in the presence of greatness. 'Exactly, Miss Evans,' said Mr Dibble. 'It's a dramatic vision.'

He opened his notebook once more and began to scribble again. Then he threw down his carefully sharpened HB pencil on the table. His repressed artistic temperament was beginning to surface.

'It's no good!' he declared. 'I've no pussy willow

213

and where do I get irises if I'm here in school all day and most of tomorrow? It will have to be daffodils and a few sprigs of blossom.' The agony of thwarted creation was etched upon his pale face.

Vera took off her steel-framed spectacles and cleaned them. The tension for Mr Dibble was almost unbearable. Then she uttered the words that were music to his ears.

'Mr Dibble,' said Vera, with a finality that surprised even her, 'we will do it together tomorrow before you leave Ragley. I will collect a few helpful items from the vicarage and I know where we can find some pussy willow. What time shall we meet tomorrow?'

'I complete my inspection at morning break and I will be giving my report to the staff at twelve-fifteen. So, if it's convenient for you, we could do it at eleven o'clock.'

'I'm usually at my Cross-Stitch class on Thursday mornings,' said Vera, studying her pocket diary very carefully. 'However, I'm sure they won't miss me on this occasion.'

Mr Dibble looked at Vera in admiration. 'Thank you so much, Miss Evans.'

That afternoon, while Mr Dibble's attention was fixed on Anne's class listening to a Bible story, a discussion among Jo's children about Noah's Ark, followed by Sally's lesson on the Good Samaritan, his mind kept returning to the flower arrangement of his dreams. Occasionally, he walked back into the school office to attempt to solve the Rubik Cube.

At four o'clock, Mr Dibble took his leave. 'I'll see

you tomorrow, Mr Sheffield, and, don't forget, I shall be observing your class at nine o'clock and I shall give you my report at lunchtime,' he said, with depressing finality.

'Thank you, Mr Dibble,' I said, but without enthusiasm. My *faux pas* on his arrival would certainly count against his judgement on our school and, in particular, my leadership of this Church of England School.

Then his eyes fell on the Rubik Cube. 'I wonder if I might borrow this?' he said. 'Just to show it to a few colleagues, of course, and then return it tomorrow. I understand these toys are becoming all the rage.'

'Of course, Mr Dibble, be my guest.'

He slipped it quickly into his briefcase and left.

Vera walked into the office and smiled. 'Don't worry, Mr Sheffield, it will be fine,' she said.

'But I made such a hash of things this morning. Mr Dibble won't forget that in a hurry.'

'Let's wait and see, shall we?' she said, with a Mona Lisa smile.

'Thank you, Vera,' I said, but my spirits were low.

'Oh, and by the way, Miss Henderson rang and hopes you can meet her tonight at The Royal Oak at half past seven.'

My spirits shot up again.

The conversation in The Royal Oak was familiar as I stood at the bar to order a drink for Beth and myself. Deke Ramsbottom, resplendent in a new vividly checked cowboy shirt and a crimson neckerchief, was regaling Don, the barman.

'Ah never thought ah'd live t'see the day,' said Deke. 'A million pound for a footballer.'

Trevor Francis had recently become the United Kingdom's first one-million-pound footballer when he was transferred to Nottingham Forest from Birmingham City.

'World's goin' mad, Deke,' said Don, as he pulled another pint. 'They'll put prices up t'watch football, you wait 'n' see.'

'If y'beer goes up t'thirty pence a pint, Don,' said Deke, 'ah'll 'ave t'choose between beer an' football. Ah can't afford both.'

'Well, at least y'can watch football f'nowt on telly,' said Don. 'They'll never tek that away.'

'Mebbe so,' said Deke, supping his sixth pint of Tetley's bitter and not sounding entirely convinced.

Back at the bay-window table, Beth was obviously bursting to tell me her news.

'I've got an interview, Jack,' she said. 'It's for that headship I told you about at Hartingdale Primary School. I drove through the village today and it's only a few miles from where I work now.' She thrust an official-looking letter across the table for me to read. 'It's on the first Monday of the Easter holidays at County Hall,' she said, pointing to the underlined date of the interview.

A surge of joy ran through my veins. 'That's great news, Beth,' I said. I felt like lifting her up in my arms.

We talked excitedly about the new opportunity and the lovely village of Hartingdale with its beautiful church, its pretty High Street and the

216

old stocks in the middle of the village green. Beth had brought with her a recent magazine article showing the ten most attractive Yorkshire villages and Hartingdale was featured. In the background of the aerial photograph, the Hartingdale Hunt could be seen with red-coated fox-hunters galloping across the North Yorkshire Moors.

Darkness had fallen outside and I stared into Beth's eyes and noticed how similar they were to Laura's. The arrival of our food shattered the images flickering through my mind. Sheila, the barmaid, in a skin-tight, bright-pink sweater that left little to the imagination, served piping-hot stew in giant Yorkshire puddings, along with a refill of Chestnut mild for me and white wine for Beth.

'Enjoy y'meals, you two lovebirds,' said Sheila, as she collected the empty glasses and wiggled in her black leather miniskirt back to the bar.

Beth smiled and changed the subject. 'I hear you've got someone from the Diocesan Board of Education in school, Jack. Everyone's talking about where he will go to next.'

'No idea, Beth. Sadly, I didn't make a good impression, so I'm hopeful tomorrow will improve.'

Beth nodded and we ate in silence for a while, both filled with our own thoughts. By nine o'clock, we had said our goodbyes and made the excuse that we both needed an early night. When I closed the curtains of Bilbo Cottage, I prayed the next day would bring a good report from Mr Nicholas Dibble.

The next morning, everyone arrived early in school and Vera, true to her word, missed her twice-weekly Cross-Stitch class in the village hall and came in to help. When I walked into the staff-room, she looked relaxed as she read her *Daily Telegraph* and studied the front-page photo of a nurse preparing to stand outside parliament in a silent vigil over pay, after the Royal College of Nurses had pledged not to strike. The outside world was still turbulent.

Surprisingly, next to Vera's desk was a large cardboard box tied up with baling twine.

'What's in the box, Vera?' asked Sally, as she rushed in to collect her class register.

'Something for Mr Dibble,' said Vera mysteriously.

Sally Pringle's transcendental experiences, at a wide variety of open-air rock concerts in her youth, had moulded her relaxed attitude to apparent mysteries and she pursued it no further.

Mr Dibble looked tired when he arrived in the office and sat down at my desk. From his briefcase he produced the Rubik Cube and put it down on the desk top with a long sigh. For a moment he stared at it forlornly, as if he was saying goodbye to a half-finished crossword. I noticed the faces of the cube were still an uncoordinated collection of different colours.

The morning went slowly and Mr Dibble sat in the corner of my classroom and his unblinking stare missed nothing. He wrote pages of notes but, at half past ten, he returned his notebook to his briefcase. His scrutiny was over.

'I should like to read my report to the whole

218

staff in the staff-room at twelve-fifteen, Mr Sheffield,' said Mr Dibble.

After morning break, we returned to our class-rooms and Vera and Mr Dibble were alone in the school office. Vera had made sure that everything was prepared. Mr Dibble took off his jacket, rolled up his sleeves and waited for his first instruction.

'First,' said Vera, 'you put Plasticine on the base of a dry, oval Pyrex dish.'

Mr Dibble pressed the Plasticine into place.

'Then you push this heavy lead pin holder into the Plasticine.'

Step by step, Mr Dibble did exactly what Vera told him to do and gradually the irises, the *Bergenia crassifolia* and the pussy willow were added and the base was covered in fine gravel. The result was a masterpiece.

Mr Dibble stood back, buttoned the cuffs of his shirt and replaced his jacket. Then with Vera's help he put his creation into her cardboard box and they carried it to the boot of his car.

When he returned to the office with Vera, he sat at my desk and took his notes out of his briefcase. In front of him was the Rubik Cube.

'Challenging little blighters, aren't they, Miss Evans?' said Mr Dibble, holding up the cube.

'Really?' said Vera. 'One of our six-year-olds solved it in a few minutes. We're lucky having such good teachers in Ragley School.'

Mr Dibble looked up in surprise. 'That's very interesting, Miss Evans,' he said. Then he sifted through his papers and added another sentence to the report.

At twelve-fifteen, I walked into the staff-room with Anne, Sally and Jo. Mr Dibble was already in his seat with his report clutched tightly in his hand. Vera was sitting calmly alongside him.

By twenty minutes to one, Mr Dibble had almost completed reading his report and he had praised us all for our hard work. Anne, Sally and Jo were beginning to breathe a collective sigh of relief, while my stomach was in knots as I waited for the final verdict.

'To conclude, I must say, Mr Sheffield, that you are indeed fortunate in having such an excellent secretary in Miss Evans.'

Vera beamed from ear to ear.

'An outstanding team of teachers,' continued Mr Dibble.

Anne, Sally and Jo looked suitably modest.

'And leadership,' he paused to consult his notes, while I held my breath, 'is, er, interesting.'

You could have heard a pin drop.

He picked up the Rubik Cube. 'For example, a headmaster who not only fosters a very good Christian ethos, based on care and love of one another, but encourages a curriculum through which children have the opportunity to solve complex problems by using, er,' Mr Dibble consulted the final sentence of his notes, 'advanced spatial awareness,' he looked at me and smiled, 'is to be congratulated.'

I was dumbstruck. Somehow we had survived. Then, to add to my confusion, Vera gave me a wink.

Mr Dibble stood up and returned his report to his briefcase. 'So, well done, everybody,' he said, and he stood up and shook hands with Anne, Sally and Jo. Then he turned to me. 'Congratulations, Mr Sheffield. Ragley School is in good hands.'

Next Mr Dibble picked up his briefcase and turned to Vera. 'Thank you, Miss Evans, for all, er, your support.'

'I'll walk you to your car if I may, Mr Dibble,' said Vera.

From the staff-room window, we watched them part in the manner of old friends.

Finally, Mr Dibble drove away very slowly in his Triumph 2500 'S' saloon, making sure his flower arrangement rode undisturbed.

When Vera walked back into the staff-room, we all stared in astonishment.

'Whatever you did, Vera,' I said, 'thank you.'

'Let's celebrate with a cup of tea and a Bourbon biscuit,' she said.

Everybody began talking at once, when there was a knock on the door.

'Oh no,' I said. 'He's come back.'

Fearing the worst, I opened the staff-room door gingerly.

Heathcliffe Earnshaw was standing outside with a strained smile on his face. 'Please can I 'ave m'cube back, please, Mr Sheffield, please,' said Heathcliffe, who had clearly grasped the importance of the magic word.

Jo picked up the Rubik Cube from the desk, walked to the doorway and crouched down. 'You're a clever boy, Heathcliffe,' said Jo, with a reassuring smile. 'How did you get all the colours to be the same on each side?'

'S'easy, Miss,' said Heathcliffe, taking the cube and swiftly removing one of the sticky squares from the surface of a cube. 'You jus' peel 'em off an' stick 'em on again.'

With that, he walked away, whistling tunelessly.

I closed the door and everybody burst out laughing.

'Advanced spatial awareness,' muttered Anne.

After Vera had regaled us with the story of the flower arrangement, we were all still chuckling when I rang the one o'clock bell for afternoon school.

That evening, I was sitting on my sofa with Beth at Bilbo Cottage, watching television and eating a fish-and-chips supper. Terry Wogan was presenting the twelve United Kingdom songs competing for the chance to sing in the Euro-vision Song Contest in Jerusalem. The group Black Lace was about to win, when the telephone rang. It was Vera calling.

'Sorry to disturb your evening, Mr Sheffield, but I thought you would like to know that Mr Dibble has just telephoned to say his flower arrangement won first prize in the Branton village Spring Flower Show.'

'So he's a happy man, Vera,' I said. 'Thanks for all your help.'

'All in the line of duty, Mr Sheffield,' said Vera. 'Good evening and I'll see you tomorrow.'

'Who was that?' asked Beth, as I returned to the sofa.

'Just Vera,' I said. 'She told me that Mr Dibble was impressed with our school.'

'Really?' said Beth. 'And what impressed him most?'

I put my arm round her shoulder and whispered in her ear, 'He said something about me encouraging advanced spatial awareness.'

'Oh yes?' said Beth, and snuggled closer.

Chapter Fourteen

The Age of Miracles

County Hall sent out a circular asking for responses to the proposal for a common curriculum for all schools in England and Wales.
Extract from the Ragley School Logbook:
Friday, 23 March 1979

'Ah'd need a miracle,' said Ruby.

'Something will turn up,' said Vera optimistically. 'Maybe your Ronnie will get a job this week.'

Ruby picked up Vera's litter bin and emptied the contents into her black bag. 'An' pigs might fly, beggin' y'pardon, Miss Evans,' she said, replacing the bin with a clatter.

It was shortly before nine o'clock on the morning of Friday, 23 March, and Ruby did not look her usual happy self.

'So how much do these new wardrobes cost,

223

Ruby?' asked Vera.

Ruby had brought a furniture catalogue into school. She put it on Vera's desk and opened it at the bedroom furniture section.

'A 'undred pounds, Miss Evans, an' they're on sale in MI5,' said Ruby.

Vera did not correct Ruby's mistake. Instead she studied the MFI catalogue and then passed it over to me. I stared in wonderment at the brightly coloured bedroom wardrobes and dressing tables and wondered if they came supplied with a pair of free sunglasses.

'They look really cheerful, Ruby,' I said, handing back the catalogue.

'Thank you, Mr Sheffield,' she said. 'Ah jus' wanted t'know what Miss Evans thought before ah started savin' up for 'em.'

'I'm sure they will be perfect for you, Ruby,' said Vera.

Reassured, Ruby picked up the catalogue, took one last longing look at her dream bedroom and set off for the school hall, dragging the black bag behind her.

Vera shook her head sadly. 'If only Ronnie would earn some money for a change, poor Ruby might have an easier life.'

'Now that would be a miracle,' I said.

Three miles away in Easington, Ruby's unemployed husband, Ronnie Smith, had another purchase on his mind.

He looked in admiration at a shiny 1968 Honda 747 motorcycle and patted the handlebars.

Clyde Dlambulo, the big friendly West Indian

who worked in Morrissey's Motorcycle Mart as a general labourer and part-time salesman, put his arm round Ronnie's frail shoulders. 'S'only a 'undred pound, Ronnie, mon – you know it be a bargain.'

'Ah'd need a miracle,' said Ronnie mournfully. 'Ah've only got a fiver.' As if to prove the point he pulled out of his pocket a crumpled five-pound note and proceeded to flatten out the creases.

'If you 'ad fifty quid, Ronnie, mon, y'could pay me de rest on de never-never,' said Clyde.

'Ah know, Clyde, but Ruby's a bit tight where money's concerned. Las' time we 'ad a windfall she went an' bought a three-piece suite. An' now she's on about some new wardrobes.'

Clyde looked shocked. 'Who wears de trousers, mon, in your 'ouse?' he exclaimed.

Ronnie shook his head wearily. 'Give us a few days, Clyde: summat'll turn up,' he said hopefully. 'Ah might be lucky on tomorrow's Gran' National.'

Clyde's eyes were like saucers. 'An' what you be backing, Ronnie, mon?' he asked hopefully.

'Not sure yet, Clyde, but ah'll let y'know if ah get a good tip,' said Ronnie, tapping the side of his nose with his index finger.

Clyde looked thoughtful. 'Ah suppose we do goes back de long way, Ronnie, mon.'

Ronnie stared into space and looked wistful. 'Y'reight there, Clyde. Ah remember when we joined t'boy scouts.'

'Dat's right, Ronnie, mon,' said Clyde, recalling the days when he and Ronnie were a pair of Baden-Powell misfits. 'It was you dat showed me 'ow t'make fire by rubbin' de two sticks together.'

Something flickered in the back of Ronnie's mind, something important. 'It were a good fire, Clyde,' he said, somewhat absent-mindedly.

Clyde nodded in appreciation of this significant moment in his young life and decided not to mention the fact that the scoutmaster had to telephone the fire brigade. 'Well, as you be a mate, Ronnie, mon, one week, but no more,' he said, as he lovingly polished the handlebars with the sleeve of his blue overalls.

Ronnie took one last look at the object of his desire, jumped into Big Dave's bin wagon parked outside, and squeezed onto the front bench seat next to Little Malcolm. 'Thanks f'lift, lads,' he said.

'Bike looked good, Ronnie,' said Big Dave, as he crunched into first gear.

'Y'reight there, Dave,' said Little Malcolm. 'Looked a winner t'me.'

'Problem is Ruby,' said Ronnie, staring at his five-pound note. 'This is m'last fiver. Ah could mebbe buy it on t'never-never but she'd create summat rotten.'

'That's women f'you,' said Big Dave. 'Can't see a proper bargain, when it's not shoes an' dresses an' suchlike.'

'Y'reight there, Dave – speshully shoes,' said Little Malcolm knowingly.

Ronnie pulled his bobble hat further down over his furrowed brow.

'Mebbe you'll 'ave a winner on t'Gran' National,' said Big Dave hopefully.

'Mebbe it'll jus' come t'you in a flash,' added

226

Little Malcolm, as the bin wagon turned onto the narrow back road to Ragley through Easington woods.

It was then Ronnie remembered. Although years of backing horses with names such as 'Rocket Ronnie' and 'Lucky Pigeon' had never produced a winner, he knew that one day he would get a *feeling*. Today was that day. It hit him like a thunderbolt. He sat up in his seat and stared through the windscreen. It was something Clyde had said: something that Ronnie knew for certain was about to change his life and provide him with the motorbike of his dreams. He took out his *Racing Post* and as he studied the runners and riders of the Aintree Grand National one name sprang out from the page, and Ronnie Smith knew with absolute certainty that he was about to back a winner.

Back in school, it was almost lunchtime and I had just finished reading the next chapter in our class story, *Prince Caspian* by C.S. Lewis, when Jungle Telegraph Jodie announced, 'Mr Smith's comin' up t'drive, Mr Sheffield.'

Ronnie Smith, shoulders hunched in a baggy grey suit and wearing his best Leeds United bobble hat, looked smarter and more sprightly than usual. As I walked into the entrance hall, Ruby had finished putting out the dining tables and chairs and was locking her caretaker's store. She was surprised to see Ronnie.

'Ah thought you were goin' t'York t'sign on for a job,' said Ruby sternly.

'Ah'm goin' soon,' said Ronnie, flinching under

her gaze. 'Ah've gorra himportant job t'do first.'

I opened the office door. 'Hello, Ronnie. Come on through,' I said. 'You too, Ruby.'

Vera was sitting at her desk. She looked up from reading a County Hall circular entitled 'The School Curriculum: the case for a common curriculum for all schools in England and Wales'.

'So what is it, Ronnie?' I said. 'Is everything all right?'

He rattled the cocoa tin he was carrying. 'Ah'm collectin', Mr Sheffield.'

'Who are you collecting for?' asked Vera.

'It's Billy Two-Sheds, Miss Evans. 'Is funeral's on Monday, an' we're buying some flowers,' said Ronnie forlornly. ''E's passed on t'great bird loft in t'sky.' He gazed theatrically out of the office window as bright sunshine pierced through the rain-washed clouds.

We all followed his gaze, half expecting to see a white-painted garden shed being pulled across the heavens by a host of winged angels wearing flat caps and carrying bags of birdseed.

It was a poignant moment. Ronnie lowered his head in reverence.

'Who's Billy Two-Sheds?' I asked, breaking the awkward silence.

''E were in our Ronnie's Pigeon Club,' explained Ruby.

'Why was he called Billy Two-Sheds?' I asked rather lamely.

'Well, er, 'e 'ad two sheds, Mr Sheffield,' said Ronnie.

Vera rolled her eyes at me, took fifty pence from her purse and put it in the tin.

'It's William Braithwaite, Mr Sheffield,' explained Vera. 'He lived on the Morton Road and always supported the church. He was well into his eighties.'

''E were a lovely man,' said Ruby, dabbing a tear from her eye with the hem of her bright orange, Extra-Large, Double X overall.

'He collected all kinds of bric-a-brac and had a stall in Easington Market,' said Vera. 'He kept all his stock in two enormous sheds in his garden.'

I put another fifty-pence piece in the tin.

'You can go round the rest of the staff if you like, Ronnie,' I said. 'It sounds like a good cause.'

'"God loveth a cheerful giver",' recited Vera. 'Two Corinthians, chapter nine, verse seven.'

For a moment Ronnie looked perplexed. He thought Corinthians was a football team. 'Thanks, Mr Sheffield. Thanks, Miss Evans. Ah'll be off, then,' said Ronnie, and set off in the direction of the hall.

''E's supposed t'be tryin' t'get a job,' said Ruby mournfully.

'I'm sure he'll try his best,' I said, more in hope than expectation.

'Y'can't trust 'im, Mr Sheffield,' said Ruby. ''Is benefit's just gone up t'eighteen pound fifty a week, an' 'e thinks ah don't know.'

A few minutes later Ronnie and Ruby were in heated discussion in the entrance hall. Ruby still wasn't happy.

'Ah want you t'go straight t'York t'sign on, Ronnie,' said Ruby, brushing a few bird droppings from the lapel of his suit.

'But ah've not even filled in me "Mark the Ball"

229

Competition,' said Ronnie, in desperation, taking a rolled-up *Yorkshire Evening Post* from his pocket.

Every football season for the past ten years, with religious devotion Ronnie opened his newspaper to the sports page, studied the photograph of a moment of soccer action, from which the ball had been erased, and then neatly drew twelve crosses to guess the exact position of the football. Ronnie used his foolproof system of triangulation, by following the steely gaze of the diving centre forward who was about to head the ball, and those of the helpless defenders stranded in the muddy goalmouth. The fact his foolproof system never worked did not deter Ronnie's scheming mind. All he knew was that for a ten-pence stake the winning prize was the massive sum of a hundred pounds.

Each week, as he handed his entry to Miss Prudence Golightly in the Ragley General Stores & Newsagent, he thought of what he would buy with a hundred pounds, and each week Miss Golightly's view that nearly all men were gullible fools was steadily reinforced.

To Ronnie's amazement, Ruby snatched the rolled-up newspaper from his grasp. 'Y'can forget about wasting money on that, Ronnie,' she shouted. Then she stood back and surveyed him from top to toe. 'An' y'look a disgrace in that old suit; we need t'get shut of it.'

'Well, y'said t'get smart f'signing on,' retorted Ronnie.

'Y'should ah gone in y'best suit,' said Ruby. 'Y'need t'make a good impression.'

'Nay, there's a bit o' life left in this un yet,' he replied, scratching at the tomato ketchup stains on his cuffs.

'But, if y'get a job, we can buy them new wardrobes from MI5,' pleaded Ruby.

'MI5! That's secret service, y'daft ha'porth,' said Ronnie in disgust.

Ronnie's bobble hat muffled the sound of the sharp slap of the rolled-up newspaper on the back of his head that ended the conversation.

By the time Saturday morning arrived, Ronnie and Ruby were far from my mind. To my surprise, Laura telephoned to say she had got Saturday morning free and would I like a lift into York to do my weekend shopping. There seemed to be only minutes between my saying 'Yes' and the sound of the tyres of her mother's brand-new Mini Clubman screeching to a halt outside Bilbo Cottage.

When I opened the door Laura strode in confidently. ''Morning, Jack. You ready?' she asked.

I couldn't help but notice the black flared jeans she was wearing and the black leather jacket that was styled to accentuate her slim waist. She carefully rearranged her delicate pink scarf that matched her lipstick perfectly.

Laura appeared to be in a hurry and she playfully grabbed my hand and tugged me through the door.

Her driving matched her lifestyle: definitely faster than mine. On the outskirts of York we pulled into a garage for fuel. The five gallons of petrol cost four pounds, but, to my surprise, instead of paying by cash Laura produced a plastic Trustcard with the word VISA printed on it. The garage assistant made an imprint of the card on a grey carbonized receipt and Laura signed the top copy.

'I've never seen one of those newfangled plastic cards used before,' I said.

'It's all the rage in London, Jack,' said Laura, with a smile. 'You're still in the dark ages up here, I see.'

'But you might go accidentally into debt,' I said.

'I've got six weeks to clear it,' said Laura, as she replaced the card and receipt in her purse. 'So there's no problem.'

I wasn't convinced and didn't tell Laura that I could never imagine using one myself.

Minutes later I breathed a sigh of relief as we parked in an impossibly small space in Lord Mayor's Walk alongside the city walls. I felt a little strange as we walked side by side towards York's medieval streets without Beth. Laura was relaxed but quiet and, once again, I was aware of her perfume. It was as if we were both waiting for the other to speak. Off to our right, the great grassy banks were studded with the arrowheads of daffodils, waiting for the trigger of sunshine to burst into life.

Laura suggested we meet up again in a coffee shop in Stonegate and we went our separate ways to do our shopping.

An hour later, and weighed down by two large bags containing enough food to last me another week, I sat down opposite Laura, who was stirring her hot chocolate thoughtfully.

'I've found a flat in York,' she said. 'It's perfect.'

'What's it like?' I asked.

'It's got a lovely lounge and a bedroom that overlooks the museum gardens.' She pursed her lips and blew on her hot drink before she drank it, just the same as Beth always did.

'When do you move in?'

'As soon as I can find a big strong man to help me,' she said, looking up from her drink with a hint of mischief in her eyes.

I smiled and stood up to order a cup of tea.

We chatted about life and work and Laura appeared fascinated by the seemingly mundane tasks of a village school headmaster.

Later, we walked down Stonegate as watery spring sunshine broke through the clouds.

'So what's your horse for the National?' asked Laura.

'I haven't backed one, I'm afraid,' I said apologetically. 'In fact, I've never even been into a betting shop.'

Laura's eyes crinkled into a smile. It was another of her mannerisms that I liked. 'Then it's time we did something about that,' she said, with a grin.

Moments later she was guiding me down a side street, off Parliament Street, and through a bookmaker's doorway.

I stared in confusion at the long list of horses.

Laura walked confidently up to the counter. She took five pounds from her neat, businesslike handbag. 'Now give me five pounds, Jack,' she said, holding out her hand.

I took a five-pound note from my wallet and handed it over.

Laura put the two five-pound notes on the counter. 'Five pounds each way on Rough and Tumble,' she said to the bookmaker's assistant, who was looking at me, anticipating that I would make the bet.

She picked up the betting slip and we walked back to the car. Then we drove, at Laura's familiar breakneck speed, back to Kirkby Steepleton. Outside Bilbo Cottage I collected my shopping from the back seat of her car and crouched by her open window to say goodbye.

'Thanks, Laura. It's been an enjoyable morning.'

'Don't forget: cheer for Rough and Tumble this afternoon. The odds are fourteen to one, so if we win there should be enough for a night out.'

As she drove away, I thought a night out with Beth sounded a good idea, but as I turned and walked through the door I began to wonder whether Laura had meant a night out with her. By the time I had unpacked my shopping, such an idea seemed far-fetched, but perhaps interesting.

In an exciting race, Rough and Tumble came third, beaten by Zongalero and, the winner, Rubstic. I couldn't work out if Laura and I had won any money and the phone didn't ring.

Little did I know that at number 7, School View, in Ragley village, a certain unemployed pigeon-racer had been watching the same race and biting his knuckles in an attempt not to alert Ruby to the fact he had just won the biggest bet of his life.

On Monday lunchtime, I walked into the staff-room. Vera had finished checking the dinner registers and was talking to Ruby.

'I'm going with Ruby to stand in the High Street, Mr Sheffield,' said Vera, as she buttoned her royal-blue overcoat. 'We just want to pay our last respects.'

'It's Billy Two-Sheds' funeral, Mr Sheffield,' explained Ruby. 'An' our Duggie will be walking be'ind t'hearse in 'is black 'at.'

Ruby's son, Duggie Smith, was the assistant to the local undertaker, and he would regularly boast to his team mates in the Ragley Rovers Football Club that he never got any complaints from his customers.

I glanced across the staff-room to where Anne was showing Jo Maddison how to fill in an order form for large tins of powder paint.

'Could you hold the fort, Anne?' I asked. 'I think I'll go with Vera and Ruby.'

Anne looked up from the complicated order form with its triplicate carbon sheets and nodded. She looked preoccupied. Last year, Jo had mistakenly written '144' in the 'no. of units' column and had received 144 boxes of white chalk. As each box contained 144 sticks, we were now the proud owners of over twenty thousand sticks of chalk!

Ruby, Vera and I walked down the school drive.

The High Street was lined with villagers and shopkeepers, as per the local tradition, while the shiny black hearse paused outside The Royal Oak

235

as a mark of respect. The members of the dominoes team removed their flat caps and bowed their heads.

'Doesn't our Duggie look smart,' said Ruby proudly.

Duggie looked like a Victorian gentleman in his tall black hat and tightly buttoned black overcoat. Fortunately, the half-smoked Castella cigar, propped absent-mindedly behind his left ear, was largely covered by his Bay City Rollers hairstyle and appeared to go unnoticed by the tearful throng.

As the hearse and the small procession of mourners passed by, I bowed my head with everyone else and thought for a moment about Billy, a man I had never met. He had lived in the village all his life, attended Ragley School at the turn of the century and served his country in two World Wars. It seemed appropriate that, as a sudden shaft of sunlight illuminated the bright flowers scattered over the oak coffin, the echoes of children's voices filled the air.

Suddenly, Ronnie Smith appeared from the direction of the council estate. He sidled up to Ruby and removed his bobble hat. As he bowed his balding head, I noticed he was dressed in his best suit and I had never seen him look so smart. I had also never seen him look so anxious. There was clearly something on his mind.

As the cortège made its way slowly towards the row of shops in the High Street, Ronnie gave Ruby a glassy-eyed smile. 'Ah were jus' lookin' f'me other suit, Ruby, luv,' he said.

'That ol' thing,' said Ruby dismissively. 'Ah got

shut of it.'

Ronnie's eyes bulged. 'Y'got shut of it? Who to?'

'Ah gave it t'our Duggie.'

Ronnie looked momentarily relieved. 'Oh, that's all right, then, luv. Is it in 'is bedroom, then?'

'No, Ronnie,' said Ruby tersely. 'Y'suit's jus' gone by.' She pointed towards the hearse.

Ronnie was puzzled. 'What d'you mean, it's jus' gone by?' he asked.

'Our Duggie said poor Billy Two-Sheds only 'ad an ol' boiler suit, so ah gave 'im your ol' suit. It's jus' gone by in t'coffin,' explained Ruby.

Ronnie grabbed Ruby's arm. 'Did y'by any chance empty t'pockets?' he gasped.

Ruby watched the hearse pause again outside Piercy's Butcher's Shop, where for the last fifty years Billy Two-Sheds had bought his weekly supply of pig's trotters.

'No, luv, ah didn't,' said Ruby finally. 'What y'askin' for?'

Ronnie couldn't reply. In fact, he could barely breathe. Ronnie's dilemma was clear. Last Friday he had been to the bookmaker's in York and put his last five pounds on Rubstic to win at odds of twenty-five to one. His winning bookmaker's slip was worth £130 and he knew he only had to get the bus into York to collect his winnings. As Ruby disapproved of his gambling, there was no way he could admit this, particularly as he had no intention of buying a set of bedroom furniture.

'Ah might 'ave left summat in me pocket,' stuttered Ronnie.

'Ah 'ope y'not thinkin' of running after our Duggie an' asking 'im t'open t'coffin,' said Ruby, in disbelief.

Ronnie stared at the hearse as it turned the corner towards Pratt's Garage. The thought had crossed his mind. 'Who d'you think I am, Seb bleedin' Coe?' he said, in disgust.

Ruby gave Ronnie a withering look and set off for the council estate. Vera and I walked back to school and, at the gate, we looked back at the distraught Ronnie, who was staring helplessly down the empty High Street.

At the end of afternoon school, Jodie Cuthbertson made an unexpected announcement. 'Mrs Buttle's runnin' up t'drive, Mr Sheffield.'

No one had ever seen Betty Buttle run before. While she would move quickly to collect her prizes at the local bingo parlour, no one could ever recall her actually running. But there was no doubt: Betty Buttle was running towards the school entrance like Steve Ovett going for his gold medal. She was also clutching a copy of the *Yorkshire Evening Post*.

She was soon in deep conversation with Ruby in the school entrance hall. As the children put their chairs on top of their tables and we said our end-of-day prayer, we could hear Betty and Ruby uttering high-pitched screams of delight.

By the time I reached the staff-room, Betty had sprinted back down the school drive and Anne, Sally, Jo and Vera were already sharing Ruby's news.

'Oh, Mr Sheffield, ah'm all of a fluster,'

shouted Ruby.

'What is it, Ruby?' I asked.

She held up the *Yorkshire Evening Post*. 'Ah've won "Mark the Ball", Mr Sheffield,' she said, pointing to her name in the newspaper. 'Ah jus' put a load o' crosses on that football photo in our Ronnie's paper, paid me ten pence, an' gave it t'Miss Golightly in t'General Stores. An' ah've won a 'undred pound!'

Sally and Jo gave Ruby a big hug.

Vera smiled with affection at her loyal friend who worked so hard and always put the needs of her family above her own. 'You can have your new bedroom now,' she said, gently squeezing Ruby's hand.

At that moment Joseph Evans walked in after completing his duties at Billy Two-Sheds' funeral. 'Hello, Ruby. There's an African gentleman looking for you in the school car park,' he said.

Curious, we all followed Joseph out of the school to investigate.

Clyde Dlambulo removed his Biggles-like goggles, kicked down the chromium stand and parked his gleaming 1968 Honda 747 motorcycle. 'Ah'm lookin' f'your Ronnie,' he said.

'Hello, Clyde,' said Ruby. 'What d'you want my Ronnie for?'

'Look no further,' said Joseph, as Ronnie suddenly appeared at the school gate.

'Ah've just 'eard y'news, Ruby my luv, from Betty Buttle,' said the panting Ronnie.

Ronnie looked in admiration at the motorcycle as if all his prayers had mysteriously been

239

answered, but then Clyde pulled a five-pound note out of his back pocket and offered it to Ronnie.

'What's all this abart, Clyde?' asked Ronnie, looking perplexed.

'It's de big thank you from me, Ronnie, mon, 'cause it were you be talkin' about rubbing dem sticks together when we be in de scouts. It be a lucky omen when ah went into de bookies las' Saturday.'

'What d'you mean?' asked Ronnie.

'Ah backed de winner in dat Gran' National 'orse race, Ronnie, mon. De winner, he be called Rubstic and ah won de fortune. In fact, ah won so much, ah bought dis bike off Mr Morrissey. It be a real beauty. Ah know you was keen t'buy it but no 'ard feelings, Ronnie, mon.'

Ronnie looked as if the sky had just fallen in.

'It be a miracle, Ronnie, mon, so 'ere be a fiver t'say thank you.'

With that, Clyde climbed on his bike, replaced his goggles and sped off down the High Street.

Ruby looked in amazement at Ronnie. 'Now ah know why they used t'call you Bonnie 'n' Clyde an' not Ronnie 'n' Clyde,' she shouted. 'Gamblin' our 'ard-earned money again, Ronnie!' She snatched the five-pound note from his trembling fist. 'An' this'll pay for a new bedspread,' she shouted, and stormed off towards the council estate, dragging Ronnie by his shirt collar.

I recalled with some embarrassment the bet that Laura had placed on my behalf at the bookmakers and wondered about the outcome.

'"He that diggeth a pit shall fall into it".

Ecclesiastes, chapter ten, verse eight,' said Joseph solemnly.

We stood there, Joseph, Vera and I, in the bright spring sunshine, staring after the downcast Ronnie.

'I think Ronnie's in for a tough time,' I said.

'Someone needs to explain,' said Joseph, looking bewildered.

I looked expectantly at Vera.

'"The price of wisdom is above rubies". Job, chapter twenty-eight, verse eighteen,' said Vera, with a wink in my direction.

We both looked at Vera with admiration.

'I still don't understand,' said Joseph.

'Let's just say the secret service will be delivering a new bedroom to Ruby's house in the very near future,' said Vera.

'Ah,' said Joseph.

'"And God said, Let there be light: and there was light",' said Vera.

'Genesis, chapter one, verse three,' recited Joseph.

Vera smiled proudly at her brother, took him by the arm and, with light steps, walked back into school.

As I followed them up the cobbled driveway, it occurred to me that miracles were like buses. You wait ages for one to arrive and then two come at once.

Chapter Fifteen

A Different Déjà Vu

School closed today for the Easter holidays. 87 children on roll. End-of-term reports were sent out to all parents.
Extract from the Ragley School Logbook:
Friday, 30 March 1979

Victor Pratt trudged out of his little garage to the single pump on the forecourt. 'Ah s'ppose y'want it fillin'?' he asked, with a frown.

'Yes, please, Victor,' I said, noting that he looked even more miserable than usual. 'How are you?'

'Ah've got bronchitis an' aches that start 'ere,' he said, pointing to his knees. 'An' they go right up m'legs into m'back an' finish up 'ere.' He pointed to his neck, which was swathed with a thick woollen scarf.

'I'm sorry to hear that,' I said.

'An' ah've got toothache an' earache,' he added for good measure.

'Oh dear,' I said, remembering the last time Victor had described his ailments. 'It sounds like déjà vu.'

'No, I 'aven't got that,' said Victor, shaking his head. 'An' ah wouldn't go t'France anyway.'

It was early Friday morning, 30 March, the last

242

day of the spring term, and Victor's mood was matched by the cold, unfriendly weather. I drove off, turned into Ragley High Street, stopped to buy my morning newspaper at the General Stores and parked in the school car park. The pale petals of a few brave primroses bordering the cobbled school drive were struggling to open up in the raw, biting wind and the first daffodils shivered with each sudden gust.

The staff-room had an end-of-term feel to it, as if everyone had begun to relax at last. Vera was reading her *Daily Telegraph* and chuckling to herself; Jo was engrossed in an article in her monthly science magazine on how to grow cress on soggy cotton wool; Sally and Anne were sitting in the corner, flipping through Sally's *Cosmopolitan* and drinking black coffee. Sally was cutting down on milky drinks and Anne was providing loyal support. Everybody seemed to be busy with their own thoughts.

'Good morning, everyone,' I said.

'It certainly is,' said Vera, with a broad smile. 'Listen to this. "Labour have lost a vote of no confidence and a general election has been called for 3 May".'

Sally shook her head sadly and carried on browsing. As an ardent Labour supporter, she guessed that time might be up for Prime Minister Jim Callaghan.

Jo looked across at Vera's newspaper and the headline BEARDED BOBBIES caught her eye. She pointed it out to Vera, who scanned the article next to a photograph of a policeman sporting a formidable growth of facial hair.

'Hey, listen to this, everyone,' said Jo. 'Go on, Vera.'

'It says here that "Police Superintendent Harry Potter has complained that eight per cent of all policemen now have a beard",' Vera read.

'I wonder if that includes Dan's moustache,' said Jo, a dreamy look in her eyes.

'Pity a senior policeman hasn't got something more important to think about with everything that's going on,' said Sally rather grumpily.

'Dan says this Superintendent's a really important person in the police,' said Jo.

'What was his name again, Vera?' asked Anne.

'Harry Potter,' said Vera.

'Well, that's a name we won't hear again,' said Sally defiantly. She rummaged in her trendy open-weave shoulder-bag and produced an old copy of *Cosmopolitan* featuring wedding dresses for the seventies bride. 'By the way, Jo, I brought this in for you,' she said, suddenly brightening up. 'It's got some terrific wedding dresses in it.'

Margaret Thatcher, Harry Potter and facial hair were suddenly forgotten as the four women began to pore over the colourful photographs of perfectly formed brides posing, without a care in the world, amid idyllic English countryside.

Sally had been a regular *Cosmopolitan* reader for the past seven years, ever since its inaugural copy in 1972, when a certain article had caught her eye. She had found 'What makes men fantastic lovers' by Jilly Cooper to be excellent reading. Sadly, when she tried to share these new ideas with her husband, Colin, he did not even look up from the section 'Mitre joints made easy' in his

Woodwork for Beginners:Volume 1. At that moment, Sally realized that ever since the long-haired, peace-loving Colin had said he was too old to wear flowers in his hair at the Isle of Wight music festival at the end of August 1970, their relationship had become rather more grey than psychedelic. Then, Sally recalled, when he returned home and bought a Rolf Harris Stylophone, it was about that time she began to find comfort in digestive biscuits.

The day passed by quickly and, finally, the children rushed home for their two-week holiday with thoughts of an absence of essays and an abundance of Easter eggs. I was sitting at my desk in the school office, checking the carbon copies of the other teachers' end-of-term reading test results on each pupil, when Anne walked in.

'I hope it goes well for Beth next Monday, Jack,' she said.

Once again, Beth's interview filled my thoughts. 'I'm giving her a lift to County Hall on Monday morning,' I said.

'Give her my best wishes, Jack. Beth would make an excellent headmistress.'

I pushed my papers to one side. 'What about you, Anne? Wouldn't you like your own school?'

She gave me that familiar gentle smile and I guessed her answer. 'I'm content with what I've got, Jack, and I'm happy here. I wouldn't want the extra responsibility. I'd rather go home and spend time with John than write curriculum documents and policies.'

I nodded. Anne had found her niche. 'Perhaps you and John would like to come over to Bilbo

Cottage for a meal during the holiday?'

Anne smiled. 'Thanks, Jack. That would be lovely.'

With that, she walked towards the classroom door, when a thought occurred to me.

'You've not tasted my cooking yet,' I said.

'It can't be worse than John's,' said Anne, with a grin, and closed the door behind her.

Gradually, the school emptied and I heard Ruby in the distance singing 'Climb Every Mountain'. She was moving all the furniture in my classroom into the hall in order to give the floor her 'holiday polish'.

I had just written 'School closed today for the Easter holidays' in the school logbook, when the telephone rang. It was Beth on the line.

'Just confirming Monday morning, Jack.'

'I'll pick you up at nine o'clock and, don't worry, everything will be fine.'

'Thanks,' she said.

'Shall I come over?' I asked.

There was a pause. 'I've got lots of reading to do.'

'Well, I'm here if you need me.'

'OK, Jack. See you on Monday.'

'Bye, Beth.'

I put the receiver down slowly and wondered what Monday would bring.

Later that evening, in front of a roaring fire, with Simon and Garfunkel on the turntable, and sustained by a bottle of full-bodied red wine, I read *The Return of the King*, the final part of Tolkien's epic trilogy. That night I dreamed that Beth and I were staggering up the steep sides of

246

Mount Doom, until we reached the entrance to a dark cave, above which the label 'Interviews This Way' burned in fiery letters.

The peace and warmth of my bed on Saturday morning was shattered by the ringing of my telephone on the hall table. I grabbed my dressing gown and hurried downstairs. At first my sleepy brain thought the voice was Beth's and then I realized it wasn't.

'Wake up, Jack: the weekend has begun,' said a cheerful voice.

'Oh, hello, Laura,' I mumbled.

'Remember Rough and Tumble?' said Laura.

'You mean in the Grand National?'

'That's right.'

'I remember giving you five pounds,' I said.

'Well, it's payback time, Jack.'

'Is it?' I said, rubbing the sleep out of my eyes.

'It's time to spend our winnings,' said Laura triumphantly.

I was intrigued and woke up quickly. 'What had you in mind?'

'Lunch today, at a rather nice place in York. My surprise – you'll love it. It's near the Minster. I asked Beth this morning if she would like to come, but she's too busy preparing for her interview.'

'Oh, well, er, fine,' I said.

'I only do half-days at Liberty's on Saturday so I'll see you when I've finished work. Meet me outside the Minster at one o'clock.'

She rang off and I recalled that Laura had started her new job as a manager in the fashion

247

department of the up-market Liberty's.

Dressed in my best sports jacket and my Yorkshire Cricket Club tie, I waited on the steps outside York Minster and shivered in the cold wind. Heads turned when Laura appeared along Petergate and strode confidently across the road towards me, dressed in a figure-hugging business suit. She kissed me on the cheek, took my arm and we walked into Duncombe Place and up the steps of the Dean Court Hotel.

Two strikingly dressed women, a redhead and a brunette, were sitting at the first table in the elegant dining room. Both were wearing fashionable maxiskirts, each with a long slit down the side, and leather maxicoats that afforded a seductive glimpse of their long legs.

Laura saw me glance in their direction, as the maître d'hôtel showed us to our table. She leaned towards me and whispered, 'I'm going back to Liberty's this afternoon to buy a coat just like that, Jack. I get a huge discount. You can help me choose.'

The conversation of the two women drifted over to us as we examined the endless menu.

'"Marry in haste, repent at leisure",' said the brunette.

'I couldn't agree more, darling,' said the redhead, while checking her immaculate lipstick in a small mirror.

Laura raised her eyebrows and smiled wickedly.

Soon, we were chatting happily. Laura was an engaging conversationalist and a good listener. The meal was excellent, the service spectacular,

248

and an hour and a half later Laura insisted on paying the bill. She held onto my arm again, as we dodged the tourists and Easter shoppers, and walked into the entrance of Liberty's. The spacious department store was on three floors and there was a feeling of grandeur within the dark-panelled walls. Laura was treated royally by the shop assistants and I sat in a comfortable wickerwork chair close to the changing rooms. Two other reluctant men were sitting in the same area and both nodded profusely each time their respective wives appeared in a new outfit. Laura seemed to spend an age encouraging me to help her select the perfect black leather coat and then kissed me on the cheek in full view of every employee in the department when we parted.

That night, I reflected on an enjoyable day, until my thoughts returned to Beth and her interview and I hoped it would go well.

By Monday morning, the cold wind had gone and the long winter was finally laid to rest. As Beth and I drove towards Northallerton, the country-side was waking from its frozen slumber and the bright April sunlight reflected off the sharp buds of the hawthorn hedgerows. The drive was spec-tacular as the giant mass of the Hambleton Hills stretched out before us, towering like a guardian over the plain of York.

Next to me, Beth was silent. She sat upright in the passenger seat, clutching her letter of invi-tation to attend for the headship of Hartingdale Primary School.

I reached across to squeeze her hand. 'You'll be

fine, Beth,' I said.

There was a flicker of a response and we drove on in silence.

As we drove further north, the green fringes of the North Yorkshire Moors were dotted with ewes, protecting their new-born lambs, and swathes of primroses splashed the grassy banks with colour. It was a time of new life and new beginnings.

I glanced across at Beth again and hoped with all my heart that this would be her day. I knew how much she wanted to become a headteacher and, with her reputation as one of the brightest young deputy heads in North Yorkshire, this opportunity was a great chance to achieve her dream. I also knew that, if successful, it would mean that Beth would be a local headteacher and could remain in my life. As we neared the sprawling market town of Northallerton, we stopped in heavy traffic alongside a Clarks shoe shop. In the centre of the window a pair of 'Aviemore' sheepskin-lined, genuine-leather boots at £25 had caught the attention of two well-dressed ladies. I couldn't help but think of Laura. Beth glanced but her mind was on more pressing matters.

County Hall was a huge, imposing building and dominated everything round it. As Beth reported to the reception desk, busy office workers hurried past carrying bulky manila files and bundles of brown envelopes. It wasn't long before a stern-looking assistant, with a burgundy clipboard, beckoned us to follow her up a magnificent staircase that wouldn't have been out of place on the set of *Gone with the Wind*.

The soles of my leather shoes tapped out a rapid heartbeat on the wide marble stairs and echoed round the vast, ornate ceiling and Corinthian columns as I followed Beth to the first floor.

'Miss Henderson should wait in the reception area outside Room 109,' said the lady with the clipboard. She pointed to a large brown door with a shiny brass handle. 'Wait here until you're called.'

'Good luck, Beth,' I whispered.

She smiled a nervous smile.

'This is where I waited for my interview,' I explained, and I squeezed her hand.

Miss Clipboard glanced up at me with a slight air of irritation. 'Your friend can wait in the reception room at the far end of the corridor.'

It was a command rather than a request.

I mouthed a final good-luck message to Beth and walked with loud, echoing footsteps to the far end of the wide first-floor corridor. The reception room was furnished like a stately home, elegant but uncomfortable.

A large, dark and highly polished mahogany table filled the middle of the room and in its exact centre a vase of dried flowers added to the funereal atmosphere. Countless tiny specks of dust hovered in the sharp shafts of sunlight that bisected the room from the high leaded windows. I sat down, picked up an educational publication and noted that the lobby supporting a common curriculum in schools in England and Wales appeared to be gathering momentum.

Beth walked into the waiting room outside Room 109. Three interviewees were already

251

there: two females in smart skirts and jackets and a portly, grey-haired man in a shiny and well-worn three-piece suit with a very crumpled waistcoat. They were sitting upright in stiff-backed chairs as if they were auditioning for *Pride and Prejudice*.

Shiny Suit glanced up forlornly. 'Hello,' he said weakly, and lowered his head again.

His voice, though quiet, sounded like a pistol crack in this large echo chamber and Beth nodded in recognition and forced a smile.

One of the women looked pensive and rocked gently forwards and backwards in a tense manner, as if in a trance. The other smiled with the inner glow of absolute confidence. She strode over to Beth and shook her hand.

'Good luck,' said Miss Confidence, in a loud voice. 'Hope you do yourself justice. If we all perform well there can be no complaints.'

She looked as though she would have been at home introducing the Eurovision Song Contest. 'I'm Sally, deputy head of Ollerthorpe Infants and Nursery,' she continued, in animated style. 'Julie over there is deputy of Westbrook Primary and David is already a head of a small school in the Dales and looking for a new challenge. And you are?'

Even Miss Pensive looked up to listen to Beth's reply.

'I'm Beth Henderson, deputy at Thirkby Primary School,' replied Beth, clearly trying to sound confident. 'This is my first interview for a headship in North Yorkshire,' she added.

'Don't worry,' said Miss Confidence. 'This is

my third. You'll soon get the hang of giving the answers they want to hear.'

Miss Confidence was one of the carousel of interviewees who turned up regularly for the cycle of headship interviews. Eventually, one by one, they were appointed or cast aside. For the next twenty minutes, Miss Confidence grilled everyone. She was keen to know all she could about the opposition.

Eventually, the assistant with the charisma bypass returned and explained they were to be interviewed in alphabetical order. Beth was to be third. Miss Confidence was first and clipped across the hard floor as if on a catwalk. Depression settled heavily on Shiny Suit, who was due to be last and complained he was desperate for a cigarette. Apart from his mutterings, the only sound during the next forty minutes was the creaking of Miss Pensive's chair as she rocked gently forwards and backwards as if she was in the front row of a Hare Krishna concert. Beth sat perfectly still, concentrating for all she was worth. As the minutes ticked by, the angle of the sun changed subtly until a shaft of pale sunlight lit up her honey-blonde hair.

With a sudden squeak of heavy doors and a clip-clop of shoes, Miss Confidence re-entered the waiting room, brimming with even more confidence. She glanced at her watch. 'Exactly forty minutes,' she said, with a forced smile.

Miss Pensive was summoned next and dropped her handbag with a resounding clatter as she hurried to keep up with the officious assistant. She reappeared thirty minutes later, looking as if she was about to burst into tears, and then it was Beth's turn.

The journey for Beth from the doorway of the vast interview room to the interviewee's isolated chair took an age. Back in the waiting area, a huge, circular oak-framed clock with faded Roman numerals counted out the minutes. Beneath it Shiny Suit squirmed in his seat, while Miss Confidence continued her monologue on successful interview strategies. Miss Pensive seemed to be close to collapse.

When Beth reappeared, her face was white. Miss Clipboard ushered Shiny Suit to the condemned cell and Miss Confidence began her interrogation. For Beth, this was almost as demanding as the interview. Miss Confidence wanted to know everything Beth had been asked. Eventually, a leaden-footed Shiny Suit trudged wearily into the room and sank heavily onto a chair.

'Another one bites the dust,' he grumbled. 'Doesn't help when old Mr Know-It-All asks what educational research has had an impact on your work and I say I'm too busy teaching, preparing topics, marking books and putting up library shelves for all that high-brow stuff.'

After a thirty-five-minute wait, in which time all of them vowed they would not go through this again, the assistant from the Colditz Charm School popped her head round the door, scanned their faces, looked down at her clipboard and announced, 'Miss Henderson, could you come with me, please? The rest of you will wait here.'

There was a moment's pause and then everyone spoke at once.

'Well done – they must be going to offer you the job,' said Miss Pensive, looking relieved.

'Good luck,' said Shiny Suit, reaching for his cigarettes.

'Oh no, not again!' said a distraught Miss Confidence.

Beth was whisked quickly through the door for the second time. While the odds were on her being offered the post, there had been occasions when the interviewing panel wanted to confirm some details and had called one of the interviewees back before making their decision.

Everyone looked up as the door creaked again and Miss Clipboard reappeared like a genie from a magic lamp.

'Could the rest of you come with me, please?' she said, with smooth rhetorical authority.

They all trooped out to be told they were the unsuccessful candidates but they could go home safe in the knowledge that the interviewing panel thought they had all done well and could be proud of their performances. It was the third time Miss Confidence had heard this speech.

It seemed an eternity but eventually Beth reappeared at the far end of the corridor. For a moment, she stood in a shaft of sunlight, getting her bearings, and I stood up and waved. Baron Von Trapp could not have moved more quickly towards his Maria across an Austrian mountainside. I sped down the length of the room and, forgetting all decorum, wrapped my arms round her waist.

'Well, what news?'

'I got it, Jack. They offered me the post and I

said yes.'

'Well done, Beth. I'm so proud of you.'

I gave her a hug and we descended the magnificent staircase.

During the journey home, Beth gave me an in-depth account of her interview. She related every question and every answer. Her excitement was obvious.

'How about going out tonight to celebrate?' she said, as we approached the outskirts of York.

'Where would you like to go?'

'I know just the place,' she said. 'I've been wanting to go for ages.'

'Where's that?' I asked.

'That really smart hotel on Duncombe Place, close to the Minster.'

'Oh, you mean the Dean Court Hotel?' I said, in surprise.

'Yes, that's the one. Do you know it?'

'Yes, it's lovely. I went there on Saturday. In fact, I went with Laura.'

Beth looked shocked. 'Laura told me she was going out to lunch in York with a friend, but she didn't say where. And she didn't say who with.'

'Oh. She mentioned that she had asked you, but you were too busy because of your interview.'

I was perplexed for a moment, wondering why Beth appeared concerned that I had gone out to lunch with her sister.

'Our meal, Jack, will be very different,' she said, and squeezed my arm.

I wondered what she had in mind and, as I joined the Easington Road and headed towards

Morton village, I mused on Beth's reaction to my having lunch with Laura. For the first time, I pondered the possibility that Beth might even be a little jealous, and the grin on my face gradually widened.

Later that evening, Beth and I drove into York together and we parked outside the Dean Court. Beth looked wonderful in a forget-me-not-blue dress and appeared to hold my arm tighter than usual. I was pleased that my one and only grey suit had recently been to the dry cleaner's.

'Good evening, sir,' said the maître d'hôtel. 'Welcome back.'

He obviously had a good memory for faces.

I saw the same two long-legged women at the next table, sporting even more daring maxiskirts. I presumed they must be residents. They both glanced up as we walked in and nodded briefly in acknowledgement. They appeared to look rather quizzical about my having been accompanied by two different and very attractive women in almost as many days. Far from being embarrassed, I was rather enjoying the feeling, especially as Beth was particularly attentive.

It was a memorable evening and, as we raised our glasses of champagne to celebrate Beth's success, I recalled the last time I had sat in this luxurious dining room. There was, of course, something different this time.

Beth was sitting across the table from me.

It may have felt like déjà vu, but on this occasion, it was a different déjà vu.

Chapter Sixteen

Beware of the Ducks

PC Hunter took a road safety assembly and introduced the Green Cross Code. Class 1 visited the Ragley duck pond as part of their 'Pond Life' project.
Extract from the Ragley School Logbook:
Wednesday, 18 April 1979

The bright-yellow posters were on every telegraph pole in the village. Each one blared out, 'It's Time to Go, and Vote for Coe', and I stared in dismay at the message. If Stan Coe was elected onto the local council, it could only spell trouble for Ragley School.

It was early morning, on Wednesday, 18 April. The Easter holiday was over and the summer term had begun. I was crouching alongside the village duck pond, staring at the teeming pond life and making a few notes in an old school exercise book.

The sun shone through a powder-blue sky and warmed the back of my neck. The air, fragrant with the scent of spring wallflowers, was clean and fresh after the overnight rain. Around me, the new leaves on the weeping willow weighed down the graceful branches and caressed the fresh green sward of grass, like gentle swordplay between respected friends. It was good to be alive on a day such as this.

My class had begun a 'Pond Life' project and, that afternoon, I intended to bring them out to our village pond armed with nets, jam jars, magnifying glasses, sketch pads and clipboards. The ducks on the pond glanced up, hopeful of titbits, as the Ragley ladies' jogging group wobbled by in their Lycra outfits and multi-coloured leg-warmers. They, like me, knew that it was important not to disturb the harmonious lives of the resident duck population. In Ragley, they were definitely a protected species. While they regularly caused traffic delays, as they played follow-my-leader across the High Street, no one ever complained about the ducks.

The notable exception was Stan Coe, who suddenly appeared from the Morton Road, turned left in front of The Royal Oak, and roared by at a crazy speed in his Land Rover. He veered at the last moment, swerved onto the grass next to the pond and swore at the ducks that scattered before him with a frantic flapping of wings.

''E wants tekkin' down a peg or two,' said Tommy Piercy, who was sitting on the bench at the side of the pond. Old Tommy had brought a bag of bread crusts to feed the ducks.

'Good morning, Tommy,' I said, standing up and staring after the speeding Land Rover as it turned left and tore up the Easington Road. 'He was certainly in a hurry.'

'Allus is, that one,' grumbled Old Tommy, and he broke the crusts into bite-size chunks.

As I retraced my steps across the village green, I felt tempted to tear down the yellow poster of

Stan Coe that had been pasted on the telegraph pole immediately outside school. It had come as a surprise to all the staff and governors that Stan, the local bully and pig-farmer, had put his name forward for election.

Last year, Albert Jenkins had done some shrewd detective work and discovered from the school logbook that, way back in 1933, Stan Coe had been suspended for bullying. Since then, the corpulent Stan had made his fortune and was determined to become the most powerful man in the village by browbeating his opponents. There had been dark rumours among the locals of land deals and shady building contracts and all the stories included the name of Stan Coe. Now, undeterred, he was running for the office of county councillor and that spelled trouble for anyone who crossed his path.

Back in school, a different type of poster was in evidence.

Police Constable Dan Hunter and Jo Maddison were preparing a road safety assembly. Dan had come into school to advertise the Green Cross Code campaign, aimed at showing children how to cross the road safely. He had a handful of drawing pins and was pinning up some large-scale pictures of David Prowse, the ex-Mr Universe, who was now the superhero Green Cross Man. Throughout it all, Jo smiled adoringly at her own moustached superhero.

The giant policeman proved to be very popular with the children and, at the end of the assembly, he answered their many questions carefully and accurately. At ten-thirty, Anne rang the bell for morning playtime and we all met in the staff-room. Dan was packing up some of his equipment into a police-issue bag before taking it out to his little grey van.

'What's that?' asked Jo, pointing to a small green plastic box with a hinged lid, about the size of a soap dish.

'It's one of the new breathalyser kits,' said Dan, opening the box.

We all looked inside at a collection of tubes that appeared to be full of crystals.

'It's an electronic Alcometer SL2,' said Dan proudly. He laid out all the parts for us to see.

'How does it work?' asked Sally.

'You cut the end off one of the tubes, fix one end to the mouthpiece and the other to the plastic bag. Then you blow, with one continuous breath, into the mouthpiece, and the change in the colour of the crystals gives the result.'

It was a well-rehearsed routine. He had been well trained.

'So you know when a driver is over the limit?' asked Jo.

Dan nodded. 'All the lads at the station are looking forward to trying it out,' he said, with a huge grin.

Sally pointed to one of Dan's posters that read 'Think Before You Drink Before You Drive'.

'I'm putting that on the notice board outside the village hall,' said Dan, rolling up the poster and putting a rubber band round it.

'I'll have to be careful,' said Sally thoughtfully. 'Colin will have to drive me to the pub quiz at the Oak tonight.'

'You're in a quiz team, Sally?' I asked, in surprise.

'Well, yes,' she said, rather sheepishly. 'All the girls in the Ladies' Keep Fit evening class decided to end the evening with a chat in the pub after class. Then Don and Sheila asked us if we wanted to enter a team in their monthly quiz.'

'I'm sure you'll do very well,' said the ever-supportive Vera.

'Remember to stay on soft drinks, or even that new bottled water,' said Jo. 'Just in case any of Dan's uniformed friends are lurking outside.'

'That's right,' said Dan, zipping up the bag. 'They'll have you for "Drunk and Disorderly" or "Conduct Liable to Cause Breach of the Peace".'

For the remainder of morning playtime, Dan was only too willing to help his fiancée recycle a multicoloured ball of slightly hard Plasticine in preparation for her next lesson. True love clearly manifested itself in many ways.

After a lunch of spam fritters and baked beans followed by semolina, I walked across to the village green, carrying a chair and a collection of pond life identification charts. Soon all the children were sitting round the pond, observing, dipping and sketching.

'These water boatmen are swimmin' back-stroke, Mr Sheffield,' said Tony Ackroyd, full of his usual enthusiasm. He pointed to a group of strange aquatic insects, each about half an inch long, with a brown body and reddish eyes. With their long back legs like oars, they paddled around without a care in the world.

Eleven-year-old Micky Buttle had sketched a

wonderfully detailed drawing of the dark, slender body of a pond-skater that was balancing, incredibly, on the surface tension of the water. Jodie Cuthbertson and Dominic Brown were stretched out by the water's edge, watching the slow progress of pond snails, and eleven-year-old Mandy Ollerenshaw was doing a colourful pastel drawing of a mallard with a dark-green head and a ring of white feathers around its neck.

After half an hour, Sheila Bradshaw came out of The Royal Oak and propped outside the front door a large chalkboard announcing 'Pub Quiz Tonight'. She glanced up, saw all the children and quickly reappeared with four jugs of orange juice and a stack of plastic beakers. We all stopped work for a welcome break and sat in the sunshine, enjoying the unexpected refreshment.

'Nice t'see 'em working so 'ard,' said Sheila, as she walked round topping up our beakers.

'Thanks a lot, Sheila,' I said. 'You're very kind.'

'Anything for t'children ... and, of course, you, Mr Sheffield,' she whispered as she stooped to give me a refill and, in doing so, displayed her ample bosom.

The revving of an engine suddenly shattered the peaceful scene.

'Ah'm paying 'igh taxes f'you t'sit 'aving a bloody picnic,' yelled Stan Coe from the open window of his Land Rover. He had just visited the Pig and Ferret in Easington and enjoyed five pints of Tetley's bitter with a group of his duck-shooting friends. Before Sheila or I had the chance to reply, he put his foot down and accelerated back up the Morton Road.

''E needs t'watch 'is language in front o' t'children,' muttered Sheila, as she collected the beakers and tottered away, rather shakily, her high heels sinking into the grass with each step.

Albert Jenkins, our school governor, had just walked up the High Street and witnessed the whole scene. He was a tall, smartly dressed sixty-six-year-old and he shook his head in annoyance. "O! it is excellent to have a giant's strength, but it is tyrannous to use it like a giant",' he quoted.

Albert was a very well-read and astute man. He loved his Shakespeare.

'*Macbeth,*' I said, in acknowledgement.

Albert nodded. 'I see he's at it again,' he said, pointing towards the yellow posters. 'I thought we'd frightened him off last summer when he resigned as a school governor.'

'So did I, Albert.'

He nodded towards Sheila's chalkboard. 'I'm here to sign up our dominoes team for the quiz night,' he said.

'With your general knowledge, you should have a good chance, Albert.'

'I'm better at long ago than recent times.'

I looked at him, slightly puzzled.

'Memories are strange things, Jack,' he said. 'Mine are vivid and sharp like the still water at the bottom of a full bucket.'

'How do you mean?' I asked.

'Well, it's like this,' he replied, hooking his thumbs in his waistcoat pockets and leaning back against the weeping willow. 'All the old memories are cold and clear at the bottom of the bucket; whereas my new memories from recent times just splash on the surface and trickle over the sides. They're lost for ever.'

His face creased into a well-worn smile and he walked away, looking relaxed in his three-piece suit, in spite of the warm weather.

Eventually, we replaced all our specimens into the pond, where they could presumably get reacquainted and multiply, and carried all our equipment, notebooks and artwork back into the classroom. When Jodie Cuthbertson rang the school bell for the end of the day, she shouted, 'That was a smashing day, Mr Sheffield.' I walked out to the playground, where Jodie's twelve-year-old sister, Anita, was waiting for her. She was leaning against the school gate with Kenny Kershaw, who had also been in my class last year. Both were now in their first year at Easington Comprehensive School.

''Ello, Mr Sheffield,' said Anita. 'Me an' Kenny 'ad a lib'ry period.'

Kenny just nodded. Anita always had been the spokesperson for the class and nothing had changed.

She rummaged in her bag. 'Look what I got,' she said enthusiastically. 'It's a Casio calculator, Mr Sheffield. Look, when you press the buttons to do sums, they make a noise and then you get the answer. It's easy.'

'She's not s'pposed t'use it, though,' said Jodie.

'No! Don't y'think it's daft, Mr Sheffield?' said Anita. 'Ol' Chalky, our maths teacher, goes ballistic if 'e sees 'em in class. He meks us use slide rules an' I get all confused moving that plastic sliding thing up 'n' down t'ruler. All that loggyrhythm stuff don't mek sense t'me.'

Kenny was holding the handlebars of a racy new bicycle. Anita continued in full flow. No one got a word in when Anita was talking.

'Kenny's got a Chopper bike, Mr Sheffield. It's called "The 'ot One". In t'cycle shop in Easington it says it 'as "muscles t'spare an' snap-action shift gears".'

With its coil spring shock absorbers, chrome roll bar and 'apehanger' handlebars it looked like something from *Star Wars*.

'Anyway, got to rush t'do ol' Chalky's 'omework an' see Tucker in *Grange 'ill*, Mr Sheffield. Bye.'

With that, she rushed off home, still chattering at the top of her voice, with Jodie and Kenny following on behind. Later that evening, she helped Jodie to construct a Bay City Rollers self-assembly lampshade. When you're twelve years old, you can pack a lot into one day.

Jo and I were the last to leave school that afternoon and we walked into the car park together.

'Dan's on duty tonight, Jack,' she said. 'I thought I'd call in to the Oak and give Sally some moral support. Why not come along?'

'Thanks, Jo. I'll see how the evening goes.'

Happily, I made what turned out to be an excellent decision and, at seven o'clock, I drove back into Ragley and parked by the village green.

When I walked into The Royal Oak, Rod Stewart was singing 'Maggie May' on the jukebox and a heated discussion among the football team was taking place at the bar.

Big Dave was beside himself with absolute astonishment. 'Bottled water!' he said. 'Bottled water!' Big Dave was so exasperated he could do no more than repeat himself.

'Y'reight there, Dave,' said Little Malcolm. 'It's water in bottles.'

'Ah'm tellin' y'straight,' said Don, the barman, as he expertly cleaned a pint pot with a York City tea towel.

'Y'mean it's summat diff'rent t'soda water an' tonic water?' asked Chris 'Kojak' Wojciechowski, the Bald-Headed Ball-Wizard.

'That's reight,' said Don.

'But y'drink tonic water wi' gin, an' soda water wi' whisky,' said Clint Ramsbottom. 'So 'ow d'you drink this bottled water?'

'Y'jus' drink it as it is,' said Don.

'Y'mean it's jus' water in bottles an' y'drink it?' asked Big Dave, shaking his head in disbelief.

Little Malcolm was speechless, so he just shook his head in sympathy.

Don continued to pursue the point and reveal the sum total of his newly acquired knowledge. 'It's from t'Continent,' he said. 'An' it's called Evian or summat.'

'Ah, so it's 'eavy water, then, is it?' said Big Dave. 'Maybe that's why people buy it.'

'That's reight, Dave, it'll be 'eavy,' said Little Malcolm.

'Not 'eavy,' shouted Stevie 'Supersub' Cole-clough, who was proud that he was the only member of the football team who had been to college. 'It's from France an' it's called Evian. It's full o' minerals.'

267

'Mebbe that's why it's 'eavy,' said Don, frowning at the bottle of Evian water in his huge fist.

Everyone stared at the bottle dubiously.

'Well, ah'll tell y'summat f'nowt,' said Big Dave: 'it'll never catch on.'

'Y'reight there, Dave,' said Little Malcolm. 'Who's gonna buy water when y'get it from t'tap f'nowt?'

Don put the bottle of water back behind the counter, grabbed the hand pump in his wrestler's fist and pulled a foaming pint of Chestnut mild and put it on the counter. 'Twenty-eight and a half pence, please, Mr Sheffield.'

I gave Don thirty pence.

'Ah'm fed up wi' these half pences,' said Don mournfully and he struggled to extract the tiny coins from the till with his thick fingers. 'Still, way inflashun's goin', pints'll soon be thirty pence.'

By the time Sheila turned down the Eagles singing 'Hotel California', the crowded lounge bar was full of excitement. The various teams huddled round each table with their pens and quiz sheets.

'Number one,' said Sheila into her crackly microphone: 'Where are thee gods?'

'Y'what?' shouted Big Dave. The four brightest members of the football team, including ex-college boy Stevie 'Supersub' Coleclough, had been chosen and Big Dave had been feeling confident until then.

'That's what it sez 'ere,' said Sheila unflinchingly. 'Where are thee gods?'

Albert Jenkins and his dominoes team looked

puzzled and started talking about the seats in the upper circle in York Theatre Royal. However, Sally Pringle smiled confidently and whispered to the already well-lubricated ladies of the Keep Fit evening class. Their teacher, a plump lady in pink flares and four-inch platform shoes, lit up a Silk Cut Ultra Mild and wrote down their first answer.

'Question two,' said Sheila: 'What hinstrument did that Jack Lemming play in *Some Like It 'ot?*'

Timothy Pratt looked at his brother, Victor, and his sister, Nora, and shook his head. He was the undisputed leader of the Pratts' quiz team.

'It were Lemmon, not Lemming,' said Timothy.

Tidy Tim liked correct questions.

'All right, keep yer 'air on,' shouted Sheila. 'Number three: Who were Billy J. Kramer's backin' group?'

Ronnie Smith, the captain of the Pigeon Club team, scratched his head and prayed that this month there would be a question about football or pigeons.

At the end, Sheila read out the answers on her printed sheet. While she could remember twelve different drinks and four different bar-meal orders without blinking, reading unfamiliar words was not her strength.

'Number one: Mount Holym-pus,' said Sheila hesitantly, staring, puzzled, at the clipboard. 'Number two: a double bass,' said Sheila, unfortunately pronouncing it like the fish.

Sally's team and Albert Jenkins' team tied on sixteen points each.

'OK, this is y'tie-break question,' said Sheila.

'Put yer 'and up if y'know it. What do you find once in a minute, twice in a moment and never in a 'undred years?'

'Dakotas,' shouted Ronnie Smith, who had just remembered going to a Billy J. Kramer concert with Ruby in 1964.

'Shurrup, Ronnie,' shouted Sheila.

The tension was unbearable. Absolute silence descended on The Royal Oak. It was the moment of truth.

Then, very calmly, Albert Jenkins raised his hand. 'The letter "m",' he said simply.

'Y'reight,' said Sheila.

Albert Jenkins received the first prize, a crate of Guinness, and Sally got the runner-up prize, six packets of Smith's Crisps.

One person who never displayed his ignorance in a quiz competition was Stan Coe and, at that moment, he lurched out of his seat in the taproom and staggered towards the door. Seven pints of bitter and two whisky chasers had made it difficult to walk in a straight line. His Land Rover was parked partly on the gravel road outside The Royal Oak and partly on the village green. After leaning back against the bonnet and rummaging around in his pockets for his keys, Stan finally slumped into the seat and revved up the engine.

Suddenly, silhouetted against a pair of dazzling headlights, two huge policemen walked towards him, and Stan panicked. As he released the clutch pedal, the Land Rover's nearside tyres bit into the gravel, while the offside tyres met no resistance in the soft grass. The result was the car slewed in an arc of flying mud and gravel and bounced down towards the edge of the pond. A duck flew angrily towards his open window and Stan took his hands off the wheel to beat it off.

Both policemen dived out of the way: one onto the gravel, the other into the mud thrown up by Stan's tyres. By the time they had stood up and dusted down their uniforms, Stan was bonnet-deep in the pond, screaming for help and surrounded by a lynch mob of ducks.

The Quiz Night forgotten, everyone piled out of the Oak to watch the entertainment.

'They're two of the constables from Easington,' said Jo.

'And they don't look too pleased,' I replied.

One of the policemen had gone back to the police van.

'There's not many rushing to 'elp,' said Big Dave.

'Y'reight there, Dave,' agreed Little Malcolm.

'Ducks don't look 'appy,' said Kojak, as a mallard pecked repeatedly at Stan Coe's flat cap, which was now floating on the surface like a lily pad.

Stan pushed open his driver's door, thrashed his way through a cordon of irate ducks and sat down on the bank. He appeared to be, literally, spitting feathers.

The policeman who had gone back to the van reappeared with a plastic bag attached to a tube and a mouthpiece.

'We know what's coming next, Jack,' said Jo, with a grin.

'And it couldn't happen to a nicer man,' I said.

Alongside me, Brian Crowther, the editor of the *Easington Herald & Pioneer*, was busy making notes on the back of a beer mat before rushing back to use the Oak's telephone to ring his photographer.

So it was that on that late April evening, Stan Coe, with soaking-wet trousers and a waterlogged engine, had his political ambitions dashed amid a flurry of duck feathers.

Instead, Albert Jenkins decided to stand for the local council and was elected by a massive majority. At his first council meeting, Albert made a special request to the Highways Department and, one month later, he had a positive response.

Now alongside the village green stands a rare and peculiar road sign. Beneath a red warning triangle it carries a stark but poignant message: 'Beware of the Ducks'.

Chapter Seventeen

The Handbag Election

At the end of school today, we closed for one day and the hall was prepared to be used as the Ragley polling station for the General Election on Thursday, 3 May.
Extract from the Ragley School Logbook:
Wednesday, 2 May 1979

'I can now announce the short list of nominations for President of our Women's Institute,' said Mrs Patterson-Smythe. 'There are three names, as follows.'

It was Wednesday, 2 May, and the village hall was packed for the Annual General Meeting of the Ragley and Morton Women's Institute. Forty-eight pairs of eyes were concentrated on the President. Vera gripped her handbag so tightly, her knuckles had gone white. Mrs Patterson-Smythe scanned the room as if checking the three members were all present. Then she read out their names.

'Miss Deirdre Coe, Mrs Joyce Davenport and Miss Vera Evans.'

There was a collective intake of breath.

'Voting forms are being distributed now. Please write down the name of your choice and put it in the voting box as you leave the meeting. The box is situated on the table at the back of the hall, where our two independent voting supervisors are seated. They will scrutinize the votes, inform me of the number awarded to each candidate, and then I shall display the official result on the notice board tomorrow at 7.30 p.m.'

Allan Bickerstaff, the local accountant, and Peter Duddleston, the manager of one of Easington's two banks, both nodded soberly in acknowledgement. The gravity of the situation had not escaped them. They knew that if they got this wrong their lives would no longer be worth living.

Vera sighed as she looked across the hall at Deirdre Coe, who was surrounded by her hangers-on. Deirdre looked confident and was laughing as she filled in her voting form.

273

'Well, we won't be 'avin' Bible readings every month if ah get in,' said Deirdre, with a sly look in Vera's direction. Her friends tittered in response and Vera looked away, pretending she hadn't heard.

'Good luck, Vera. May the best woman win,' said a voice in her ear.

'Oh, hello, Joyce,' said Vera. 'And good luck to you as well.' She smiled at Joyce Davenport, the doctor's wife, who too had served her apprenticeship in the Women's Institute, and was noted for the excellence of her sponge cakes and her cold-cure remedies.

'If I don't get it, Vera, I hope you do,' said Joyce, with a genuine smile of friendship. Joyce knew how much it meant to Vera and she squeezed her hand. She recalled the young and carefree Vera of forty years ago when they were at school together. It was a girls' boarding school in Thirkby and their lives had been governed by a regime based on alphabetical order. Joyce Davenport had always sat at the desk in front of Vera Evans. Her name was always read out before Vera's and she hoped it would be so on this occasion. She had often puzzled why Vera had dedicated her life to the Church and her brother's work. While many men had tried to court Vera, none had succeeded, and Joyce wondered if the chance had finally gone.

When Vera arrived back home at the vicarage and walked into the hall, she was surprised to hear Joseph swapping stories with me about his home-made wine. This particular variety had not only the potency of rocket fuel but also, sadly, the aftertaste.

'Just a little adjustment to the ingredients and the bouquet should be fine,' said Joseph, taking another sip that made his eyes water.

'Not quite your best, Joseph,' I said unconvincingly. 'But it's definitely up there among them.'

We both looked up at Vera when she walked into the kitchen, but her face was inscrutable.

'Good evening, Vera,' I said. 'Any news?'

Vera looked disparagingly at the empty wine bottles. 'I'm in the final three, and I'll find out tomorrow evening,' she said in a matter-of-fact manner. It seemed as though she didn't want to discuss it. She picked up a dishcloth, wiped the table and removed our glasses as she did so. 'There are strict rules and regulations, you understand,' she explained, anticipating Joseph's next question.

We all sat in silence for a few moments, until I decided to change the subject.

'I called in to confirm arrangements for tomorrow, Vera.'

Ragley School, along with other schools in the area, was to be used as a polling station for the General Election and Vera had been appointed the officer-in-charge. Voting started at 7.00 a.m. and I had volunteered to help her prepare the school hall.

'Thank you, Mr Sheffield,' said Vera. 'I do appreciate your support.' She picked up her *Daily Telegraph* and read the small print underneath the front-page photograph of a beaming Mrs Thatcher and an elderly woman. '"This lady is looking forward to a wonderful life ahead with the Conservatives",' read Vera, with a smile.

Joseph looked over her shoulder and read the same text. 'Yes, but she's 102 years old!' he exclaimed.

'Even so,' said Vera, 'you must admit that she does look pleased.'

It was my cue to depart. 'Well, I'll be on my way,' I said. 'Big day tomorrow.'

'Yes, indeed,' said Vera, a faraway look in her eyes. 'Margaret's Day.'

'Don't count your chickens,' said Joseph gently.

'I'm not,' said Vera, picking up the newspaper again. 'Although it says here that *The Archers* programme has already been recorded assuming Margaret will win.'

'I wonder if Prime Minister Callaghan knows,' chuckled Joseph, reaching for another wine bottle.

'We have a very early start tomorrow, Joseph,' said Vera firmly, removing the bottle and taking it to the kitchen.

'She's a bit tense,' whispered Joseph, looking wistful, as his nettle-and-dandelion *vin blanc* disappeared from sight.

'The Election?'

'Both of them, Jack,' said Joseph, with a strained smile.

As I drove back to Kirkby Steepleton, I reflected that the next twenty-four hours would mark Vera's destiny.

Election Day arrived. It was a morning of forgotten suns and gun-metal clouds, a still day, frozen in time, one without past or future. As I drove slowly up the Morton Road and through the vicarage gates, above my head branches of cherry blossom hung heavily, unmoving, pink and fragrant. Soon the first winds of May would come and scatter the petals like confetti on the newly mown grass. But now all was silent as stone. It was as if the world was holding its breath.

I paused, wound down the window of my car, and breathed in the fragrance. The grounds of the vicarage were always beautiful, but never more so than when the May blossom lifted the spirit as well as the soul.

Suddenly a flock of black-headed gulls broke the spell. They swooped in graceful formation over the spire of St Mary's Church and on towards the woods beyond, where the harsh cawing of rooks shattered the silence of the sycamores.

The lace curtains behind the hall window twitched and I caught a fleeting glimpse of Vera's nervous face; in that moment, I wished with all my heart that the day would bring good news for her.

The gravel crunched beneath as I drove past the wild-raspberry canes along the Victorian brick wall. As I parked my car, Joseph appeared at the front door, carrying a wickerwork picnic basket.

'Good morning, Jack,' he said, with a tired smile. He showed me the contents of the wonderfully packed basket: 'Vera's elevenses, lunch, afternoon tea and a light supper.'

Every meal was expertly colour-coded, a triumph of Tupperware.

I opened the back doors of my car and Joseph put the basket on the violently coloured, checked-patterned car-rug, one of my mother's less embarrassing presents.

Vera stood in front of the hall mirror, making final adjustments to her mother's Victorian brooch that she always wore on special occasions.

'Good morning, Vera. Your carriage awaits,' I said, trying to sound light-hearted.

She nodded appreciatively but was clearly anxious.

'I've told her she'll be fine, Jack,' said Joseph.

'Sadly, I shall have to leave this behind, Mr Sheffield,' said Vera. 'I'm supposed to remain impartial.' Her blue-and-white rosette was the size of a dinner plate. She propped it against a pair of candlesticks on the hall table.

'Very wise, Vera,' I said.

The school was silent and dark until the fluorescent lights in the hall hummed into life. A large black metal box had been delivered, along with a set of wooden voting booths that resembled a construction kit for a series of Punch and Judy shows. I began to assemble these while Vera prepared her list of voters and the special hole-punch that would validate each voting slip. Together we mounted on the school gate a large sign that read 'POLLING STATION' and made sure that the arrow underneath was pointing the right way. When all was ready I went into the staff-room and made Vera a cup of coffee.

This reversal of roles clearly amused her. 'Thank you for all your help, Mr Sheffield – and the warm coffee,' said Vera. 'I think everything is in place now.' She glanced at her wristwatch. It was 6.45 a.m. 'Oh dear,' she said, looking at a portly figure walking up the drive. 'Here comes my assistant for the day.'

Delia Morgetroyd, the milkman's wife from Morton village, was coming up the drive with two heavy Co-op carrier bags.

'Well, at least she's brought some food, by the look of it,' said Vera.

'I'm sure it will be fine,' I said.

'I don't think so, Mr Sheffield,' said Vera gloomily. 'Delia only stops talking when she's eating and, even then, she tries very hard to do both at the same time. Her hobby is collecting spoons, so the next fifteen hours should be interesting!'

As I left, Mrs Morgetroyd was getting her teeth into a family-sized pork pie while describing in detail to Vera the set of soup spoons she had bought in Filey. Vera, for her part, appeared to be beginning a crash-course in transcendental meditation.

As I drove back to Kirkby Steepleton, I thought about my meeting with Beth. Her school in Thirkby was also closed for the day, so we had arranged to meet at Bilbo Cottage for morning coffee and then go shopping in York.

When she arrived, as usual she despaired at the state of my kitchen. 'It's a shambles, Jack,' she said, staring at the assortment of pans stacked on the draining board. 'For such a supposedly organized man, you really have no idea.'

'I keep trying, Beth,' I said apologetically. 'Don't you like my latest gadget I've just fixed to

279

the wall?' I pointed to my state-of-the-art manual can opener with its large metal handle.

Beth shook her head. 'It's lethal there. I bet you've bumped your head on it a dozen times. You need to fit it here.' She pointed to a space under the storage cupboards.

She was right but, then again, she usually was.

As we drove into York together, I knew she would make an excellent headmistress. If she could organize my kitchen, she should have no problems with her school and staff!

York was busy with the early influx of tourists as we wandered hand in hand down Coney Street and stopped outside Debenhams. The shop window display advertised a new look called 'the Romantic Revival', and Beth giggled as she read the words on the large poster. '"The look of Debenhams is soft and fluid, with fabrics that beg to be touched",' she read, with a knowing stare.

'You'd look good in that,' I said, and pointed to a mannequin wearing a button-through shirt-waister in blues and pinks with a £19.95 price tag.

'You're right,' she said, and pulled me through the door.

I lost count of the number of times Beth emerged from the changing cubicle, but I tried hard on each occasion to respond to her questions. She finished up buying the two dresses she had tried on right at the beginning, one in blue and one in pink. It reminded me of another day with Laura.

'I can always take one back at the weekend,' said Beth, which reinforced one of my theories about women and shopping.

'Good idea,' I said. 'Although you look lovely in both,' I added hastily.

'Laura was right,' said Beth. 'You are different from other men.'

I picked up her bags and we walked back into the street.

I was curious. 'In what way?' I asked.

She looked up at me and straightened the rumpled collar of my old sports jacket and then examined the frayed stitching round the leather strips attached to my cuffs. 'You listen,' she said simply, and then we walked on.

I sighed. I had given up trying to understand women.

On our way back to Kirkby Steepleton, Beth and I stopped at school to call in and vote. There was a steady stream of voters going in and out as we made our way to Vera's table. It was significant that when I left in the morning the two tables had been together. Now there was a clear division between Vera's tidy table with her lists, hole-punch and different-coloured pens and that of Delia Morgetroyd's, with her half-eaten pork pie, slab of seed-cake, flask of strong tea and her *Spoons Through the Ages* library book from the mobile-library van.

Vera looked pleased to see us and quickly underlined our names on the electoral list, punched our voting slips and passed them over.

Deirdre Coe and two of her friends were deep in conversation next to the voting booths. I walked into the first empty booth and picked up the pencil that was attached to the shelf by a long piece of string. Suddenly, Deirdre was at my shoulder.

'Was there something you wanted, Miss Coe?' I said sharply.

She stepped back quickly. 'Not from likes o' you,' she said, and with a swagger she walked out past Vera's table.

'Judgement Day, Vera,' said Deirdre, with an evil laugh.

Vera shook her head in dismay.

Suddenly Mrs Patterson-Smythe swept in, chatting with Mary Hardisty. As Vera gave her a voting slip she smiled in acknowledgement and walked confidently into the booth.

When she emerged, she walked to Vera's table and put the folded slip through the slit in the top of the metal box. Then she gave Vera a knowing wink and spoke quietly in her ear. 'Don't worry,' whispered Mrs Patterson-Smythe. 'In case of a tie, the President has the casting vote.'

Vera looked up expectantly but dared not say a word.

'The note I put up in the village hall at seven-thirty will announce you as the next President,' said Mrs Patterson-Smythe. 'I'm so pleased for you.'

'I don't know what to say,' said Vera.

'Nothing to say, Vera,' said the smiling Mrs Patterson-Smythe. 'Just keep it under your hat until this evening.' With that, she caught up with Mary Hardisty and together they walked out into the sunshine.

Vera quickly gathered herself, waved goodbye

to Beth and me, and looked across at Delia Morgetroyd. 'Now what were you saying, Delia, about your Hornsea Pottery salad spoon?' asked Vera politely.

News spread round the local villages like wildfire and it was Joseph who finally broke the news officially, although Anne had already walked to the village hall, read the notice and telephoned all the staff.

On Friday morning, a guard of honour was waiting to greet Vera in the school entrance hall. I stood by the open staff-room door and, next to me, Anne, Sally, Jo, Ruby and Shirley waited in line. We all clapped as Vera walked in, waving her copy of the *Daily Telegraph* in triumph. The headline read THATCHER SET FOR NO. 10 and below it was a photograph of a beaming Mrs Thatcher outside Finchley Town Hall.

'She's done it,' said Vera. 'I knew she would.' Then she paused, realizing something was different.

'And so have you, Vera,' said Anne, and beckoned her into the office.

'Well done, Miss Evans,' shouted Ruby, giving a passable imitation of a drum roll with the wooden handle of her mop against the side of her galvanized bucket.

'Congratulations, Vera,' said Jo, waving her correctly filled-in Attendance Register, of which she was becoming almost too proud.

'Good news, Vera,' said Sally. 'You deserve it.'

We all piled into the staff-room, closely followed by Ruby's galvanized bucket, and Vera took in the scene before her.

Anne had made a large 'Congratulations' card and this was standing on the coffee table. Inside the card Sally had penned in beautiful italic lettering, 'To our new President from all the staff at Ragley School', and we had all written a personal message underneath. Ruby had sat up late into the night sewing a small cross-stitch pattern on a tiny strip of a cast-off pillowcase and this had been mounted on a small rectangle of white card.

In the centre of the table was Shirley's non-alcoholic fruit punch, with tinned raspberries floating on the surface and seven school tumblers lined up alongside. Jo had surprised everyone by baking a scrumptious lemon meringue pie. We later discovered it was Dan's favourite and Jo was fast becoming an expert at making it.

Vera was overwhelmed and gave everyone a hug, including a huge one for Ruby, who was wiping a stream of teardrops from her flushed cheeks with the clean side of her chamois leather. 'Oh, thank you all so much,' she said. 'What a wonderful surprise from all my special friends.'

We all stood around, feeling a little awkward, until Ruby said, 'That lemon meringue wants putting in t'fridge, Shirley, unless y'thinkin' of 'aving a bit now.'

Everybody laughed and Shirley rushed into the kitchen to gather up plates, forks and a cake slice.

It was an unusual but happy start to the day, as we chatted, drank Shirley's excellent fruit punch and gorged ourselves on Jo's delicious lemon meringue. At two minutes to nine we were all hastily wiping our mouths with tissues and clearing the staff-room of plates.

'Almost time for the bell,' said Anne, with a sense of urgency.

We all glanced at the clock.

'Mr Sheffield, please could ah ring it today in 'onour of Miss Evans, as it's a speshul day?' asked Ruby.

'That's a very kind thought, Ruby,' said Vera.

Ruby sped off like a child about to play with a new toy.

In the hundred-year history of Ragley School, the school bell had never pealed with such vigour. Ruby and the art of campanology were not natural allies.

As a result, on the stroke of nine o'clock Timothy Pratt, assuming a fire engine was approaching the High Street, dropped his new supply of hedgehog-shaped boot scrapers. Old Tommy Piercy, sitting on the bench next to the duck pond by the village green, dropped his box of Swan Vesta matches in the damp grass as he tried to light his pipe and thought for a moment it was an air raid. Prudence Golightly smiled confidently at her new hearing aid and Peter Miles-Humphreys, the local bank clerk, forgot his habitual stammer of twenty years, as he drove past the school on his way to York and yelled, 'Bloody hell!'

His wife, Felicity, in the passenger seat, looked delighted. 'Well done, darling,' she said. 'I knew it was just a passing phase.'

Peter grasped the steering wheel a little tighter and refrained to mention the 'passing phase' had begun in August 1958 on the day he had married Felicity.

At lunchtime, Vera and I drove to the vicarage and collected a huge box of brand-new crockery, recently purchased by Vera from Brown's in York on behalf of the Women's Institute.

Vera looked at her watch. 'If you'd be kind enough to take me straight to the village hall, Mr Sheffield, we should be just in time. Perhaps you wouldn't mind putting the crockery in the kitchen. You know the way,' she said, with a smile.

As we drove down the High Street, the women of Ragley and Morton were coming out in force to welcome Vera.

'Good luck, Vera,' I said, as we pulled up outside the village hall. 'I'll look after the crockery.'

Vera got out of the car with a determined expression, clutched her handbag tightly, and walked through the milling crowds to the wooden steps in front of the main entrance. The members of the new committee shuffled to the front, anxious to bathe in Vera's reflected glory. This was a significant day in their calendar.

Right on cue, the sun came out and a breeze sprang up. Vera was bathed in bright sunlight and a few petals of cherry and almond blossom blew through the air and fell onto her shoulders. It was as if she had been blessed from on high.

'Speech!' shouted Mary Hardisty.

'Speech!' echoed Bridget Crowther.

'Say a few words, Vera,' encouraged Joyce Davenport.

Mrs Patterson-Smythe modestly stepped down

from the top step leading to the main entrance of the village hall, and ushered Vera to take her place. In that moment there was a subtle shift of power.

I stood at the back of the throng, put down the heavy box of crockery and leaned back against one of the flowering cherry trees.

Vera rummaged in her handbag and took out a postcard on which she had written a few notes. 'It is a great honour to become President of the Ragley and Morton Women's Institute,' said Vera, her voice calm and sure.

Two hundred miles away, on the steps of 10 Downing Street, Vera's idol, Margaret Thatcher, was addressing a similar throng.

'And I would just like to remember some words of St Francis of Assisi which I think are really just particularly apt at the moment,' said Margaret.

Back in Ragley, Vera glanced down at her post-card. 'And I would just like to remember some words of the late Violet Parkinson,' read Vera, 'who was the President of our Women's Institute twenty-five years ago when I first became a member.'

Margaret Thatcher half-closed her eyes and recited:

'Where there is discord, may we bring harmony.
Where there is error, may we bring truth.
Where there is doubt, may we bring faith.
And where there is despair, may we bring hope.'

Vera held up her postcard and recited:

'Let us uphold the ideals of truth, justice, tolerance and fellowship in order to provide a friendly atmosphere where women can be inspired and enlightened.'

The crowd cheered.

Margaret Thatcher was now in full flow.

'And to all the British people, howsoever they voted, may I say this. Now that the Election is over, may we get together and strive to serve and strengthen the country of which we're so proud to be a part.'

This was followed by polite applause. Then Margaret Thatcher walked into 10 Downing Street and began to plan her Cabinet posts.

Vera scanned her audience, pausing briefly at the chain-smoking Deirdre Coe. 'And may I remind you,' she said, 'that however you voted we should be united from now on in helping women to lead fulfilling lives and to be of value in the community.'

This was inspirational stuff and everyone cheered again, with the exception, of course, of Deirdre Coe. Then Vera walked proudly into the village hall and supervised the creation of her new Committee.

Everyone, with the notable exception of Deirdre Coe, had moved up the pecking order. Vera was officially installed as the new President, resplendent in her green sash; Joyce Davenport became Vice-President; the retiring President, Mrs Patterson-Smythe, took up the post of Secretary again; Mrs Bronwyn Bickerstaff, the accountant's wife, was press-ganged into becoming the Treasurer, largely because her husband, Allan, offered his services free of charge; Mrs Mary Hardisty became a hugely popular Produce and Handicrafts Secretary; Miss Prudence Golightly was an obvious choice as Outings Secretary; Mrs Bridget Crowther, wife of the editor of the *Easington Herald & Pioneer*, became Press Secretary; Vera volunteered to continue to coordinate Flowers for the Sick; Miss Amelia Duff from the Post Office was in charge of Magazines; the striking and vivacious Madame Jacqueline Laporte, a French teacher at Easington Comprehensive School, took responsibility for Stallholders and New Members; Mrs Patterson-Smythe also took on the additional role of coordinating the rota for the monthly Hostesses; and, finally, Deirdre Coe was given the job of Cupboard Supervisor. So, on the day Vera was crowned queen, her arch-rival was awarded the key to a cupboard full of crockery.

In London, Margaret Thatcher announced to her husband, Denis, 'I feel a sense of change and an aura of calm,' and Denis looked surprised.

In Yorkshire, Vera announced to her brother, Joseph, 'I think it's about time I sampled a bottle of your wine,' and Joseph looked astonished.

So, on a sunlit day in May 1979, two women achieved their life's ambition. Margaret Thatcher, the fifty-three-year-old grocer's daughter, became the United Kingdom's first woman Prime Minister; Vera Evans, the fifty-six-year-old vicar's daughter, became President of the Ragley and Morton Women's Institute.

With equal forcefulness both women promised significant change. Margaret Thatcher pledged a complete transformation of British industry, including drastic reform for trade unions. Vera Evans, in her maiden speech, confirmed she would revolutionize the present catering system by introducing her new set of elegant white crockery that boasted a distinctive green-patterned ring round all the cups, saucers, side plates, milk jugs and sugar bowls.

Also, following many complaints relating to soggy biscuits, a new Marks & Spencer's air-tight biscuit tin would be purchased, with a separate compartment for chocolate digestives.

Meanwhile, in her office, Margaret Thatcher was looking at wallpaper catalogues.

Chapter Eighteen

Kel and Stinger

A group of 'Travellers' have camped just outside Ragley village on the Kirkby Steepleton Road. Joseph Starkey has joined Class 4 and Roy Davidson, EWO, has offered Section 11 support. This will commence after the Spring Bank Holiday on Monday, 4 June.
Extract from the Ragley School Logbook:
Thursday, 24 May 1979

The smell of wood smoke drifted through my car window and I slowed as I approached the bend in the road. On a broad, grassy area of wasteland stood a brightly painted gypsy caravan and, next to it, crouched over a camp fire, a young boy was cooking breakfast.

It was shortly before eight o'clock on Thursday, 24 May. Our one-week Spring Bank Holiday was only two days away and I was in good spirits. The three-mile drive from Kirkby Steepleton to Ragley village was always picturesque, but on this bright and breezy day the countryside looked especially beautiful. I sped the first mile through open pasture-land, ignored by the grazing cattle and sheep, until I reached the avenue of sycamore trees. The longer days and the warm weather had broadened the leaves and the road ahead was dark with shadows.

In the dappled shade, three cobs – the traditional, sturdy, short-legged horses favoured by gypsies – munched the grass. Two were black and white, one was brown and white, and all were strong-boned, with the build of miniature shire-horses. Next to the caravan stood a swarthy, stocky man, who was whittling wood, and a slim, black-haired woman, who was erecting a makeshift washing-line. As I drove past, the boy glanced up and pushed his unkempt, wavy black hair from out of his eyes. He was small and wiry, with skin the colour of a walnut. He waved and gave me a smile that would have brightened up the darkest day. I waved back and wondered where they were heading.

During morning playtime, my question was answered.

'There's a gypsy lady who would like to see you,' said Vera, very evenly and with no sense of prejudice. 'She has a delightful eleven-year-old boy she would like to enrol. I knew you would want me to contact Mr Davidson, and he's calling in later today.'

Vera's efficiency never failed to amaze me. Roy Davidson was our Education Welfare Officer and his knowledge of specialist educational support was second to none.

In the office was the little boy I had seen by the camp fire. His mother was a striking Romany woman.

'Thank you for seeing us, sir. This kind lady said you might be able to 'elp us,' she said politely.

Vera smiled in acknowledgement. 'This is Joe

Starkey. He's old enough to go into your class, Mr Sheffield,' she said. 'Mrs Starkey says they expect to be in the area for most of the time up to the summer holidays.'

Young Joe Starkey gave me that broad smile again.

'Fine,' I said. 'Miss Evans will take all the necessary information and then I'll show you round.'

Long before lunchtime, the gregarious and confident Joe looked relaxed as he sat next to Tony Ackroyd and listened intently to the mathematics lesson. I had written '36 x 7' on the chalkboard.

'So, what's thirty-six multiplied by seven?' I asked.

Jodie Cuthbertson's hand shot in the air, which surprised me. 'My sister's got one o' them new calc'lators, Mr Sheffield. She could tell you, dead easy.' Jodie always meant well.

'Thank you, Jodie, but does anyone know the answer?'

Joe Starkey looked around him, while everyone scribbled in their mathematics books, and raised his hand.

'Yes, Joe?'

'It's same as twenty-one dozen, Mr Sheffield,' said Joe. 'So it's two hundred an' fifty-two.'

It quickly became apparent that, while Joe's reading and writing were weak, his mental arithmetic was excellent.

At lunchtime, I sat down with a group of the children in my class including Joe Starkey. As we ate our beefburgers, chips and mushy peas, I asked them to tell me what they intended to do during the Spring Bank Holiday.

Tony Ackroyd, eager as usual, put up his hand. Unfortunately, this was the hand holding his fork and he startled Mrs Critchley.

'Watch what y'doin' wi' that fork, Tony Ackroyd,' snarled Mrs Critchley. She walked to the next table and glowered at the eight innocent faces. 'Now then, who's s'pposed to be one o' them vegetarians?'

Wisely, no one spoke. In Mrs Critchley's eyes, vegetarians were either communists or, worse still, from the southern counties.

Undeterred, Tony Ackroyd lowered his fork and continued. 'Ah'm goin' t'Saturday morning cinema, Mr Sheffield. It'll be great. There's *Zorro, Tom and Jerry* an' *Champion the Wonder 'orse.*'

Mandy Ollerenshaw appeared excited. 'We're getting a new push-button telephone, Mr Sheffield.'

I recalled the considerable psychological pressure put on consumers by Buzby, the orange cartoon bird in the advertisements for Trimphones. It looked like the Ollerenshaws had been converted to the concept that 'a Trimphone gives style to your home'.

'Ah'm gettin' a new top wi' a designer label...' Jodie Cuthbertson paused to give this the full effect, 'and it 'as t'label on the *outside.*'

Labels on the outside seemed an interesting gimmick but, even in this strange world of glam rock, platform shoes and denim jeans – flared from the knee and, apparently, known as loons – I couldn't imagine it catching on.

'My dad's gorra skin'ead 'aircut,' said Dominic

294

Brown triumphantly.

Menacing skinheads with crew cuts and bovver boots had recently begun to become more fashionable, and I guessed that, if you had the misfortune to live with Winifred Brown, you needed something to keep your spirits up.

Joe Starkey, clearly a boy with a good appetite, had polished off his beefburger, scraped the last of his rhubarb crumble and pink custard off his plastic tray and raised his hand.

'Yes, Joe?'

'Ah'm goin' t'Appleby 'orse Fair, Mr Sheffield,' said Joe.

Mandy Ollerenshaw put down her spoon and gazed at Joe. She had fallen in love with Joe from the moment she had first offered him a cheese-and-onion crisp.

'When we get t'Appleby we all go to Gallows Hill,' said Joe excitedly.

'Gallows Hill!' said Mandy, in alarm. 'That sounds awful.'

'Don't be frightened, Mandy,' said Joe gently. 'It's really a lovely place.'

It was good to see the caring side of Joe's character. Mandy relaxed and listened intently to her swashbuckling hero. She knew she would never, ever, eat rhubarb crumble again without remembering the way Joe had said her name.

'There's about five thousand of us an' fifteen 'undred caravans. An' we all know each other like a big family. There's a big river there called t'River Eden where 'orses get washed. Then we run 'em up and down t'main street shoutin', "Mind yer backs. Mind yer backs". It's mainly gypsy cobs, but sometimes trotters and pacers, and we earn a lot o' money.'

'It sounds wonderful, Joe,' I said.

Joe's face simply beamed with pride. He clearly loved telling stories about his unusual life.

Back in the quiet of the staff-room, Jo was reading the local paper. 'It says here they've just made a baby in a test tube,' she said, astonished.

'Let's hope they've given it a better personality than my Colin,' said Sally.

'And there's more about that dreadful Yorkshire Ripper,' continued Jo. 'And this woman is his eleventh victim.'

'I pray to God they catch him,' said Vera.

There was an uneasy silence as we all considered this blight on our lives.

'That gypsy boy looks a livewire,' said Sally, lightening the gloom. 'What was he saying to you at lunchtime, Jack?'

'He's looking forward to going to Appleby Horse Fair.'

'He's sure to enjoy it. Appleby Fair is the best-known of all the fairs attended by Romany gypsies,' said Sally, our amateur historian. 'It was given the protection of a charter by King James the Second in 1685.'

'Impressive,' said Jo.

'They're interesting people,' said Sally. 'Every summer, they camp near my village and do the fruit-picking.'

Everyone suddenly had an opinion on life on the road, but then there was a tap on the door. It was Roy Davidson, our Education Welfare

Officer. He was a tall, gaunt man in his mid-forties with a shock of prematurely grey hair. His support for Ragley School was considerable and his local knowledge was legendary. I walked into the school office with him and he came straight to the point.

'It's Section Eleven,' said Roy simply.

Section 11 was the name of the local authority's provision that enabled schools to offer specialist support. This was usually in the form of a peripatetic teacher who would visit school for around two hours per week.

'Joe Starkey obviously needs help with his reading and writing,' said Roy, looking at the handwritten report from his last school.

'We'll do what we can, Roy.'

'Problem is, Jack, I doubt he will stay around for long,' he said. 'I've met the father and he seems very wary. He says they get the blame for any local trouble that may occur.'

'What are Joe's chances of attending secondary school?' I asked.

Roy looked serious and shook his head. 'Almost negligible. Not many of them stay in education after primary school. Latest estimates suggest there are around ten thousand children of gypsies and travellers not registered for education in English schools. I doubt Joe Starkey will be here for long.'

'OK, Roy. I'll keep you informed.'

Secretly, I made my mind up to persuade Joe's parents that continued education for Joe was vital.

The opportunity came sooner than I thought.

The following morning, I drove to school earlier than usual and the familiar smell of wood smoke was there again. By the side of the road, next to the caravan, was a large wicker basket with a sign in front of it that read 'FOR SALE'. I pulled off the road, walked towards the basket and looked in it at the posies of lucky heather, carved animals and bags of clothes pegs.

'Mornin', Mr Sheffield,' shouted Joe. He was crouched over his camp fire.

'Hello, Joe,' I said.

Mrs Starkey walked down the steps of the caravan. I glimpsed inside and saw a raised double bed with a set of drawers underneath. Over a small stove, a mantelpiece, ornately carved and covered in gold leaf, gave the interior an aura of grandeur. A mirrored cupboard reflected the bright morning light and on a small wooden table sat a china pot filled with fresh wild flowers. It looked neat and tidy.

Mrs Starkey appeared pleased to see me, whereas Mr Starkey kept his thoughts to himself.

'Please sit down, Mr Sheffield,' she said. 'You're welcome to join us for a little bit of breakfast.'

Mr Starkey brushed some wood shavings from the top of a small wooden stool and placed it next to the fire. It felt like a place of honour, reserved for a special guest. 'Please sit down,' he said.

It seemed disrespectful not to comply.

Mr Starkey leaned back against one of the large yellow wheels of the caravan and began to whittle away with a razor-sharp hunting knife. A two-pronged clothes peg miraculously emerged from the finger-width branch in his strong hands. With a careless flick of the wrist, he threw it into the wicker basket next to him and immediately began to carve another.

Joe looked up from the food he was preparing. 'We allus 'ave some bread wi' a little bit o' kel an' stinger, Mr Sheffield,' he said.

'Kel and stinger?' I asked.

Joe smiled and pointed to a block of cheese and the onion he was peeling. 'Cheese an' onion, Mr Sheffield,' he translated. 'We call it kel and stinger.'

I decided to grasp the opportunity. 'I was just thinking about Joe's education, Mr Starkey. He should be starting secondary school next September.'

Joe glanced up at his mother and father as if to judge their reaction.

Mrs Starkey was cutting thick slices of fresh bread. She stopped to ruffle Joe's black, wavy hair. ''E's a good boy is our Joe,' she said. ''E works 'ard an' 'e's good wi' 'orses.'

'An' 'e can barter wi' men twice 'is age,' said Mr Starkey proudly.

'I was hoping you would give him the chance of an education.'

Mr Starkey stopped his whittling and studied me with eyes that were deep pools of wisdom. 'Joe 'as t'work,' he said.

'But he's only eleven years old, Mr Starkey.'

'It's our way,' he said simply.

Mrs Starkey put a slice of bread on an enamel plate and passed it to Joe. 'We ask f'nothing an' we expect nothing,' she said.

Joe kept his head down, stirred the onions with a fire-blackened wooden spoon and then put a portion of sizzling, golden-brown fried onions on the slice of bread. Alongside it, Mrs Starkey added a generous slice of crumbly Wensleydale cheese. Suddenly, I felt ravenous.

It was a strange breakfast, very different from sitting in the kitchen of Bilbo Cottage and eating Kellogg's Cornflakes from a china cereal bowl.

There was silence while we ate, apart from birdsong and the whisper of the trees.

Mrs Starkey smiled as I tucked into my unusual breakfast. 'Our Joe does a good bit o' kel an' stinger,' she said proudly.

'It's delicious, Mrs Starkey, and eating in the open air makes it taste even better.'

She smiled and everyone appeared to relax.

A large enamel mug of a fresh-ground coffee I had never tasted before was to follow and the conversation began again.

'We're allus movin',' said Mr Starkey.

Mrs Starkey collected the plates. 'Every week there's a new village, a new river, a new field,' she said.

'It's in the blood,' said Mr Starkey. 'We'll never change.'

The passing of time was forgotten as we exchanged stories. It was clear that Joe had grown up to be proud of his cultural inheritance. Story-telling formed the building bricks of his life and, piece by piece, he learned the traditions of his extended family.

'Ah got this when ah sold m'first 'orse, Mr Sheffield.' He pointed to a bracelet on his wrist.

'It's a band o' gold,' he said proudly.

I noticed that Mrs Starkey had gold coins woven into her black hair and she told me that this tradition, along with her dark complexion, came from one of her ancestors: namely, an Egyptian princess. I learned that they could speak a version of the Romany language, a mixture of Sanskrit words and Elizabethan rhyming slang. Among gypsy families, I was told, Mrs Starkey had a reputation for fortune-telling and performing feats of simple magic.

Soon, it was time for me to leave and I gave Mrs Starkey and Joe a lift into Ragley and dropped them outside the school gate.

'Good luck with all y'chavvies,' said Mrs Starkey, with a smile.

'It means "little children",' said Joe helpfully.

As Mrs Starkey walked up the school drive, I heard Mrs Brown shouting in a voice that carried across the playground, 'We don't want no gypsies 'ere, thank you very much. Y'can't trust them lot.'

Mrs Starkey simply lowered her head and walked on. I admired the passive way she dealt with such a cruel taunt and I reflected on how little Winifred Brown knew about this proud lady and her family.

That afternoon, as Joe Starkey was leaving school, I was standing in the playground.

'Bye, Mr Sheffield,' shouted Joe. 'Thanks for a good day.'

'See you when you get back from the fair, Joe,' I shouted back.

He gave me a wave and that familiar happy

smile and walked off into the distance.

Three weeks later, during afternoon playtime, Anne and I were in the school office, checking the results of the Schonell Word Recognition Test for every child in the infants' classes. The telephone rang and Anne picked it up.

'It's Roy Davidson,' she said.

Five minutes later, I replaced the receiver and put my head in my hands.

'What's wrong, Jack?' she asked.

I found it difficult to form the words. 'He's not coming back, Anne... I've failed Joe.'

Anne closed the door between the office and the staffroom, sat down in Vera's chair and turned to face me. 'How can you say that, Jack? You did everything you could.'

'I should have taken his father to see the secondary school. He might have become aware of the opportunities there.'

'Jack, don't you see? It's their culture. You're not going to change that overnight.'

'I just feel I could have done more.'

There was silence between us. On the office wall, the clock ticked. Outside, on the school field, children played. Their yells of laughter floated on a midsummer breeze and I wished that Joe Starkey could have been among them.

'Jack ... Jack.' Anne's voice was insistent. 'Joe Starkey is a good boy. He's honest and hard-working. But more than that, he's happy. He has a loving family and he's learning a different set of skills. Who are we to say what's right and what's wrong?'

I had never heard Anne speak to me in this way before. She was determined to make me understand.

'But to me, education is so important, Anne. You, of all people, know that.'

Anne stood up and looked out of the window. 'Come here, Jack,' she said.

I stood up and walked to the window.

'Look out there. We have more than eighty happy children. But how many can shoe a horse? How many can survive outdoors in cold weather or do complicated mental arithmetic? How many can hammer metal or cook breakfast? Joe has skills that most of these children can only dream about. There are different kinds of education. So don't say you've failed. You did your best with the knowledge you have.'

This was a long speech for the usually quiet Anne and I smiled at her. 'Thanks, Anne. I think I understand.'

'So you should,' she said, with a reassuring grin. 'And now, Jack, it's time for the bell.'

With that, she walked out and I wandered back to my classroom to teach long multiplication.

Many years later, the local council dug up the little grassy glade where I first saw Joe Starkey. They replaced it with black tarmac and a sign that read 'Picnic Area'. It is featureless now, frequented by families who have no wish to venture far from their cars. An orderly row of identical garden-centre tables stand under the mature sycamores and a large, rectangular wire-mesh basket now occupies the exact spot where Joe's camp fire burned merrily.

When the harvest is over and the farmers burn the stubble in their fields, the smell of smoke drifts across the road from Kirkby Steepleton to Ragley. On those late autumn days, I am often reminded of a long-ago morning when an eleven-year-old boy made me a breakfast I shall never forget.

Occasionally, I wonder what became of him and I imagine a man leading his horses down the main street at the Appleby Horse Fair. He would have long, wavy, black hair and a band of gold round his wrist. He would barter quickly and skilfully with a smile that would soften the heart of any horse-trader.

Then he would return to his caravan and, in the morning, he would light his fire and prepare a simple breakfast.

And, in the sanctuary of sycamores, he would enjoy his kel and stinger.

Chapter Nineteen

Engelbert and the Pet Show

I contacted Miss Celia Etheringshaw, the Special Needs teacher from Easington Comprehensive School, and invited her to visit Ragley to meet Michael Buttle, age 11, whom she will be supporting from September. Mrs Grainger and Mrs Pringle provided a collection of artwork from all classes to be displayed at the Morton

and Ragley Agricultural Show on Saturday, 30 June.
Extract from the Ragley School Logbook:
Friday, 29 June 1979

'Don't worry about our Engelbert, Mr Sheffield,' said Mrs Betty Buttle apologetically. 'Ah've jus' tied 'im t'school railings.'

'Engelbert?'

'Yes, our Engelbert 'umperdinck,' said Mrs Buttle.

'Engelbert Humperdinck?'

''E's got fleas.'

'Fleas?'

'You've gorrit now, Mr Sheffield. Our Engelbert's got fleas,' said Mrs Buttle, with a reassuring smile. 'Ah'm tekkin' 'im to gerrit seen to.'

'Who's Engelbert, Mrs Buttle?' I asked.

'Our Afghan 'ound, Mr Sheffield, an' a reight beauty 'e is an' all. Our Micky wants t'tek 'im t'tomorrow's pet show.'

The interview with Mrs Betty Buttle hadn't got off to the start I had expected.

It was Friday, 29 June, the day before the annual Ragley and Morton Agricultural Show, and the villagers were making final preparations, cleaning horse-boxes, picking choice vegetables and grooming pets. It was the biggest annual gathering of the year for the two villages and excitement was rising.

'Anyway, it's about your Michael that I wanted to see you, Mrs Buttle. So, thank you for calling in.'

I gestured to the spare chair in the school office and Mrs Buttle sat down. Michael Buttle was an

305

affable eleven-year-old in my class but, in spite of all our efforts, he still had the reading age of a seven-year-old. I had decided to invite Miss Celia Etheringshaw, the Special Needs teacher from our local comprehensive school, to call in and meet Michael prior to his transfer to Easington in September.

'So what's our Micky been up to, Mr Sheffield? He's allus been a good lad.'

'I agree, Mrs Buttle,' I said. 'He's a lovely boy, gentle and kind. It's just that I'm still concerned about his reading. I think your Michael could do with extra special needs support when he goes to Easington.'

Betty Buttle immediately cheered up. 'Ah allus knew our Micky were summat special,' she said. 'It runs in t'family. He teks after 'is Uncle Barry.'

'Uncle Barry?'

''E were a painter an' decorator,' explained Mrs Buttle. 'Y'should 'ave seen 'is ceilings. 'E allus used t'say, y'can keep that Michelangelo da Vinci and 'is Pristine Chapel. No one did ceilings like our Barry.'

'Well, I must confess, Michael is good at art,' I said, feeling a little confused. 'It's just that he struggles with reading and writing and he doesn't seem to see the world in the same way as you and I.'

'Neither did 'is Uncle Barry, Mr Sheffield,' said Betty enthusiastically: 'y'should 'ave seen 'is ceilings.'

Undeterred, I pressed on. 'We need to find out what he's really interested in, Mrs Buttle, and make special efforts to encourage him and find

306

success before he moves on to Easington,' I said.

Mrs Buttle pondered this. 'Well, ah know 'e's looking forward t'going t'big school,' she said.

'I've invited the teacher in charge of Special Needs at Easington to come and meet Michael. I was hoping you would come in as well.'

'Who's that, then?' asked Mrs Buttle suspiciously.

'It's Miss Celia Etheringshaw,' I said.

'Ah know that lady,' said Mrs Buttle, suddenly looking relaxed.

'Oh, well, that's good,' I said, feeling reassured. 'So, how do you know her, Mrs Buttle?'

'Our Barry did 'er ceiling,' she replied.

I took a deep breath, smiled politely and carried on. By the time Mrs Buttle had left we had resolved what to do with Michael and I had promised I would contact Barry if I ever needed my ceilings painted.

On this sunny morning, I was trying to make good use of a welcome free period by seeing a few parents. As we were a Church of England primary school, the Revd Joseph Evans was taking a Religious Education lesson with the top class.

Sadly, as usual, when the bell rang for morning playtime, Joseph looked glum as he walked back into the staff-room and trawled his way through a pile of exercise books. Jodie Cuthbertson had written: 'Lot's wife was a pillar of salt during the day and a ball of fire during the night'; Tony Ackroyd had written: 'Noah's wife was Joan of Ark'; and Dominic Brown insisted that 'Solomon

307

had 300 wives and 700 porcupines'. Worst of all, in Joseph's eyes, but much to the delight of Sally Pringle and Anne Grainger, who were also reading the exercise books in the staff-room, Billy McNeill had written: 'Christians only have one spouse, this is called monotony.'

'Too true,' said Sally, as she was reminded of her previous night's boring conversation with her husband about the benefits of dove-tail joints, following his weekly woodwork evening class.

She and Anne excused themselves and set off to search for paintings and drawings that could be put on display in the children's art marquee on Saturday morning. It was an onerous task, but one that the two of them had done for a few years now and the effort was always worthwhile. Each year, parents admired the work of their children and agreed that their little pride-and-joy was a future David Hockney.

All was almost ready for the grandest event in the village calendar. According to Ruby it was 'a proper Yorkshire show'.

A short car journey up the Morton Road, alongside Major Forbes-Kitchener's manor house and his daughter's riding stable, there were vast acres of flat grazing land. Each year, since the 1920s, this had been the chosen site of the Ragley and Morton Agricultural Show. During the past week, on my way to visit Beth I had watched the giant marquees being erected and the show-jumping fences being positioned in the centre of the main show ring. As the week progressed, the activity had increased, so that by Friday afternoon all was ready.

It was also a big day for Vera and she had been tireless in making sure everything was in place in the Women's Institute tent. I had been asked by the organizing committee to oversee the Pets' Competition at one o'clock and work alongside Major Forbes-Kitchener, who was to be the judge. All we needed was fine weather.

Saturday morning dawned bright and clear. As far as I could see from my bedroom window in Bilbo Cottage, the landscape quivered in the sultry heat and, around me, the earth held its breath. There was an air of expectancy in the two villages as the big day arrived. Riding hats were being dusted, jodhpurs pressed, guinea pigs groomed, fresh lettuces picked and washed and, somewhere in Ragley village, an Afghan hound was enjoying his first day of flea-free living.

During the early morning, resplendent in her green sash, Vera was already organizing the competition displays in the Women's Institute tent. Here, the fiercest inter-village rivalries would be played out in the afternoon and, as Vera put a neat label in front of a vase of fragrant sweet peas, she knew this would be the first big test of her Presidency.

I spent half an hour polishing my Morris Minor Traveller, as it was gradually becoming a 'classic car' and it caught the eye at shows like this.

The journey along the narrow lanes to Ragley was always a joy in summer. The cow parsley stood tall over the wild grasses, while the magenta bells of foxgloves competed for attention in the midst of unfurling bracken. Red Admiral butterflies danced among the nettles and the young tendrils of ivy invaded the dense quickthorn hedges. A reddish-brown grouse dashed across the narrow road on scampering, feathered feet and I swerved to avoid it. Eventually, I caught up with the traffic jam of horse-boxes, tractors and classic cars and we followed an old-fashioned, steam-driven threshing machine at a sedate pace into the show field.

It seemed as if all the inhabitants of both villages had descended on this small corner of 'God's Own Country' and the bright-red uni-forms of the marching brass band and the ladies in their summer dresses added colour to this special Yorkshire day.

Everyone I met said the organization in the Women's Institute tent could not be faulted and the lunchtime judging went like clockwork. I met Anne and John Grainger and we joined the throng to hear Vera read out the names of the prize winners. She was her confident and regal self as she presented the certificates and trophies to the various ladies of Ragley and Morton. As was the custom, the prizes for the best sponge cake, iced cake and fruit flan created the most interest. The large crowd listened intently as each lady, in her vote of thanks, revealed a special secret about the perfect sifting of self-raising flour or how brushing the centre of a cored apple with lemon juice prevents discoloration.

Vera, in the words of Baron Pierre de Coubertin, impressed upon the multitude in her closing remarks that 'everyone is a winner and no one is a loser'. However, the responses of the

310

competitors did not entirely support this Olympian attitude.

Ruby's sixty-five-year-old mother, Agnes, who had been taught to hand-decorate chocolates at the Rowntree factory before the Second World War, won the Betty Winship Trophy for her iced chocolate cake.

'Ah'm a winner, Ruby,' said Agnes in triumph.

Peter Miles-Humphreys, the stuttering bank clerk, looked dejectedly at the 'Unplaced' card in front of his lopsided sponge cake, which was studded with concentric circles of Smarties, in the Dads' Cake-Making Competition.

'I-I-I'm a l-l-loser, F-F-Felicity,' said Peter to his wife, who had secretly thought this to be the case since the first Valentine's Day of their married life, in 1959.

After congratulating Vera, we walked out to see Dan and Jo rolling out the tug-of-war rope. Dan, as the local bobby, had been asked to judge the annual competition between the two villages. However, the decisive win by two pulls to nil by the Ragley team was a foregone conclusion. This was largely because Whistling John Paxton's wife, Pauline, was the 'anchor' at the end of the rope and our kitchen assistant, Doreen Critchley, had positioned herself at the front of the team. Her rippling muscles and frightening snarl were enough to frighten the life out of the eight men of Morton. Their 'anchor', Ernie Morgetroyd, the Morton milkman, had just supped eight pints of Guinness in the refreshment tent and for him the phrase 'the earth moved' took on a new meaning.

After looking at Anne and Sally's display in the 'Children's Art' tent, I wandered round the pens of sheep, cattle and pigs. Stan Coe and some of his farming friends glanced in my direction and then laughed loudly. Stan, pint pot in hand and sporting a bright-yellow checked waistcoat that bulged over his huge belly, was clearly enjoying himself.

I frowned in his direction and wondered what plot he was hatching.

'A long face doesn't suit you, Mr Jack Sheffield,' said a singsong voice behind me.

'Laura,' I said. 'Lovely to see you.'

'Likewise, Jack,' said Laura.

Her bare shoulders were golden brown and her hair had been bleached by the sun. Her green eyes softened as she kissed me lightly on my cheek.

'Where's Beth?' I asked, looking around beyond the rows of horse-boxes, the candy-floss stall and the tossing-the-sheaf competition.

'Over there with her new Robert Redford,' said Laura at little coyly. 'Rather dishy, don't you think, Jack?'

I spotted Beth and at the same moment heard her cheer as her strapping, flaxen-haired companion almost atomized a coconut with a wooden ball on the coconut shy.

'So, who's he?' I asked, a little too abruptly.

'That's Simon,' said Laura. 'He will be Beth's new Deputy Head at Hartingdale.'

'Oh,' I said, weighing up the tall young man with the film-star looks.

'He loves old fast cars,' said Laura enthusiastically. 'And he's got this dear little bright-red Morgan. He's taking Beth for a spin in it later.'

'Is he?'

Laura tugged my sleeve. 'Come on, I'll buy you an ice cream,' she said.

I looked at my watch. It was time for the Pets' Competition. 'Damn!' I said. 'Sorry, Laura, I have to go. I promised to be at the pet show.'

Laura took my arm. 'Let's go, then,' she said. 'I'll come with you. We can catch up with my big sister later.'

The smell of fur and feathers in the Pets' Competition marquee filled our nostrils as we walked in. Before us, on a long line of trestle tables, the most diverse menagerie of local pets that could be imagined was lined up in front of their owners. Miss Tripps, the sixty-four-year-old headmistress of Morton Primary School, gave me a wave and a friendly smile. She was close to retirement and many of her parents and children stood alongside her. The children of Ragley School were represented in force and they stood behind the cages on which the name of their pet was written on a bright-yellow card.

Tony Ackroyd had brought a tortoise called Yul Brynner and there was no doubt that, on the few occasions his head appeared from under his shell, he had the unblinking, hypnotic stare of a gunfighter.

Sarah Louise Tait had brought her black-and-white rabbit, Nibbles, and had taught him not only to high jump but also to leap over a series of low hurdles at remarkable speed. As she stroked his long ears lovingly, he appeared to fall asleep –

which was surprising, since the next exhibit crashed repeatedly into the wire netting at the end of its wooden box. Dominic Brown had brought in Frankenstein, his father's psychopathic ferret, which had the personality of a drug-crazed werewolf.

Jimmy Poole was restraining his lively little Yorkshire Terrier, called Scargill – or, as Jimmy called him, 'Thcargill' – and it seemed appropriate that it was attempting to bite the ankles of everyone in authority.

Charlotte Ackroyd's Dwarf Russian hamster, Lenin, stared out of his wire-meshed cage and appeared to be attempting to hypnotize Dawn Phillips's English Crested guinea pig in the next cage and presumably convert him to Communism.

Next in line, Hazel Smith had brought her father's champion racing pigeon, Caesar, which was clearly trying to start a romantic relationship with the occupant of the next cage. Cleopatra, Jodie Cuthbertson's talking parrot, was unimpressed. Unfortunately, the extent of the parrot's vocabulary consisted of a small selection of two-word expletives, all of which ended in 'off!' so, on this occasion, Caesar did not invade Egypt.

At the end of the line stood Micky Buttle, cheerfully oblivious of the barking, squeaking and blaspheming that was going on next to him. On the table in front of him stood a screw-top jar with holes punched in the lid. In the jar there was a sprig of privet but, seemingly, nothing else.

I walked over to him. 'Where's your Engelbert, Michael?' I asked.

'Gone, Mr Sheffield,' said Michael glumly. ''E ran off, so ah brought Twiggy instead.'

'Twiggy?'

'See here, Mr Sheffield,' said Micky, pointing to a superbly camouflaged stick insect in his jar.

'Well, good luck, Michael.'

I patted Micky on the shoulder and he beamed with pleasure.

Major Rupert Forbes-Kitchener suddenly strode confidently into the marquee after watching his daughter Virginia jump a clear round on her sprightly horse, Banjo. All the young men of Ragley and Morton had also watched, mainly because she was one of the most curvaceous young women in the neighbourhood. Her riding stables did a roaring trade and many an adolescent young man spent an enjoyable summer evening ogling Virginia Anastasia Forbes-Kitchener in a pair of skin-tight jodhpurs.

'So, we're here to judge the children's pet show, what?' said the Major, surveying the expectant line of children from the two primary schools.

'Yes, please, Major,' I said. 'You can ask the children any questions you like. Just do it your way and then we announce the first, second and third in reverse order.'

'Roger and out, old boy,' said the Major.

The children responded well to the huge, formidable figure of the Major and answered his questions as well as they could. He was patient and friendly and spoke to each child in turn. Even when Scargill, the Yorkshire Terrier, almost bit through his regimental tie he remained undeterred.

Finally he came to Michael Buttle. 'And what's in here, young man?'

'It's Twiggy, sir,' said Micky. 'She's a stick insect.'

'So it's a she, is it?' asked the Major, peering into the jar.

'Yes, sir,' said Micky politely. 'T'females live in trees an' make eggs that drop down t'ground an' then they 'atch out.'

'Good lad,' said the Major appreciatively.

'An' they grow to 'bout one and a 'alf inches long, sir, an' they 'ave really tiny wings or no wings at all.'

'You certainly know a lot about your pet,' said the Major.

'Thank you, sir,' said Micky. 'Ah love animals, speshully 'orses.'

'So you like horses, do you?'

'Yes, sir,' said Michael.

'Well, young man, my daughter runs the riding school next door,' said the Major. 'Come round early next Saturday and you can meet the horses and do a few jobs.'

'Thank you, sir,' said Micky, beaming from ear to ear.

After a few minutes the Major announced the prize winners. Cleopatra Cuthbertson, the talking parrot, was third; Nibbles Tait, the hurdling rabbit, was second; and first, much to everyone's amazement, was Twiggy Buttle, the stick insect.

'You've got a good lad there, Jack,' said the Major. 'He knows everything about his pet.'

Mrs Buttle rushed into the tent just in time to

316

see the Major presenting Micky with a certificate and a small trophy.

'Sorry ah'm late, Mr Sheffield,' said the breathless Mrs Buttle. 'Ah've jus' been t'chemist t'collect a description f'me mother.'

Micky showed her his certificate and, with faltering words, she tried to read it to him. Then he looked up at me and held his trophy in the air. In that instant I knew it was an image I would carry with me. Michael Buttle's broad smile was full of pride and confidence. It was a far cry from the hesitant reader and the struggling writer we had come to know.

Micky Buttle's life changed from that day on. In years to come, he became one of the Major's most trusted workers and a talented trainer of horses. While he carried his writing difficulties throughout his life, he did so with skill and wit and wisdom. It left me to reflect that every child has a talent and, occasionally, we have to search that little bit harder to find it.

Sometimes, like Twiggy, it's right in front of your face.

Chapter Twenty

Curd Tarts and Crumpets

Many parents and governors supported Class 3's 'How We Used to Live' project. School governors, members of the teaching staff and their partners have been invited to a summer garden party on Saturday, 7 July at Old Morton Manor, as guests of Major Forbes-Kitchener.

Extract from the Ragley School Logbook:
Friday, 6 July 1979

Sally's class were in the middle of their 'How We Used to Live' project and Vera was proving to be a popular storyteller. It was a hot, sunny morning on Friday, 6 July, and a refreshing breeze drifted through the open windows in the school hall.

'What was it like when you were a little girl, Miss Evans?' asked nine-year-old Tracy Crabtree.

'Let me see ... I was about the same age as you in 1932,' said Vera. 'And, on special occasions, I used to go out with my mother and my brother to Betty's Tea Rooms in York or Harrogate. In those days, you could order a four-course lunch for two shillings. That's only ten pence in modern money.'

Simon Nelson, the eight-year-old grandson of the local dentist, waved his hand in the air. 'Miss

318

Evans ... Miss Evans. What did you eat when you got there?'

'Well, a lady with a white apron used to bring a tall, three-tier cake stand and it was full of buttery crumpets and a selection of pastries. It made me feel like a princess. Then after I had eaten a crumpet, I always picked a delicious curd tart. That was my favourite.' Vera was caught up in the memory and remained quiet for a few moments.

'Excuse me, Miss Evans,' said the ever-polite, nine-year-old Katy Ollerenshaw. 'Did you ever go on holiday?'

'Oh yes, Katy,' said Vera. 'My father was a vicar and he used to have a week's holiday in the summer. We travelled by train to the seaside on the "Scarborough Flyer". I had my Shirley Temple doll and my *Bobby Bear's Annual*. It was so exciting. And when we got there, my mother bought me a Walls Brickette ice cream, which I ate between two wafers. It cost two old pence and I made it last and last. And then, if I was a really good girl, my father bought one of the new Mars bars for me. That cost two old pence as well.'

Vera was in full flow and the children listened in wonder at the tales of a far-off world with an endless supply of cheap sweets.

The dining tables in the school hall had been put out early by Ruby and, at each one, a group of children sat with one of our visitors. They included a few parents of children in Sally's class, and Major Forbes-Kitchener, Albert Jenkins, Old Tommy Piercy, Miss Amelia Duff from the Post Office, Mary Hardisty, our caretaker Ruby Smith, and Shirley the cook. All of them had brought in old artefacts and photographs and the children looked at them in awe and wonder.

At the next table to Vera, the Major had brought in his old camera. 'This is my Box Brownie,' he explained. 'My mother gave it to me on my thirteenth birthday. It cost seven shillings.'

Miss Duff was showing the children her 1935 King George V Silver Jubilee mug, while Mary Hardisty had brought in her posser tub and corrugated washboard. Albert Jenkins was surrounded by an eager group of boys who were reading his huge collection of 1930s comics, including *The Wizard*, *The Dandy*, *The Beano*, *The Hotspur* and *The Triumph*, all priced at two old pence. Tommy Piercy had a remarkable collection of biscuit and chocolate tins, celebrating the British Empire Exhibition that took place during 1924 and 1925; whereas the relatively youthful Shirley and Ruby were leafing through their collection of old recipes, including a battered edition of *Gert and Daisy's Wartime Cookery Book*. The hall was a hive of activity and the children learned about a world without mail-order catalogues, decimal currency and *Starsky and Hutch*.

When the bell rang for morning playtime, Shirley and Ruby had a surprise for all the children. They put a plate of assorted biscuits on every table and enough beakers of orange juice for every child in the school. Jo Maddison walked into the hall with the Revd Joseph Evans and all the children in her class. The vicar had visited school for his weekly Religious Education lesson and, on this occasion, he had been reading Bible stories to Class 2. This meant that Joseph had suffered the varied delights of teaching Heathcliffe Earnshaw.

Jo gathered the children round her. 'Now, children, please take one biscuit and a beaker of orange juice.'

Joseph immediately spotted Heathcliffe walking towards the nearest plate of biscuits and announced in a stern voice, 'Don't pick your nose, Heathcliffe. Remember, God is watching you.'

Heathcliffe stopped in his tracks and glanced up at the sky outside the huge arched window. Although not entirely convinced, he wiped his finger on his sleeve and picked up a beaker and a chocolate digestive biscuit.

Next to Heathcliffe, Jimmy Poole stared at the plate of biscuits but couldn't decide between a custard cream and a ginger-nut. He resolved this dilemma by taking both.

Behind him in the queue, the sharp-eyed Elisabeth Amelia Dudley-Palmer intervened. 'Excuse me, Jimmy, but you took two biscuits,' she said, in the style of a budding head girl.

Jimmy grinned. 'Ith OK, Elithabeth,' he lisped. 'God ith watchin' Heathcliffe pickin' hith nothe.'

Elisabeth Amelia Dudley-Palmer considered the seemingly indisputable logic of Jimmy's reply and glanced through the window at the sun peeping through the clouds. 'Are you sure?' she asked.

'Pothitive,' said Jimmy, through a mouthful of biscuit crumbs.

Satisfied, she selected two Bourbon biscuits

and retreated to a quiet corner of the hall.

In the staff-room, Vera was smiling. She had just read in her *Daily Telegraph* that Margaret Thatcher was busy changing the décor at Chequers and had introduced a tasteful range of beautiful china bowls filled with fragrant pot-pourri. She was pondering that we were undoubtedly at the outset of a new, golden age of government, when the Major popped his head round the door.

'Splendid morning, everybody. Well done. Sadly, must dash. Duty calls, what?'

'Would you like to stay for coffee, Major?' asked Vera, her cheeks becoming a little flushed again.

'Sorry, Miss Evans, but I shall look forward to seeing you at the Manor tomorrow at twelve hundred hours with all your friends. So until then, farewell.' With a dignified bow, and a gentle smile in the direction of Vera, the Major departed in his chauffeur-driven classic Bentley.

'So, I'll call for you and Joseph at eleven-thirty, Vera,' I said. 'And we're picking up Beth on the way.'

But Vera didn't hear me. She was staring at the gleaming black Bentley as it purred down the drive.

All the teaching staff and members of the school governing body, along with their partners, had been invited by the Major to attend a grand garden party at Old Morton Manor House. It was meant as a thank-you gesture and an opportunity for staff and governors to relax in lovely surroundings. Vera had been asked by the Major to send out all the invitations.

'I invited Beth Henderson, Mr Sheffield,' she had informed me. Then, as an afterthought, 'Hope you don't mind. I didn't know Laura Henderson very well when I was asked to organize it.' She gave me an inquisitive look and then returned to checking the dinner-money registers.

The afternoon passed by uneventfully, apart from Jimmy Poole grazing his knees in the playground. In a lively re-enactment of *Star Wars*, six-year-old Jimmy, in the role of a slightly-lisping Obi-Wan Kenobi, had defeated five-year-old Terry Earnshaw, the considerably vertically challenged Darth Vader, by using the anti-gravity powers of a Jedi warrior. Unfortunately, Newtonian theory persisted and he fell off the school wall. Elisabeth Amelia Dudley-Palmer, who had asked, very politely, if she could play the part of Princess Leia, had been rebuffed thrice. She told him that if Jedi warriors cried when they fell down, she didn't want to play anyway.

'But it thtings,' moaned Jimmy, as he limped bravely off the battlefield and into school to ask Jo Maddison to put a plaster on his sore knee.

Standing to attention against the school wall, the twins Rowena and Katrina Buttle, as the two androids, C3PO and R2D2, decided *Star Wars* was boring and set off to follow their new leader, Elisabeth Amelia, who was the proud owner of a new Tressy doll. Tressy's hair could be combed into a variety of styles and Rowena and Katrina had just perfected side-plaits so, in their opinion, Empire domination could wait.

When the school bell rang out to announce the

end of the school week, everyone seemed to be in a hurry.

'What's happening, Anne?' I asked. 'You don't normally rush off so quickly.'

She gave me a harassed look. 'I don't know why I let myself in for it,' she said, with a touch of desperation.

Vera, Sally and Jo suddenly appeared at Anne's classroom door. 'See you tonight,' they said, in unison, and hurried off to their cars.

'It's just that she was so persuasive,' said Anne, quickly tidying away a box of Cuisenaire counting rods.

Ruby rattled by the open doorway with her galvanized bucket. 'Can ah bring our Racquel, Mrs Grainger?' she asked, mopping the floor as if there was no tomorrow.

'Of course, Ruby,' said Anne, through clenched teeth. 'The more the merrier.'

Then she picked up her handbag and pulled out a garish-yellow invitation card. It read **TUPPERWARE PARTY** in bold capitals.

'Mrs Ackroyd runs Tupperware parties, Jack, and she's doing one at my house tonight. Apparently, they're all the rage now, and I get some free samples. I just provide drinks and nibbles.'

I looked at the card in horror, desperately searching for a good excuse.

'Oh, don't worry, Jack. It's women only.'

I breathed a sigh of relief and walked out to my car.

An hour later I received a heartbreaking call from John Grainger. He was surrounded by strange women, some of whom were even examining the new fridge in the garage. There was nowhere to go and he wondered if he could come round for a couple of hours.

John arrived at Bilbo Cottage carrying a huge can of Watney's Party Seven draught bitter. We switched on the Wimbledon television highlights and, by the time we had drained the last drop, we were convinced that, while Chris Evert Lloyd's dress was undoubtedly prettier, Martina Navratilova's powerful forehand would eventually be too strong for the darling of the Centre Court.

Three miles away, in Anne's overcrowded lounge, twenty-five women had devoured every crisp, peanut and walnut whip and Anne had retired to the kitchen to locate sufficient cups for a hot drink.

Margery Ackroyd was berating her audience with the enthusiasm of an evangelist. 'Y'can trust Tupperware,' said Margery. 'Not like some men ah could mention.'

Everyone laughed, although in a few cases it was forced laughter.

'Tupperware is 'ygienic,' said Margery, replacing a lid on a container and pointing at the trapped air inside.

Everyone nodded in approval, as if Margery had just invented comfortable high heels.

'It's a well-known fact that nasty little bugs can crawl round inside the spiral lid of a screw-top jar,' said Margery. 'But t'evil little vermin can't get into Tupperware.'

Anne walked in from the kitchen, unscrewing her family-size jar of Maxwell House. 'How many for coffee?' she asked.

She was puzzled when everyone chose tea.

As darkness finally fell, each clutching a tower block of Tupperware, the ladies of Ragley village tottered home and began to fill their plastic containers with postcards, wax crayons and spare buttons.

On Saturday morning, as I drove along the Morton Road, an armada of cirrus clouds raced across the sky and glinted gold in the sunlight. It was a fine day for the society event of the year. I collected Joseph and Vera from the vicarage and then Beth from her cottage. Both women looked attractive in their summer hats and dresses.

As we turned into the back road out of Morton, William Featherstone, the driver of the local cream-and-green Reliance bus, had just pulled up ahead, outside his tiny cottage. This was a regular unofficial stop and none of the passengers faltered in their conversations about the latest events of Ragley and Morton.

For over thirty years William Featherstone had driven his bus each morning from the outlying villages into York and then back again in the mid-afternoon in time for farmers' wives to prepare the evening meal. His steady pace never altered and he would stop to feed his hens, collect a few duck eggs and deliver these, along with a few parcels, to York market. In his brown bus driver's jacket and his peaked cap, he cut a distinctive figure in the life of the villages, and in 1979 no one could imagine a day when the bus service no longer existed. Life, like a slowly moving mill wheel, simply trundled by, just like William's bus.

Eventually, we came to a narrow track of crushed stone and the first few outbuildings that formed part of the Major's estate. I had never been here before and I stopped the car to take in the view.

In this quiet backwater of the village, Mother Nature had spread out a carpet of new grass and given us clean air that filled our lungs and purified the soul. Beyond a narrow cobbled yard there was a row of individual cottages with bright painted doors, leaded windows and hanging baskets, ablaze with bright-red trailing geraniums, green-and-cream variegated ivy and cool cascades of blue lobelia. In the farmyard alongside, hens pecked contentedly and a lone pig snuffled round in an overgrown corner, oblivious of the sharp thistles. It was as if time had passed by and left the scenery untouched, and I wondered how many generations of North Yorkshire farmers had paused to admire this simple rural scene.

I parked alongside John Grainger's Cortina and half a dozen other cars in a small grassy field. We got out and walked through a gap in the tall yew hedge and along an avenue of espaliered pears towards the manor house. Vera paused by a low row of lavender and stooped to enjoy the scent of the mauve flower spikes. As she did so, a gardener appeared with a barrow-load of horse dung.

Vera recognized him. 'Good morning, Thomas,' she said.

He touched the peak of his frayed flat cap in acknowledgement. ''Ow do, Miss Evans,' he said. 'Ah'm jus' seein' t'floribunda roses.'

'They look magnificent,' said Vera.

'Thank you, Miss Evans.' He tipped the fresh dung onto the rose beds. 'As my granddad used t'say, "Where there's muck, there's brass".' And with a chuckle he walked away, pushing his barrow.

The Major's garden was the most beautiful I had ever seen. As we walked along the pebbled path, the scent of old-fashioned roses filled the air. A walkway of metal arches had been constructed, encouraging the Victorian roses to scramble for space and light among the honeysuckle and clematis. The sounds and scents of summer lifted our spirits and, as a light breeze caressed Beth's summer dress, I sensed the whisper of silk against her skin.

In front of the turreted, Yorkshire-stone manor house stood the Major, next to a pretty window box teeming with pendulous fuchsias and trailing pelargoniums. Immaculate in a cream suit, crisp white shirt and regimental tie with a smart straw hat shielding his steel-blue eyes, he bowed and then walked towards us. Surprisingly, he carried a rose in each hand.

With a graceful bow he handed one to Beth. 'For you, Miss Henderson,' he said, 'a *Rosa mundi* with a splash of crimson to match your zest for life.'

Beth was obviously thrilled. She gave a mock curtsy and smiled broadly at the giant ex-military man. 'Thank you, kind sir,' she said sweetly.

The Major bowed again, this time very low. 'For the elegant Miss Evans,' he said, 'a pale-pink

328

Blush Noisette to match the complexion of a very fine English lady.'

The colour rose in Vera's cheeks but, apart from that, she remained serenely composed. 'Thank you, Major,' said Vera. 'You're very kind.'

Joseph looked uncertainly at his sister, who was staring thoughtfully at the beautiful rose. For a moment, she was in a world of her own.

'You have a wonderful garden, Major,' said Joseph, breaking the spell.

'Thank you, Joseph. Now, if you will come with me, there are some comfortable seats under the willow tree and the champagne should be just the right temperature.'

An hour later, after a champagne lunch, Joseph and John Grainger set off to explore the garden and Beth and I sat with Anne and Sally, enjoying a second helping of strawberries and cream.

Anne touched my arm and nodded towards Vera. 'She's enjoying herself,' she said quietly.

Vera was sitting nearby on a wickerwork chair, listening to one of the Major's animated stories. They seemed to be enjoying each other's company. There was no doubt that the Major was completely besotted with her and he treated her with dignity and the utmost respect. Vera looked relaxed as she sipped her chilled white wine in a ladylike manner without appearing to get her lips wet. All her actions were calm and graceful and I wondered about her life.

Age had touched her with cool fingertips and her hair was beginning to be flecked with grey, but on this day, with the dappled sun on her summer dress she looked a young woman again.

Almost as if she was aware that Beth and I were looking at her, she turned in our direction, peered from under her stylish broad-brimmed lavender hat and gave us a little wave.

The Major's daughter, the confident and curvaceous Virginia, arrived and offered a tour of the house and Anne and Sally got up to join her. They set off with Jo and Dan and left Beth and me in the welcome shade of the weeping willow.

'What a wonderful day, Jack,' said Beth. She stretched out and her dress was taut against her slim, suntanned figure.

'I'm glad you're here to share it with me, Beth.'

Her sun-bleached hair fell over her face and, with her long fingers, she parted it and tucked it behind her ears. For a brief moment, I was reminded of Laura.

Then Beth looked up at me. 'Pass me your spectacles, Jack.'

'Pardon?'

'Your spectacles. I want to see what you look like without them.'

I removed my thick, black-framed spectacles and handed them to her. The world suddenly became fuzzy and I stared vacantly at her.

'Laura's right,' said Beth. 'You are really handsome without them.'

She passed them back. I put them on and tried to judge the expression on her face. But the moment had gone and she was looking at the Major, who was walking towards the open French windows that led to his study.

The Major walked in, pushed back the chintz curtains, and sunlight lit up his antique record player on the huge walnut sideboard. It was a 'His Master's Voice Portable Model 102' gramophone, purchased in 1933 for five pounds, twelve shillings and sixpence, a fortune in those days. A small tin box, once containing two hundred stylus needles, stood alongside the dark hardwood carcass. The price in 1933 was nine old pence, which appeared to represent value for money as, forty-six years later, over half the needles remained.

The Major lifted the lid, placed a shiny black long-playing record on the rubber turntable and carefully lowered the metal arm, with its sharp stylus, onto the precise track he wanted.

Satisfied, he walked towards Vera and paused as the first familiar notes of Vera Lynn's 'We'll Meet Again' floated through the open French windows and lingered in the air. The Major took Vera's hand gently in his and ushered her onto the stone-flagged courtyard. They danced slowly, their bodies a respectful distance apart, and the Major's eyes never once left Vera's face.

With the formal grace of a guardsman, the Major escorted Vera back to their table. When they were seated, he waved to his daughter, Virginia, who had completed her house tour and was in animated conversation with her current boyfriend, the son of the local Member of Parliament. Virginia smiled at her father and quickly skipped into the house.

'Miss Evans, forgive me, but yesterday in school I overheard your wonderful story about going into Betty's Tea Rooms as a child,' said the Major. 'I thought this might bring back a few happy memories.'

Vera looked puzzled and then broke into laughter as Virginia reappeared carrying an elegant three-tiered cake stand. She was accompanied by the Major's cook, Doris, and, with great ceremony, they put it on the table in front of Vera and curtsied. On the cake stand, neatly displayed on white doilies, was a selection of crumpets and curd tarts. The crumpets were liberally covered in local Yorkshire butter and the curd tarts had been freshly made by Doris that morning.

'Thank you so much,' said Vera. 'You really shouldn't have gone to so much trouble.'

'Our pleasure, Miss Evans,' said Virginia.

'Eat 'em while they're warm, Miss Evans,' said Doris.

As they walked away, Vera turned to the Major. 'You're very kind, Major,' said Vera. 'Thank you so much.'

He leaned forward and put his hand very lightly on top of Vera's. 'Would you do me the honour of calling me Rupert?' he asked.

Vera looked thoughtful but she did not withdraw her hand. 'Of course, Rupert.'

The Major lifted his hand and picked up the wine bottle. 'More wine, Miss Evans?'

'Just a little, Rupert.'

The Major poured the wine.

There was a long silence.

'And you may call me Vera if you wish.'

The Major lifted his glass to propose a toast. 'To you, Vera, and to happy times.'

Vera raised her glass. 'Happy times,' she said.

Chapter Twenty-one

Mister Teacher

Miss Maddison received gifts from staff, parents and children prior to her marriage on Saturday, 21 July, to Police Constable Hunter. School closed today for the summer holiday with 87 children on roll.
Extract from the Ragley School Logbook:
Friday, 20 July 1979

'Mister Teacher' was printed in a childlike hand on the side of a long grey cardboard tube.

'It's for you, Mr Sheffield,' said Vera. 'Mrs Phillips called in on her way to work.'

'Thank you, Vera,' I said, taking out the roll of A3 paper.

'She says it's from that little boy, Sebastian, and that he's getting better now.'

'That's wonderful news.'

A snowy day at York hospital flickered through my mind. It seemed long ago now. I glanced out of the office window and watched the children playing on the school field. It was lunchtime on Friday, 20 July, and the smiling suns of dandelions were lighting up the last day of the school year.

Inside the cardboard tube was a wonderful drawing. A boy and girl were holding hands and stepping through the doorway of a magical ward-

333

robe, which led to a long pathway through a forest, towards a fairytale castle. It was Sebastian's Narnia, but now it was springtime in his new land and the drawing was full of colour. I pinned it on the notice board and stood back and admired it.

Then I followed Vera into the staff-room. She had finished checking the end-of-year reports and attendance figures and was leafing through her *Daily Telegraph*. Jo, Sally and Anne were leaning over her shoulder, staring at photographs of three men in the news.

'Now, that's my perfect man,' drooled Sally, pointing at Bjorn Borg, who had beaten Roscoe Tanner and won Wimbledon for the fourth consecutive time.

Jo, who had more youthful tastes, appeared to forget that she was about to marry a policeman from Sunderland. *'He's* definitely my heart throb,' she said, swooning over the photograph of the handsome twenty-two-year-old Seve Ballesteros, who had just won the British Open Golf Championship.

'Actually, this one's more my type,' said Anne. 'There's a hint of danger about him. Looks as though he might make a name for himself.' She pointed to the picture of the newly elected President of Iraq.

'Who is he, Vera?' asked Anne.

'It's a young man called Saddam Hussein,' said Vera. 'Looks like trouble to me. It's all in the eyes, you know.'

Vera closed the newspaper, looked at Jo with a smile and said, 'Now, young lady, tell me once more about this wonderful dress you're wearing tomorrow.'

Anne and Sally gathered round as if it was class story time and I walked out onto the school playground.

It was a day of goodbyes. The fourth-year juniors in my class gathered in the cool shade of the horse chestnut trees, by the stone wall at the front of the school, and I walked out to talk to them.

'Easington'll be great, Mr Sheffield,' said Jodie Cuthbertson. 'Our Anita says we go swimmin' on Tuesdays.'

'An' they've got a big gym wi' a trampoline,' said Billy McNeill, wiping his nose with the back of his sleeve.

'Ah'll miss bein' milk monitor, Mr Sheffield,' said Micky Buttle mournfully.

'Ah were told they sell ginger biscuits an' chocolate Wagon Wheels in t'toilets at playtime,' said Dominic Brown, eyes wide in expectation of future culinary feasts.

Everyone relaxed and smiled at this unexpected news.

I looked at their eager faces and wondered what would become of them. They were another generation of Ragley children who were about to move on in their lives and become the youngest pupils once again. School uniform would unite their appearance and, in time, the nonconformists would reduce the width of their ties, or the length of their skirts, and refuse to tuck in shirts and blouses. The girls would rush headlong through puberty, leaving puzzled boys in their wake, while streaming for English and mathematics would thrust lifelong friends into separate groups. A new dawn beckoned, a new world awaited.

The solid walls of this school were familiar to me now. Above the grey slate roof, the Yorkshire stone tower was mellow in the amber sunlight and, finally, at a quarter to four, the giant bell rang out and announced the end of another school year. I waved goodbye as another generation of eleven-year-olds walked down the drive for the last time as primary school pupils.

Feeling a little sad, I returned to the school office and took out the school logbook. My pen was poised over an empty page when Anne walked in.

'Another year over, Jack.'

'Almost,' I said. 'I've just got to add an entry for the last day, but my brain's tired.'

'Do it over the weekend,' said Anne. 'Vera and I will be calling in tomorrow afternoon to return the crockery after the wedding reception.'

I recalled that Jo and Dan had booked the Ragley village hall for their wedding breakfast.

'Good idea,' I said, closing the logbook.

'Coffee?' she said, switching on the kettle.

'Thanks, Anne.' I put the top back on my pen and looked up at her. 'I'd be lost without your support,' I said.

Anne gave me that familiar calm smile. 'It's been another good year, Jack,' she said. 'Let's just hope the government don't introduce that common curriculum they keep talking about. That's the only dark cloud on the horizon for me.'

We sipped our coffee in silence, pondering the

state of education, until Jo and Sally burst in, overloaded with wedding presents from children and parents.

'We'll need a van for all these,' said Sally, tipping a pile of brightly wrapped boxes onto the coffee table.

'Look what John Grainger gave to me, Jack,' said Jo, holding up a hand-carved oak name-plate for her classroom door. It read 'Mrs J. Hunter'.

John Grainger had left work early to help Anne load up the school crockery for the wedding reception. Along with Vera's collection of Women's Institute crockery, there would be just enough. Half an hour later, we left Ruby to begin her 'holiday cleaning' and I drove out of the school gate. I had completed my second year as headmaster of Ragley-on-the-Forest Church of England Primary School.

Next day, the wedding morning was bright and sunny and, probably for the first time in my life, I felt really smart. I had bought a brand-new, three-piece grey suit from Marks & Spencer's for the extravagant sum of £39.95. The lapels were wide and the flares were fashionable. I spent an age trying to iron my best white shirt, and the bright flower-power tie, which Beth had bought for me last summer, added the finishing touch. Our holiday a year ago seemed a distant but pleasant dream and I polished my black shoes vigorously, erasing the scuffs but not the memories.

There had been a time when I had hoped that Beth and I would be more than just good friends, but there was a lot going on in her life. Her new headship had dominated the last few months for her and she had made it clear that she did not want any commitment. At least not yet. And then, there was Laura.

As I drove up the Morton Road, I was happy for Jo and Dan, who had found each other and wanted to be man and wife.

The bells of St Mary's were ringing, summoning us to church, and the Revd Joseph Evans was preparing himself for another wedding ceremony. By his side, as always, Vera went through her part of their ritual. They had both done this many times. Like slow-motion dancers they moved with quiet assurance through the still air of the church, brother and sister in well-rehearsed harmony.

In the peaceful sanctuary of the silent vestry, Joseph unlocked the old oak wardrobe and Vera took out his cassock, a long black robe that fitted comfortably over Joseph's lanky frame and showed off his spotlessly clean clerical collar. Vera scrutinized the cassock for specks of dust or rogue cat hairs and then stood back, satisfied. She glanced down at his black shoes with their gleaming military shine and nodded with pride. Her gentle smile was sufficient for Joseph; there was no need for words.

Outside, on the vicarage lawn, alongside the church, the wedding guests were gathering. There is something very special about a wedding on an English summer's day. Men in sombre suits provided the backdrop for a riot of bright colour. Elegant ladies in spectacular dresses and with hats of all shapes and sizes chatted in happy groups. A cluster of young policemen in smart ceremonial uniforms and pristine-white gloves leaned against the church wall and admired the young women. As I walked through the church gateway, I spotted Beth and Laura talking to Sally Pringle. Beth saw me and waved. I waved back. She was clutching a single, carmine-pink rose and she walked to meet me.

In the stillness of the nave, Joseph greeted the bridegroom and his best man. After a few quiet words, he ushered them into the vestry to complete the formalities of payments for the legal fees, bell ringers, flower ladies, and the Valium-sedated organist. Vera put her beautifully embroidered wedding kneeler in place on the steps in front of the altar. Joseph gave the best man his final instructions, checked the location of the ring in his uniform pocket and sent both him and Dan back to their front pew.

Beth looked stunning in a cream suit and matching wide-brimmed hat.

'I brought this for you, Jack. It's from that lovely climbing rose next to my front door. It's called Zephirine Drouhin.' She slipped it into the buttonhole on my lapel.

'Thank you, Beth. It's beautiful.' I sniffed it appreciatively. 'And so fragrant.'

Before I could say any more, a vision in bright pink appeared.

Sally Pringle's vivid dress drew a few wide-eyed stares as she walked towards us, clutching a huge carton of confetti. Her dramatic hat, which resembled an explosion of flamingo feathers, would have fitted in beautifully on Ladies' Day at Ascot.

'Hello, Jack. Hi, Beth,' shouted Sally. 'Isn't Jo lucky to have such a perfect day?'

'Sally, you look lovely,' I said, ever the diplomat.

'Thanks, Jack. Come on, Beth. Let's find an end pew.'

With that, she linked arms with Beth and marched her off towards the church entrance.

'Laura, we're going in now,' called Beth to her sister.

Suddenly, out of a crowd of admiring policemen, Laura appeared and waved to Beth. 'Save me a place,' she called out and then turned to face me.

'Hi, Jack. Great suit,' she said, smoothing the wide lapels.

'Hello, Laura,' I said, with a grin. 'Great dress.'

Laura was wearing a beautifully tailored, forget-me-not blue dress, with her long hair hanging free over her bare, suntanned shoulders. She looked lovely.

'I'm having a relaxing night in tonight, Jack. I was hoping you might like to join me for a meal.'

Up ahead, Beth turned round and stared. Laura's interest in my new suit seemed to surprise her and, before I had a chance to reply to Laura's invitation, I heard Beth call out, 'Come on, Laura.'

We joined the procession that was moving slowly into the church.

It was filling rapidly with families, friends and schoolchildren, and we mingled as we made our way up the aisle. The usher, a uniformed policeman, directed us into the pews in the style of a traffic controller. Beth waved at Laura and pointed to the last available seat on her pew and Laura sat down next to her. I followed Anne and John Grainger and we sat down behind Laura, Beth and Sally.

Anne, in an understated steel-grey hat, smiled and pointed back up the aisle. 'Look, Jack, there's Jo's mother,' she whispered.

The bridesmaids, in matching lilac dresses, had gathered in the porch behind us. Jo's younger sister, as maid of honour, was showing her tiny nieces how to hold their posies, and Jo's mother, in a neat beige suit and matching hat over the familiar jet-black hair, was walking quickly down the aisle.

In the vestry, Joseph opened the wardrobe once again and put on his white surplice and a wonderfully trimmed, full-length garment known as a cope. Vera added the final touch round his neck, a white stole stitched with intricate gold crosses along the edge. She stood back to admire him, her eyes full of pride. The moment had come for Joseph to meet the bride and for Vera, looking the picture of elegance in a lavender two-piece suit, to stand alongside Elsie Crapper at the organ to tell her when to begin to play the 'Bridal March'.

All was ready and the hushed whispers among the congregation indicated that at any moment the bride was about to arrive. A collective intake of breath swept round the church when Jo, in a fabulous wedding dress trimmed with white lace, walked down the aisle with her very proud father. Some of the small children who had been in her class waved as she passed them and Jo smiled at each one of them. Her mother was wiping away tears long before the radiant bride had joined Dan in front of the altar.

Ruby, in the pew behind me, had treated herself to a perm at Diane's Hair Salon, and was wearing a straw hat smothered in red roses supplied by Vera. She squeezed Ronnie's hand so tightly he thought he might never play darts again. Sadly, he, resplendent in his best suit, felt naked without his bobble hat and was looking forward to the reception, when he reckoned he could put it on again.

The ceremony passed by with joy and tears in equal measure. We sang 'Morning Has Broken', a choice made by Jo especially for the children, and 'Lord of all Hopefulness'. Next to me, when the couple repeated their wedding vows, John Grainger put his arm round Anne's shoulders and I glanced across at Beth. To my surprise, Laura was smiling at me, while Beth was deep in thought.

When the couple walked into the vestry to sign the register, Beth glanced my way with questioning green eyes. I smiled and she smiled back. Her thoughts were broken as Laura whispered something in her ear.

Suddenly, Elsie Crapper attacked the organ keyboard with chemically enhanced gusto, and almost raised the roof as the bride and groom returned down the aisle. The smiling congregation slowly filed out and Beth and Laura stood by me as we gathered on the lawn once again for the official photographs.

Beth squeezed my hand. 'Lovely service, Jack,' she said.

'I loved Jo's dress,' said Laura. 'One day, I'll have one like that.'

Everyone stopped to stare at Jo and Dan, who were holding each other tightly. The official photographer was going through his ritual of interchanging their parents for the family photographs. Jo's mother, when Dan's handsome six-foot-three-inch father stood beside her and gave her an all-enveloping bear hug, finally stopped crying.

As we walked to our cars to follow the procession down the Morton Road to Ragley village hall, Laura caught me up. Again, she stood close and gently smoothed the creases in my jacket. I could smell her perfume.

'Ring me later, Jack,' she said, 'and we can talk about that meal.'

Her green eyes looked a little more determined than before. It was an interesting prospect. She squeezed my hand and then trotted to catch up with Beth, who was unlocking her Volkswagen Beetle.

The village hall committee, marshalled by Anne and Vera, had worked wonders inside this ancient wooden building. A magnificent, three-tiered wedding cake took pride of place on the stage. White cloths covered the trestle tables, small vases of sweet peas scented the air and Sheila from The Royal Oak had set up a temporary bar in the corner.

After the buffet came the speeches and then the dancing. Clint Ramsbottom was gritting his teeth behind his disco kit while playing his least favourite record, 'Congratulations' by Cliff Richard. To his alarm, he realized that he was the only person in the hall who did not know all the words. Dan Hunter's seventy-year-old grandmother was dancing with little Jimmy Poole, who had been dressed in his first pair of long trousers and a tartan bow-tie. Sally Pringle persuaded a reluctant John Grainger to dance with her.

'That's a first,' said Anne. 'I'd forgotten he could dance.'

When Clint put Abba's 'Take a Chance on Me' on the turntable, Laura grabbed my hand and we danced. Her hair was soft against my face and the dance seemed to end so quickly.

'You've improved,' said Laura, with a smile, as she left me to join a group of friends.

Suddenly, to my surprise, a short, stocky man was by my side. 'For you, Mr Sheffield,' he said, holding out a glass of Yorkshire pale ale. It was Jo's father.

'Thank you, Mr Maddison.'

We touched glasses and drank.

'Thank you for all you've done for my daughter. She loves her work.'

'We're lucky to have her. She's a fine teacher.'

We both looked at Jo, who was walking onto the stage with Dan to cut the cake.

'Fathers and daughters,' he said softly.

I looked at him curiously.

344

He smiled and patted me on the back. 'You'll understand ... one day.'

After the cutting of the cake and as the celebrations drew to a close, Dan and Jo prepared to roar off in a wedding car, which had been festooned with streamers and tin cans, to get changed at Jo's house and then depart for a honeymoon destination known only to Dan.

A tired but happy group washed dishes and tidied up. I helped Anne and John Grainger load up their Cortina Estate with the school crockery and they drove off up the High Street to school.

'I'll see you there,' I called after them.

Soon Vera and I had collected the school cutlery in carrier bags and loaded it, along with a few tablecloths, in the back of my car. Everyone spilled out of the village hall and said their goodbyes.

Beth and Laura walked over to me.

'I'll talk to you in the holidays about joining the choir, Vera,' said Beth, with a smile.

'I shall look forward to it,' said Vera.

'Bye, Vera,' said Laura. 'Bye, Jack.' She stretched up and kissed me on the cheek. 'See you soon,' she whispered in my ear, and walked across the street to her car, which was parked next to Beth's.

Beth looked curiously at her sister and walked towards me. As she made a slight adjustment to the rose in my lapel, she said, 'I wanted you to have this because it reminded me of the roses you bought for me last summer in Cornwall.'

I didn't know what to say.

'It would be good to see you tonight, if you

345

want to come back to Morton.'

I smiled. This was unexpected.

'We've got some catching up to do,' she said. Then she stretched up and kissed me gently on the lips.

Nothing more was said. She crossed the road to her Volkswagen Beetle and looked back.

Laura glanced once at her sister and then her green eyes rested on me. Then, with fast acceleration, she drove down the High Street towards York.

I looked at Beth as she got into her car and set off towards Morton. She slowed as she drew alongside. Her driver's window was open and she smiled. Her green eyes were steady and unwavering.

'What are you thinking about, Mr Sheffield?' asked Vera softly.

'A girl with green eyes,' I murmured, almost to myself.

Vera stared at me thoughtfully and then glanced each way at the two disappearing cars. Yes, but which one? thought Vera.

We climbed into my car and drove in silence to the school car park.

Behind my desk in the office, I looked at Sebastian's picture on the notice board. The two children were holding hands and running into their enchanted world and, once again, I recalled the letter addressed to 'Mister Teacher' at the beginning of the school year. Sebastian had written, 'I would also like to go on a magical journey with a special friend,' and I guessed that

346

the small boy in the drawing was really Sebastian and the little girl was his imaginary friend.

'Penny for them, Mr Sheffield.' It was Vera, standing in the doorway.

'Hello, Vera. I'm sorry, I didn't see you there.'

'Can I help?' she said. 'You do seem to be deep in thought.'

'I was just looking at Sebastian's drawing and thinking what a wonderful artist he is.'

Vera studied the picture. 'It's got a sense of movement. It looks as though the little boy has decided to move on with his life. He's a free spirit now.'

'You're right, Vera.'

She rested a pile of tea towels on top of the filing cabinet and then stared back at the picture. 'Perhaps we could all learn from him, Mr Sheffield. Maybe we all need to move on from time to time and not stagnate in the past.'

Vera gave me a knowing glance. I recognized the look. I had seen it often during the past two years, but usually when I had made some administrative error and Vera hinted at the direction I should take.

'I'll leave you to your logbook, Mr Sheffield,' said Vera. 'And thank you for another good year.' With a gentle smile, she closed the door.

The school was quiet as I wrote my final entry in the school logbook. Then I blotted the page carefully, closed the ancient, leather-bound volume and unlocked the bottom drawer of my desk.

The bright-yellow envelope with the words 'Mister Teacher' printed on the front was still

347

there. Inside was Sebastian's letter and, once again, I read his three wishes. The first had come true. He was an artist already and I knew that one day he would achieve his second wish and build his snowman. His third wish was special and his 'magical journey' was about to begin. He had already taken the first brave steps.

I stared at the letter and smiled. Sebastian's words were simple and honest, uncluttered by adult reticence. They spelled out a message of hope and I, too, knew what I must do. Vera was right. We all need to move on and not dwell in the past.

I locked the logbook away in the bottom drawer of my desk for another summer. I had now completed two years as headmaster of Ragley School and I wondered what the next year would bring.

As the early-evening sun reflected from the high arched windows of the school, I drove out of the gates and left the academic year of 1978/1979 behind me.

Then I turned towards the High Street and stopped by the side of the village green.

To my left was the City of York. To my right was the Morton Road.

The decision was not easy.

I switched on my indicator.

And in a heartbeat I knew which road to take.

The publishers hope that this book has given you enjoyable reading. Large Print Books are especially designed to be as easy to see and hold as possible. If you wish a complete list of our books please ask at your local library or write directly to:

Magna Large Print Books
Magna House, Long Preston,
Skipton, North Yorkshire.
BD23 4ND

This Large Print Book for the partially sighted, who cannot read normal print, is published under the auspices of

THE ULVERSCROFT FOUNDATION